The AMBASSADORS

By

HENRY JAMES

With Introductions by

MARTIN W. SAMPSON

and

JOHN C. GERBER

D1498472

HARPER & ROW, PUBLISHERS

NEW YORK, EVANSTON, AND LONDON

G-Q

INTRODUCTION

THE main purpose of an introduction, as usually written, seems to be the statement of a critical opinion of the literary work concerned. Possibly the best place for such an opinion would be not as prologue but as epilogue, to be read when the book was finished and when one's own tentative judgment had been formed. The comparison of that judgment with the critic's judgment would then be an interesting thing. But there is another function that an introduction may have, and indeed should have, if it is to be true to its name: to clear away obstacles, to pave the way, to lead up to the work, that will then be really introduced to the reader; in a word, to try to say something that will make the reader appreciate the book for himself, rather than to tell him in advance what his appreciation should be. It so happens that Henry James seems markedly in need of preliminary explanation. Many readers find him difficult, many readers miss his best points. But he is an author who has something to say, and what he has to say is so admirable that it is eminently worth the trouble to master his style, his method, and his substance. What should be the untried but willing reader's preliminary attitude? I speak to such a reader.

You need, to read *The Ambassadors* of Henry James, an inquisitive patience. The process of reading should be leisurely but not halting; the attitude of mind acute but not carping. This story does not rush, it unfolds: personages reveal themselves through a natural consecutive display of their traits, much as they might reveal themselves in actual life; situations grow to their significance through the aid of your intelligent awareness—they are not suddenly flashed at you as from a moving-picture screen—and you bring your own knowledge of life to bear on the interpretation of the underlying motives. Apprehending thus the problems and perplexities of your fellow beings as they pass before you in print, you see them fortunately working their way out of the mazes of life or unfortunately working their way into them. Apprehending motives, you come to your own appraisal of the actions to which the motives give rise. James is interested in delicate, yet impressive, scruples; he likes to deal with the predicaments of more or less subtle consciences. It is by being delicate and scrupulous in your own estimates of the presented situations that you enjoy the author's clear-sighted, careful revelation of human character. For if you would appreciate fineness, you must apprehend it quietly and finely and with your own sense of balance: no one ever galloped through Henry James and got much from him, and probably no one ever brought much to him who did not take away more.

This, then, is a fine story: if one accepts fineness as meaning intellectual and moral refinement, perhaps the finest novel ever written. From first to last it is the exposition of a clean, noble, and retiring nature—Strether's—and as such natures in life gradually grow on one, so the process for one who reads the book for the first time is to allow it to make its point in the same way, quietly, deliberately, accumulatingly. That is a good way to approach any great piece of art, for great art is not primarily sensational, and, by virtue of making a deep appeal, calls thereby for a deep response.

In beginning acquaintance with the work of an artist, it is wise to learn something about his aims and methods. To discuss fully the technique and accomplishment of a writer like Henry James would require the space of a volume; we must confine ourselves here to one or two essentials. Nothing is more essential to the understanding of James than is the device of the point of view. Indeed, care in handling the point of view is a distinguishing feature of modern fiction. The technical term means the standpoint or angle from which incidents are told, or characters described. Since it is a matter of concern in the art of fiction, and markedly of concern in the art of Henry James, a word should be said about it.

The point of view in the novelists of the older school is, so to say, the omniscient one; that is, the author, knowing all that is to be known about his characters, being in all their secrets, aware of the motives for all their actions, being in short the absolute creative author of his story, knows thereby every reason for everything that occurs. If two persons are talking together, each unaware of the other's real feelings, the author, knowing the feelings of both, may reveal to us why John, speaking thus and so, says what he does;

and then, promptly shifting the point of view from John's side to Mary's, may tell us not only what Mary replies, but why she replies to the effect that she does; and so on through the story. In one way this may be counted illuminating, but in another way it may overdo the matter, and may remove from the reader the impression of life-likeness. For in life you or I have but a single point of view, and listening to some one, we hear what he says from our own angle; or speaking ourselves, we know why we say what we do, but may only guess at what is going on in our listener's mind: we quite lack the omniscient point of view. A narrative method that reproduces the natural way may be more in accord with art than the artificial way that explains everything. Moreover, our interest is concentrated and enhanced if the story goes on in the lifelike way. Thus to sink ourselves in one character, hear with his ears, respond with his lips, think with his mind, and with these only, brings us into closer relationship with him than when we are transferring our interest rapidly from one person to another and back again.

Moreover, the limited point of view permits, on the whole, a more dramatic way of narrating. And still again, it permits a more uni-fied way of narrating. The closing in of the interest gains for us more in concentration than it loses for us in comprehensiveness. At any rate, modern novelists have been solicitous in choosing the points of view that they will maintain; and many of them have found the single point of view—all things seen, heard, interpreted, from a given person's angle—more productive of the desired effect of veri-similitude, not to say reality, than any other method. This focusing of attention—for that is what the process amounts to—brings its reward in an intensification of the reader's interest. Certainly there can be no doubt that the character whose point of view is selected tends to become familiar, natural, and real.

In *The Ambassadors* James has chosen to present from the point of view of the hero of the story, Strether, literally everything that is to be presented. We are to see things as he sees them, and we are to know at first hand what he thinks, why he acts or keeps from acting, and what the whole action means to him. All the other personages are to appear to us only when they appear to Strether; we shall hear them speak only when they speak to him; when they are out of his presence, they are out of ours. It does not follow that we shall accept his judgments of these personages: we preserve our independence there as definitely as we preserve it when an acquaintance tells us what he has heard and seen; we may accept wholly, or we may discount, in accord with our recognition of the speaker's accuracy and wisdom. But there it is: it is through him and through him only that the case has come into our experience; and at the end we shall know him through and through.

One other matter of technique must be mentioned, and then we shall be ready to proceed to the substance of the novel. This matter is the use of one or more nominally important but actually subordinate characters, whose function it is to expand the field of the point-of-view character. To appreciate the need of this expansion when the single point of view is chosen, imagine the extreme case of a taciturn, hermit-like character: the author then is bound to have difficulty in giving sufficient variety to the story, and we the readers shall be too strictly limited to a very limited character's experience. But, on the other hand, if the main character is quick and eager to talk to others, above all if he is naturally ready to confide his perplexities to some one else, and if this some one else is highly intelligent and prompt to give sympathy and counsel, the field of our main character's experience is vitally enlarged, and we the readers shall be by way of gaining a far more comprehensive view of the ensuing situations. By the use of this device, the author who chooses the single or selective point of view for his method gains something of the value of the omniscient point of view, but gains it without the disadvantages of that latter method.

The technical name for such a listening character is the confidant. It is obvious that in artistic writing the confidant will not be presented in a purely mechanical way. He or she, however subordinate to the main personages, will be portrayed as a real and vivid personality and will hold our interest for his or her own sake. Indeed, as a story progresses, such a person may acquire a definite narrative significance and be, as it were, intrusted with important functions in solving complexities of plot. A notable example in *The Ambassadors* of this emergence into essential, organic value is Maria Gostrey, who gradually and felicitously grows from a mere pleasant listener into a character of such significance that to her is allotted the right to share beautifully in the final moment as the curtain falls. In our novel, since Strether is in disposition frank and open, much use is made of confidants, or interlocutors, as the author sometimes calls them. The most important of these personages is Miss Gostrey; then follow in order of value Waymarsh, Bilham, Miss Barrace, and at a long distance Jim Pocock. Through their use the story gains greatly in vividness and breadth.

The problem in conscience presented in *The Ambassadors* is one for which no such light word as "attractive" will serve. One needs a word that will mean profound and fascinating at the same time: "penetrating," perhaps, or "poignant." At any rate, it is the problem of a man of fine nature, endowed with the conscientiousness that we think of as indigenous to New England, who has been drawn into a situation whose import is apparently clear and whose solution apparently calls for simple straightforward action. But the implications of the situation change under his very eyes as he comes closer and closer to its core. If he solves the matter as he is expected to do, loyally in behalf of those who have intrusted him with his mission, he must act on the basis of their inadequate information and in the light of their too narrow preconceptions. If in accordance with the new knowledge he has gained, he solves the matter in behalf of the person apparently most deeply concerned, Chad Newsome, he must seem recreant to the powers of which he is ambassador. Moreover, his success in accordance with the original plans means his worldly happiness and prosperity, and his failure means the loss of all that. Further, if he acts in accordance with all the revelations that have come to him, acts, in short, in a way to square with his own conscience, he must find that the person most deeply concerned is one previously counted as negligible in the real issue; and that not to that person, not to the object of his quest, not to those who sent him, and not to himself will ultimate reward come. How, then, shall he act?

Let us put all this concretely. Chad Newsome, the son of a wealthy manufacturing New England family, has been staying in Paris long enough to be a source of great worry to his widowed mother and to all his friends and acquaintances at home. The reason for his prolonged sojourn abroad in flagrant disregard of all the possibilities awaiting him in Woollett, Massachusetts, is in the eyes of the home people obvious and a bit unspeakable: no youth would stay so long in an alien land were there not some wicked woman, some hussy, holding him in her clutches. Family feeling calls on him to return, honor calls him, business calls him. But he doesn't, he won't, either return or discuss returning. Therefore he must be brought back, and, just as obviously, not by force but by persuasion. Some one must be sent over to Paris to induce him to break away from the reprehensible woman. Strether is chosen as ambassador.

Strether is an elderly friend of the family, related to it by ties of long acquaintance, by tried and trusted association with the family interests, and finally by the prospective ties of marriage with the elderly, anxious, and wealthy widow. The choice of the legate is a natural and happy one: he is intelligent, sympathetic, and gentle, and the young man has always liked him. Let him then go to Paris and spy out the way the land lies; let him appeal to the young man's sense of morality to break off the base entanglement; let him adjure Chad in the name of duty, in the name of filial affection, in the name of his financial future, in the name shall we say of Americanism, to come back to Woollett and take up the advertising opportunities of the prosperous manufacturing enterprise. As opposed to the brilliant business future, what are the unworthy charms of Paris? Surely it will be easy for Chad to see, once the claims of the practical are asserted with firmness and serenity, that the specious attractions of an alien civilization must be abandoned for the lucrative certainties of large production. Indeed, only a young man caught in the toils of a vile enchantress could have failed to see long ago the necessity of turning over a new leaf and beginning afresh in a career in which unite all the claims of morality, filial affection, and pecuniary gain. So much for the attitude of Woollett.

And who better than the kindly Strether to drive home the necessary point to the erring youth? For Strether is a person given to the ideal. In Woollett he has held aloft the banner of culture by editing a periodical, by lecturing on literature, and doubtless most of all by being a close friend of the Newsome family. He is a gentleman by birth, nurture, and lifelong habit, a natural minister plenipotentiary *in partibus infidelium*.

Well, Strether goes to Europe, landing at Liverpool and proceeding to Chester. Here the novel opens. The man at once begins to feel again the old-world charm, first aroused by a long-ago journey in the days of his young manhood, and persisting in his memories through all the intervening years. Chester, London, Paris (where the temporary absence of Chad gives the envoy time to orient himself), delightful scenes, delightful weather, delightful people—all these renew, enhance, create a spell in the heart of the elderly sojourner, contrasting all too vividly with the earnest, bustling New England factory town. There is a difference, there *would* be a difference, between Paris and Woollett, Mass. It is not on the side of Woollett that our traveler's imaginative balance dips. The finest and the best of the charm of Paris enters Strether's very soul. Is this the atmosphere in which to fling the duteous spokesman of Woollett interests?

The essential situation, however, remains: degenerate Chad, the wicked hussy, the yearning mother, the grand business opening; and most of all there remains the fine conscience of Strether. He is here to see the thing through, to do his duty, to bring back the redeemed prodigal son. And at last Chad returns to Paris and Strether sees him. But it isn't a reprobate Chad, it is a Chad so vastly improved that his prospective mentor may hardly recognize him for the same fellow. It is a Chad of charm and vigorous manhood, accomplished in the ways of the world, assured of himself, easy of approach, ready to discuss the whole situation amiably, and eager to have Strether learn at first hand what this wonderful foreign civilization is, that has so marvelously made over the home product. And, as if this daunting revelation of the young man's improvement were not enough, the enchantress turns out to be not a creature of the dance hall, studio, or stage, but a lady to the manner born, a woman of exquisite grace and breeding. In short, it is—as Chad's friends give Strether to understand—a virtuous attachment, that has done for the young man a world of wonders. What now is the ambassador's duty? He has come over to rescue a misguided idle rich youth, and has found an admirably poised young man, already in possession of more values than Woollett at its best could ever give him. One must begin to take stock all over again, and readjust oneself to the new situation. The very lack of opposition from Chad makes Strether's task the more difficult and searching. Strether needs time.

But time, even with the ample explanations conscientiously elaborated in Strether's copious letters home, is the last thing that Woollett is disposed to give him; and soon enough there arises in the Puritan-descended family the suspicion, the fear, the dread, the certainty that the ambassador himself has succumbed to the insidious wiles of Europe. He himself needs looking after, perhaps even more than Chad; for after all—so one may imagine Woollett animatedly saying—"there is no fool like an old fool," and Strether is no longer young. Therefore, still to rescue Chad, and to give Strether a last chance to rescue himself, there proceeds from the western shores a new ambassador, Chad's sister, Mrs. Jim Pocock, Sarah Newsome that was. Now we shall see what we shall see. For no Frenchwoman born, countess though she be, may pull the wool over the eyes of the lady from Woollett. And as a part of the new embassy, perhaps as ambassador, or perhaps only—to put it more bluntly—as bait, there is a fine specimen of the blooming American girl, Mamie Pocock, Jim's sister. What could better turn Chad from his devious ways than a pretty, wholesome, marriageable product of his native land? And of course there is Jim Pocock himself, but Jim, a mere American husband accompanying women, doesn't count.

What now? Sarah is indeed immune to the charm of Madame de Vionnet, and sees evil abundantly. To Sarah there is no improvement in Chad: Chad is hideous, and his entanglement indecent beyond speech. Now the blame is fixed fast on poor Strether: for Chad is willing to leave when Strether says so, and Strether hasn't yet said so, because he is still uncertain that Chad ought to go. Has not Chad chosen the better part, light and warmth and culture, against the commercial attractions of Woollett? Moreover, is it honest and kindly to leave Madame de Vionnet in the lurch?

And now, to cut our long summary short, Sarah turns out to be right, at bottom; right, as it were, for the wrong reasons, right in her fact and wrong in her conception of the truth, narrowly, mercilessly, unrightly right. And Strether finds out the fact with his own eyes. Now, since he knows the situation, he is filled with deepest compassion for Madame de Vionnet, and his last act in the case is to plead with Chad not to desert the woman who has made him what he is. Then by way of beautifully ironic ending, a new vista of real happiness opens out to Strether, and this happiness he denies himself, because out of all the bewildering experience through which he has moved there must come to him no personal profit.

In this novel there is story, as we have just seen, and there is an underlying idea or theme. Moral is hardly the right word for it, since it is not a notion evolved from the tale, but is the inspiring idea which set the whole narrative in motion, which preceded the narrative, indeed, and caused it to take shape at all. This underlying, animating idea sprang from the words of an elderly man (it is no secret, I believe, that it was our distinguished novelist Howells) addressed to a younger man, "Don't neglect your opportunities to live . . . you have only one life . . . live it to the full. If you haven't had that, what have you had?" Hence our author's embodiment in a story of a man who has not lived life to the full, but who none the less appreciates what he has lost or has never had, and who urges the listening youth not to make the same mistake. Hence the creation of a sequence of incidents that shall make plausible the opening of the eyes of the man who has largely missed life, by the spectacle of the younger man who is not missing life. Hence the unfolding of a story that shall carry to its logical conclusion the things involved in that recognition of a great meaning in life. And hence, finally, the adjuration to youth to accept the consequences of happy daring and to exult in a life that is free and well-rounded. But for all this, turn to the second chapter of Part Fifth; and for an account of the way the story sprang from the idea, read James's preface to this novel in the definitive edition of his works, that preface, incidentally, being one of James's best pieces of critical writing.

In the process of this superb novel there is, I believe, no weak spot, no unnecessary situation, no irrelevant detail; and yet amid all the closely woven excellence certain parts stand out as superfine. A positively magnificent piece of writing is the pair of chapters in Part Eleventh recounting Strether's little journey into the French country-side and his discovery there of Chad and Madame de Vionnet. Hardly less splendid is the scene in Gloriani's garden. Perfectly done, and only less effective than the two just named are a score of incidents, of which it may suffice to mention a very few: Strether and Maria Gostrey at the London theater, the dinner in Chad's apartment, the first call on Madame de Vionnet, Mamie on the hotel balcony, Strether at Notre Dame.

Scattered through the book are many admirable descriptions—of things seen, it should be remembered, through Strether's eyes and thereby given a tinge of personality. Moreover, since Strether is, broadly speaking, a man of James's own type, the author may use to the full his own delicacy of fancy and of speech. Some of these descriptions are long, some short; some record a visual image, others create an atmosphere; every one of them has a function in the story, and there is no description for description's sake. And these descriptions do what only perfect writing can do: they call up the thing described, they are evocative. At their best, as in the already instanced picture of rural France, they proceed gently, insinuatingly, mentioning things just in the order they would occur to the observer, having just the clean note that his mind would take them in with, possessing the color and shade that his mood would endow them with, seeming indeed not to be description at all, but the natural outflowing response of him who sees beautiful things wisely and happily —a consummate fusion of nature and of art. To have a little anthology of felicities, turn to the description of Chester wall, of the Luxembourg garden, of the dining room in the little Paris hotel, of Maria's apartment, of Madame de Vionnet's drawing room, of Notre Dame.

An even finer anthology might be made of passages of keen, sympathetic revelations of the spirit, interpretations of what goes on inside a man's mind and heart. But these things it is hardly fair to cite as separate passages, for they depend not only on the situation that gives rise to them, but also on the whole flow of preceding narrative. They are culminations, often phrased in the simplest of words, of a succession of dramatic moments skillfully marshaled to produce at the given instant the right and illuminating touch, no more, no less.

Several odds and ends of comment remain to be mentioned: the constant unseen pressure of the character of Mrs. Newsome—it is really a triumph to have her presence incessantly felt without her appearance on the scene; the variety of well-chosen places in which the scenes occur; the sense of unity present in each one of the twelve parts, separate yet contributing to the unity of the whole book; the naturalness with which Strether's mood responds to the environment; the constantly implied contrast, not of America with Europe, but of the hard and fast quality of the American factory town with the flower of European urban civilization. Incidentally, if piqued by this

INTRODUCTION

last point, the reader may take comfort in remembering that Strether is American of the Americans.

Here then is the novel, a book that the author rightly thought his masterpiece. Not now—let us beware of prejudgments—but after reading it, the reader, one hopes, may feel like acclaiming it one of the masterpieces of fiction

Martin W. Sampson.

Cornell University

1843 Henry James born, 15 April
1876 *Roderick Hudson*
1877 *The American*
1878 *The Europeans*
1879 *Daisy Miller*
     Hawthorne
1881 *The Portrait of a Lady*
1885 *A Little Tour in France*
1886 *The Bostonians*
     The Princess Casamassima
1888 *The Aspern Papers*
     Partial Portraits
1890 *The Tragic Muse*
1892 *The Lesson of the Master*
1893 *The Real Thing*
1894 *Theatricals*
1895 *Terminations*
1897 *The Spoils of Poynton*
     What Maisie Knew
1898 *In the Cage*
     The Turn of the Screw
1899 *The Awkward Age*
1900 *The Soft Side*
1901 *The Sacred Fount*
1902 *The Wings of the Dove*
1903 *The Beldonald Holbein*
     The Ambassadors
1904 *The Golden Bowl*
1905 *English Hours*
1907 *The American Scene*
1913 *A Small Boy and Others*
1916 James died, 28 February
     The Ivory Tower, unfinished
     The Sense of the Past, unfinished

FOREWORD

IN 1930 when this edition of *The Ambassadors* was first published there appeared also a biography of James, a bibliography, a set of his letters, an edition of *The Turn of the Screw*, and five scholarly articles about his work. But 1930 marked only the start of what since has become a revival of astonishing proportions. Since then there have been new editions of seven of James's longer novels, two collections of selected novels, eight collections of his short stories and short novels, two collections of his critical writing, one edition of his notebooks, and one collection of letters. In the same period he has been the subject of four biographies, four extended critical studies, one collection of critical essays, over one hundred articles in the learned journals, and scores of critical and biographical accounts in newspapers and magazines and general works on American literature.

Such evidence would indicate that James's popularity in recent years has been widespread and that those who dub him merely a "writer's writer" have not examined all the facts. It is true that he has a special appeal for other writers since he is preeminently a literary theoretician and craftsman. But he appeals also to scholars and critics and, as the new editions of his works demonstrate, to a growing body of general readers. Despite his limited range of interest—he wrote almost exclusively about the upper social group of which he was a part—he offers a minute analysis of human action and an almost uncanny insight into human motives. What seems apparent is that as readers become more skilled, more perceptive, his reputation grows.

For any study of James, *The Ambassadors* is admirably suited. Indeed, James himself called the novel "quite the best, 'all round,' of my productions." There were good reasons for his thinking so. The situation was a favorite one: an American exposed to the older and richer culture of Europe. He had treated facets of it in earlier works like *Roderick Hudson*, *The American*, *Daisy Miller*, and *The Portrait of a Lady*. The theme was one he had mulled over for five years, or ever since the day in October of 1895 when he had first heard it. It had been an admonition from William Dean Howells to Jonathan Sturges: "Live all you can: it's a mistake not to. It doesn't so matter what you do—but live. This place makes it all come over me. I see it now. I haven't done so—and now I'm old. It's too late. It has gone past me—I've lost it. You have time. You are young. Live." At the time, James had jotted these words in his notebook and had speculated there about the action and characters that could transmute the idea into a novel.

He began the actual work in the summer of 1900 when he was never fresher or more eager for novel-writing. For reasons not now altogether clear, he had spent the late eighties and early nineties dabbling in play-writing, for which he had no special talent. Despite the failure of his plays, he felt that the experience had not been all loss since it gave him a renewed sense of "all the big, suggestive, swarming world around me, with all its life and motion—in which I only need to dip my ladle." By the late nineties he was eager to return to the novel. The first two or three he tried, like *The Spoils of Poynton* and *The Awkward Age*, were sound enough technically but largely uninspired. Then he began *The Ambassadors*, and somehow caught fire immediately. It was a perfect combination: a favorite situation, an exciting theme, a fresh interest in novel-writing. To Howells he wrote, "My genius, I may even say, absolutely thrives."

What he did first was to write the story in synopsis form, a synopsis in 20,000 words! This he sent first to *Harper's Magazine* and then to the *North American Review*, the latter agreeing to print the complete novel in ten or twelve installments. It ran the full twelve and almost 155,000 words. The same year that it appeared in the *Review* (1903), it was published in book form by Harper's in this country and by Methuen in England. Four different stages in the creation of the novel are now easily available: the original notebook jotting and the synopsis, printed in *The Notebooks of Henry James* as edited by Professors Matthiessen and Murdock; the complete novel in an edition like this one; and the preface written for the New York Edition but now more readily obtainable in the collection of James's prefaces entitled *The Art of the Novel*. Taken together, these four give us the most detailed record of literary production that we have for any of James's novels or, for that matter, for any novel you might want to mention.

One gets the impression that James thought *The Ambassadors* his best book because it demanded so much of him in the way of technical accomplishment. In the preface he speaks glowingly of "the thrilling ups and downs, the intricate ins and outs of the compositional problem." To measure the extent of his accomplishment we might ask ourselves what some of the "ins and outs" of this compositional problem were. Professor Sampson in his delightful introduction to this edition mentions two when he discusses the single point of view and the use of a confidant. The list could be continued at some length: (1) how to make consistent a central character who has lived by duty and conscience but who can yet understand and even defend impulse and pleasure, (2) how to adapt content to the twelve-installment form so that the two will seem organically rather than mechanically related, (3) how to keep the center of interest in Strether's mind and yet introduce events which are objective and dramatic enough to sustain the reader's interest, (4) how to have Strether announce the basic theme—as James thought he should—somewhere near the middle of the book, (5) how to show Strether's growing approval of Chad's way of life without seeming to imply that Strether—or James—countenanced Bohemianism in general, (6) how to portray Chad as immensely improved without making him seem implausibly perfect, (7) how to demonstrate Mrs. Newsome's effect on the other characters without having her actually present, (8) how to enlist the American reader's sympathy for Mme. de Vionnet even though she represents a type of life Americans generally disapprove, (9) how to present the Pococks as stiffly provincial without making them caricatures or seeming to be nasty about Americans as a whole, and (10) how to have Strether come out of the experience grand and noble and not profiting by it in some mean and conventional way.

One suspects that it was more than technical accomplishment that endeared *The Ambassadors* to James. For consciously or unconsciously he must have known that the "great central intelligence" of which he was so fond was really his own. In several very real senses Strether was James and the novel is an autobiography. Strether's attitude toward Europe as contrasted with America was James's attitude. Strether's wistful regret that he had not lived more fully in the past was James's regret. Strether's ability to receive in the present "an amount of experience out of any proportion to his adventures" was James's ability. James's, too, were Strether's lack of animal passion,

FOREWORD

his reserve if not timidity, his acute awareness of human motives, and his rigid integrity. In short, we may do much worse than try to understand James through the character he thought his greatest achievement.

The final word should be about style. Admittedly James's later novels, of which *The Ambassadors* is one, are not easy for many people to read, especially if they have read nothing else by James or if they have no notion of what he is about. Dissatisfied with interpretations placed upon his earlier and more simply written books, James tested each sentence of the later ones, each word even, to see that sentence and word communicated what he thought to be just the right shade of meaning. The result is an involved style that is peculiarly his in diction, syntax, and word order—an idiom that is often more personal than conventional. Even the characters in a work like *The Ambassadors* speak in this idiom. Though many readers have had misgivings about the effectiveness of such highly individualized writing, James himself apparently had none. For he took time late in life to rewrite his more important earlier works in his later and more complicated style. Furthermore, after doing this he asserted that the person who reads an unrevised version of an early novel "forfeits half, or much more than half, my confidence." People accustomed to the terseness of contemporary prose may not at first be willing to agree with James, believing that many of his stylistic devices obscure rather than clarify the meaning. On continued acquaintance, however, most readers come to admit that for James's characters and the world in which they live, for James's own interest in analysis and speculation and artistic form, the style is the natural and often admirable consequence.

JOHN C. GERBER

The State University of Iowa

PART FIRST

THE AMBASSADORS

I

STRETHER'S first question, when he reached the hotel, was about his friend; yet on his learning that Waymarsh was apparently not to arrive till evening he was not wholly disconcerted. A telegram from him bespeaking a room "only if not noisy," with the answer paid, was produced for the inquirer at the office, so that the understanding that they should meet at Chester rather than at Liverpool remained to that extent sound. The same secret principle, however, that had prompted Strether not absolutely to desire Waymarsh's presence at the dock, that had led him thus to postpone for a few hours his enjoyment of it, now operated to make him feel that he could still wait without disappointment. They would dine together at the worst, and, with all respect to dear old Waymarsh—if not even, for that matter, to himself—there was little fear that in the sequel they should not see enough of each other. The principle I have just mentioned as operating had been, with the most newly disembarked of the two men, wholly instinctive—the fruit of a sharp sense that, delightful as it would be to find himself looking, after so much separation, into his comrade's face, his business would be a trifle bungled should he simply arrange that this countenance should present itself to the nearing steamer as the first "note," for him, of Europe. Mixed with everything was the apprehension, already, on Strether's part, that it would, at best, throughout, prove the note of Europe in quite a sufficient degree.

That note had been meanwhile — since the previous afternoon, thanks to this happier device— such a consciousness of personal

freedom as he had not known for years; such a deep taste of change,
and of having, above all, for the moment, nobody and nothing to
consider, as promised already, if headlong hope were not too foolish, to color his adventure with cool success. There were people
on the ship with whom he had easily—so far as ease could, up to
now, be imputed to him—consorted, and who for the most part
plunged straight into the current that set, from the landing-stage,
to London; there were others who had invited him to a tryst at
the inn and had even invoked his aid for a "look round" at the
beauties of Liverpool; but he had stolen away from every one alike;
had kept no appointment and renewed no acquaintance; had been
indifferently aware of the number of persons who esteemed themselves fortunate in being, unlike himself, "met"; and had even,
independently, unsociably, alone, without encounter or relapse and
by mere quiet evasion, given his afternoon and evening to the
immediate and the sensible. They formed a qualified draught of
Europe, an afternoon and an evening on the banks of the Mersey, but
such as it was he took his potion at least undiluted. He winced
a little, truly, at the thought that Waymarsh might be already at
Chester; he reflected that, should he have to describe himself at
Chester as having "got in" so early, it would be difficult to make
the interval look particularly eager; but he was like a man who,
finding in his pocket, with joy, more money than usual, handles
it awhile and idly, pleasantly chinks it before addressing himself
to the business of spending. That he was prepared to be vague
to Waymarsh about the hour of the ship's touching, and that he
both wanted extremely to see him and enjoyed extremely the duration of delay—these things, it is to be conceived, were early signs
in him that his relation to his actual errand might prove none of
the simplest. He was burdened, poor Strether—it had better be
confessed at the outset—with the oddity of a double consciousness.
There was detachment in his zeal and curiosity in his indifference.

After the young woman in the glass cage had held up to him,
across her counter, the pale-pink leaflet bearing his friend's name,
which she pronounced, he turned away to find himself, in the hall,
facing a lady who met his eyes as with an intention suddenly determined, and whose features—not freshly young, not markedly fine,
but expressive and agreeable—came back to him as from a recent

4

vision. For a moment they stood confronted; then the moment placed her: he had noticed her, the day before, at his previous inn, where—again in the hall—she had been briefly engaged with some people of his own ship's company. Nothing had actually passed between them, and he would as little have been able to say what had been the sign of her face for him on the first occasion as to name the ground of his present recognition. Recognition, at any rate, appeared to prevail on her own side as well—which would only have added to the mystery. All she now began by saying to him, none the less, was that, having chanced to catch his inquiry, she was moved to ask, by his leave, if it were possibly a question of Mr. Waymarsh of Milrose, Connecticut—Mr. Waymarsh the American lawyer.

"Oh yes," he replied, "my very well-known friend. He's to meet me here, coming up from Malvern, and I supposed he would already have arrived. But he doesn't come till later, and I'm relieved not to have kept him. Do you know him?" Strether wound up.

It was not till after he had spoken that he became aware of how much there had been in him of response; when the tone of her own rejoinder, as well as the play of something more in her face—something more, that is, than its apparently usual restless light—seemed to notify him. "I've met him at Milrose—where I used sometimes, a good while ago, to stay; I had friends there who were friends of his, and I've been at his house. I won't answer for it that he would know me," Strether's interlocutress pursued; "but I should be delighted to see him. Perhaps," she added, "I shall—for I'm staying over." She paused an instant, while our friend took in these things, and it was as if a good deal of talk had already passed. They even vaguely smiled at it, and Strether presently observed that Mr. Waymarsh would, no doubt, be easily to be seen. This, however, appeared to affect the lady as if she might have advanced too far. She was frank about everything. "Oh," she said, "he won't care!"—and she immediately thereupon remarked that she believed Strether knew the Munsters; the Munsters being the people he had seen her with at Liverpool.

But he didn't, as it happened, know the Munsters well enough to give the case much of a lift; so that they were left together as if over the mere laid table of conversation. Her qualification of the

5

mentioned connection had rather removed than placed a dish, and there seemed nothing else to serve. Their attitude remained, none the less, that of not forsaking the board; and the effect of this, in turn, was to give them the appearance of having accepted each other with an absence of preliminaries practically complete. They moved along the hall together, and Strether's companion remarked that the hotel had the advantage of a garden. He was aware by this time of his strange inconsequence: he had shirked the intimacies of the steamer and had muffled the shock of Waymarsh only to find himself forsaken, in this sudden case, both of avoidance and of caution. He passed with his new friend, before he had so much as gone up to his room, into the garden of the hotel, and at the end of ten minutes had agreed to meet her there again as soon as he should have made himself tidy. He wanted to look at the town, and they would forthwith look together. It was almost as if she had been in possession and received him as a guest. Her acquaintance with the place presented her in a manner as a hostess, and Strether had a rueful glance for the lady in the glass cage. It was as if this personage had seen herself instantly superseded.

When, in a quarter of an hour, he came down, what his hostess saw, what she might have taken in with a vision kindly adjusted, was the lean, slightly loose figure of a man of the middle height and something more, perhaps, than the middle age—a man of five-and-fifty, whose most immediate signs were a marked bloodless brownness of face, a thick, dark mustache, of characteristically American cut, growing strong and falling low, a head of hair still abundant, but abundantly streaked with gray, and a nose of bold, free prominence, the even line, the high finish, as it might have been called, of which, had a certain effect of mitigation. A perpetual pair of glasses astride of this fine ridge, and a line, unusually deep and drawn, the prolonged pen-stroke of time, accompanying the curve of the mustache from nostril to chin, did something to complete the facial furniture which an attentive observer would have seen to be catalogued, on the spot, in the vision of the other party to Strether's appointment. She waited for him in the garden, the other party, drawing on a pair of singularly fresh, soft and elastic light gloves and presenting herself with a superficial readiness which, as he approached her over the small smooth lawn and in the watery English sunshine, he might, with his rougher preparation, have marked as the model for such an occasion. She had, this lady, a perfect plain propriety, an expensive subdued suitability, that her companion was not free to analyze, but that struck him, so that his consciousness of it was instantly acute, as a quality quite new to him. He stopped on the grass, before reaching her, and went through the form of feeling for something, possibly forgotten, in the light overcoat he carried on his arm; yet the essence of the act was no more than the impulse to gain time. Nothing could have been more odd than Strether's feeling, at that moment, that he was launched in something of which the sense would be quite disconnected from the sense of his past, and which was literally beginning there and then. It had begun, in fact, already, upstairs, before the dressing-glass that struck him as blocking further, so strangely, the dimness of the window of his dull bedroom; begun with a sharper survey of the elements of Appearance than he had for a long time been moved to make. He had felt during those moments that these elements were not so much to his hand as he should have liked, and then had fallen back on the thought that they were precisely a matter as to which help was supposed to come from what he was about to do. He was about to go up to London, and hat and necktie might wait. What had come as straight to him as a ball in a well-played game— and caught, moreover, not less neatly—was just the air, in the person of his friend, of having seen and chosen, the air of achieved possession of those vague qualities and quantities that figured to him, collectively, as the advantage snatched from lucky chances. Without pomp or circumstance, certainly, as her original address to him, equally with his own response, had been, he would have sketched to himself his impression of her as: " Well, she's more subtly civilized—!" If " More subtly than *whom?*" would not have been for him a sequel to this remark, that was just by reason of his deep consciousness of the bearing of his comparison.

The amusement, at all events, of a civilization more subtle was what—familiar compatriot as she was, with the full tone of the compatriot and the rattling link, not with mystery, but only with dear dyspeptic Waymarsh — she appeared distinctly to promise.

His pause while he felt in his overcoat was positively the pause of confidence, and it enabled his eyes to make out as much of a case for her, in proportion, as her own made out for himself. She affected him as almost insolently young; but an easily carried five-and-thirty could still do that. She was, however, like himself, marked and wan; only it naturally couldn't have been known to him how much a spectator looking from one to the other might have discerned that they had in common. It would not for such a spectator have been altogether insupposable that, each so finely brown and so sharply spare, each confessing so to dents of surface and aids to sight, to a disproportionate nose and a head delicately or grossly grizzled, they might have been brother and sister. On this ground, indeed, there would still have been a residuum of difference; such a sister having known, surely, in respect to such a brother the extremity of separation, and such a brother feeling now, in respect to such a sister, the extremity of surprise. Surprise, it was true, was not, on the other hand, what the eyes of Strether's friend most showed him while she gave him, stroking her gloves smoother, the time he appreciated. They had taken hold of him straightway, measuring him up and down, as if they knew how; as if he were human material they had already in some sort handled. Their possessor was in truth, it may be communicated, the mistress of a hundred cases or categories, receptacles of the mind, subdivisions for convenience, in which, from a full experience, she pigeon-holed her fellow-mortals with a hand as free as that of a compositor scattering type. She was as equipped in this particular as Strether was the reverse, and it made an opposition between them which he might well have shrunk from submitting to if he had fully suspected it. So far as he did suspect it he was, on the contrary, after a momentary shake of his consciousness, as pleasantly passive as might be. He really had a sort of sense of what she knew. He had quite the sense that she knew things he didn't, and though this was a concession that, in general, he found not easy to make to women, he made it now as good-humoredly as if it lifted a burden. His eyes were so quiet behind his eternal nippers that they might almost have been absent without changing his face, which took its expression mainly, and not least its stamp of sensibility, from other sources, surface and grain and form.

8

He joined his guide in an instant, and he then felt that she had profited still better than he by his having been, for the moments just mentioned, so at the disposal of her intelligence. She knew even intimate things about him that he had not yet told her and perhaps never would. He was not unaware that he had told her rather remarkably many for the time, but these were not the real ones. Some of the real ones, however, precisely, were what she knew.

They were to pass again through the hall of the inn to get into the street, and it was here, presently, that she checked him with a question. "Have you looked up my name?"

He could only stop with a laugh. "Have you looked up mine?"

"Oh dear, yes—as soon as you left me. I went to the office and asked. Hadn't *you* better do the same?"

He wondered. "Find out who you are, after the uplifted young woman there has seen us thus scrape acquaintance?"

She laughed on her side now at the shade of alarm in his amusement. "Isn't it a reason the more? If what you're afraid of is the injury for me—my being seen to walk off with a gentleman who has to ask who I am—I assure you I don't in the least mind. Here, however," she continued, "is my card, and as I find there is something else again I have to say at the office, you can just study it during the moment I leave you."

She left him after he had taken from her the small pasteboard she had extracted from her pocket-book, and he had extracted another from his own, to exchange with it, before she came back. He read thus the simple designation "Maria Gostrey," to which was attached, in a corner of the card, with a number, the name of a street, presumably in Paris, without other appreciable identity than its foreignness. He put the card into his waistcoat pocket, keeping his own meanwhile in evidence; and as he leaned against the door-post he met with the smile of a straying thought what the expanse before the hotel offered to his view. It was positively droll to him that he should already have Maria Gostrey, whoever she was—and he hadn't really the least idea of it—in a place of safe keeping. He had somehow an assurance that he should carefully preserve the little token he had just tucked in. He gazed with unseeing, lingering eyes as he followed some of the implications of his act, asking himself if he really felt admonished to qualify it as disloyal. It was prompt, it was possibly even premature, and there was little doubt of the expression of face the sight of it would have produced in a certain person. But if it were " wrong "— why then he had better not have come out at all. At this, poor man, had he already—and even before meeting Waymarsh—arrived. He had believed he had a limit, but the limit had been transcended within thirty-six hours. By how long a space on the plane of manners or even of morals, moreover, he felt still more sharply after Maria Gostrey had come back to him and with a gay, decisive " So now—!" led him forth into the world. This counted, it struck him as he walked beside her with his overcoat on an arm, his umbrella under another and his personal pasteboard a little stiffly retained between forefinger and thumb—this struck him as really, in comparison, his introduction to things. It hadn't been " Europe " at Liverpool, no—not even in the dreadful, delightful, impressive streets the night before—to the extent his present companion made it so. She had not yet done that so much so as when, after their walk had lasted a few minutes and he had had time to wonder if a couple of sidelong glances from her meant that he had best have put on gloves, she almost pulled him up with an amused challenge. " But why—fondly as it's so easy to imagine your clinging to it— don't you put it away? Or if it's an inconvenience to you to carry it, one is often glad to have one's card back. The fortune one spends in them!"

Then he saw both that his way of marching with his own prepared tribute had affected her as a deviation in one of those directions he couldn't yet measure, and that she supposed this emblem to be still the one he had received from her. He handed her, accordingly, the card, as if in restitution, but as soon as she had it she felt the difference and, with her eyes on it, stopped short for apology. " I like," she observed, " your name."

" Oh," he answered, " you won't have heard of it!" Yet he had his reasons for not being sure but that she perhaps might.

Ah, it was but too visible! She read it over again as one who had never seen it. " ' Mr. Lewis Lambert Strether ' "—she sounded it almost as freely as if a stranger were in question. She repeated, however, that she liked it—" particularly the Lewis Lambert. It's the name of a novel of Balzac's."

" Oh, I know that!" said Strether.

" But the novel's an awfully bad one."

" I know that too," Strether smiled. To which he added with an irrelevance that was only superficial: " I come from Woollett, Massachusetts." It made her for some reason—the irrelevance or whatever—laugh. Balzac had described many cities, but he had not described Woollett, Massachusetts. " You say that," she returned, " as if you wanted one immediately to know the worst."

" Oh, I think it's a thing," he said, " that you must already have made out. I feel it so that I certainly must look it, speak it, and, as people say there, ' act ' it. It sticks out of me, and you knew, surely, for yourself, as soon as you looked at me."

" The worst, you mean ?"

" Well, the fact of where I come from. There, at any rate, it *is;* so that you won't be able, if anything happens, to say that I've not been straight with you."

" I see "—and Miss Gostrey looked really interested in the point he had made. " But what do you think of as happening ?"

Though he was not shy—which was rather anomalous—Strether gazed about without meeting her eyes; a motion that, in talk, was frequent with him, yet of which his words often seemed not at all the effect. " Why, that you should find me too hopeless." With which they walked on again together, while she answered, as they went, that the most " hopeless " of her countryfolk were precisely those, in general, she liked best. All sorts of other pleasant small things—small things that were yet large for him—flowered in the air of the occasion; but the bearing of the occasion itself on matters still remote concerns us too closely to permit us to multiply our illustrations. Two or three, however, in truth, we should perhaps regret to lose. The tortuous wall—girdle, long since snapped, of the little swollen city, half held in place by careful civic hands— wanders, in narrow file, between parapets smoothed by peaceful generations, pausing here and there for a dismantled gate or a bridged gap, with rises and drops, steps up and steps down, queer twists, queer contacts, peeps into homely streets and under the brows of gables, views of cathedral tower and waterside fields, of

11

nuddled English town and ordered English country. Too deep almost for words was the delight of these things for Strether; yet
as deeply mixed with it were certain images of his inward picture.
He had trod this walk in the far-off time, at twenty-five; but that,
instead of spoiling it, only enriched it for present feeling and
marked his renewal as a thing substantial enough to share. It
was with Waymarsh he should have shared it, and he was now, accordingly, taking from him something that was his due. He looked
repeatedly at his watch, and when he had done so for the fifth time
Miss Gostrey took him up.

"You're doing something that you think not right."

It so touched the place that he quite changed color, and his laugh
was almost awkward. "Am I enjoying it as much as *that?*"

"You're not enjoying it, I think, so much as you ought."

"I see"—he appeared thoughtfully to agree. "Great is my
privilege."

"Oh, it's not your privilege! It has nothing to do with *me.*
It has to do with yourself. Your failure's general."

"Ah, there you are!" he laughed. "It's the failure of Woollett.
That's general."

"The failure to enjoy," Miss Gostrey explained, "is what I
mean."

"Precisely. Woollett isn't sure it ought to enjoy. If it were it
would. But it hasn't, poor thing," Strether continued, "any one
to show it how. It's not like me. I have somebody."

They had stopped, in the afternoon sunshine—constantly pausing,
in their stroll, for the sharper sense of what they saw—and Strether
rested on one of the high sides of the old stony groove of the little
rampart. He leaned back on this support with his face to the
tower of the cathedral, now admirably commanded by their standpoint, the high red-brown mass, square and subordinately spired and
crocketted, retouched and restored, but charming to his long-sealed
eyes and with the first swallows of the year weaving their flight all
round it. Miss Gostrey lingered near him, full of an air, to which
she more and more justified her right, of understanding the effect
of things. She quite concurred. "You've indeed somebody." And
she added: "I wish you *would* let me show you how!"

"Oh, I'm afraid of you!" he declared.

She kept on him a moment, through her glasses and through his own, a certain pleasant pointedness. "Ah no, you're not! You're not in the least, thank goodness! If you had been we shouldn't so soon have found ourselves here together. I think," she comfortably said, "you trust me."

"I think I do!—but that's exactly what I'm afraid of. I shouldn't mind if I didn't. It's falling thus, in twenty minutes, so utterly into your hands. I dare say," Strether continued, "it's a sort of thing you're thoroughly familiar with; but nothing more extraordinary has ever happened to me."

She watched him with all her kindness. "That means simply that you've recognized me—which *is* rather beautiful and rare. You see what I am." As on this, however, he protested, with a good-humored headshake, a resignation of any such claim, she had a moment of explanation. "If you'll only come on further as you *have* come, you'll at any rate make out. My own fate has been too many for me, and I've succumbed to it. I'm a general guide—to 'Europe,' don't you know? I wait for people—I put them through. I pick them up—I set them down. I'm a sort of superior 'courier-maid.' I'm a companion at large. I take people, as I've told you, about. I never sought it—it has come to me. It has been my fate, and one's fate one accepts. It's a dreadful thing to have to say, in so wicked a world, but I verily believe that, such as you see me, there's nothing I don't know. I know all the shops and the prices—but I know worse things still. I bear on my back the huge load of our national consciousness, or, in other words—for it comes to that—of our nation itself. Of what is our nation composed but of the men and women individually on my shoulders? I don't do it, you know, for any particular advantage. I don't do it, for instance—some people do, you know—for money."

Strether could only listen and wonder and weigh his chance. "And yet, affected as you are then to so many of your clients, you can scarcely be said to do it for love." He waited a moment. "How do we reward you?"

She had her own hesitation, but "You don't!" she finally ex-claimed, setting him again in motion. They went on, but in a few minutes, though while still thinking over what she had said, he once more took out his watch; but mechanically, unconsciously, and as if made nervous by the mere exhilaration of what struck him as her strange and cynical wit. He looked at the hour without seeing it, and then, on something again said by his companion, had another pause. "You're really in terror of him."

He smiled a smile that he almost felt to be sickly. "Now you can see why I'm afraid of you."

"Because I've such illuminations? Why, they're all for your help! It's what I told you," she added, "just now. You feel as if this were wrong."

He fell back once more, settling himself, as if to hear more about it, against the parapet. "Then get me out!"

Her face fairly brightened for the joy of the appeal, but, as if it were a question of immediate action, she visibly considered "Out of waiting for him?—of seeing him at all?"

"Oh no—not that," said poor Strether, looking grave. "I've got to wait for him—and I want very much to see him. But out of the terror. You did put your finger on it a few minutes ago. It's general, but it avails itself of particular occasions. That's what it's doing for me now. I'm always considering something else; something else, I mean, than the thing of the moment. The obsession of the other thing is the terror. I'm considering at present, for instance, something else than *you*."

She listened with charming earnestness. "Oh, you oughtn't to do that!"

"It's what I admit. Make it, then, impossible."

She continued to think. "Is it really an 'order' from you?—that I shall take the job? *Will* you give yourself up?"

Poor Strether heaved his sigh. "If I only could! But that's the deuce of it—that I never can. No—I can't."

She was not, however, discouraged. "But you desire to, at least!"

"Oh, unspeakably!"

"Ah then, if you'll try!"—and she took over the job, as she had called it, on the spot. "Trust me!" she exclaimed; and the action of this, as they retraced their steps, was presently to make him pass his hand into her arm in the manner of a kind, dependent, paternal old person who wishes to be "nice" to a younger one. If he drew it out again, indeed, as they approached the inn, this may have been because, after more talk had passed between them, the relation of age, or at least of experience—which, for that matter, had already played to and fro with some freedom—affected him as incurring a readjustment. It was at all events perhaps lucky that they arrived in sufficiently separate fashion within range of the hotel-door. The young lady they had left in the glass cage watched as if she had come to await them on the threshold. At her side stood a person equally interested, by his attitude, in their return, and the effect of the sight of whom was instantly to determine for Strether another of those responsive arrests that we have had so repeatedly to note. He left it to Miss Gostrey to name, with the fine, full bravado, as it almost struck him, of her "Mr. Waymarsh!" what was to have been, what—he more than ever felt as his short stare of suspended welcome took things in—would have been, but for herself, his doom. It was already upon him, even at that distance, that Mr. Waymarsh was, for *his* part, joyless.

II

HE had none the less to confess to this friend that evening that he knew almost nothing about her, and it was a deficiency that Waymarsh, even with his memory refreshed by contact, by her own prompt and lucid allusions and inquiries, by their having partaken of dinner, in the public room, in her company, and by another stroll, to which she was not a stranger, out into the town to look at the cathedral by moonlight—it was a blank that the resident of Milrose, though admitting acquaintance with the Munsters, professed himself unable to fill. He had no recollection of Miss Gostrey, and two or three questions that she put to him about those members of his circle had, to Strether's observation, the same effect he himself had already more directly felt—the effect of appearing to place all knowledge, for the time, on this original woman's side. It interested him indeed to mark the limits of any such relation for her with his friend as there could possibly be a question of, and it particularly struck him that they were to be marked altogether in Waymarsh's quarter. This added to his own sense of having gone far with her—gave him an early illustration of a much shorter course. There was a certitude he immediately grasped—a conviction that Waymarsh would quite fail, as it were, and on whatever degree of acquaintance, to profit by her.

There had been, after the first interchange among the three, a talk of some five minutes, in the hall, and then the two men had adjourned to the garden, Miss Gostrey, for the time, disappearing. Strether, in due course, accompanied his friend to the room he had bespoken, and had, before going out, scrupulously visited; where, at the end of another half hour, he had no less discreetly left him. On leaving him he repaired straight to his own room, but with the effect, very soon, of feeling the compass of that chamber resented by his condition. There he had, on the spot, the first consequence

of their reunion. A place was too small for him after
seemed large enough before. He had awaited it with
that he would have been sorry, have been almost ashame
recognize as emotion, yet with a tacit assumption, at t
time, that emotion would in the event find itself relieve
actual oddity was that he was only more excited; and his
ment—to which, indeed, he would have found it difficult ins
to give a name—brought him once more downstairs and cause
for some minutes vaguely to wander. He went once more t
garden; he looked into the public room, found Miss Gostrey v
ing letters and backed out; he roamed, fidgeted and wasted ti
but he was to have his more intimate session with his friend bef
the evening closed.

It was late—it was not till Strether had spent an hour upstair
with him—that this subject consented to betake himself to doubt
ful rest. Dinner and the subsequent stroll by moonlight—a dream
on Strether's part, of romantic effects rather prosaically merged in
a mere missing of thicker coats—had measurably intervened, and
this midnight conference was the result of Waymarsh's having—
when they were free, as he put it, of their fashionable friend—
found the smoking-room not quite what he wanted, and yet bed
what he wanted still less. His most frequent form of words was
that he knew himself, and they were applied on this occasion t
his certainty of not sleeping. He knew himself well enough t
know that he should have a night of prowling unless he shou'
succeed, as a preliminary, in getting as tired as he wanted.
the effort directed to this end involved, till a late hour, the pr
ence of Strether—consisted, that is, in the detention of the la
for full discourse—there was yet an impression of minor discip
involved, for our friend, in the picture Waymarsh made as he
in trousers and shirt, on the edge of his couch. With his long
extended and his large back much bent, he nursed alternatel
an almost incredible time, his elbows and his beard. He str
visitor as extremely, as almost wilfully, uncomfortable; ye
had this been for Strether, from that first glimpse of him
certed in the porch of the hotel, but the predominant n
was a discomfort that was in a manner contagious, as wel
in a manner, inconsequent and unfounded; the visitor

unless he should get used to it — or unless Waymarsh himself should—it would constitute a menace for his own prepared, his own already confirmed, consciousness of the agreeable. On their first going up together to the room that Strether had selected for him Waymarsh had looked it over, in silence, with a sigh that represented for his companion, if not the habit of disapprobation, at least the despair of felicity; and this look had recurred to Strether as the key of much that he had since observed. "Europe," he had begun to gather from these things, had, as yet, then, for him, rather failed of its message; he had not got into tune with it, and had almost, at the end of three months, renounced any such expectation.

He really appeared at present to insist on that by just perching there with the gas in his eyes. This of itself somehow conveyed the futility of single rectifications in a multiform failure. He had a large, handsome head, and a large, sallow, seamed face—a striking, significant physiognomic total, the upper range of which, the great political brow, the thick, loose hair, the dark, fuliginous eyes, recalled even to a generation whose standard had dreadfully deviated the impressive image, familiar by engravings and busts, of some great national worthy of the earlier part of the mid-century. He was of the personal type—and it was an element in the power and promise that in their early time Strether had found in him— of the American statesman, the statesman of "Congressional halls," of an elder day. The legend had been, in later years, that, as the lower part of his face, which was weak, and slightly crooked, spoiled the likeness, this was the real reason for the growth of his beard, which might have seemed to spoil it for those not in the secret. He shook his mane; he fixed, with his admirable eyes, his auditor or his observer; he wore no glasses and had a way, partly formidable, yet also partly encouraging, as from a representative to a constituent, of looking very hard at those who approached him. He met you as if you had knocked and he had bidden you enter. Strether, who had not seen him for a long interval, apprehended him now with a freshness of taste, and had perhaps never done him such ideal justice as on this occasion. The head was bigger, the eyes finer, than they need have been for the career; but that only meant, after all, that the career was itself expressive.

What it expressed at midnight in the gas - glaring bedroom **at** Chester was that the subject of it had, at the end of years, barely escaped, by flight in time, a general nervous collapse. But this very proof of the full life, as the full life was understood at Milrose, would have made, to Strether's imagination, an element in which Waymarsh could have floated easily had he only consented to float. Alas, nothing so little resembled floating as the rigor with which, on the edge of his bed, he hugged his posture of prolonged impermanence. It suggested to his comrade something that always, when kept up, worried him—a person established in a railway-coach with a forward inclination. It represented the angle at which poor Waymarsh was to sit through the ordeal of Europe.

Thanks to the stress of occupation, the strain of professions, the absorption and embarrassment of each, they had not, for some five years before this sudden brief and almost bewildering reign of comparative ease, found, at home, so much as a day for a meeting; a fact that was in some degree an explanation of the sharpness with which, for Strether, most of his friend's features stood out. Those he had lost sight of since the early time came back to him; others that it was never possible to forget struck him now as sitting, clustered and expectant, like a somewhat defiant family-group, on the doorstep of their residence. The room was narrow for its length, and Strether's friend on the bed thrust so far a pair of slippered feet that he had almost to step over them in his re-current rebounds from his chair to fidget back and forth. There were marks they made on things to talk about, and on things not to, and one of the latter, in particular, fell like the tap of chalk on the blackboard. Married at thirty, Waymarsh had not lived with his wife for fifteen years, and it came up vividly between them in the glare of the gas that Strether was not to ask about her. He knew they were still separate and that she lived at hotels, travelled in Europe, painted her face, and wrote her husband abusive letters, of not one of which, to a certainty, that sufferer spared himself the perusal; but he respected without difficulty the cold twilight that had settled on this side of his companion's life. It was a province in which mystery reigned, and as to which Waymarsh had never spoken the informing word. Strether, who wanted to do him the highest justice wherever he *could* do it, singularly admired him **for** the dignity of this reserve, and even counted it as one of the grounds—grounds all handled and numbered—for ranking him, in the range of their acquaintance, as a success. He *was* a success, Waymarsh, in spite of overwork, of prostration, of sensible shrinkage, of his wife's letters and of his not liking Europe. Strether would have reckoned his own career less futile had he been able to put into it anything so handsome as so much fine silence. One might, oneself, easily have left Mrs. Waymarsh; and one would assuredly have paid one's tribute to the ideal in covering with that attitude the derision of having been left by her. Her husband had held his tongue, and had made a large income; and these were the achievements, in especial, as to which Strether envied him. Our friend had had indeed, for his part too, a subject for silence, which he fully appreciated; but it was a matter of a different sort, and the figure of the income he had arrived at had never been high enough to look any one in the face.

"I don't know as I quite see what you require it for. You don't appear sick to speak of." It was of Europe that Waymarsh thus finally spoke.

"Well," said Strether, falling as much as possible into step, "I guess I don't *feel* sick now that I've started. But I had pretty well run down before I did start."

Waymarsh raised his melancholy look. "Ain't you about up to your usual average?"

It was not quite pointedly sceptical, but it seemed somehow a plea for the purest veracity, and affected our friend, proportionately, as the very voice of Milrose. He had long since made a mental distinction—though never, in truth, daring to betray it—between the voice of Milrose and the voice, even, of Woollett. It was the former, he felt, that was most in the real tradition. There had been occasions in his past when the sound of it had reduced him to temporary confusion, and the present, for some reason, suddenly became such another. It was no light matter, none the less, that the very effect of his confusion should be to make him again prevaricate. "That description hardly does justice to a man to whom it has done such a lot of good to see *you*."

Waymarsh fixed on his washing-stand the silent, detached stare with which Milrose in person, as it were, might have marked the unexpectedness of a compliment from Woollett; and Strether, on his side, felt once more like Woollett in person. " I mean," his friend presently continued, " that your appearance isn't as bad as I've seen it: it compares favorably with what it was when I last noticed it." On this appearance Waymarsh's eyes yet failed to rest; it was almost as if they obeyed an instinct of propriety, and the effect was still stronger when, always considering the basin and jug, he added: " You've filled out some since then."

" I'm afraid I have," Strether laughed: " one does fill some with all one takes in, and I've taken in, I dare say, more than I've natural room for. I was dog-tired when I sailed." It had the oddest sound of cheerfulness.

" *I* was dog-tired," his companion returned, " when I arrived, and it's this wild hunt for rest that takes all the life out of me. The fact is, Strether—and it's a comfort to have you here at last to say it to; though I don't know, after all, that I've really waited; I've told it to people I've met in the cars—the fact is, such a country as this ain't my *kind* of country, any way. There ain't a country I've seen over here that *does* seem my kind. Oh, I don't say but what there are plenty of pretty places and remarkable old things; but the trouble is that I don't seem to feel anywhere in tune. That's one of the reasons, I suppose, I've gained so little. I haven't had the first sign of that lift I was led to expect." With this he broke out more earnestly. " Look here — I want to go back."

His eyes were all attached to Strether's now, for he was one of the men who fully face you when they talk of themselves. This enabled his friend to look at him hard and immediately to appear in his own eyes, by doing so, to the highest advantage. " That's a genial thing to say to a fellow who has come out on purpose to meet you!"

Nothing could have been finer than, on this, Waymarsh's sombre glow. " *Have* you come out on purpose?"

" Well—very largely."

" I thought, from the way you wrote, there was something back of it."

Strether hesitated. " Back of my desire to be with you?"

" Back of your prostration."

Strether, with a smile made more dim by a certain consciousness, shook his head. "There are all the causes of it!"

"And no particular cause that seemed most to drive you?"

Our friend could at last conscientiously answer. "Yes. One. There *is* a matter that has had much to do with my coming out."

Waymarsh waited a little. "Too private to mention?"

"No, not too private—for *you*. Only rather complicated."

"Well," said Waymarsh, who had waited again. "I *may* lose my mind over here, but I don't know as I've done so yet."

"Oh, you shall have the whole thing. But not to-night."

Waymarsh seemed to sit stiffer and to hold his elbows tighter "Why not—if I can't sleep?"

"Because, my dear man, I *can!*"

"Then where's your prostration?"

"Just in that—that I can put in eight hours;" and Strether brought it out that if Waymarsh didn't "gain" it was because he didn't go to bed: the result of which was, in its order, that, to do the latter justice, he permitted his friend to insist upon his really getting settled. Strether, with a kind coercive hand for it, assisted him to this consummation, and again found his own part in their relation auspiciously enlarged by the smaller touches of lowering the lamp and seeing to a sufficiency of blanket. It somehow ministered for him to indulgence to feel Waymarsh, who looked unnaturally big and black in bed, as much tucked in as a patient in a hospital and, with his covering up to his chin, as much simplified by it. He hovered in vague pity, in fine, while his companion challenged him out of the bedclothes. "Is she really after you? Is that what's behind?"

Strether felt an uneasiness at the direction taken by his companion's vision, but he played a little at uncertainty. "Behind my coming out?"

"Behind your prostration, or whatever. It's generally felt, you know, that she follows you up pretty close."

Strether's candor was never very far off. "Oh, it has occurred to you that I'm literally running away from Mrs. Newsome?"

"Well, I haven't *known* but what you are. You're a very attractive man, Strether. You've seen for yourself," said Waymarsh

22

"what that lady downstairs makes of it. Unless indeed," he rambled on with an effect between the ironic and the anxious, " it's you that are after *her*. Is Mrs. Newsome *over* here?" He spoke as with a droll dread of her.

It made his friend—though rather dimly—smile. " Dear no; she's safe, thank goodness—as I think I more and more feel—at home. She thought of coming, but she gave it up. I've come in a manner instead of her; and come, to that extent—for you're right in your inference—on her business. So you see there *is* plenty of connection."

Waymarsh continued to see at least all there was. "Involving accordingly the particular one I've referred to?"

Strether took another turn about the room, giving a twitch to his companion's blanket and finally gaining the door. His feeling was that of a nurse who had earned personal rest by having made everything straight. " Involving more things than I can think of breaking ground on now. But don't be afraid—you shall have them from me: you'll probably find yourself having quite as much of them as you can do with. I shall—if we keep together—very much depend on your impression of some of them."

Waymarsh's acknowledgment of this tribute was characteristically indirect. " You mean to say you don't believe we *will* keep together?"

" I only glance at the danger," Strether paternally said, " because when I hear you wail to go back I seem to see you open up such possibilities of folly."

Waymarsh took it—silent a little—like a large snubbed child. " What are you going to do with me?"

It was the very question Strether himself had put to Miss Gostrey, and he wondered if he had sounded like that. But *he* at least could be more definite. " I'm going to take you right down to London."

" Oh, I've *been* down to London!" Waymarsh more softly moaned. " I've no use, Strether, for anything down there."

" Well," said Strether, good-humoredly, " I guess you've some use for *me.*"

" So I've got to go?"

" Oh, you've got to go further yet."

"Well," Waymarsh sighed, "do your damnedest! Only you *will* tell me before you lead me on all the way—?"

Our friend had again so lost himself, both for amusement and for contrition, in the wonder of whether he had made, in his own challenge that afternoon, such another figure, that he for an instant missed the thread. "Tell you—?"

"Why, what you've got on hand."

Strether hesitated. "Why, it's such a matter as that, even if I positively wanted, I shouldn't be able to keep it from you."

Waymarsh gloomily gazed. "What does that mean, then, but that your trip is just *for* her?"

"For Mrs. Newsome? Oh, it certainly is, as I say. Very much."

"Then why do you also say it's for me?"

Strether, in impatience, violently played with his latch. "It's simple enough. It's for both of you."

Waymarsh at last turned over with a groan. "Well, *I* won't marry you!"

"Neither, when it comes to that—!" But Strether had already laughed and escaped.

III

HE had told Miss Gostrey that he should probably take, for departure with Waymarsh, some afternoon train, and it thereupon in the morning appeared that this lady had made her own plan for an earlier one. She had breakfasted when Strether came into the coffee-room; but, Waymarsh not having yet emerged, he was in time to recall her to the terms of their understanding and to pronounce her discretion overdone. She was not, surely, to break away at the very moment she had created a want. He had met her as she rose from her little table in a window, where, with the morning papers beside her, she reminded him, as he let her know, of Major Pendennis breakfasting at his club—a compliment of which she professed a deep appreciation; and he detained her as pleadingly as if he had already—and notably under pressure of the visions of the night—learned to be unable to do without her. She must teach him at all events, before she went, to order breakfast as breakfast was ordered in Europe, and she must especially sustain him in the problem of ordering for Waymarsh. The latter had laid upon his friend, by desperate sounds through the door of his room, dreadful divined responsibilities in respect to beefsteak and oranges—responsibilities which Miss Gostrey took over with an alertness of action that matched her quick intelligence. She had weaned the expatriated before from traditions compared with which the matutinal beefsteak was but the creature of an hour, and it was not for her, with some of her memories, to falter in the path; though she freely enough declared, on reflection, that there was always, in such cases, a choice of opposed policies. "There are times when to give them their head, you know—!"

They had gone to wait together in the garden for the dressing of the meal, and Strether found her more suggestive than ever. "Well, what?"

"Is to bring about for them such a complexity of relations—unless indeed we call it a simplicity!—that the situation *has* to wind itself up. They want to go back."

"And you want them to go!" Strether gayly concluded.

"I always want them to go, and I send them as fast as I can."

"Oh, I know—you take them to Liverpool."

"Any port will serve in a storm. I'm—with all my other functions—an agent for repatriation. I want to re-people our stricken country. What will become of it else? I want to discourage others."

The ordered English garden, in the freshness of the day, was delightful to Strether, who liked the sound, under his feet, of the tight, fine gravel, packed with the chronic damp, and who had the idlest eye for the deep smoothness of turf and the clean curves of paths. "Other people?"

"Other countries. Other people—yes. I want to encourage our own."

Strether wondered. "Not to come? Why then do you 'meet' them?—since it doesn't appear to be to stop them?"

"Oh, that they shouldn't come is, as yet, too much to ask. What I attend to is that they come quickly and return still more so. I meet them to help it to be over as soon as possible, and though I don't stop them I've my way of putting them through. That's my little system; and, if you want to know," said Maria Gostrey, "it's my real secret, my innermost mission and use. I only seem, you see, to beguile and approve; but I've thought it all out and I'm working all the while underground. I can't perhaps quite give you my formula, but I think that, practically, I succeed. I send you back spent. So you stay back. Passed through my hands—"

"We don't turn up again?" The further she went, always, the further he seemed to see himself able to follow. "I don't want your formula—I feel quite enough, as I hinted yesterday, your abysses. Spent!" he echoed. "Thank you—if that's how you're arranging so subtly to send me—for the warning."

For a minute, in the pleasant place—poetry in tariffed items, but all the more, for guests already convicted, a challenge to consumption—they smiled at each other in confirmed fellowship. "Do you call it subtly? It's a plain, poor tale. Besides, you're a special case."

"Oh, special cases—that's weak!" She was weak enough, further still, to defer her journey and agree to accompany the gentlemen on their own, might a separate carriage mark her independence; though it was, in spite of this, to befall, after luncheon, that she went off alone, and that, with a tryst taken for a day of her company in London, they lingered another night. She had, during the morning—spent in a way that he was to remember, later on, as the very climax of his foretaste, as warm with presentiments, with what he would have called collapses—had all sorts of things out with Strether; and among them the fact that though there was never a moment of her life when she wasn't "due" somewhere, there was yet scarce a perfidy to others of which she was not capable for his sake. She explained, moreover, that wherever she happened to be she found a dropped thread to pick up, a ragged edge to repair, some familiar appetite in ambush, jumping out as she approached, yet appeasable with a temporary biscuit. It became, on her taking the risk of the deviation imposed on him by her insidious arrangement of his morning meal, a point of honor for her not to fail with Waymarsh of the larger success too; and her boast, later, to Strether, was that she had made their friend fare—and quite without his knowing what was the matter—as Major Pendennis would have fared at the Megatherium. She had made him breakfast like a gentleman, and it was nothing, she forcibly asserted, to what she would yet make him do. She made him participate in the slow reiterated ramble with which, for Strether, the new day amply filled itself; and it was by her art that he somehow had the air, on the ramparts and in the Rows, of carrying a point of his own.

The three strolled and stared and gossiped, or at least the two did; the case really yielding, for their comrade, if analyzed, but the element of stricken silence. This element, indeed, affected Strether as charged with audible rumblings, but he was conscious of the care of taking it, explicitly, as a sign of pleasant peace. He wouldn't appeal too much, for that provoked stiffness; yet he wouldn't be too freely tacit, for that suggested giving up. Waymarsh himself adhered to an ambiguous dumbness that might have represented either the growth of a perception or the despair of one; and at times

27

and in places—where the low-browed galleries were darkest, the opposite gables queerest, the solicitations, of every kind, densest—the others caught him fixing hard some object of minor interest, fixing even at moments nothing discernible, as if he were indulging it with a truce. When he met Strether's eye on such occasions he looked guilty and furtive, fell the next minute into some attitude of retractation. Our friend couldn't show him the right things for fear of provoking some total renouncement, and was tempted even to show him the wrong in order to make him differ with triumph. There were moments when he himself felt shy of professing the full sweetness of the taste of leisure, and there were others when he found himself feeling as if his passages of interchange with the lady at his side might fall upon the third member of their party very much as Mr. Burchell, at Dr. Primrose's fireside, was influenced by the high flights of the visitors from London. The smallest things so arrested and amused him that he repeatedly almost apologized—brought up afresh, in explanation, his plea of a previous grind. He was aware at the same time that his grind had been as nothing to Waymarsh's, and he repeatedly confessed that, to cover his frivolity, he was doing his best for his previous virtue.

Do what he might, however, his previous virtue was still there, and it seemed fairly to stare at him out of the windows of shops that were not as the shops of Woollett, fairly to make him want things that he shouldn't know what to do with. It was, by the oddest, the least admissible, of laws, demoralizing him now; and the way it boldly took was to make him want more wants. These first walks in Europe were in fact a kind of finely lurid intimation of what one might find at the end of that process. Had he come back, after long years, in something already so like the evening of life, only to be exposed to it? It was at any rate over the shop-windows that he made, with Waymarsh, most free; though it would have been easier had not the latter most sensibly yielded to the appeal of the merely useful trades. He pierced with his sombre detachment the plate-glass of ironmongers and saddlers, while Strether flaunted an affinity with the dealers in stamped letter-paper and in neckties. Strether was in fact recurrently shameless in the presence of the tailors, though it was just over the heads of the tailors that his countryman most loftily looked. This gave Miss Gostrey a grasped opportunity to back up Waymarsh at his expense. The weary law-yer—it was unmistakable—had a conception of dress; but that, in view of some of the features of the effect produced, was just what made the danger of insistence on it. Strether wondered if he by this time thought Miss Gostrey less fashionable or Lambert Strether more so; and it appeared probable that most of the re-marks exchanged between this latter pair about passers, figures, faces, personal types exemplified in their degree the disposition to talk as " society " talked.

Was what was happening to himself then, was what already *had* happened, really that a woman of fashion was floating him into so-ciety, and that an old friend, deserted on the brink, was watching the force of the current? When the woman of fashion permitted Strether—as she permitted him at the most—the purchase of a pair of gloves, the terms she made about it, the prohibition of neck-ties and other items till she should be able to guide him through the Burlington Arcade, were such as to fall upon a sensitive ear as a challenge to just imputations. Miss Gostrey was such a woman of fashion as could make without a symptom of vulgar blinking an appointment for the Burlington Arcade. Mere discriminations about a pair of gloves could thus at all events represent—always for such sensitive ears as were in question—possibilities of some-thing that Strether could make a mark against only as the peril of apparent wantonness. He had quite the consciousness of his new friend, for their companion, that he might have had of a Jesuit in petticoats, a representative of the recruiting interests of the Catholic church. The Catholic church, for Waymarsh—that was to say the enemy, the monster of bulging eyes and far-reaching, quivering, groping tentacles—was exactly society, exactly the multi-plication of shibboleths, exactly the discrimination of types and tones, exactly the wicked old Rows of Chester, rank with feudalism; exactly, in short, Europe.

There was light for observation, however, in an incident that occurred just before they turned back to luncheon. Waymarsh had been for a quarter of an hour exceptionally mute and distant, and something or other—Strether was never to make out exactly what—proved, as it were, too much for him after his comrades had stood for three minutes taking in, while they leaned on an old balustrade that guarded the edge of the Row, a particularly crooked and huddled street-view. "He thinks us sophisticated, he thinks us worldly, he thinks us wicked, he thinks us all sorts of queer things," Strether reflected; for it was wondrous, the vague quantities that our friend had, within a couple of short days, acquired the habit of conveniently and conclusively lumping together. There seemed moreover a direct connection between some such inference and a sudden grim dash taken by Waymarsh to the opposite side. This movement was startlingly sudden, and his companions at first supposed him to have espied, to be pursuing, the glimpse of an acquaintance. They next made out, however, that an open door had instantly received him, and they then recognized him as engulfed in the establishment of a jeweller, behind whose glittering front he was lost to view. The act had somehow the note of a demonstration, and it left each of the others to show a face almost of fear. But Miss Gostrey broke into a laugh. "What's the matter with him?"

"Well," said Strether, "he can't stand it."

"But can't stand what?"

"Anything. Europe."

"Then how will that jeweller help him?"

Strether seemed to make it out, from their standpoint, between the interstices of arrayed watches, of close-hung dangling gewgaws. "You'll see."

"Ah, that's just what—if he buys anything—I'm afraid of: that I shall see something rather dreadful."

Strether studied the finer appearances. "He may buy everything."

"Then don't you think we ought to follow him?"

"Not for worlds. Besides, we can't. We're paralyzed. We exchange a long, scared look; we publicly tremble. The thing is, you see, we 'realize.' He has struck for freedom."

She wondered, but she laughed. "Ah, what a price to pay! And I was preparing some for him so cheap."

"No, no," Strether went on, frankly amused now; "don't call it that: the kind of freedom _you_ deal in is dear." Then as to justify himself: "Am I not, in _my_ way, trying it? It's this."

"Being here, you mean, with me?"

"Yes, and talking to you as I do. I've known you a few hours.

30

and I've known *him* all my life; so that if the ease I thus take with you about him isn't magnificent"—and the thought of it held him a moment—"why, it's rather base."

"It's magnificent!" said Miss Gostrey, to make an end of it. "And you should hear," she added, "the ease *I* take—and I above all intend to take—with Mr. Waymarsh."

Strether thought. "About *me?* Ah, that's no equivalent. The equivalent would be Waymarsh's serving me up—his remorseless analysis of me. And he'll never do that"—he was sadly clear. "He'll never remorselessly analyze me." He quite held her with the authority of this. "He'll never say a word to you about me."

She took it in; she did it justice; yet after an instant her reason, her restless irony, disposed of it. "Of course he won't. For what do you take people, that they're able to say words about anything, able remorselessly to analyze? There are not many like you and me. It will be only because he's too stupid."

It stirred in her friend a sceptical echo which was at the same time the protest of the faith of years. "Waymarsh stupid?"

"Compared with you."

Strether had still his eyes on the jeweller's front, and he waited a moment to answer. "He's a success of a kind that I haven't approached."

"Do you mean he has made money?"

"He makes it—to my belief. And I," said Strether, "though with a back quite as bent, have never made anything. I'm a perfectly equipped failure."

He was afraid, an instant, that she would ask him if he meant he was poor; and he was glad she didn't, for he really didn't know to what the truth on this unpleasant point mightn't have prompted her. She only, however, confirmed his assertion. "Thank goodness you're a failure—it's why I so distinguish you! Anything else to-day is too hideous. Look about you—look at the successes. Would you *be* one, on your honor? Look, moreover," she continued, "at me."

For a little, accordingly, their eyes met. "I see," Strether returned. "You too are out of it."

"The superiority you discern in me," she concurred, "announces my futility. If you knew," she sighed, "the dreams of my youth!

But our realities are what has brought us together. We're beaten brothers in arms."

He smiled at her kindly enough, but he shook his head. "It doesn't alter the fact that you're expensive. You've cost me already—!"

But he had hung fire. "Cost you what?"

"Well, my past—in one great lump. But no matter," he laughed: "I'll pay with my last penny."

Her attention, however, had now been engaged by their comrade's return, for Waymarsh met their view as he came out of his shop. "I hope he hasn't paid," she said, "with *his* last; though I'm convinced he has been splendid, and has been so for you."

"Ah no—not that!"

"Then for me?"

"Quite as little." Waymarsh was by this time near enough to show signs his friend could read, though he seemed to look almost carefully at nothing in particular.

"Then for himself?"

"For nobody. For nothing. For freedom."

"But what has freedom to do with it?"

Strether's answer was indirect. "To be as good as you and me. But different."

She had had time to take in their companion's face; and with it, as such things were easy for her, she took in all. "Different—yes. But better!"

If Waymarsh was sombre he was also indeed almost sublime. He told them nothing, left his absence unexplained, and though they were convinced he had made some extraordinary purchase they were never to learn its nature. He only glowered grandly at the tops of the old gables. "It's the sacred rage," Strether had had further time to say; and this sacred rage was to become, between them, for convenient comprehension, the description of one of his periodical necessities. It was Strether who eventually contended that it did make him better than they. But by that time Miss Gostrey was convinced that she didn't want to be better than Strether.

PART SECOND

THOSE occasions on which Strether was, in association with the
exile from Milrose, to see the sacred rage glimmer through would
doubtless have their due periodicity; but our friend had meanwhile
to find names for many other matters. On no evening of his life
perhaps, as he reflected, had he had to supply so many as on the third
of his short stay in London; an evening spent, by Miss Gostrey's
side, at one of the theatres, to which he had found himself trans-
ported, without his own hand raised, on the mere expression of a
conscientious wonder. She knew her theatre, she knew her play,
as she had known, triumphantly, for three days, everything else,
and the moment filled to the brim, for her companion, that apprehension of the interesting which, whether or no the interesting
happened to filter through his guide, strained now to its limits his
brief opportunity. Waymarsh had not come with them; he had seen
plays enough, he signified, before Strether had joined him—an
affirmation that had its full force when his friend ascertained by
questions that he had seen two and a circus. Questions as to what
he had seen had on him indeed an effect only less favorable than
questions as to what he hadn't. He liked the former to be discriminated; but how could it be done, Strether asked of their
constant counsellor, without discriminating the latter?

Miss Gostrey had dined with him at his hotel, face to face over a
small table on which the lighted candles had rose-colored shades;
and the rose-colored shades and the small table and the soft fragrance of the lady—had anything to his mere sense ever been so
soft?—were so many touches in he scarce knew what positive high
picture. He had been to the theatre, even to the opera, in Boston,
with Mrs. Newsome, and been more than once her only escort; but
there had been no little confronted dinner, no pink lights, no whiff
of vague sweetness, as a preliminary: one of the results of which

fact was that at present, mildly rueful, though with a sharpish accent, he actually asked himself *why* there hadn't. There was much
the same difference in his impression of the noticed state of his
companion, whose dress was "cut down," as he believed the term
to be, in respect to shoulders and bosom, in a manner quite other
than Mrs. Newsome's, and who wore round her throat a broad red
velvet band with an antique jewel—he was rather complacently
sure it was antique—attached to it in front. Mrs. Newsome's dress
was never in any degree "cut down," and she never wore round her
throat a broad red velvet band: if she had, moreover, would it ever
have served so to carry and complicate, as he now almost felt, his
vision?

It would have been absurd of him to trace into ramifications the
effect of the ribbon from which Miss Gostrey's trinket depended,
had he not, for the hour, at the best, been so given over to uncontrolled perceptions. What was it but an uncontrolled perception
that his friend's velvet band somehow added, in her appearance, to
the value of every other item—to that of her smile and of the way
she carried her head, to that of her complexion, of her lips, her
teeth, her eyes, her hair? What, certainly, had a man conscious of
a man's work in the world to do with red velvet bands? He
wouldn't, for anything, have so exposed himself as to tell Miss
Gostrey how much he liked hers; yet he *had,* none the less, not only
caught himself in the act—frivolous, no doubt, idiotic, and above all
unexpected—of liking it: he had, in addition, taken it as a starting-point for fresh backward, fresh forward, fresh lateral flights.
The manner in which Mrs. Newsome's throat *was* encircled suddenly represented for him, in an alien order, almost as many things
as the manner in which Miss Gostrey's was. Mrs. Newsome wore,
at operatic hours, a black silk dress—very handsome, he knew it
was "handsome"—and an ornament that his memory was able
further to identify as a ruche. He had his association indeed with
the ruche, but it was rather imperfectly romantic. He had once
said to the wearer—and it was as "free" a remark as he had ever
made to her—that she looked, with her ruff and other matters, like
Queen Elizabeth; and it had after this, in truth, been his fancy that,
as a consequence of that tenderness and an acceptance of the idea,
the form of this special tribute to the "frill" had grown slightly

more marked. The connection, as he sat there and let his imagina‹
tion roam, was to strike him as vaguely pathetic; but there it all
was, and pathetic was doubtless, in the conditions, the best thing
it could possibly be. It had existed, assuredly, at any rate; for it
seemed now to come over him that no gentleman of his age, at Woollett, could ever, to a lady of Mrs. Newsome's, which was not much
less than his, have embarked on such a simile.

All sorts of things in fact now seemed to come over him, comparatively few of which his chronicler can hope for space to mention.
It came over him for instance that Miss Gostrey looked perhaps
like Mary Stuart: Lambert Strether had a candor of fancy which
could rest for an instant gratified in such an antithesis. It came
over him that never before—no, literally, never—had a lady dined
with him at a public place before going to the play. The publicity
of the place was just, in the matter, for Strether, the rare, strange
thing; it affected him almost as the achievement of privacy might
have affected a man of a different experience. He had married,
in the far-away years, so young as to have missed the natural time,
in Boston, for taking girls to the Museum; and it was absolutely
true of him that—even after the close of the period of conscious
detachment occupying the centre of his life, the gray middle desert
of the two deaths, that of his wife and that, ten years later, of his
boy—he had never taken any one anywhere. It came over him in
especial—though the monition had, as happened, already sounded,
fitfully gleamed, in other forms—that the business he had come
out on had not yet been so brought home to him as by the sight of
the people about him. She gave him the impression, his friend, at
first, more straight than he got it for himself—gave it simply by
saying with off-hand illumination: "Oh yes, they're types!"—but
after he had taken it he made to the full, both while he kept silence
for the four acts and while he talked in the intervals, his own use
of it. It was an evening, it was a world of types, and this was a
connection, above all, in which the figures and faces in the stalls
were interchangeable with those on the stage.

He felt as if the play itself penetrated him with the naked elbow
of his neighbor, a great stripped, handsome, red-haired lady, who
conversed with a gentleman on her other side in stray dissyllables
which had for his ear, in the oddest way in the world, so much

sound that he wondered they hadn't more sense; and he recognized by the same law, beyond the footlights, what he was pleased to take for the very flush of English life. He had distracted drops in which he couldn't have said if it were actors or auditors who were most true, and the upshot of which, each time, was the consciousness of new contacts. However he viewed his job it was " types " he should have to tackle. Those before him and around him were not as the types of Woollett, where, for that matter, it had begun to seem to him that there must only have been the male and the female. These made two exactly, even with the individual varieties. Here, on the other hand, apart from the personal and the sexual range—which might be greater or less—a series of strong stamps had been applied, as it were, from without; stamps that his observation played with as, before a glass case on a table, it might have passed from medal to medal and from copper to gold. It befell that in the drama, precisely, there was a bad woman, in a yellow frock, who made a pleasant, weak, good-looking young man, in perpetual evening dress, do the most dreadful things. Strether felt himself, on the whole, not afraid of the yellow frock, but he was vaguely anxious over a certain kindness into which he found himself drifting for its victim. He hadn't come out, he reminded himself, to be too kind, or indeed to be kind at all, to Chadwick Newsome. Would Chad also be in perpetual evening dress? He somehow rather hoped it—it seemed so to add to *this* young man's general amenability; though he wondered too if, to fight him with his own weapons, he himself (a thought almost startling,) would have likewise to be. This young man, furthermore, would have been much more easy to handle—at least for *him*—than appeared probable in respect to Chad.

It came up for him with Miss Gostrey that there were things of which she would really perhaps, after all, have heard; and she admitted when a little pressed that she was never quite sure of what she heard as distinguished from things such as, on occasions like the present, she only extravagantly guessed. " I seem, with this freedom, you see, to have guessed Mr. Chad. He's a young man on whose head, at Woollett, high hopes are placed, whom a wicked woman has got hold of, and whom his family, over there, have sent you out to rescue. You've accepted the mission of separating him from the wicked woman. Are you quite sure she's very bad for him?"

Something in his manner showed it as quite pulling him up. "Of course we are. Wouldn't *you* be?"

"Oh, I don't know. One never does—does one?—beforehand. One can only judge on the facts. Yours are quite new to me; I'm really not in the least, as you see, in possession of them; so it will be awfully interesting to have them from you. If you're satisfied, that's all that's required. I mean if you're sure that you *are* sure: sure that it won't do."

"That he should lead such a life? Rather!"

"Oh, but I don't know, you see, about his life; you've not told me about his life. She may be charming—his life!"

"Charming?"—Strether stared before him. "She's base, venal—out of the streets."

"I see. And *he—?*"

"Chad, wretched boy?"

"Of what type and temper is he?" she went on as Strether had hesitated.

"Well—the obstinate." It was as if for a moment he had been going to say more and had then controlled himself.

That was scarce what she wished. "Do you like him?"

This time he was prompt. "No. How *can* I?"

"Do you mean because of your being so saddled with him?"

"I'm thinking of his mother," said Strether after a moment. "He has darkened her admirable life." He spoke with austerity. "He has worried her half to death."

"Oh, that's of course odious." She had a pause as if for renewed emphasis of this truth, but it ended on another note. "Is her life very admirable?"

"Extraordinarily."

There was so much in the tone that Miss Gostrey had to devote another pause to the appreciation of it. "And has he only *her?* I don't mean the bad woman in Paris," she quickly added—" for I assure you I shouldn't, even at the best, be disposed to allow him more than one. But has he only his mother?"

"He has also a sister, older than himself and married; and they're both remarkably fine women."

"Very handsome, you mean?"

This promptitude—almost, as he might have thought, this precipitation, gave him a brief drop; but he came up again. "Mrs. Newsome, I think, is handsome, though she's not, of course, with a son of twenty-eight and a daughter of thirty, in her very first youth. She married, however, extremely young."

"And is wonderful," Miss Gostrey asked, "for her age?"

Strether seemed to feel with a certain disquiet the pressure of it. "I don't say she's wonderful. Or rather," he went on the next moment, "I do say it. It's exactly what she *is*—wonderful. But I wasn't thinking of her appearance," he explained—"striking as that doubtless is. I was thinking—well, of many other things." He seemed to look at these as if to mention some of them; then took, pulling himself up, another turn. "About Mrs. Pocock people may differ."

"Is that the daughter's name—'Pocock'?"

"That's the daughter's name," Strether sturdily confessed.

"And people may differ, you mean, about *her* beauty?"

"About everything."

"But *you* admire her?"

He gave his friend a glance as to show how he could bear this. "I'm perhaps a little afraid of her."

"Oh," said Miss Gostrey, "I see her from here! You may say then I see very fast and very far, but I've already shown you I do. The young man and the two ladies," she went on, "are at any rate all the family?"

"Quite all. His father has been dead ten years, and there's no brother, nor any other sister. They'd do," said Strether, "anything in the world for him."

"And you'd do anything in the world for *them*?"

He shifted again; she had made it perhaps just a shade too affirmative for his nerves. "Oh, I don't know!"

"You'd do at any rate this, and the 'anything' they'd do is represented by their *making* you do it."

"Ah, they couldn't have come—either of them. They're very busy people, and Mrs. Newsome, in particular, has a large, full life. She's moreover highly nervous—and she's not strong."

"You mean she's a bad invalid?"

40

He carefully distinguished. "There's nothing she likes less than to be called one. But she's delicate, sensitive, high-strung. She puts so much of herself into everything—"

Ah, Maria knew these things. "That she has nothing left for anything else? Of course she hasn't. To whom do you say it? High-strung? Don't I spend my life, for them, jamming down the pedal? I see moreover how it has told on you."

Strether took this more lightly. "Oh, I jam down the pedal too!"

"Well," she lucidly returned, "we must from this moment bear on it together with all our might." And she reappeared further on. "Have they money?"

But it was as if, while her energetic image still held him, her inquiry fell short. "Mrs. Newsome," he wished further to explain, "hasn't moreover your courage on the question of contact. If she had come it would have been to see the person herself."

"The woman? Ah, but that's courage."

"No—it's exaltation, which is a very different thing. Courage," he, however, accommodatingly threw out, "is what *you* have."

She shook her head. "You say that only to patch me up—to cover the nudity of my want of exaltation. I've neither the one nor the other. I've mere battered indifference. I see that what you mean," Miss Gostrey pursued, "is that if your friend *had* come she would take great views, and the great views, to put it simply, would be too much for her."

Strether looked amused at her notion of the simple, but he adopted her formula. "Everything's too much for her."

"Ah then, such a service as this of yours—"

"Is more for her than anything else? Yes—far more. But so long as it isn't too much for *me*—!"

"Her condition doesn't matter? Surely not; we leave her condition out; we take it, that is, for granted. I see it, her condition, as behind and beneath you; yet at the same time I see it as bearing you up."

"Oh, it does bear me up!" Strether laughed.

"Well then, as yours bears *me*, nothing more is needed." With which she put again her question. "Has Mrs. Newsome money?"

This time he heeded. "Oh, plenty. That's the root of the evil.

There's money, in quantities, in the concern. Chad has had the free use of a great deal. But if he'll pull himself together and come home, all the same, he'll find his account in it."

She had listened with all her interest. "And I hope to goodness you'll find yours!"

"He'll take up his definite material reward," said Strether without acknowledgment of this. "He's at the parting of the ways. He can come into the business now—he can't come later."

"Is there a business?"

"Lord, yes—a big, brave, bouncing business. A roaring trade."

"A great shop?"

"Yes—a workshop; a great production, a great industry. The concern's a manufacture—and a manufacture that, if it's only properly looked after, may well be on the way to become a monopoly. It's a little thing they make—make better, it appears, than other people can, or than other people, at any rate, do. Mr. Newsome, being a man of ideas, at least in that particular line," Strether explained, "put them on it with great effect, and gave the place altogether, in his time, an immense lift."

"It's a place in itself?"

"Well, quite a number of buildings; almost a little industrial colony. But above all it's a thing. The article produced."

"And what *is* the article produced?"

Strether looked about him as in slight reluctance to say; then the curtain, which he saw about to rise, came to his aid. "I'll tell you next time." But when the next time came he only said he would tell her later on—after they should have left the theatre; for she had immediately reverted to their topic, and even for himself the picture of the stage was now overlaid with another image. His postponements, however, made her wonder—wonder if the article referred to were anything bad. And she explained that she meant improper or ridiculous or wrong. But Strether, so far as that went, could satisfy her. "Unmentionable? Oh no, we constantly talk of it; we are quite familiar and brazen about it. Only, as a small, trivial, rather ridiculous object of the commonest domestic use, it's rather wanting in—what shall I say? Well, dignity, or the least approach to distinction. Just here, therefore, with everything about us so grand—!" In short he shrank.

" It's a false note ? "

" Sadly. It's vulgar."

" But surely not vulgarer than this." Then on his wondering as she herself had done: " Than everything about us." She seemed a trifle irritated. " What do you take this for ? "

" Why, for—comparatively—divine ! "

" This dreadful London theatre ? It's impossible, if you really want to know."

" Oh then," laughed Strether, " I *don't* really want to know ! "

It made between them a pause, which she, however, still fascinated by the mystery of the production at Woollett, presently broke. " Rather ridiculous ? Clothes-pins ? Saleratus ? Shoe-polish ? "

It brought him round. " No—you don't even ' burn.' I don't think, you know, you'll guess it."

" How then can I judge how vulgar it is ? "

" You'll judge when I do tell you "—and he persuaded her to patience. But it may even now frankly be mentioned that he, in the sequel, never *was* to tell her. He actually never did so, and it moreover oddly occurred that, by the law, within her, of the in-calculable, her desire for the information dropped, and her attitude to the question converted itself into a positive cultivation of igno-rance. In ignorance she could humor her fancy, and that proved a useful freedom. She could treat the little nameless object as indeed unnamable—she could make their abstention enormously definite. There might indeed have been for Strether the portent of this in what she next said.

" Is it perhaps then because it's so bad—because your industry, as you call it, *is* so vulgar—that Mr. Chad won't come back ? Does he feel the taint ? Is he staying away not to be mixed up in it ? "

" Oh," Strether laughed, " it wouldn't appear—would it ?—that he feels ' taints '! He's glad enough of the money from it, and the money's his whole basis. There's appreciation in that—I mean as to the allowance his mother has hitherto made him. She has of course the resource of cutting this allowance off ; but even then he has, unfortunately, and on no small scale, in money left him by his grandfather, her own father, his independent supply."

" Wouldn't the fact you mention then," Miss Gostrey asked " make it, precisely, more easy for him to be particular ? Isn't he

43

conceivable as fastidious about the source—the apparent and public source—of his income?"

Strether was able quite good-humoredly to entertain the proposition. "The source of his grandfather's wealth—and thereby of his own share in it—was not particularly noble."

"And what source was it?"

Strether hesitated. "Well—practices."

"In business? Infamies? He was an old swindler?"

"Oh," Strether said with more emphasis than spirit, "I sha'n't describe *him* nor narrate his exploits."

"Lord, what abysses! And the late Mr. Newsome then?"

"Well, what about him?"

"Was he like the grandfather?"

"No—he was on the other side of the house. And he was different."

Miss Gostrey kept it up. "Better?"

Her friend for a moment hung fire. "No."

Her comment on his hesitation was scarce the less marked for being mute. "Thank you. *Now* don't you see," she went on, "why the boy doesn't come home? He's drowning his shame."

"His shame? What shame?"

"What shame? *Comment donc? The* shame."

"But where and when," Strether asked, "is '*the* shame'—where is any shame—to-day? The men I speak of—they did as every one does; and—besides being ancient history—it was all a matter of appreciation."

She showed how she understood. "Mrs. Newsome has appreciated?"

"Ah, I can't speak for *her!*"

"In the midst of such doings—and, as I understand you, profiting by them, she at least has remained exquisite?"

"Oh, I can't talk of her!" Strether said.

"I thought she was just what you *could* talk of. You *don't* trust me," Miss Gostrey after a moment declared.

It had its effect. "Well, her money is spent, her life conceived and carried on with a large beneficence—"

"That's a kind of expiation of wrongs? Gracious," she added before he could speak, "how intensely you make me see her!"

"If you see her," Strether dropped, "it's all that's necessary."

She really seemed to have her. "I feel that. She *is,* in spite of everything, handsome."

This at least enlivened him. "What do you mean by everything?"

"Well, I mean *you.*" With which she had one of her swift changes of ground. "You say the concern needs looking after; but doesn't Mrs. Newsome look after it?"

"So far as possible. She's wonderfully able, but it's not her affair, and her life's a good deal overcharged. She has many, many things."

"And you also?"

"Oh yes—I've many too, if you will."

"I see. But what I mean is," Miss Gostrey amended, "do you also look after the business?"

"Oh no, I don't touch the business."

"Only everything else?"

"Well, yes—some things."

"As for instance—?"

Strether obligingly thought. "Well, the Review."

"The Review?—you have a Review?"

"Certainly, Woollett has a Review—which Mrs. Newsome, for the most part, magnificently pays for, and which I, not at all magnificently, edit. My name's on the cover," Strether pursued. "and I'm really rather disappointed and hurt that you seem never to have heard of it."

She neglected for a moment this grievance. "And what kind of a Review is it?"

His serenity was now completely restored. "Well, it's green."

"Do you mean in political color as they say here?—in thought."

"No; I mean the cover's green—of the most lovely shade."

"And with Mrs. Newsome's name on it too?"

He hesitated. "Oh, as for that, you must judge if she peeps out. She's behind the whole thing; but she's of a delicacy and a discretion—!"

Miss Gostrey took it all. "I'm sure. She *would* be. I don't underrate her. She must be rather a swell."

"Oh yes, she's rather a swell!"

"A Woollett swell—*bon!* I like the idea of a Woollett swell. And you must be rather one too, to be so mixed up with her."

"Ah no," said Strether, "that's not the way it works."

But she had already taken him up. "The way it works—you needn't tell me!—is of course that you efface yourself."

"With my name on the cover?" he lucidly objected.

"Ah, but you don't put it on for yourself."

"I beg your pardon—that's exactly what I do put it on for. It's exactly the thing that I'm reduced to doing for myself. It seems to rescue, a little, you see, from the wreck of hopes and ambitions, the refuse-heap of disappointments and failures, my one presentable little scrap of an identity."

She looked at him an instant, on this, as if to say many things; but what she at last simply said was: "She likes to see it there. You're the bigger swell of the two," she immediately continued, "because you think you're not one. She thinks she *is* one. However," Miss Gostrey added, "she thinks you're one too. You're at all events the biggest she can get hold of." She embroidered, she abounded. "I don't say it to interfere between you, but on the day she gets hold of a bigger one—!" Strether had thrown back his head as in silent mirth over something that struck him in her audacity or felicity; and her flight, meanwhile, was already higher. "Therefore close with her—!"

"Close with her?" he asked as she seemed to hang poised.

"Before you lose your chance."

Their eyes, with it, met a moment. "What do you mean by closing?"

"And what do I mean by your chance? I'll tell you when you tell me all the things *you* don't. Is it her *greatest* fad?" she briskly pursued.

"The Review?" He seemed to wonder how he could best describe it. This resulted, however, but in a sketch. "It's her tribute to the ideal."

"I see. You go in for tremendous things."

"We go in for the unpopular side—that is so far as we dare."

"And how far *do* you dare?"

"Well, she very far. I much less. I don't begin to have her faith. She provides," said Strether, "three-fourths of that. And she provides, as I've confided to you, *all* the money."

It evoked somehow a vision of gold that held for a little Miss

Gostrey's eyes, and she looked as if she heard the bright dollars shovelled in. "I hope then you make a good thing—"

"I *never* made a good thing!" he promptly declared.

She just waited. "Don't you call it a good thing to be loved?"

"Oh, we're not loved. We're not even hated. We're only just sweetly ignored."

She had another pause. "You don't trust me!" she once more repeated.

"Don't I when I lift the last veil?—tell you the very secret of the prison-house?"

Again she met his eyes, but with the result that, after an instant, her own turned away with impatience. "You don't sell? Oh, I'm glad of *that!*" After which, however, and before he could protest, she was off again. "She's just a *moral* swell."

He accepted gayly enough the definition. "Yes—I really think that describes her."

But it had for his friend the oddest connection. "How does she do her hair?"

He laughed out. "Beautifully!"

"Ah, that doesn't tell me. However, it doesn't matter—I know. It's tremendously neat—a real reproach; quite remarkably thick and without, as yet, a single strand of white. There!"

He blushed for her realism, but he gaped at her truth. "You're the very deuce."

"What else *should* I be? It was as the very deuce I pounced upon you. But don't let it trouble you, for everything but the very deuce—at our age—is a bore and a delusion, and even he himself, after all, but half a joy." With which, on a single sweep of her wing, she resumed. "You assist her to expiate—which is rather hard when you've yourself not sinned."

"It's she who has not sinned," Strether returned. "I've sinned the most."

"Ah," Miss Gostrey cynically laughed, "what a picture of *her!* Have you robbed the widow and the orphan?"

"I've sinned enough," said Strether.

"Enough for whom? Enough for what?"

"Well, to be where I am."

"Thank you!" They were disturbed at this moment by the

passage between their knees and the back of the seats before them of a gentleman who had been absent during a part of the perform- ance and who now returned for the close; but the interruption left Miss Gostrey time, before the subsequent hush, to express as a sharp finality her sense of the moral of all their talk. "I knew you had something up your sleeve!" This finality, however, left them, in its turn, at the end of the play, as disposed to hang back as if they had still much to say; so that they easily agreed to let every one go before them—they found an interest in waiting. They made out from the lobby that the night had turned to rain; yet Miss Gostrey let her friend know that he was not to see her home. He was simply to put her, by herself, into a four-wheeler; she liked so, in London, of wet nights, after wild pleasures, thinking things over, on the return, in lonely four-wheelers. This was her great time, she intimated, for pulling herself together. The delays caused by the weather, the struggle for vehicles at the door, gave them occasion to subside on a divan at the back of the vestibule and just beyond the reach of the fresh, damp gusts from the street. Here Strether's comrade resumed that free handling of the subject to which his own imagination of it already owed so much.

"Does your young friend in Paris like you?"

It had almost, after the interval, startled him. "Oh, I hope not! Why *should* he?"

"Why shouldn't he?" Miss Gostrey asked. "That you're coming down on him need have nothing to do with it."

"You see more in it," he presently returned, "than I."

"Of course I see *you* in it."

"Well then, you see more in me!"

"Than you see in yourself? Very likely. That's always one's right. What I was thinking of," she explained, "is the possible par- ticular effect on him of his *milieu.*"

"Oh, his *milieu*—!" Strether really felt that he could now imagine it better than three hours before.

"Do you mean it can only have been so lowering?"

"Why, that's my very starting-point."

"Yes, but you start so far back. What do his letters say?"

"Nothing. He practically ignores us—or spares us. He doesn't write."

"I see. But there are, all the same," she went on, "two quite distinct things that—given the wonderful place he's in—may have happened to him. One is that he may have got brutalized. The other is that he may have got refined."

Strether stared—this *was* a novelty. "Refined?"

"Oh," she said quietly, "there *are* refinements."

The way of it made him, after looking at her, break into a laugh. "*You* have them!"

"As one of the signs," she continued in the same tone, "they constitute perhaps the worst."

He thought it over, and his gravity returned. "Is it a refinement not to answer his mother's letters?"

She hesitated, but she brought it out. "Oh, I should say the greatest of all."

"Well," said Strether, "*I'm* quite content to let it, as one of the signs, pass for the worst that I know he believes he can do what he likes with me."

This appeared to strike her. "How do you know it?"

"Oh, I know it. I feel it in my bones."

"Feel that he *can* do it?"

"Feel that he believes he can. It may come to the same thing!" Strether laughed.

She wouldn't, however, have this. "Nothing, with you, will ever come to the same thing as anything else." And she understood what she meant, it seemed, sufficiently to go straight on. "You say that if he does break he'll come in for things at home?"

"Quite positively. He'll come in for a particular chance—a chance that any properly constituted young man would jump at. The business has so developed that an opening that scarcely existed three years ago, but which his father's will took account of as, in certain conditions, possible, attaching to Chad's availing himself of it a large contingent advantage—this opening, the conditions having come about, now simply waits for him. His mother has kept it for him, holding out against strong pressure, till the last possible moment. It requires, naturally, as it carries with it a handsome 'part,' a large share in profits, his being on the spot and making a big effort for a big result. That's what I mean by his chance. If he misses it he comes in, as you say, for nothing. And *to* see that he doesn't miss it is, in a word, what I've come out for."

She let it all sink in. "What you've come out for then is simply to render him an immense service."

Well, poor Strether was willing to take it so. "Ah, if you like."

"He stands, as they say, if you succeed with him, to gain—"

"Oh, a lot of advantages." Strether had them, clearly, at his fingers' ends.

"By which you mean, of course, a lot of money."

"Well, not only. I'm acting with a sense, for him, of other things too. Consideration and comfort and security—the general safety of being anchored by a strong chain. He wants, as I see him, to be protected. Protected, I mean, from life."

"Ah *voilà!*"—her thought fitted with a click. "From life. What you *really* want to get him home for is to marry him."

"Well, that's about the size of it."

"Of course," she said, "it's rudimentary. But to any one in particular?"

He smiled at this—he looked a little more conscious. "You get everything out."

For a moment again their eyes met. "You put everything in!"

He acknowledged the tribute by telling her. "To Mamie Pocock."

She wondered; then gravely, even exquisitely, as if to make the oddity also fit: "His own niece?"

"Oh, you must yourself find a name for the relation. His brother-in-law's sister. Mrs. Jim's sister-in-law."

It seemed to have on Miss Gostrey a certain hardening effect. "And who in the world's Mrs. Jim?"

"Chad's sister—who was Sarah Newsome. She's married—didn't I mention it?—to Jim Pocock."

"Ah yes," she tacitly replied; but he had mentioned things—! Then, however, with all the sound it could have, "Who in the world's Jim Pocock?" she asked.

"Why, Sally's husband. That's the only way we distinguish people at Woollett," he good-humoredly explained.

"And is it a great distinction—being Sally's husband?"

He considered. "I think there can be scarcely a greater—unless it may become one, in the future, to be Chad's wife."

"Then how do they distinguish *you?*"

"They *don't*—except, as I've told you, by the green cover."

Once more their eyes met on it, and she held him an instant "The green cover won't—nor will *any* cover—avail you with me. You're of a depth of duplicity!" Still, she could in her own large grasp of the real condone it. "Is Mamie a great *parti?*"

"Oh, the greatest we have—our prettiest, brightest girl."

Miss Gostrey seemed to fix the poor child. "I know what they *can* be. And with money?"

"Not perhaps with a great deal of that—but with so much of everything else that we don't miss it. We *don't* miss money much, you know," Strether added, "in general, in America, in pretty girls."

"No," she conceded; "but I know also what you do sometimes miss. And do you," she asked, "yourself admire her?"

It was a question, he indicated, that there might be several ways of taking; but he decided after an instant for the humorous. "Haven't I sufficiently showed you how I admire *any* pretty girl?"

Her interest in his problem was, however, by this time such that it scarce left her freedom, and she kept close to the facts. "I supposed that at Woollett you wanted them—what shall I call it?—blameless. I mean your young men for your pretty girls."

"So did I!" Strether confessed. "But you strike there a curious fact—the fact that Woollett too accommodates itself to the spirit of the age and the increasing mildness of manners. Everything changes, and I hold that our situation precisely marks a date. We *should* prefer them blameless, but we have to make the best of them as we find them. Since the spirit of the age and the increasing mildness send them so much more to Paris—"

"You've to take them back as they come. When they *do* come. *Bon!*" Once more she embraced it all, but she had a moment of thought. "Poor Chad!"

"Ah," said Strether cheerfully, "Mamie will save him!"

She was looking away, still in her vision, and she spoke with impatience and almost as if he hadn't understood her. "*You'll* save him. That's who'll save him."

"Oh, but with Mamie's aid. Unless indeed you mean," he added, "that I shall effect so much more with yours!"

It made her at last again look at him. "You'll do more—as you're so much better—than all of us put together."

"I think I'm only better since I've known *you!*" Strether bravely returned.

The depletion of the place, the shrinkage of the crowd and now comparatively quiet withdrawal of its last elements had already brought them nearer the door and put them in relation with a messenger of whom he bespoke Miss Gostrey's cab. But this left them a few minutes more, which she was clearly in no mood not to use. "You've spoken to me of what—by your success—Mr. Chad stands to gain. But you've not spoken to me of what you do."

"Oh, I've nothing more to gain," said Strether very simply.

She took it as even quite too simple. "You mean you've got it all 'down'? You've been paid in advance?"

"Ah, don't talk about payment!" he murmured.

Something in the tone of it pulled her up, but as their messenger still delayed she had another chance and she put it in another way. "What—by failure—do you stand to lose?"

He still, however, wouldn't have it. "Nothing!" he exclaimed, and on the messenger's at this instant reappearing he was able to sink the subject in their responsive advance. When, a few steps up the street, under a lamp, he had put her into her four-wheeler and she had asked him if the man had called for him no second conveyance, he replied before the door was closed. "You won't take me with you?"

"Not for the world."

"Then I shall walk."

"In the rain?"

"I like the rain," said Strether. "Good-night!"

She kept him a moment, while his hand was on the door, by not answering; after which she answered by repeating her question. "What do you stand to lose?"

Why the question now affected him as other he couldn't have said; he could only, this time, meet it otherwise. "Everything."

"So I thought. Then you shall succeed. And to that end I'm yours—"

"Ah, dear lady!" he kindly breathed.

"Till death!" said Maria Gostrey. "Good-night."

V.

STRETHER called, his second morning in Paris, on the bankers, in the Rue Scribe, to whom his letter of credit was addressed, and he made this visit attended by Waymarsh, in whose company he had crossed from London two days before. They had hastened to the Rue Scribe on the morrow of their arrival, but Strether had not then found the letters the hope of which prompted this errand. He had had as yet none at all; had not expected them in London, but had counted on several in Paris, and now, disconcerted, had presently strolled back to the Boulevard with a sense of injury which he presently felt himself taking for as good a start as any other. It would serve, this spur to his spirit, he reflected, as, pausing at the top of the street, he looked up and down the great foreign avenue, it would serve to begin business with. His idea was to begin business immediately, and it did much for him the rest of that day that the beginning of business awaited him. He did little else, till night, but ask himself what he should do if he had not fortunately had so much to do; but he put himself the question in many different situations and connections. What carried him hither and yon was an admirable theory that nothing he could do would not be in some manner related to what he fundamentally had on hand, or *would* be—should he happen to have a scruple—wasted for it. He did happen to have a scruple — a scruple about taking no definite step till he should get letters; but this reasoning carried it off. A single day to feel his feet — he had felt them as yet only at Chester and in London—was, he could consider, none too much; and having, as he had often privately expressed it, Paris to reckon with, he threw these hours of freshness consciously into the reckoning. They made it continually greater, but that was what it had best be if it was to be anything at all, and he gave himself up till far into the evening, at the theatre and on the return, after the

53

theatre, along the bright, congested Boulevard, to feeling it grow. Waymarsh had accompanied him this time to the play, and the two men had walked together, as a first stage, from the Gymnase to the Café Riche, into the crowded " terrace " of which establishment—the night, or rather the morning, for midnight had struck, being bland and populous—they had wedged themselves for refreshment. Waymarsh, as a result of some discussion with his friend, had made a marked virtue of his having now let himself go; and there had been elements of impression in their half-hour over their watered beer-glasses that gave him his occasion for conveying that he held this compromise with his stiffer self to have become extreme. He conveyed it—for it was still, after all, his stiffer self that gloomed out of the glare of the terrace—in solemn silence; and there was indeed a great deal of critical silence, every way, between the companions, even till they gained the Place de l'Opéra, as to the character of their nocturnal progress.

This morning there *were* letters—letters which had reached London, apparently all together, the day of Strether's journey, and had taken their time to follow him; so that, after a controlled impulse to go into them in the reception-room of the bank, which, reminding him of the post-office at Woollett, affected him as the abutment of some transatlantic bridge, he slipped them into the pocket of his loose gray overcoat with a sense of the felicity of carrying them off. Waymarsh, who had had letters yesterday, had had them again to-day, and Waymarsh suggested, in this particular, no controlled impulses. The last one, clearly, at all events, he was likely to be observed to struggle with was that of bringing to a premature close any visit to the Rue Scribe. Strether had left him there yesterday; he wanted to see the papers, and he had spent, by what his friend could make out, a succession of hours with the papers. He spoke of the establishment, with emphasis, as a post of superior observation; just as he spoke generally of his actual damnable doom as a device for hiding from him what was going on. Europe was best described, to his mind, as an elaborate engine for dissociating the confined American from that indispensable knowledge, and was accordingly only rendered bearable by these occasional stations of relief, traps for the arrest of wandering western airs. Strether, on his side, set himself to walk again—he had his relief in his pocket;

and indeed, much as he had desired his budget, the growth of restlessness might have been marked in him from the moment he had
assured himself of the superscription of most of the missives it
contained. This restlessness became therefore his temporary law; he
knew he should recognize as soon as he should see it the best place
of all for settling down with his chief correspondent. He had for
the next hour an accidental air of looking for it in the windows of
shops; he came down the Rue de la Paix in the sun and, passing
across the Tuileries and the river, indulged more than once—as if
on finding himself determined—in a sudden pause before the book-
stalls of the opposite quay. In the garden of the Tuileries he had
lingered, on two or three spots, to look; it was as if the wonderful
Paris spring had stayed him as he roamed. The prompt Paris
morning struck its cheerful notes—in a soft breeze and a sprinkled
smell, in the light flit, over the garden-floor, of bareheaded girls with
the buckled strap of oblong boxes, in the type of ancient thrifty
persons basking betimes where terrace-walls were warm, in the blue-
frocked, brass-labelled officialism of humble rakers and scrapers, in
the deep references of a straight-pacing priest or the sharp ones of
a white-gaitered, red-legged soldier. He watched little brisk figures,
figures whose movement was as the tick of the great Paris clock.
take their smooth diagonal from point to point; the air had a taste
as of something mixed with art, something that presented nature
as a white-capped master-*chef*. The palace was gone; Strether
remembered the palace; and when he gazed into the irremedia-
ble void of its site the historic sense in him might have been freely at play—the play under which in Paris indeed it so often winces
like a touched nerve. He filled out spaces with dim symbols of
scenes; he caught the gleam of white statues at the base of which,
with his letters out, he could tilt back a straw-bottomed chair. But
his drift was, for reasons, to the other side, and it floated him un-
spent up the Rue de Seine and as far as the Luxembourg.

In the Luxembourg gardens he pulled up: here at last he found
his nook, and here, on a penny chair from which terraces, alleys,
vistas, fountains, little trees in green tubs, little women in white
caps and shrill little girls at play all sunnily " composed " together,
he passed an hour in which the cup of his impressions seemed truly
to overflow. But a week had elapsed since he quitted the ship, and

there were more things in his mind than so few days could account for. More than once, during the time, he had regarded himself as admonished; but the admonition, this morning, was formidably sharp. It took as it had not done yet the form of a question—the question of what he was doing with such an extraordinary sense of escape. This sense was sharpest after he had read his letters, but that was also precisely why the question pressed. Four of the letters were from Mrs. Newsome and none of them short; she had lost no time, had followed on his heels while he moved, so expressing herself that he now could measure the probable frequency with which he should hear. They would arrive, it would seem, her communications, at the rate of several a week; he should be able to count, it might even prove, on more than one by each mail. If he had begun yesterday with a small grievance he had therefore an opportunity to begin to-day with its opposite. He read the letters successively and slowly, putting others back into his pocket but keeping these for a long time afterwards gathered in his lap. He held them there, lost in thought, as if to prolong the presence of what they gave him; or as if, at the least, to assure them their part in the constitution of some lucidity. His friend wrote admirably, and her tone was even more in her style than in her voice—it was almost as if, for the hour, he had had to come to this distance to get its full carrying quality; yet the enormity of his consciousness of difference consisted perfectly with the deepened intensity of the connection. It was the difference, the difference of being just where he was and *as* he was, that formed the escape—this difference was so much greater than he had dreamed it would be; and what finally he sat there turning over was the strange logic of his finding himself so free. He felt it in a manner his duty to think out his state, to approve the process, and when he came in fact to trace the steps and add up the items they sufficiently accounted for the sum. He had never expected—that was the truth of it—again to find himself young, and all the years and other things it had taken to make him so were exactly his present arithmetic. He had to make sure of them to put his scruple to rest.

It all sprang at bottom from the beauty of Mrs. Newsome's desire that he should be worried with nothing that was not of the essence of his task; by insisting that he should thoroughly intermit and break she had so provided for his freedom that she would, as it were, have only herself to thank. Strether, however, could not at this point indeed have completed his thought by the image of what she might have to thank herself *for:* the image, at best, of his own likeness—poor Lambert Strether washed up on the sunny strand, thankful for breathing-time, stiffening himself while he gasped, by the waves of a single day. There he was, and there was nothing in his aspect or his posture to scandalize: it was only true that if he had seen Mrs. Newsome coming he would instinctively have jumped up to walk away a little. He would have come round and back to her bravely; but he would have had to pull himself together. She abounded in news of the situation at home, proved to him how perfectly she was arranging for his absence, told him who would take up this and who take up that exactly where he had left it, gave him in fact chapter and verse for the moral that nothing would suffer. It filled for him, this tone of hers, all the air; yet it struck him at the same time as the hum of vain things. This latter effect was what he tried to justify—and with the success that, grave though the appearance, he at last lighted on a form that was happy. He arrived at this form by the inevitable recognition of his having been a fortnight before one of the weariest of men. If ever a man had come off tired Lambert Strether was that man; and hadn't it been distinctly on the ground that he *was* tired that his wonderful friend at home had so felt for him and so contrived? It seemed to him somehow at these instants that, could he only maintain with sufficient firmness his grasp of this truth, it might become in a manner his compass and his helm. What he wanted most was some idea that would simplify, and nothing would do that so much as the fact that he was done for and finished. If it had been in such a light that he had just detected in his cup the dregs of youth, that was a mere flaw of the surface of his scheme. He was so distinctly fagged-out that it must serve precisely as his convenience, and if he could but consistently be good for little enough he might do everything he wanted.

Everything he wanted was comprised moreover in a single boon—the common, unattainable art of taking things as they came. He appeared to himself to have given his best years to an active appreciation of the way they didn't come; but perhaps—as they would

seemingly here be things quite other—this long ache might at last
drop to rest. He could easily see that from the moment he should accept the notion of his foredoomed collapse the last thing he would
lack would be reasons and memories. Oh, if he *should* do the sum,
no slate would hold the figures! The fact that he had failed, as he
considered, in everything, in each relation and in half a dozen
trades, as he liked luxuriously to put it, might have made, might
still make, for an empty present; but it stood solidly for a crowded
past. It had not been, so much achievement missed, a light yoke
nor a short road. It was at present as if the backward picture had
hung there, the long crooked course, gray in the shadow of his solitude. It had been a dreadful, cheerful, sociable solitude, a solitude of life, of choice, of community; but though there had been
people enough all round it, there had been but three or four persons
in it. Waymarsh was one of these, and the fact struck him just
now as marking the record. Mrs. Newsome was another, and Miss
Gostrey had of a sudden shown signs of becoming a third. Beyond,
behind them was the pale figure of his real youth, which held against
its breast the two presences paler than itself—the young wife he
had early lost and the young son he had stupidly sacrificed. He had
again and again made out for himself that he might have kept
his little boy, his little dull boy, who had died at school, of rapid
diphtheria, if he had not in those years so insanely given himself
to merely missing the mother. It was the soreness of his remorse
that the child had, in all likelihood, not really been dull—had been
dull, as he had been banished and neglected, mainly because the
father had been unwittingly selfish. This was doubtless but the
secret habit of sorrow, which had slowly given way to time; yet
there remained an ache sharp enough to make the spirit, at the
sight, now and again, of some fair young man just growing up,
wince with the thought of an opportunity lost. Had ever a man,
he had finally fallen into the way of asking himself, lost so much
and even done so much for so little? There had been particular
reasons why, all yesterday, beyond other days, he should have had
in one ear this cold inquiry. His name on the green cover, where
he had put it for Mrs. Newsome, expressed him doubtless just
enough to make the world—the world as distinguished, both for
more and for less, from Woollett—ask who he was. He had in-

curred the ridicule of having to have his explanation explained. He was Lambert Strether because he was on the cover, whereas it should have been, for anything like glory, that he was on the cover because he was Lambert Strether. He would have done anything for Mrs. Newsome, have been still more ridiculous—as he might, for that matter, have occasion to be yet; which came to saying that this acceptance of fate was all he had at fifty-five to show.

He judged the quantity as small because it *was* small, and all the more egregiously so since it couldn't, as he saw the case, so much as thinkably have been larger. He had not had the gift of making the most of what he tried, and if he had tried and tried again—no one but himself knew how often—it appeared to have been that he might demonstrate what else, in default of that, *could* be made. Old ghosts of experiments came back to him, old drudgeries and delusions and disgusts, old recoveries with their relapses, old fevers with their chills, broken moments of good faith, others of still better doubt; adventures, for the most part, of the sort qualified as lessons. The special spring that had constantly played for him the day before was the recognition—frequent enough to surprise him—of the promises to himself that, after his other visit, he had never kept. The reminiscence that to-day most revived for him was that of the vow taken in the course of the pilgrimage that, newly-married, with the War just over, and helplessly young in spite of it, he had recklessly made with the creature who was so much younger still. It had been a bold dash, for which they had taken money set apart for necessities, but consecrated for them at the moment in a hundred ways, and in none more so than by this private pledge of his own to treat the occasion as a relation formed with the higher culture, to see that, as they said at Woollett, it should bear a good harvest. He had believed, as he sailed home again, that he had gained something great, and his theory—with an elaborate, innocent plan of reading, digesting, coming back, even, every few years—had then been to preserve, cherish and extend it. As such plans as these had come to nothing, however, in respect to acquisitions still more precious, it was doubtless little enough of a marvel that he should have lost account of that handful of seed. Buried for long years in dark corners, at any rate, these few germs had sprouted again under forty-eight hours of

59

Paris. The process of yesterday had really been the process of feeling the general stirred life of connections long since individually dropped. Strether had become acquainted even on this ground with short gusts of speculation—sudden flights of fancy in Louvre galleries, hungry gazes through clear plates behind which lemon-colored volumes were as fresh as fruit on the tree.

These were instants at which he could ask whether, since there had been, fundamentally, so little question of his keeping anything, the fate after all decreed for him hadn't been only to *be* kept. Kept for something, in that event, that he didn't pretend, didn't possibly dare, as yet, to divine; something that made him hover and wonder and laugh and sigh, made him advance and retreat, feeling half ashamed of his impulse to plunge and more than half afraid of his impulse to wait. He remembered for instance how he had gone back in the sixties with lemon-colored volumes in general on the brain as well as with a dozen—selected for his wife too—in his trunk; and nothing had at the moment shown more confidence than this invocation of the finer taste. They were still somewhere at home, the dozen—stale and soiled and never sent to the binder; but what had become of the sharp initiation they represented? They represented now the mere sallow paint on the door of the temple of taste that he had dreamed of raising up—a structure that he had practically never carried further. Strether's present highest flights were perhaps those in which this particular lapse figured to him as a symbol, a symbol of his long grind and his want of odd moments, his want moreover of money, of opportunity, of positive dignity. That the memory of the vow of his youth should, in order to throb again, have had to wait for this last, as he felt it, of all his accidents—that was surely proof enough of how his conscience had been encumbered. If any further proof were needed it would have been to be found in the fact that, as he perfectly now saw, he had ceased even to measure his meagreness, a meagreness that sprawled, in this retrospect, vague and comprehensive, stretching back like some unmapped Hinterland from a rough coast-settlement. His conscience had been amusing itself, for the forty-eight hours, by forbidding him the purchase of a book; he held off from that, held off from everything; from the moment he didn't yet call on Chad he wouldn't for the world have taken any other step. On this evidence, however, of the way they actually affected him, he glared at the lemon-colored covers with the fancy of the subconsciousness that, all the same, in the great desert of the years, he must have had of them. The green covers at home comprised, by the law of their purpose, no tribute to letters; it was of a mere rich kernel of economics, politics, ethics that, glazed and, as Mrs. Newsome maintained, rather against *his* view, pre - eminently pleasant to touch, they formed the specious shell. Without, therefore, any needed instinctive knowledge of what was coming out, in Paris, on the bright highway, he struck himself at present as having more than once flushed with a suspicion: he couldn't otherwise at present be feeling so many fears confirmed. There were " movements " he was too late for—weren't they, with the fun of them, already spent? There were sequences he had missed and great gaps in the procession: he might have been watching it all recede in a golden cloud of dust. If the playhouse was not closed, his seat at least had fallen to somebody else. He had had an uneasy feeling the night before that if he was at the theatre at all—though he indeed justified the theatre, in the specific sense, and with a grotesqueness to which his imagination did all honor, as something he owed poor Waymarsh — he should have been there with, and as might have been said, *for* Chad.

This suggested the question of whether he could properly have taken him to such a play, and what effect—it was a point that suddenly rose—his peculiar responsibility might be held to have, in general, on his choice of entertainment. It had literally been present to him at the Gymnase—where one was held moreover comparatively safe—that having his young friend at his side would have been an odd feature of the work of redemption; and this quite in spite of the fact that the picture presented might well, confronted with Chad's own private stage, have seemed the pattern of propriety. He hadn't, clearly, come out in the name of propriety only to visit unattended equivocal performances; yet still less had he done so to undermine his authority by sharing them with the graceless youth. Was he to renounce all amusement for the sweet sake of that authority? and *would* such renouncement give him for Chad a moral glamour? The little problem bristled the more by reason of poor Strether's fairly open sense of the irony of things. Were there then sides on which his predicament threatened to look rather droll to him? Should he have to pretend to believe—either to himself or the wretched boy—that there was anything that could make the latter worse? Was not some such pretence on the other hand involved in the assumption that there were processes that would make him better? His greatest uneasiness seemed to peep at him out of the possible impression that almost any acceptance of Paris might give one's authority away. It hung before him this morning, the vast bright Babylon, like some huge iridescent object, a jewel brilliant and hard, in which parts were not to be discriminated nor differences comfortably marked. It twinkled and trembled and melted together, and what seemed all surface one moment seemed all depth the next. It was a place of which, unmistakably, Chad was fond; wherefore, if he, Strether, should like it too much, what on earth, with such a bond, would become of either of them? It all depended, of course— which was a gleam of light—on how the " too much " was measured; though indeed our friend fairly felt, while he prolonged the meditation I describe, that for himself, even already, a certain measure had been reached. It will have been sufficiently seen that he was not a man to neglect any good chance for reflection. Was it at all possible, for instance, to like Paris enough without liking it too much? He luckily, however, hadn't promised Mrs. Newsome not to like it at all. He was ready to recognize at this stage that such an engagement *would* have tied his hands. The Luxembourg gardens were, incontestably, just so adorable at this hour by reason—in addition to their intrinsic charm—of his not having taken it. The only engagement he had taken, when he looked the thing in the face, was to do what he reasonably could.

It upset him a little, none the less, after a while, to find himself at last remembering on what current of association he had been floated so far. Old imaginations of the Latin Quarter had played their part for him, and he had duly recalled its having been with this scene of rather ominous legend that, like so many young men in fiction as well as in fact, Chad had begun. He was quite out of it, with his " home," as Strether figured the place, in the Boulevard Malesherbes, now; which was perhaps why, repairing, not to fail of justice either, to the elder neighborhood, our friend had felt that he could allow for the element of the usual, the immemorial, without courting perturbation. He was not, in other words, in danger of seeing the youth and the particular Person flaunt by together; and yet he was in the very air of which—just to feel what the early, natural note must have been—he wished most to take counsel. It became, on the spot, vivid to him that he had originally had, for a few days, an almost envious vision of the boy's romantic privilege. Melancholy Mürger, with Francine and Musette and Rodolphe, at home, was, in the company of the tattered, one—if he was not in his single self two or three—of the unbound, the paper-covered dozen on the shelf; and when Chad had written, five years ago, after a sojourn then already prolonged to six months, that he had decided to go in for economy and the real thing, Strether's fancy had quite fondly accompanied him in this migration, which was to convey him, as they somewhat confusedly learned at Woollett, across the bridges and up the Montagne Sainte-Geneviève. This was the region—Chad had been quite distinct about it—in which the best French, and many other things, were to be learned at least cost, and in which all sorts of clever fellows, compatriots there for a purpose, formed an awfully pleasant set. The clever fellows, the friendly countrymen, were mainly young painters, sculptors, architects, medical students; but they were, Chad sagely opined, a much more profitable lot to be with—even on the footing of not being quite one of them—than the " terrible toughs " (Strether remembered the edifying discrimination,) of the American bars and banks roundabout the Opera. Chad had thrown out, in the communications following this one—for at that time he did once in a while communicate—that several members of a band of earnest workers under one of the great artists had taken him right in, making him dine every night, almost for nothing, at their place, and even pressing him not to neglect the hypothesis of there being as much " in him " as in any of them. There had been literally a moment at which it appeared that there might be something in him; there had been at any rate a moment at which he had written that he didn't know but what a month or two more might see him enrolled in some *atelier*. The season had been one at which Mrs. Newsome was moved to gratitude for small mercies; it had broken on them all as a blessing that their absentee *had* perhaps a conscience—that he was sated, in short, with idleness, was ambitious of variety. The exhibition was doubtless as yet not brilliant, but Strether himself, even by that time much enlisted and immersed, had determined, on the part of the two ladies, a temperate approval and in fact, as he now recollected, a certain austere enthusiasm.

But the very next thing that happened had been a dark drop of the curtain. The son and brother had not browsed long on the Montagne Sainte-Geneviève—his effective little use of the name of which, like his allusion to the best French, appeared to have been but one of the notes of his rough cunning. The light refreshment of these vain appearances had not, accordingly, carried any of them very far. On the other hand it had gained Chad time; it had given him a chance, unchecked, to strike his roots, had paved the way for initiations more direct and more deep. It was Strether's belief that he had been comparatively innocent before this first migration, and even that the first effects of the migration would not have been, without some particular bad accident, to have been deplored. There had been three months—he had sufficiently figured it out—in which Chad had wanted to try. He *had* tried, though not very hard—he had had his little hour of good faith. The weakness of that principle in him was that almost any accident that was bad enough was stronger. This had at any rate markedly been the case for the precipitation of a special series of impressions. They had proved, successively, these impressions—all of Musette and Francine, but Musette and Francine vulgarized by the larger evolution of the type—irresistibly sharp: he had " taken up," by what was at the time to be shrinkingly gathered, as it was scantly mentioned, with one ferociously " interested " little person after another. Strether had read somewhere of a Latin motto, a description of the hours, observed on a clock by a traveller in Spain; and he had been led to apply it in thought to Chad's number one, number two, number three. *Omnes vulnerant, ultima necat* —they had all morally wounded, the last had morally killed. The last had been longest in possession—in possession, that is, of whatever was left of the poor boy's finer mortality. And it had not been she, it had been one of her early predecessors, who had determined the second migration, the expensive return and relapse, the exchange again, as was fairly to be presumed, of the vaunted best French for some special variety of the worst.

He pulled himself then at last together for his own progress back; not with the feeling that he had taken his walk in vain. He prolonged it a little, in the immediate neighborhood, after he had quitted his chair; and the upshot of the whole morning for him was that his campaign had begun. He had wanted to put himself in relation, and he would be hanged if he were *not* in relation. He was at no moment so much so as while, under the old arches of the Odéon, he lingered before the charming open-air array of literature classic and casual. He thought the effect of tone and tint, in the long charged tables and shelves, delicate and appetizing; the impression—substituting one kind of low - priced *consommation* for another—might have been that of one of the pleasant cafés that overlapped, under an awning, to the pavement; but he edged along, grazing the tables, with his hands firmly behind him. He wasn't there to dip, to consume—he was there to reconstruct. He wasn't there for his own profit—not, that is, the direct; he was there on some chance of feeling the brush of the wing of the stray spirit of youth. He felt it in fact, he had it beside him; the old arcade indeed, as his inner sense listened, gave out the faint sound, as from far-off, of the wild waving of wings. They were folded now over the breasts of buried generations; but a flutter or two lived again in the turned page of shock-headed, slouch-hatted loiterers whose young intensity of type, in the direction of pale acuteness, deepened his vision, and even his appreciation, of racial differences, and whose manipulation of the uncut volume was too often, however, but a listening at closed doors. He reconstructed a possible groping Chad of three or four years before, a Chad who had, after all, simply—for that was the only way to see it—been too vulgar for his privilege. Surely it *was* a privilege to have been young and happy just there. Well, the best thing Strether knew of him was that he had had such a dream.

But his own actual business, half an hour later, was with a third floor on the Boulevard Malesherbes—so much as that was definite; and the fact of the enjoyment by the third-floor windows of a continuous balcony, to which he was helped by this knowledge, had perhaps something to do with his lingering for five minutes on the opposite side of the street. There were points as to which he had quite made up his mind, and one of these bore precisely on the wisdom of the abruptness to which events had finally committed him, a policy that he was pleased to find not at all shaken as he now looked at his watch and wondered. He *had* announced himself—six months before; had written out, at least, that Chad was not to be surprised should he see him some day turn up. Chad had thereupon, in a few words of rather carefully colorless answer, offered him a general welcome; and Strether, ruefully reflecting that he might have understood the warning as a hint to hospitality, a bid for an invitation, had fallen back upon silence as the corrective most to his own taste. He had asked Mrs. Newsome moreover not to announce him again; he had so distinct an opinion on attacking his job, should he attack it at all, in his own way. Not the least of this lady's high merits for him was that he could absolutely rest on her word. She was the only woman he had known, even at Woollett, as to whom his conviction was positive that to lie was beyond her art. Sarah Pocock, for instance, her own daughter, though with social ideals, as they said, in some respects different—Sarah who *was,* in her way, æsthetic, had never refused to human commerce that mitigation of rigor; there were occasions when he had distinctly seen her apply it. Since, accordingly, at all events, he had had it from Mrs. Newsome that she had, at whatever cost to her more strenuous view, conformed, in the matter of preparing Chad, wholly to his restrictions, he now looked up at the fine continuous balcony with a safe sense that if the case had been bungled the mistake was at least his property. Was there perhaps just a suspicion of that in his present pause on the edge of the Boulevard and well in the pleasant light?

Many things came over him here, and one of them was that he should doubtless presently know whether he had been shallow or sharp. Another was that the balcony in question didn't somehow show as a convenience easy to surrender. Poor Strether had at this very moment to recognize the truth that, wherever one paused in Paris, the imagination, before one could stop it, reacted. This perpetual reaction put a price, if one would, on pauses; but it piled up consequences till there was scarce room to pick one's steps among them. What call had he, at such a juncture, for instance, to like Chad's very house? High, broad, clear—he was expert enough to make out in a moment that it was admirably built—it fairly embarrassed our friend by the quality that, as he would have said, it "sprang" on him. He had struck off the fancy that it might,

as a preliminary, be of service to him to be seen, by a happy accident, from the third-story windows, which took all the March sun;
but of what service was it to find himself making out after a moment that the quality "sprung," the quality produced by measure
and balance, the fine relation of part to part and space to space, was
probably—aided by the presence of ornament as positive as it was
discreet, and by the complexion of the stone, a cold, fair gray,
warmed and polished a little by life—neither more nor less than a
case of distinction, such a case as he could only feel, unexpectedly,
as a sort of delivered challenge? Meanwhile, however, the chance
he had allowed for—the chance of being seen, in time, from the
balcony—had become a fact. Two or three of the windows stood
open to the violet air; and, before Strether had cut the knot by
crossing, a young man had come out and looked about him, had
lighted a cigarette and tossed the match over, and then, resting on
the rail, had given himself up, while he smoked, to watching the
life below. His arrival contributed, in its order, to keeping Strether
in position; the result of which, in turn, was that Strether soon felt
himself noticed. The young man began to look at him as in acknowledgment of his being himself in observation.

This was interesting so far as it went, but the interest was affected by the young man's not being Chad. Strether wondered at
first if he were perhaps Chad altered; then he saw that this was
asking too much of alteration. The young man was light, bright
and alert—with an air too pleasant to have been arrived at by patching. Strether had conceived Chad as patched, but not beyond recognition. He was in presence, he felt, of amendments enough as
they stood; it was a sufficient amendment that the gentleman up
there should be Chad's friend. He was young too then, the gentleman up there—he was very young; young enough, apparently,
to be amused at an elderly watcher, to be curious even to see what
the elderly watcher would do on finding himself watched. There
was youth in that, there was youth in the surrender to the balcony,
there was youth, for Strether, at this moment, in everything but
his own business; and Chad's thus pronounced association with
youth had given, the next instant, an extraordinary quick lift
to the issue. The balcony, the distinguished front testified suddenly, for Strether's fancy, to something that was up and up;

they placed the whole case materially, and as by an admirable image, on a level that he found himself at the end of another moment rejoicing to think he might reach. The young man looked at him still; he looked at the young man; and the issue, by a rapid process, was that this knowledge of a perched privacy appeared to him the last of luxuries. To him too the perched privacy was open, and he saw it now but in one light—that of the only domicile, the only fireside in the great ironic city on which he had the shadow of a claim. Miss Gostrey had a fireside; she had told him of it, and it was something that doubtless awaited him; but Miss Gostrey had not yet arrived—she mightn't arrive for days; and the sole attenuation of his excluded state was his vision of the small, the admittedly secondary hotel in the by-street from the Rue de la Paix, in which her solicitude for his purse had placed him, which affected him somehow as all in-door chill, glass-roofed court and slippery staircase, and which was, by the same token, pervaded by Waymarsh even at times when Waymarsh might have been certain to be round at the bank. It came to pass before he moved that Waymarsh, and Waymarsh alone, Waymarsh not only undiluted but positively strengthened, struck him as the present alternative to the young man in the balcony. When he did move it was fairly to escape that alternative. Taking his way over the street at last and passing through the *porte-cochère* of the house was like consciously leaving Waymarsh out. However, he would tell him all about it.

PART THIRD

VI.

STRETHER told Waymarsh all about it that very evening, on their dining together at the hotel; which needn't have happened, he was all the while aware, had he not chosen to sacrifice to this occasion a rarer opportunity. The mention to his companion of the sacrifice was moreover exactly what introduced his recital—or, as he would have called it with more confidence in his interlocutor, his confession. His confession was that he had been captured, and that one of the features of the affair had just failed to be his engaging himself on the spot to dinner. As by such a freedom Waymarsh would have lost him, he had obeyed his scruple; and he had likewise obeyed another scruple—which bore on the question of his himself bringing a guest.

Waymarsh looked gravely ardent, over the finished soup, at this array of scruples; Strether had not yet got quite used to being so unprepared for the consequences of the impression he produced. It was comparatively easy to explain, however, that he hadn't felt sure his guest would please. The person was a young man whose acquaintance he had made but that afternoon in the course of rather a hindered inquiry for another person—an inquiry that his new friend had just prevented, in fact, from being vain. "Oh," said Strether, "I've all sorts of things to tell you!"—and he said it in a way that was a virtual hint to Waymarsh to help him to enjoy the telling. He waited for his fish, he drank of his wine, he wiped his long mustache, he leaned back in his chair, he took in the two English ladies who had just creaked past them and whom he would even have articulately greeted if they hadn't rather chilled the impulse; so that all he could do was—by way of doing something—to say "*Merci, François!*" out quite loud when his fish was brought. Everything was there that he wanted, everything that could make the moment an occasion that would do beautiful-

71

ly—everything but what Waymarsh might give. The little waxed *salle-à-manger* was sallow and sociable; François, dancing over it, all smiles, was a man and a brother; the high-shouldered *patronne,* with her high-held, much-rubbed hands, seemed always assenting exuberantly to something unsaid; the Paris evening, in short, was, for Strether, in the very taste of the soup, in the goodness, as he was innocently pleased to think it, of the wine, in the pleasant coarse texture of the napkin and the crunch of the thick-crusted bread. These were things, all, congruous with his confession, and his confession was that he *had*—it would come out properly just there if Waymarsh would only take it properly—agreed to breakfast out, at twelve literally, the next day. He didn't quite know where; the delicacy of the case came straight up in the remembrance of his new friend's "We'll see; I'll take you somewhere!"— for it had required little more than that, after all, to let him right in. He was seized after a minute, face to face with his actual comrade, with the impulse to overcolor. There had already been things in respect to which he knew himself tempted by this perversity. If Waymarsh thought them bad he should at least have his reason for his discomfort; so Strether showed them as worse. Still, he was now, in his way, sincerely perplexed.

Chad had been absent from the Boulevard Malesherbes—was absent from Paris altogether; he had learned that from the concierge, but had nevertheless gone up, and gone up—there were no two ways about it—from an uncontrollable, a really, if one would, depraved, curiosity. The concierge had mentioned to him that a friend of the tenant of the *troisième* was for the time in possession; and this had been Strether's pretext for a further inquiry, an experiment carried on, under Chad's roof, without his knowledge. "I found his friend in fact there, keeping the place warm, as he called it, for him; Chad himself being, as appears, in the south. He went a month ago to Cannes, and though his return begins to be looked for it can't be for some days. I might, you see, perfectly have waited a week; might have beaten a retreat as soon as I got this essential knowledge. But I beat no retreat; I did the opposite; I stayed, I dawdled, I trifled; above all I looked round. I saw, in fine; and—I don't know what to call it—I sniffed. It's a detail, but it's as if there were something—something very good—*to* sniff."

Waymarsh's face had shown his friend an attention apparently so remote that the latter was slightly surprised to find it at this point abreast with him. "Do you mean a smell? What of it?"

"A charming scent. But I don't know."

Waymarsh gave an inferential grunt. "Does he live there with a woman?"

"I don't know."

Waymarsh waited an instant for more, then resumed. "Has he taken her off with him?"

"And will he bring her back?"—Strether fell into the inquiry. But he wound it up as before. "I don't know."

The way he wound it up, accompanied as this was with another drop back, another degustation of the Léoville, another wipe of his mustache and another good word for François, produced apparently in his companion a slight irritation. "Then what the devil *do* you know?"

"Well," said Strether almost gayly, "I guess I don't know anything!" His gayety might have been a tribute to the fact that the state he had been reduced to did for him again what had been done by his talk of the matter with Miss Gostrey at the London theatre. It was somehow enlarging; and the air of that amplitude was now doubtless more or less—and all for Waymarsh to feel—in his further response. "That's what I found out from the young man."

"But I thought you said you found out nothing."

"Nothing but that—that I don't know anything."

"And what good does that do you?"

"It's just," said Strether, "what I've come to you to help me to discover. I mean anything about anything over here. I *felt* that, up there. It regularly rose before me in its might. The young man, moreover—Chad's friend—as good as told me so."

"As good as told you you know nothing about anything?" Waymarsh seemed to look at some one who might have as good as told *him.* "How old is he?"

"Well, I guess not thirty."

"Yet you had to take that from him?"

"Oh, I took a good deal more—since, as I tell you, I took an invitation to *déjeuner.*"

"And are you *going* to that unholy meal?"

"If you'll come with me. He wants you too, you know. I told him about you. He gave me his card," Strether pursued, " and his name is rather funny. It's John Little Bilham, and he says his two surnames are, on account of his being small, inevitably used together."

"Well," Waymarsh asked with due detachment from these details, "what is he doing up there?"

"His account of himself is that he's 'only a little artist-man.' That seemed to me perfectly to describe him. But he's yet in the phase of study; this, you know, is the great art-school—to pass a certain number of years in which he came over. And he's a great friend of Chad's, and occupying Chad's rooms just now because they're so pleasant. *He's* very pleasant and curious too," Strether added—"though he's not from Boston."

Waymarsh looked already rather sick of him. "Where *is* he from?"

Strether thought. "I don't know that, either. But he's 'notoriously,' as he put it himself, not from Boston."

"Well," Waymarsh moralized from dry depths, "every one can't notoriously *be* from Boston. Why," he continued, " is he curious?"

"Perhaps just for *that*—for one thing! But really," Strether added, "for everything. When you meet him you'll see."

"Oh, I don't want to meet him," Waymarsh impatiently growled. "Why don't he go home?"

Strether hesitated. "Well, because he likes it over here."

This appeared in particular more than Waymarsh could bear. "He ought then to be ashamed of himself, and, as you admit that you think so too, why drag him in?"

Strether's reply again took time. "Perhaps I do think so myself—though I don't quite yet admit it. I'm not a bit sure—it's again one of the things I want to find out. I liked him, and *can* you like people—? But no matter." He pulled himself up. "There's no doubt I want you to come down on me and squash me."

Waymarsh helped himself to the next course, which, however, proving not the dish he had just noted as supplied to the English ladies, had the effect of causing his imagination temporarily to wander. But it presently broke out at a softer spot. "Have they got a handsome place up there?"

"Oh, a charming place; full of beautiful and valuable things. I never saw such a place—" and Strether's thought went back to it. "For a little artist-man—!" He could in fact scarce express it.

But his companion, who appeared now to have a view, insisted. "Well?"

"Well, life can hold nothing better. Besides, they're things of which he's in charge."

"So that he does doorkeeper for your precious pair? Can life," Waymarsh inquired, "hold nothing better than *that?*" Then as Strether, silent, seemed even yet to wonder, "Doesn't he know what *she* is?" he went on.

"I don't know. I didn't ask him. I couldn't. It was impossible. You wouldn't either. Besides, I didn't want to. No more would you." Strether in short explained it at a stroke. "You can't make out over here what people do know."

"Then what did you come over for?"

"Well, I suppose exactly to see for myself—without their aid."

"Then what do you want mine for?"

"Oh," Strether laughed, "you're not one of *them!* I do know what *you* know."

As, however, this last assertion caused Waymarsh again to look at him hard—such being the latter's doubt of its implications—he felt his justification lame. Which was still more the case when Waymarsh presently said: "Look here, Strether. Quit this."

Our friend smiled with a doubt of his own. "Do you mean my tone?"

"No—damn your tone. I mean your nosing round. Quit the whole job. Let them stew in their juice. You're being used for a thing you ain't fit for. People don't take a fine-tooth comb to groom a horse."

"Am I a fine-tooth comb?" Strether laughed. "It's something I never called myself!"

"It's what you are, all the same. You ain't so young as you were, but you've kept your teeth."

He acknowledged his friend's humor. "Take care I don't get

them into *you!* You'd like them, my friends at home, Waymarsh,"
he declared; "you'd really particularly like them. And I know"—
it was slightly irrelevant, but he gave it sudden and singular force—
"I know they'd like you!"

"Oh, don't work them off on *me!*" Waymarsh groaned.

Yet Strether still lingered with his hands in his pockets. "It's
really quite as indispensable as I say that Chad should be got
back."

"Indispensable to whom? To you?"

"Yes," Strether presently said.

"Because if you get him you also get Mrs. Newsome?"

Strether faced it. "Yes."

"And if you don't get him you don't get her?"

It might be merciless, but he continued not to flinch. "I think
it might have some effect on our personal understanding. Chad's
of real importance—or can easily become so if he will—to the
business."

"And the business is of real importance to his mother's husband?"

"Well, I naturally want what my future wife wants. And the
thing will be much better if we have our own man in it."

"If you have your own man in it, in other words," Waymarsh
said, "you'll marry—you personally—more money. She's already
rich, as I understand you, but she'll be richer still if the business
can be made to boom on certain lines that you've laid down."

"*I* haven't laid them down," Strether promptly returned. "Mr.
Newsome—who knew extraordinarily well what he was about—laid
them down ten years ago."

Oh well, Waymarsh seemed to indicate with a shake of his mane,
that didn't matter! "You're fierce for the boom anyway."

His friend weighed a moment in silence the justice of the charge.
"I can scarcely be called fierce, I think, when I so freely take
my chance of the possibility, the danger, of being influenced in a
sense counter to Mrs. Newsome's own feelings."

Waymarsh gave this proposition a long, hard look. "I see.
You're afraid yourself of being squared. But you're a humbug," he
added, "all the same."

"Oh!" Strether quickly protested.

"Yes, you ask me for protection—which makes you very interesting; and then you won't take it. You say you want to be squashed—"

"Ah, but not so easily! Don't you see," Strether demanded, "where my interest, as already shown you, lies? It lies in my not being squared. If I'm squared where's my marriage? If I miss my errand, I miss that; and if I miss that, I miss everything—I'm nowhere."

Waymarsh—but all relentlessly—took this in. "What do I care where you are if you're spoiled?"

Their eyes met on it an instant. "Thank you awfully," Strether at last said. "But don't you think *her* judgment of that—?"

"Ought to content me? No."

It kept them again face to face, and the end of this was that Strether again laughed. "You do her injustice. You really *must* know her. Good-night."

He breakfasted with Mr. Bilham on the morrow, and, as inconsequently befell, with Waymarsh massively of the party. The latter announced, at the eleventh hour and much to his friend's surprise, that, damn it, he would as soon join him as do anything else; on which they proceeded together, strolling in a state of detachment practically luxurious for them, to the Boulevard Malesherbes, a couple engaged that day with the sharp spell of Paris as confessedly, it might have been seen, as any couple among the daily thousands so compromised. They walked, wandered, wondered and, a little, lost themselves; Strether had not had for years so rich a consciousness of time — a bag of gold into which he constantly dipped for a handful. It was present to him that when the little business with Mr. Bilham should be over he would still have shining hours to use absolutely as he liked. There was no great pulse of haste yet in this process of saving Chad; nor was that effect a bit more marked as he sat, half an hour later, with his legs under Chad's mahogany, with Mr. Bilham on one side, with a friend of Mr. Bilham's on the other, with Waymarsh stupendously opposite, and with the great hum of Paris coming up in softness, vagueness— for Strether himself indeed already positive sweetness—through the sunny windows toward which, the day before, from below, his curiosity had raised its wings. The feeling that had been with him at that moment had borne fruit almost faster than he could taste it, and Strether literally felt, at the present moment, that there was a precipitation in his fate. He had known nothing and nobody as he stood in the street; but had not his view now taken a bound in the direction of every one and of everything?

"What is he up to, what is he up to?"—something like that was at the back of his head all the while in respect to little Bilham; but meanwhile, till he should make out, every one and everything were as good as represented for him by the combination of his host and the lady on his left. The lady on his left, the lady thus promptly and ingeniously invited to "meet" Mr. Strether and Mr. Waymarsh—it was the way she herself expressed her case—was a very marked person, a person who had much to do with our friend's asking himself if the occasion were not in its essence the most baited, the most gilded of traps. Baited it could properly be called when the repast was of so wise a savor, and gilded surrounding objects seemed inevitably to need to be when Miss Barrace—which was the lady's name—looked at them with convex Parisian eyes and through a glass with a remarkably long tortoise-shell handle. Why Miss Barrace, mature, meagre, erect and eminently gay, highly adorned, perfectly familiar, freely contradictious and reminding him of some last-century portrait of a clever head without powder— why Miss Barrace should have been in particular the note of a "trap" Strether could not on the spot have explained; he blinked in the light of a conviction that he should know later on, and know well—as it came over him, for that matter, with force, that he should need to. He wondered what he was to think exactly of either of his new friends; since the young man, Chad's intimate and deputy, had, in thus constituting the scene, practised so much more subtly than he had been prepared for, and since, in especial, Miss Barrace, surrounded clearly by every consideration, had not scrupled to figure as a feature. It was interesting to him to feel that he was in the presence of new measures, other standards, a different scale of relations, and that evidently here were a happy pair who didn't think of things at all as he and Waymarsh thought. Nothing was less to have been calculated in the business than that it should now be for him as if he and Waymarsh were comparative- ly quite at one.

The latter was magnificent—this at least was an assurance privately given him by Miss Barrace. "Oh, your friend's a type, the grand old American—what shall one call it? The Hebrew prophet, Ezekiel, Jeremiah, who used when I was a little girl in the Rue Montaigne, to come to see my father, and who was usually the American Minister to the Tuileries or some other court. I haven't seen one these ever so many years; the sight of it warms my poor old chilled heart; this specimen is wonderful; in the right quarter, you know, he'll have a *succès fou.*" Strether had not failed to ask what the right quarter might be, much as he required his presence of mind to meet such a change in their scheme. "Oh, the artist-quarter, and that kind of thing; *here,* already, for instance, as you see." He had been on the point of echoing "'Here?'—is *this* the artist-quarter?" but she had already disposed of the question with a wave of all her tortoise-shell and an easy "Bring him to *me!*" He knew on the spot how little he should be able to bring him, for the very air was by this time, to his sense, thick and hot with poor Waymarsh's judgment of it. He was in the trap still more than his companion, and, unlike his companion, not making the best of it; which was precisely what gave him, doubtless, his admirable sombre glow. Little did Miss Barrace know that what was behind it was his grave estimate of her own laxity. The general assumption with which our two friends had arrived had been that of finding Mr. Bilham ready to conduct them to one or other of those resorts of the earnest, the æsthetic fraternity which were shown among the sights of Paris. In this character it would have justified them in a proper insistence on discharging their score. Waymarsh's only proviso, at the last, had been that nobody should pay for him; but he found himself, as the occasion developed, paid for on a scale as to which Strether privately made out that he already nursed retribution. Strether was conscious across the table of what worked in him, conscious when they passed back to the small salon to which, the previous evening, he himself had made so rich a reference; conscious most of all as they stepped out to the balcony in which one would have had to be an ogre not to recognize the perfect place for easy aftertastes. These things were enhanced, for Miss Barrace, by a succession of excellent cigarettes—acknowledged, acclaimed, as a part of the wonderful supply left behind him by Chad—in an almost equal absorption of which Strether found himself blindly, almost wildly pushing forward. He might perish by the sword as well as by famine, and he knew that his having abetted the lady by an excess that was rare with him would count for little in the sum—as Waymarsh might so easily add it up—of her license. Waymarsh had smoked of old, smoked hugely; but Waymarsh did nothing now, and that gave him his advantage over people who took things up lightly just when others had laid them heavily down. Strether had never smoked, and he felt as if he flaunted at his friend that this had been only because of a reason. The reason, it now began to appear even to himself, was that he had never had a lady to smoke with.

It was this lady's being there at all, however, that was the strange, free thing; perhaps, since she *was* there, her smoking was the least of her freedoms. If Strether had been sure at each juncture of what—with Bilham in especial—she talked about, he might have traced others and winced at them and felt Waymarsh wince; but he was in fact so often at sea that his sense of the range of reference was merely general and that he on several different occasions guessed and interpreted only to doubt. He wondered what they meant, but there were things he scarce thought they could be supposed to mean, and "Oh no—not *that!*" was at the end of most of his ventures. This was the very beginning with him of a condition as to which, later on, as will be seen, he found cause to pull himself up; and he was to remember the moment duly as the first step in a process. The central fact of the place was neither more nor less, when analyzed—and a pressure superficial sufficed—than the fundamental impropriety of Chad's situation, round about which they thus seemed cynically clustered. Accordingly, since they took it for granted, they took for granted all that, in connection with it, was taken for granted at Woollett—matters as to which, verily, he had been reduced with Mrs. Newsome to the last intensity of silence. That was the consequence of their being too bad to be talked about, and was the accompaniment, by the same token, of a deep conception of their badness. It befell, therefore, that when poor Strether put it to himself that their badness was, ultimately, or perhaps even insolently, what such a scene as the one before him was, so to speak, built upon, he could scarce shirk the dilemma of reading a roundabout echo of them into almost anything that came up. This, he was well aware, was a dreadful necessity; but such was the stern logic, he could only gather, of a relation to the irregular life.

It was the way the irregular life sat upon Bilham and Miss Barrace that was the insidious, the delicate marvel. He was eager to concede that their relation to it was all indirect, for anything else, in him, would have shown the grossness of bad manners; but the indirectness was none the less consonant—*that* was striking—with a grateful enjoyment of everything that was Chad's. They spoke of him repeatedly, invoking his good name and good nature, and the worst confusion of mind for Strether was that all their mention of him was of a kind to do him honor. They commended his munificence and approved his taste, and in doing so sat down, as it seemed to Strether, in the very soil out of which these things flowered. Our friend's final predicament was that he himself was sitting down, for the time, with them, and there was a supreme moment at which, compared with his collapse, Waymarsh's erectness affected him as really high. One thing was certain—he saw he must make up his mind. He must approach Chad, must wait for him, deal with him, master him, but he must not dispossess himself of the faculty of seeing things as they were. He must bring him to *him*—not go himself, as it were, so much of the way. He must at any rate be clearer as to what—should he continue to do that for convenience—he was still condoning. It was on the detail of this quantity—and what could the fact be but mystifying?—that Bilham and Miss Barrace threw so little light. So there they were.

6

VII.

WHEN Miss Gostrey arrived, at the end of a week, she made him a sign; he went immediately to see her, and it was not till then that he could again close his grasp on the idea of a corrective. This idea, however, was luckily all before him again from the moment he crossed the threshold of the little entresol of the Quartier Marbœuf into which she had gathered, as she said, picking them up in a thousand flights and funny little passionate pounces, the makings of a final nest. He recognized in an instant that there really, there only, he should find the boon with the vision of which he had first mounted Chad's stairs. He might have been a little scared at the picture of how much more, in this place, he should know himself " in," had not his friend been on the spot to measure the amount to his appetite. Her compact and crowded little chambers, almost dusky, as they at first struck him, with accumulations, represented a supreme general adjustment to opportunities and conditions. Wherever he looked he saw an old ivory or an old brocade, and he scarce knew where to sit for fear of a misappliance. The life of the occupant struck him, of a sudden, as more charged with possession even than Chad's or than Miss Barrace's; wide as his glimpse had lately become of the empire of " things," what was before him still enlarged it; the lust of the eyes and the pride of life had indeed thus their temple. It was the innermost nook of the shrine—as brown as a pirate's cave. In the brownness were glints of gold; patches of purple were in the gloom; objects, all, that caught, through the muslin, with their high rarity, the light of the low windows. Nothing was clear about them but that they were precious, and they brushed his ignorance with their contempt as a flower, in a liberty taken with him, might have been whisked under his nose. But after a full look at his hostess he knew, none the less, what most concerned him. The circle in which they stood

together was warm with life, and every question between them would
live there as nowhere else. A question came up as soon as they
had spoken, for his answer, with a laugh, was quickly: "Well,
they've got hold of me!" Much of their talk, on this first occasion, was his development of that truth. He was extraordinarily
glad to see her, expressing to her frankly what she most showed
him, that one might live for years without a blessing unsuspected,
but that to know it at last for no more than three days was to need
it, or miss it, forever. She was the blessing that had now become
his need, and what could prove it better than that without her he
had lost himself?

"What do you mean?" she asked with an absence of alarm that,
correcting him as if he had mistaken the "period" of one of her
pieces, gave him afresh a sense of her easy movement through the
maze he had but begun to tread. "What in the name of all the
Pococks have you managed to do?"

"Why, exactly the wrong thing. I've made a frantic friend of
little Bilham."

"Ah, that sort of thing was of the essence of your case and to
have been allowed for from the first." And it was only after this
that, quite as a minor matter, she asked who in the world little
Bilham might be. When she learned that he was a friend of Chad's
and living for the time in Chad's rooms in Chad's absence, quite
as if acting in Chad's spirit and serving Chad's cause, she showed,
however, more interest. "Should you mind my seeing him? Only
once, you know," she added.

"Oh, the oftener the better: he's amusing—he's original."

"He doesn't shock you?" Miss Gostrey threw out.

"Never in the world! We escape that with a perfection—! I
feel it to be largely, no doubt, because I don't half understand him;
but our *modus vivendi* isn't spoiled even by that. You must dine
with me to meet him," Strether went on. "Then you'll see."

"Are you giving dinners?"

"Yes—there I am. That's what I mean."

All her kindness wondered. "That you're spending too much
money?"

"Dear, no—they seem to cost so little. But that I do it to
them. I ought to hold off."

She thought again—she laughed. " The money you must be spending—to think it cheap! But I must be out of it—to the naked eye."

He looked for a moment as if she were really failing him. " Then you won't meet them?" It was almost as if she had developed an unexpected personal prudence.

She hesitated. " Who are they—first?"

" Why, little Bilham—to begin with." He kept back for the moment Miss Barrace. " And Chad—when he comes—you must absolutely see."

" When then does he come?"

" When Bilham has had time to write him, and hear from him, about me. Bilham, however," he pursued, " will report favorably—favorably for Chad. That will make him not afraid to come. I want you the more, therefore, you see, for my bluff."

" Oh, you'll do yourself for your bluff." She was perfectly **easy.** " At the rate you've gone I'm quiet."

" Ah, but I haven't," said Strether, " made one protest."

She turned it over. " Haven't you been seeing what there is to protest about?"

He let her, with this, however ruefully, have the whole truth. " I haven't yet found a single thing."

" Isn't there any one *with* him then?"

" Of the sort I came out about?" Strether took a moment. " How do I know? And what do I care?"

" Oh, oh!"—and her laughter spread. He was struck in fact by the effect on her of his joke. He saw now how he meant it as a joke. *She* saw, however, still other things. But in an instant she had hidden them. " You've got at no facts at all?"

He tried to muster them. " Well, he has a lovely home."

" Ah, that, in Paris," she quickly returned, " proves nothing. That is, rather, it *dis*proves nothing. They may very well, you see, the people your mission is concerned with, have done it *for* him."

" Exactly. And it was on the scene of their doings then that Waymarsh and I sat guzzling."

" Oh, if you forbore to guzzle here on scenes of doings," she replied, " you might easily die of starvation." With which she smiled at him. " You've worse before you."

"Ah, I've *everything* before me. But on our hypothesis, you know, they must be wonderful."

"They *are!*" said Miss Gostrey. "You're not, therefore, you see," she added, "wholly without facts. They've *been,* in effect wonderful."

To have got at something comparatively definite appeared at last a little a help—a wave by which, moreover, the next moment, recollection was washed. "My young man does admit, furthermore, that they're our friend's great interest."

"Is that the expression he uses?"

Strether more exactly recalled. "No—not quite."

"Something more vivid? Less?"

He had bent, with neared glasses, over a group of articles on a small stand; and at this he came up. "It was a mere allusion, but, on the lookout as I was, it struck me. 'Awful, you know, as Chad is '—those were Bilham's words."

"'Awful, you know—'? Oh!"—and Miss Gostrey turned them over. She seemed, however, satisfied. "Well, what more do you want?"

He glanced once more at a *bibelot* or two, but everything sent him back. "But it *is,* all the same, as if they wished to let me have it between the eyes."

She wondered. "*Quoi donc?*"

"Why, what I speak of. The amenity. They can stun you with that as well as with anything else."

"Oh," she answered, "you'll come round! I must see them each," she went on, "for myself. I mean Mr. Bilham and Mr. Newsome—Mr. Bilham naturally first. Once only—once for each; that will do. But face to face—for half an hour. What is Mr. Chad," she immediately pursued, "doing at Cannes? Decent men don't go to Cannes with the—well, with the kind of ladies you mean."

"Don't they?" Strether asked with an interest in decent men that amused her.

"No; elsewhere, but not to Cannes. Cannes is different. Cannes is better. Cannes is best. I mean it's all people you know—when you do know them. And if *he* does, why, that's different too. He must have gone alone. She can't be with him."

"I haven't," Strether confessed in his weakness, "the least

idea." There seemed much in what she said; but he was able, after a little, to help her to a nearer impression. The meeting with little Bilham took place, by easy arrangement, in the great gallery of the Louvre; and when, standing with his fellow-visitor before one of the splendid Titians—the overwhelming portrait of the young man with the strangely shaped glove and the blue-gray eyes—he turned to see the third member of their party advance from the end of the waxed and gilded vista, he had a sense of having at last taken hold. He had agreed with Miss Gostrey—it dated even from Chester—for a morning at the Louvre, and he had embraced, independently, the same idea as thrown out by little Bilham, whom he had already accompanied to the museum of the Luxembourg. The fusion of these schemes presented no difficulty, and it was to strike him again that, in little Bilham's company, difficulty in general dropped.

"Oh, he's all right—he's one of *us!*" Miss Gostrey, after the first exchange, soon found a chance to murmur to her companion; and Strether, as they proceeded and paused, as a quick unanimity, between the two, appeared to have phrased itself in half a dozen remarks—Strether knew that he knew, almost immediately, what she meant, and took it as still another sign that he had got his job in hand. This was the more grateful to him that he could think of the intelligence now serving him as an acquisition positively new. He wouldn't have known even the day before what she meant —that is if she meant, what he assumed, that they were intense Americans together. He had just worked round—and with a sharper turn of the screw than any yet—to the conception of an American intense as little Bilham was intense. The young man was his first specimen; the specimen had profoundly perplexed him; at present, however, there was light. It was by little Bilham's amazing serenity that he had been at first affected, but he had inevitably, in his circumspection, felt it as the trail of the serpent, the corruption, as he might conveniently have said, of Europe; whereas the promptness with which it came up for Miss Gostrey as but a special little form of the oldest thing they knew justified it, to his own vision as well, on the spot. He wanted to be able to like his specimen with a clear good conscience, and this fully permitted it. What had muddled him was precisely the small artist-man's way—it was so complete—of being more American than anybody. But it now, for the time, put Strether vastly at his ease to have this view of a new way.

The amiable youth, then, looked out, as it had first struck Strether, at a world in respect to which he hadn't a prejudice. The one our friend most instantly missed was the usual one in favor of an occupation accepted. Little Bilham had an occupation, but it was only an occupation declined; and it was by his general exemption from alarm, anxiety or remorse on this score that the impression of his serenity was made. He had come out to Paris to paint—to fathom, that is, at large, that mystery; but study had been fatal to him so far as anything *could* be fatal, and his productive power faltered in proportion as his knowledge grew. Strether had gathered from him that at the moment of his finding him in Chad's rooms he had not saved from his shipwreck a scrap of anything but his beautiful intelligence and his confirmed habit of Paris. He referred to these things with an equal fond familiarity, and it was sufficiently clear that, as an outfit, they still served him. They were charming to Strether through the hour spent at the Louvre, where indeed they figured for him as an unseparated part of the charged, iridescent air, the glamour of the name, the splendor of the space, the color of the masters. Yet they were present too wherever the young man led, and the day after the visit to the Louvre they hung, in a different walk, about the steps of our party. He had invited his companions to cross the river with him, offering to show them his own poor place; and his own poor place, which was very poor, gave to his idiosyncrasies, for Strether— the small sublime indifferences and independences that had struck the latter as fresh—an odd, engaging dignity. He lived at the end of an alley that went out of an old, short, cobbled street, a street that went, in turn, out of a new, long, smooth avenue—street and avenue and alley having, however, in common a sort of social shabbiness; and he introduced them to the rather cold and blank little studio which he had lent to a comrade for the term of his elegant absence. The comrade was another ingenuous compatriot, to whom he had wired that tea was to await them, " regardless ", and this reckless repast, and the second ingenuous compatriot, and the faraway makeshift life, with its jokes and its gaps, its delicate daubs and its three or four chairs, its overflow of taste and conviction and its lack of nearly all else—these things wove round the occasion a spell to which our hero unreservedly surrendered.

He liked the ingenuous compatriots—for two or three others soon gathered; he liked the delicate daubs and the free discriminations —involving references indeed, involving enthusiasms and execrations that made him, as they said, sit up; he liked, above all, the legend of good-humored poverty, of mutual accommodation fairly raised to the romantic, that he soon read into the scene. The ingenuous compatriots showed a candor, he thought, surpassing even the candor of Woollett; they were red-haired and long-legged, they were quaint and queer and dear and droll; they made the place resound with the vernacular, which he had never known so marked as when figuring for the chosen language, he must suppose, of contemporary art. They twanged, with a vengeance, the æsthetic lyre —they drew from it wonderful airs. This aspect of their life had an admirable innocence; and he looked, on occasion, at Maria Gostrey, to see to what extent that element reached her. She gave him, however, for the hour, as she had given him the previous day, no further sign than to show how she dealt with boys; meeting them with the air of old Parisian practice that she had for every one, for everything in turn. Wonderful about the delicate daubs, masterful about the way to make tea, trustful about the legs of chairs and familiarly reminiscent of those, in the other time, the named, the numbered or the caricatured, who had flourished or failed, disappeared or arrived, she had accepted with the best grace her second course of little Bilham, and had said to Strether, the previous afternoon, on his leaving them, that, since her impression was to be renewed, she would reserve judgment till after the new evidence.

The new evidence was to come, as it proved, in a day or two. He soon had from Maria a message to the effect that an excellent box at the Français had been lent her for the following night; it seeming on such occasions not the least of her merits that she was subject to such approaches. The sense of how she was, in advance, always paying for something was equalled, on Strether's part, only by the sense of how she was always being paid; all of which made for his consciousness, in the larger air, of a lively, bustling traffic, the exchange of such values as were not for him to handle. She hated, he knew, at the French play, anything but a box—just as she hated at the English anything but a stall; and a box was what he was already, in this phase, girding himself to press upon her. But she had, for that matter, her resemblance to little Bilham: she too, always, on the great issues, showed as having known in time. It made her constantly beforehand with him and gave him mainly the chance to ask himself how on the day of their settlement their account would stand. He endeavored even now to keep it a little straight by arranging that if he accepted her invitation she should dine with him first; but the upshot of this scruple was that at eight o'clock on the morrow he awaited her with Waymarsh under the pillared portico. She had not dined with him, and it was characteristic of their relation that she had made him embrace her refusal without in the least understanding it. She ever caused her rearrangements to affect him as her tenderest touches. It was on that principle, for instance, that, giving him the opportunity to be amiable again to little Bilham, she had suggested his offering the young man a seat in their box. Strether had despatched, to this end, a small blue missive to the Boulevard Malesherbes, but up to the moment of their passing into the theatre he had received no response to his message. He held, however, even after they had been for some time conveniently seated, that their friend, who knew his way about, would come in at his own right moment. His temporary absence, moreover, seemed, as never yet, to make the right moment for Miss Gostrey. Strether had been waiting till to-night to get back from her in some mirrored form her impressions and conclusions. She had elected, as they said, to see little Bilham once; but now she had seen him twice and had nevertheless not said more than a word.

Waymarsh meanwhile sat opposite him, with their hostess between; and Miss Gostrey spoke of herself as an instructor of youth introducing her little charges to a work that was one of the glories of literature. The glory was happily unobjectionable, and the little charges were candid; for herself, she had travelled that road and she merely waited on their innocence. But she referred in due time to their absent friend, whom it was clear they should have to give up. "He either won't have got your note," she said, "or you won't have got his: he has had some kind of hindrance, and, of

course, for that matter, you know, a man never writes about coming to a box." She spoke as if, with her look, it might have been
Waymarsh who had written to the youth, and the latter's face
showed a mixture of austerity and anguish. She went on, however, as
if to meet this. " He's far and away, you know, the best of them."

" The best of whom, ma'am ?"

" Why, of all the long procession—the boys, the girls, or the old
men and old women as they sometimes really are; the hope, as one
may say, of our country. They've all passed, year after year; but
there has been no one in particular I've ever wanted to stop. I
feel—don't *you?*—that I want to stop little Bilham; he's so exactly right as he is." She continued to talk to Waymarsh. " He's
too delightful. If he'll only not spoil it! But they always *will;*
they always do; they always have."

" I don't think Waymarsh knows," Strether said after a moment, " quite what it's open to Bilham to spoil."

" It can't be a good American," Waymarsh lucidly enough replied; " for it didn't strike me the young man had developed much
in *that* shape."

" Ah," Miss Gostrey sighed, " the name of the good American is
as easily given as taken away! What *is* it, to begin with, to *be* one,
and what's the extraordinary hurry? Surely nothing that's so
pressing was ever so little defined. It's such an order, really, that
before we cook you the dish we must at least have your receipt.
Besides, the poor chicks have time! What I've seen so often
spoiled," she pursued, " is the happy attitude itself, the state of
faith and—what shall I call it?—the sense of beauty. You're
right about him "—she now took in Strether; " little Bilham has
them to a charm; we must keep little Bilham along." Then she was
all again for Waymarsh. " The others have all wanted so dreadfully to do something, and they've gone and done it, in too many
cases, indeed. It leaves them never the same afterwards; the
charm is always somehow broken. Now *he,* I think, you know,
really won't. He won't do the least dreadful little thing. We shall
continue to enjoy him just as he is. No—he's quite beautiful. He
sees everything. He isn't a bit ashamed. He has every scrap of the
courage of it that one could ask. Only think what he *might do.*
One wants really—for fear of some accident—to keep him in view.

At this very moment, perhaps, what mayn't he be up to? I've had my disappointments—the poor things are never really safe; or only, at least, when you have them under your eye. One can never completely trust them. One is uneasy, and I think that's why I most miss him now."

She had wound up with a laugh of enjoyment over her embroidery of her idea—an enjoyment that her face communicated to Strether, who almost wished, none the less, at this moment, that she would let poor Waymarsh alone. *He* knew more or less what she meant; but the fact was not a reason for her not pretending to Waymarsh that he didn't. It was craven of him perhaps, but he would, for the high amenity of the occasion, have liked Waymarsh not to be so sure of his wit. Her recognition of it gave him away and, before she had done with him or with that article, would give him worse. What was he, all the same, to do? He looked across the box at his friend; their eyes met; something queer and stiff, something that bore on the situation, but that it was better not to touch, passed in silence between them. Well, the effect of it for Strether was an abrupt reaction, a final impatience of his own tendency to temporize. Where was that taking him anyway? It was one of the quiet instants that sometimes settle more matters than the outbreaks dear to the historic muse. The only qualification of the quietness was the synthetic " Oh hang it!" into which Strether's share of the silence soundlessly flowered. It represented, this mute ejaculation, a final impulse to burn his ships. These ships, to the historic muse, may seem of course mere cockles, but when he presently spoke to Miss Gostrey it was with the sense at least of applying the torch. " Is it then a conspiracy?"

" Between the two young men? Well, I don't pretend to be a seer or a prophetess," she presently replied; " but if I'm simply a woman of sense he's working for you to-night. I don't quite know how—but it's in my bones." And she looked at him at last as if, little material as she yet gave him, he would really understand. " For an opinion, *that's* my opinion. He makes you out too well not to."

" Not to work for me to-night?" Strether wondered. " Then I hope he isn't doing anything very bad."

" They've got you," she portentously answered.

" Do you mean he *is*—?"

" They've got you," she merely repeated. Though she disclaimed the prophetic vision she was at this instant the nearest approach he had ever met to the priestess of the oracle. The light was in her eyes. " You must face it now."

He faced it on the spot. " They *had* arranged—?"

" Every move in the game. And they've been arranging ever since. He has had every day his little telegram from Cannes."

It made Strether open his eyes. " Do you *know* that?"

" I do better. I see it. This was what I wondered, before I met him, if I *was* to see. But as soon as I met him I ceased to wonder, and our second meeting made me sure. I took him all in. He was acting—he is still—on his daily instructions."

" So that Chad has done the whole thing?"

" Oh no—not the whole. *We've* done some of it. You and I and ' Europe.' "

" Europe—yes," Strether mused.

" Dear old Paris," she seemed to explain. But there was more, and, with one of her turns, she risked it. " And dear old Waymarsh. You," she declared, " have been a good bit of it."

He sat massive. " A good bit of what, ma'am?"

" Why, of the wonderful consciousness of our friend here. You've helped too, in your way, to float him to where he is."

" And where the devil *is* he?"

She passed it on with a laugh. " Where the devil, Strether, are you?"

He spoke as if he had just been thinking it out. " Well, quite already, in Chad's hands, it would seem." And he had had, with this, another thought. " Will that be—just all through Bilham—the way he's going to work it? It would be, for him, you know, an idea. And Chad with an idea—!"

" Well?" she asked while the image held him.

" Well, is Chad—what shall I say?—monstrous?"

" Oh, as much as you like! But the idea you speak of," she said, " won't have been his best. He'll have a better. It won't be all through little Bilham that he'll work it."

This already sounded almost like a hope destroyed. " Through whom else then?"

" That's what we shall see!" But quite as she spoke she turned,
and Strether turned; for the door of the box had opened, with the
click of the *ouvreuse,* from the lobby, and a gentleman, a stranger
to them, had come in with a quick step The door closed behind
him, and, though their faces showed him his mistake, his air,
which was striking, was all good confidence. The curtain had just
again risen, and, in the hush of the general attention, Strether's
challenge was tacit, as was also the greeting, with a quick, depre-
cating hand and smile, of the unannounced visitor. He signed,
discreetly, that he would wait, would stand, and these things, and
his face, one look from which she had caught, had suddenly worked
for Miss Gostrey. She fitted to them all an answer for Strether's
last question. The solid stranger was simply the answer—as she
now, turning to her friend, indicated. She brought it straight out
for him—it presented the intruder. " Why, through this gentleman!" The gentleman indeed, at the same time, though sounding
for Strether a very short name, did practically as much to explain.
Strether gasped the name back—then only had he seen. Miss Gostrey had said more than she knew. They were in presence of Chad
himself.

Our friend was to go over it afterwards again and again—he
was going over it much of the time that they were together, and
they were together, constantly, for three or four days: the note had
been so strongly struck during that first half-hour that everything
happening since was comparatively a minor development. The fact
was that his perception of the young man's identity—so absolutely
checked for a minute—had been quite one of the sensations that
count in life; he certainly had never known one that had acted,
as he might have said, with more of a crowded rush. And the
rush, though both vague and multitudinous, had lasted a long time,
protected, as it were, yet at the same time aggravated, by the
circumstance of its coinciding with a stretch of decorous silence.
They couldn't talk without disturbing the spectators in the part of
the balcony just below them; and it, for that matter, came to
Strether—being a thing of the sort that did come to him—that
these were the accidents of a high civilization; the imposed tribute
to propriety, the frequent exposure to conditions, usually brilliant,
in which relief has to await its time. Relief was never quite near

at hand for kings, queens, comedians and other such people, and
though you might be yourself not exactly one of those, you could
yet, in leading the life of high pressure, guess a little how they
sometimes felt. It was truly the life of high pressure that Strether
had seemed to feel himself leading while he sat there, close to Chad,
during the long tension of the act. He was in presence of a fact
that occupied his whole mind, that occupied for the half-hour his
senses themselves all together; but he couldn't without inconvenience show anything—which moreover might count really as
luck. What he might have shown, had he shown at all, was exactly
the kind of emotion—the emotion of bewilderment—that he had
proposed to himself from the first, whatever should occur, to show
least. The phenomenon that had suddenly sat down there with him
was a phenomenon of change so complete that his imagination,
which had worked so beforehand, felt itself, in the connection,
without margin or allowance. It had faced every contingency but
that Chad should not *be* Chad, and this was what it now had to face
with a mere strained smile and an uncomfortable flush.

He asked himself if, by any chance, before he should have in
some way to commit himself, he might feel his mind settled to the
new vision, might habituate it, so to speak, to the remarkable truth.
But oh, it was too remarkable, the truth; for what could be more remarkable than this sharp rupture of an identity? You could deal
with a man as himself—you couldn't deal with him as somebody
else. It was a small source of peace, moreover, to be reduced to
wondering how little he might know in such an event what a sum he
was setting you. He couldn't absolutely not know, for you couldn't
absolutely not let him. It was a *case* then, simply, a strong case,
as people nowadays called such things, a case of transformation
unsurpassed, and the hope was but in the general law that strong
cases were liable to control from without. Perhaps he, Strether
himself, was the only person, after all, aware of it. Even Miss
Gostrey, with all her science, wouldn't be, would she?—and he had
never seen any one less aware of anything than Waymarsh as he
glowered at Chad. The social sightlessness of his old friend's survey marked for him afresh, and almost in an humiliating way, the
inevitable limits of direct aid from this source. He was not certain, however, of not drawing a shade of compensation from the

privilege, as yet untasted, of knowing more about something in particular than Miss Gostrey did. His situation too was a case, for that matter, and he was now so interested, quite so privately agog, about it, that he had already an eye to the fun it would be to open up to her afterwards. He derived, during his half-hour, no assistance from her, and just this fact of her not meeting his eyes played a little, it must be confessed, into his predicament.

He had introduced Chad, in the first minutes, under his breath, and there was never the primness in her of the person unacquainted; but she had none the less, for a long time, no eyes but for the stage, where she occasionally found a pretext for an appreciative moment that she invited Waymarsh to share. The latter's faculty of participation had never had, all round, such an assault to meet; the pressure on him being the sharper for this chosen attitude, on her part, as Strether judged it, of isolating, for their natural intercourse, Chad and himself. This intercourse was meanwhile restricted to a frank, friendly look from the young man, something markedly like a smile, but falling far short of a grin, and to the vivacity of Strether's private speculation as to whether *he* carried himself like the fool. He didn't quite see how he could so feel as one without somehow showing as one. The worst of that question moreover was that he knew it as a symptom the sense of which annoyed him. "If I'm going to be odiously conscious of how I may strike the fellow," he reflected, "it was so little what I came out for that I may as well stop before I begin." This sage consideration too, distinctly, seemed to leave untouched the fact that he *was* going to be conscious. He was conscious of everything but of what would have served him.

He was to know afterwards, in the watches of the night, that nothing would have been more open to him than, after a minute or two, to propose to Chad to pass out with him to the lobby. He had not only not proposed it, but had lacked even the presence of mind to see it as possible. He had stuck there like a schoolboy wishing not to miss a minute of the show; though for that portion of the show then presented he had not had an instant's real attention. He could not when the curtain fell have given the slightest account of what had happened. He had therefore, further, not at that moment acknowledged the amenity added by this acceptance of his awkwardness to Chad's general patience. Hadn't he none the less known at the very time—known it stupidly and without reaction—that the boy was accepting something? He was modestly benevolent, the boy—that was at least what he had been capable of, the superiority of making out his chance to be; and one had one's self literally not had the gumption to get in ahead of him. If we should go into all that occupied our friend in the watches of the night we should have to mend our pen; but an instance or two may mark for us the vividness with which he could remember. He remembered the two absurdities that, if his presence of mind *had* failed, were the things that had had most to do with it. He had never in his life seen a young man come into a box at ten o'clock at night, and would, if challenged on the question in advance, have scarce been ready to pronounce as to different ways of doing so. But it was, in spite of this, definite to him, that Chad had had a way that was wonderful: a fact carrying with it an implication that, as one might imagine it, he knew, he had learned, how.

Here already then were abounding results; he had, on the spot, and without the least trouble of intention, taught Strether that, even in so small a thing as that, there were different ways. He had done, in the same line, still more than this; had, by a mere shake or two of the head, made his old friend observe that the change in him was perhaps more than anything else, for the eye, a matter of the marked streaks of gray, extraordinary at his age, in his thick black hair; as well as that this new feature was curiously becoming to him, did something for him, as characterization, also even—of all things in the world—as refinement, that had been a good deal wanted. Strether felt, however, he would have had to confess, that it would not have been easy just now, on this and other counts, in the presence of what had been supplied, to be quite clear as to what had been missed. A reflection a candid critic might have made of old, for instance, was that it would have been happier for the son to look more like the mother; but this was a reflection that at present would never occur. The ground had quite fallen away from it, yet no resemblance whatever to the mother had supervened. It would have been hard for a young man's face and air to disconnect themselves more completely than Chad's at this juncture from any discerned, from any imaginable aspect of a

New England female parent. That of course was no more than had been on the cards; but it produced in Strether, none the less, one of those frequent phenomena of mental reference with which all judgment in him was actually beset.

Again and again, as the days passed, he had had a sense of the pertinence of communicating quickly with Woollett—communicating with a quickness with which telegraphy alone would rhyme; the fruit, really, of a fine fancy in him for keeping things straight, for the happy forestallment of error. No one could explain better when needful, nor put more conscience into an account or a report; which burden of conscience is perhaps exactly the reason why his heart always sank when the clouds of explanation gathered. His highest ingenuity was in keeping the sky of life clear of them. Whether or no he had a grand idea of the lucid, he held that nothing ever was in fact—for any one else—explained. One went through the vain motions, but it was mostly a waste of life. A personal relation was a relation only so long as people either perfectly understood or, better still, didn't care if they didn't. From the moment they cared if they didn't it was living by the sweat of one's brow; and the sweat of one's brow was just what one might buy one's self off from by keeping the ground free of the wild weed of delusion. It easily grew too fast, and the Atlantic cable now alone could race with it. That agency would, each day, have testified for him to something that was not what Woollett had argued. He was not, at this moment, absolutely sure that the effect of the morrow's—or rather of the night's—appreciation of the crisis wouldn't be to determine some brief missive. "Have at last seen him, but oh dear!" —some temporary relief of that sort seemed to hover before him. It hovered somehow as preparing them all—yet preparing them for what? If he might do so more luminously and cheaply he would tick out in four words: "Awfully old—gray hair." To this particular item in Chad's appearance he constantly, during their mute half-hour, reverted; as if so very much more than he could have said had been involved in it. The most he could have said would have been: "If he's going to make me feel young—!" which indeed, however, carried with it quite enough. If Strether was to feel young, that is, it would be because Chad was to feel old; and an aged and hoary sinner had been no part of the scheme.

The question of Chadwick's true time of life was, doubtless, what came up quickest after the adjournment of the two, when the play was over, to a café in the Avenue de l'Opéra. Miss Gostrey had, on the spot, been perfect for such a step; she had known exactly what they wanted—to go straight somewhere and talk; and Strether had even felt that she had known what he wished to say and that he was arranging immediately to begin. She had not pretended this, as she *had* pretended, on the other hand, that she had divined Waymarsh's wish to extend to her, homeward, an independent protection; but Strether nevertheless found how, after he had Chad opposite to him at a small table in the brilliant halls that his companion straightway selected, sharply and easily discriminated from others, it was quite, to his mind, as if she heard him speak; as if, sitting up, a mile away, in the little apartment he knew, she would listen hard enough to catch. He found too that he liked that idea, and he wished that, by the same token, Mrs. Newsome might have caught as well. For what had above all been determined in him as a necessity of the first order was not to lose another hour, nor a fraction of one; was to advance, to overwhelm, with a rush. This was how he would anticipate—by a night-attack, as might be—any forced maturity that a crammed consciousness of Paris was likely to take upon itself to assert on behalf of the boy. He knew, to the full, on what he had just extracted from Miss Gostrey, Chad's marks of alertness; but they were a reason the more for not dawdling. If he was himself moreover to be treated as young, he wouldn't at all events be so treated before he should have struck out at least once. His arms might be pinioned afterwards, but it would have been left on record that he was fifty. The importance of this he had indeed begun to feel before they left the theatre; it had become a wild unrest, urging him to seize his chance. He could scarcely wait for it as they went; he was on the verge of the indecency of bringing up the question in the street; he fairly caught himself going on—so he afterwards invidiously named it—as if there would be for him no second chance should the present be lost. Not till, on the purple divan before the perfunctory *bock,* he had brought out the words themselves, was he sure, for that matter, that the present would be saved.

PART FOURTH

VIII

"I've come, you know, to make you break with everything, neither more nor less, and take you straight home; so you'll be so good as immediately and favorably to consider it!"—Strether, face to face with Chad after the play, had sounded these words almost breathlessly, and with an effect at first positively disconcerting to himself alone. For Chad's receptive attitude was that of a person who has been gracefully quiet while the messenger at last reaching him has run a mile through the dust. During some seconds after he had spoken Strether felt as if *he* had made some such exertion; he was not even certain that the perspiration was not on his brow. It was the kind of consciousness for which he had to thank the look that, while the strain lasted, the young man's eyes gave him. They reflected—and the deuce of the thing was that they reflected really with a sort of shyness of kindness—his momentarily disordered state; which fact brought on, in its turn, for our friend, the dawn of a fear that Chad might simply "take it out"—take everything out—in being sorry for him. Such a fear, any fear, was unpleasant. But everything was unpleasant; it was odd how everything had suddenly turned so. This, however, was no reason for letting the least thing go. Strether had the next minute proceeded as roundly as if with an advantage to follow up.

"Of course I'm a busybody, if you want to fight the case to the death; but, after all, mainly in the sense of having known you, and having given you such attention as you kindly permitted, when you were in jackets and knickerbockers. Yes—it was knickerbockers, I'm busybody enough to remember that, and that you had, for your age—I speak of the first far-away time—tremendously stout legs. Well, we want you to break. Your mother's heart is passionately set upon it; but she has, over and beyond that, excellent arguments and reasons. I've not put them into her head—I needn't remind you how little she's a person who needs that. But they exist—you must take it from me as a friend both of hers and yours—for myself as well. I didn't invent them, I didn't originally work them out; but I understand them, I think I can explain them —by which, I mean, make you actively do them justice; and that's why, you see, I'm here. You had better know the worst at once. It's a question of an immediate rupture and an immediate return. I've been conceited enough to dream I can sugar that pill. I take, at any rate, the greatest interest in the question. I took it, already, before I left home; and I don't mind telling you that, altered as you are, I take it still more now that I've seen you. You're older and—I don't know what to call it!—more of a handful; but you're by so much the more, I seem to make out, to our purpose."

"Do I strike you as improved?" Strether was to recall that Chad had at this point inquired.

He was likewise to recall—and it had to count for some time as his greatest comfort—that it had been "given" him, as they said at Woollett, to reply with some presence of mind: "I haven't the least idea." He was really, for a while, to like to think he had been positively hard. On the point of conceding that Chad had improved in appearance, but that to the question of appearance the remark must be confined, he checked even that compromise and left his reservation bare. Not only his moral, but also, as it were, his æsthetic sense had a little to pay for this, Chad being unmistakably —and wasn't it a matter of the confounded gray hair again?— handsomer than he had ever promised. That, however, fell in perfectly with what Strether had said. They had no desire to keep down his proper expansion, and he would not be less to their purpose for not looking, as he had too often done of old, only bold and wild. There was indeed a signal particular in which he would distinctly be more so. Strether didn't, as he talked, absolutely follow himself; he only knew he was clutching his thread and that he held it, from moment to moment, a little tighter; his mere uninterruptedness, for five minutes, helped him to do that. He had frequently, for a month, turned over what he should say on this very occasion, and he seemed at last to have said nothing he had thought of—everything was so totally different.

But in spite of all he had put the flag at the window. This

was what he had done, and there was a minute during which he affected himself as having shaken it hard, flapped it with a mighty flutter, straight in front of his companion's nose. It gave him really almost the sense of having already acted his part. The momentary relief—as if from the knowledge that nothing of *that* at least could be undone—sprang from a particular cause, the cause that had flashed into operation, in Miss Gostrey's box, with direct apprehension, with amazed recognition, and that had been concerned, since then, in every throb of his consciousness. What it came to was that with an absolutely *new* quantity to deal with one could simply not know. The new quantity was represented by the fact that Chad had been made over. That was all; whatever it was, it was everything. Strether had never seen the thing so done before; it was perhaps a speciality of Paris. If one had been present at the process one might little by little have mastered the result; but he was face to face, as matters stood, with the finished business. It had freely been noted for him that he might be received as a dog among skittles; but that was on the basis of the old quantity. He had originally thought of lines and tones as things to be taken, but these possibilities had now quite melted away. There was no computing at all what the young man before him would think or feel or say on any subject whatever. This intelligence Strether had afterwards, to account for his nervousness, reconstituted as he might, just as he had also reconstituted the promptness with which Chad had corrected his uncertainty. An extraordinarily short time had been required for the correction, and there had ceased to be anything negative in his companion's aspect as soon as it was made. "Your engagement to my mother has become then what they call here a *fait accompli?*"—it had consisted, the determinant touch, in nothing more than that.

Well, that was enough, Strether had felt while his answer hung fire. He had felt at the same time, however, that nothing could less become him than that it should hang fire too long. "Yes," he said brightly, "it was on the happy settlement of the question that I started. You see therefore to what tune I'm in your family. Moreover," he added, "I've been supposing you'd suppose it."

"Oh, I've been supposing it for a long time; and what you tell me helps me to understand that you should want to do something.

To do something, I mean," said Chad, "to commemorate an event so—what do they call it?—so auspicious. I see you make out, and not unnaturally," he continued, "that bringing me home in triumph as a sort of wedding-present to mother would commemorate it better than anything else. You want to make a bonfire in fact," he laughed, "and you pitch me on. Thank you, thank you!" he laughed again.

He was altogether easy about it, and this made Strether now see how, at bottom, and in spite of the shade of shyness that really cost him nothing, he had from the first moment been easy about everything. The shade of shyness was mere good taste. People with manners formed could apparently have, as one of their best cards, the shade of shyness too. He had leaned a little forward to speak; his elbows were on the table; and the inscrutable new face that he had got somewhere and somehow was brought by the movement nearer to his companion's. There was a fascination for that companion in its not being, this ripe physiognomy, the face that, under observation at least, he had originally carried away from Woollett. Strether found a certain freedom on his own side in defining it as that of a man of the world—a formula that indeed seemed to come now in some degree to his relief; that of a man to whom things had happened and were variously known. In gleams, in glances, the past did perhaps peep out of it; but such lights were faint and instantly merged. Chad was brown and thick and strong, and, of old, Chad had been rough. Was all the difference therefore that he was actually smooth? Possibly; for that he *was* smooth was as marked as in the taste of a sauce or in the rub of a hand. The effect of it was general—it had retouched his features, drawn them with a cleaner line. It had cleared his eyes and settled his color and polished his fine square teeth—the main ornament of his face; and at the same time that it had given him a form and a surface, almost a design, it had toned his voice, established his accent, encouraged his smile to more play and his other motions to less. He had formerly, with a great deal of action, expressed very little; and he now expressed whatever was necessary with almost none at all. It was as if, in short, he had really, copious perhaps, but shapeless, been put into a firm mould and turned successfully out. The phenomenon—Strether kept eyeing it as a phenomenon, an eminent case—was marked enough to be touched by the finger. He finally put his hand across the table and laid it on Chad's arm. "If you'll promise me—here on the spot and giving me your word of honor—to break straight off, you'll make the future the real right thing for all of us alike. You'll ease off the strain of this decent, but none the less acute, suspense in which I've for so many days been waiting for you, and let me turn in to rest. I shall leave you with my blessing and go to bed in peace."

Chad again fell back at this, and, with his hands in his pockets, settled a little in his chair; in which posture he looked, though he rather anxiously smiled, only the more earnest. Then Strether seemed to see that he was really nervous, and he took that as what he would have called a wholesome sign. The only mark of it hitherto had been his more than once taking off and putting on his wide-brimmed crush hat. He had at this moment made the motion again to remove it, then had only pushed it back, so that it hung informally on his strong young grizzled crop. It was a touch that gave the note of the familiar—the intimate and the belated—to their quiet colloquy; and it was indeed by some such trivial aid that Strether became aware at the same moment of something else. The observation was at any rate determined in him by some light too fine to distinguish from so many others, but it was none the less sharply determined. Chad looked unmistakably during these instants—well, as Strether put it to himself, all he was worth. Our friend had a sudden apprehension of what, on certain sides, that would be. He saw him, in short, in a flash, as the young man marked out by women; and for a concentrated minute the dignity, the comparative austerity, as he funnily fancied it, of this character, affected him almost with awe. There was an experience on his interlocutor's part that looked out at him from under the displaced hat, and that looked out moreover by a force of its own, the deep fact of its quantity and quality, and not through Chad's intending bravado or swagger. That was then the way men marked out by women *were*—and also the men by whom the women were doubtless in turn sufficiently distinguished. It affected Strether for thirty seconds as a relevant truth; a truth which, however, the next minute, had fallen into its relation. "Can't you imagine there being some questions," Chad asked, "that a fellow

THE AMBASSADORS

—however much impressed by your charming way of stating things —would like to put to you first?"

"Oh yes—easily. I'm here to answer everything. I think I can even tell you things, of the greatest interest to you, that you won't know enough to ask me. We'll take as many days to it as you like. But I want," Strether wound up, "to go to bed now."

"Really?"

Chad had spoken in such surprise that he was amused. "Can't you believe it?—with what you put me through?"

The young man seemed to consider. "Oh, I haven't put you through much—yet."

"Do you mean there's so much more to come?" Strether laughed. "All the more reason then that I should gird myself." And as if to mark what he felt he could by this time count on he was already on his feet.

Chad, still seated, stayed him, with a hand against him, as he passed him between their table and the next. "Oh, we shall get on!"

The tone was, as it were, everything Strether could have desired; and quite as good the expression of face with which the speaker had looked up at him and kindly held him. All these things lacked was perhaps not showing quite so much as the fruit of ex- perience. Yes, experience was what Chad did play on him, if he didn't play any grossness of defiance. Of course experience was in a manner defiance; but it wasn't, at any rate—rather indeed quite the contrary!—grossness; which was so much gained. He fairly grew older, Strether thought, while he himself so reasoned. Then, with his mature pat of his visitor's arm, he also got up; and there had been enough of it all, by this time, to make the visitor feel that something *was* settled. Wasn't it settled that he had at least the testimony of Chad's own belief in a settlement? Strether found himself treating Chad's profession that they would get on as a sufficient basis for going to bed. He had not, however, after this, gone to bed directly; for after they had again passed out together into the mild bright night a check had virtually sprung from noth- ing more than a small circumstance which might have acted only as confirming quiescence. There were people, expressive sound, pro- jected light, still abroad, and after they had taken in for a moment, through everything, the great, clear architectural street, they turned off, in tacit union, to the quarter of Strether's hotel. "Of course," Chad here abruptly began, " of course mother's making things out with you about me has been natural—and of course also you've had a good deal to go upon. Still, you must have filled out."

He had stopped, leaving his friend to wonder a little what point he wished to make; and this it was that enabled Strether meanwhile to make one. " Oh, we've never pretended to go into detail. We weren't in the least bound to *that*. It was 'filling out' enough to miss you as we did."

But Chad rather oddly insisted, though, under the high lamp at their corner, where they paused, he had at first looked as if touched by Strether's allusion to the long sense, at home, of his absence. " What I mean is you must have imagined."

" Imagined what ?"

" Well—horrors."

It affected Strether: horrors were so little—superficially at least —in this robust and reasoning image. But he was none the less there to be veracious. " Yes, I dare say we *have* imagined horrors. But where's the harm if we haven't been wrong ?"

Chad raised his face to the lamp, and it was one of the moments at which he had, in his extraordinary way, most his air of designedly showing himself. It was as if, at these instants, he just presented himself, his identity so rounded off, his palpable presence and his massive young manhood, as such a link in the chain as might practically amount to a kind of demonstration. It was as if—and how but anomalously ?—he couldn't, after all help thinking sufficiently well of these things to let them go for what they were worth. What could there be in this for Strether but the hint of some self-respect, some sense of power, oddly perverted; something latent and beyond access, ominous and perhaps enviable ? The intimation had, the next thing, in a flash, taken on a name—a name on which our friend seized as he asked himself if he were not perhaps really dealing with an irreducible young pagan. This description—he quite jumped at it—had a sound that gratified his mental ear, so that, of a sudden, he had already adopted it. Pagan —yes, that was, wasn't it ? what Chad *would* logically be. It was what he must be. It was what he was. The idea was a clue and, instead of darkening the prospect, projected a certain clearness. Strether made out in this quick ray that a pagan was perhaps, at the pass they had come to, the thing most wanted at Woollett. They would be able to do with one—a good one; he would find an opening—yes; and Strether's imagination even now prefigured and accompanied the first appearance there of the rousing personage. He had only the slight discomfort of feeling, as the young man turned away from the lamp, that his thought had, in the momentary silence, possibly been guessed. "Well, I've no doubt," said Chad, "you've come near enough. The details, as you say, don't matter. It *has* been generally the case that I've let myself go. But I'm coming round—I'm not so bad now." With which they walked on again to Strether's hotel.

"Do you mean," the latter asked as they approached the door, "that there isn't any woman with you now?"

"But pray what has that to do with it?"

"Why, it's the whole question."

"Of my going home?" Chad was clearly surprised. "Oh, not much! Do you think that when I want to go any one will have any power—"

"To keep you"—Strether took him straight up—"from carrying out your wish? Well, our idea has been that somebody has hitherto —or a good many persons perhaps—kept you pretty well from 'wanting.' That's what—if you're in anybody's hands—may again happen. You don't answer my question"—he kept it up; "but if you aren't in anybody's hands, so much the better. There's nothing, then, but what makes for your going."

Chad turned this over. "I don't answer your question?" He spoke quite without resenting it. "Well, such questions have always a rather exaggerated side. One doesn't know quite what you mean by being in women's 'hands.' It's all so vague. One is when one isn't. One isn't when one is. And then one can't quite give people away." He seemed kindly to explain. "I've *never* got stuck—so very hard; and, as against anything at any time really better, I don't think I've ever been afraid." There was something in it that held Strether to wonder, and this gave him time to go on. He broke out as with a more helpful thought. "Don't you know how I like Paris itself?"

The upshot was indeed to make our friend marvel. "Oh, if *that's* all that's the matter with you—!" It was *he* who almost showed resentment.

Chad's smile, however, more than met it. "But isn't that enough?"

Strether hesitated, but it came out. "Not enough for your mother!" Spoken, however, it sounded a trifle odd—the effect of which was that Chad broke into a laugh. Strether, at this, succumbed as well, though with extreme brevity. "Permit us to have still our theory. But if you *are* so free and so strong, you're inexcusable. I'll write in the morning," he added with decision. "I'll say I've got you."

This appeared to open for Chad a new interest. "How often do you write?"

"Oh, perpetually."

"And at great length?"

Strether had become a little impatient. "I hope it's not found too great."

"Oh, I'm sure not. And you hear as often?"

Again Strether paused. "As often as I deserve."

"Mother writes," said Chad, "a lovely letter."

Strether, before the closed *porte - cochère,* fixed him a moment. "It's more, my boy, than *you* do! But our suppositions don't matter," he added, "if you're actually not entangled."

Chad's pride, however, seemed a little touched. "I never *was* that—let me insist. I always had my own way." With which he pursued: "And I have it at present."

"Then what are you here for? What has kept you," Strether asked, "if you *have* been able to leave?"

It made Chad, after a stare, throw himself back. "Do you think one's kept only by women?" His surprise and his verbal emphasis rang out so clear in the still street that Strether winced till he remembered the safety of their English speech. "Is that," the young man demanded, "what they think at Woollett?" At the good faith in the question Strether had changed color, feeling that, as he would have said, he had put his foot in it. He had appeared, stupidly, to misrepresent what they thought at Woollett; but before he had time to rectify Chad again was upon him. "I must say then you show a low mind!"

It so fell in, unhappily for Strether, with that reflection of his own prompted in him by the pleasant air of the Boulevard Malesherbes, that its disconcerting force was rather unfairly great. It was a dig that, administered by himself—and administered even to poor Mrs. Newsome—was no more than salutary; but administered by Chad—and quite logically—it came nearer drawing blood. They *hadn't* a low mind—nor any approach to one; yet, incontestably, they had worked, and with a certain smugness, on a basis that might be turned against them. Chad had at any rate pulled his visitor up; he had even pulled up his admirable mother; he had absolutely, by a turn of the wrist and a jerk of the far-flung noose, pulled up, in a bunch, Woollett browsing in its pride. There was no doubt Woollett *had* insisted on his coarseness; and what he at present stood there for in the sleeping street was, by his manner of striking the other note, to make of such insistence a preoccupation compromising to the insisters. It was exactly as if they had imputed to him a vulgarity which he had by a mere gesture caused to fall from him. The devil of the case was that Strether felt it, by the same stroke, as falling straight upon himself. He had been wondering a minute ago if the boy weren't a pagan, and he found himself wondering now if he weren't by chance a gentleman. It didn't in the least, on the spot, spring up helpfully for him that a person couldn't at the same time be both. There was nothing at this moment in the air to challenge the combination; there was everything, on the contrary, to give it something of a flourish. It struck Strether, into the bargain, as doing something to meet the most difficult of the questions; though perhaps indeed only by substituting another. Wouldn't it be precisely by having learned to be a gentleman that he had mastered the consequent trick of looking so well that one could scarce speak to him straight? But what in the world was the clue to such a prime producing cause? There were too many clues then that Strether still lacked, and these clues to clues were among them. What it accordingly amounted to for him was that he had to take full in the face a fresh attribution of ignorance. He had grown used, by this time, to reminders, especially from his own lips, of what he didn't know; but he had borne them because in the first place they were private and because in the second they practically conveyed a tribute. He didn't **know** what was bad, and—as others didn't know how little he knew it—he could put up with his state. But if he didn't know, in so important a particular, what was good, Chad at least was now aware he didn't; and that, for some reason, affected our friend as curiously public. It was in fact an exposed condition that the young man left him in long enough for him to feel its chill—till he saw fit, in a word, generously again to cover him. This last was in truth what Chad quite gracefully did. But he did it as with a simple thought that met the whole of the case. " Oh, I'm all right!" It was what Strether had rather bewilderedly to go to bed on.

IX

It really looked true, moreover, from the way Chad, after this, behaved. He was full of attentions to his mother's ambassador; in spite of which, remarkably, however, the latter's other relations still contrived to assert themselves. Strether's sittings, pen in hand, with Mrs. Newsome up in his own room were broken, but they were richer; and they were more than ever interspersed with the hours in which he reported himself, in a different fashion, but with scarce less earnestness and fulness, to Maria Gostrey. Now that, as he would have expressed it, he had really something to talk about, he found himself, in respect to any oddity that might reside for him in the double connection, at once more aware and more indifferent. He had been fine to Mrs. Newsome about his useful friend, but it had begun to haunt his imagination that Chad, taking up again for her benefit a pen too long disused, might possibly be finer. It wouldn't at all do, he saw, that anything should come up for him at Chad's hands but what specifically *was* to have come; the greatest divergence from which would be precisely the element of any lubrication of their intercourse by levity. It was accordingly to forestall such an accident that he frankly put before the young man the several facts, just as they had occurred, of his funny alliance. He spoke of these facts, pleasantly and obligingly, as " the whole story," and felt that he might qualify the alliance as funny if he remained sufficiently grave about it. He flattered himself that he even exaggerated the wild freedom of his original encounter with the wonderful lady; he was scrupulously definite about the absurd conditions in which they had made acquaintance —their having picked each other up almost in the street; and he had—finest inspiration of all!—a conception of carrying the war into the enemy's country by showing surprise at the enemy's ignorance.

He had always had a notion that this last was the grand style of fighting; the greater therefore the reason for it, as he couldn't remember that he had ever before fought in the grand style. Every one, according to this, knew Miss Gostrey: how came it Chad didn't know her? The difficulty, the impossibility, was really to escape it; Strether put on him, by what he took for granted, the burden of proof of the contrary. This tone was so far successful as that Chad quite appeared to recognize her as a person whose fame had reached him, but against his acquaintance with whom much mischance had worked. He made the point, at the same time, that his social relations, such as they were, were perhaps not to the extent Strether supposed with the rising flood of their compatriots. He hinted at his having more and more given way to a different principle of selection; so that the moral of it seemed to be that he went about little in the " colony." For the moment, certainly, he had quite another interest. It was deep, what he understood; and Strether, for himself, could only so observe it. He couldn't see as yet how deep. Might he not all too soon! For there was really too much of their question that Chad had already committed himself to liking. He liked, to begin with, his prospective stepfather; which was distinctly what had not been on the cards. His hating him was the untowardness for which Strether had been best prepared; he had not expected the boy's actual form to give him more to do than his supposed. It gave him more through suggesting that he must somehow make up to himself for not being sure he was sufficiently disagreeable. That had really been present to him as his only way to be sure he was sufficiently thorough. The point was that if Chad's tolerance of his thoroughness were insincere, were but the best of devices for gaining time, it none the less did treat everything as tacitly concluded.

That seemed, at the end of ten days, the upshot of the abundant. recurrent talk through which Strether poured into him all it con- cerned him to know, put him in full possession of facts and figures Never cutting these colloquies short by a minute, Chad behaved, looked and spoke as if he were rather heavily, perhaps even a trifle gloomily, but none the less fundamentally and comfortably, free. He made no crude profession of eagerness to yield, but he asked the most intelligent questions, probed, at moments, abruptly, even deeper than his friend's layer of information, justified by these touches the native estimate of his latent stuff, and had in every way the air of trying to live, reflectively, into the square, bright picture. He walked up and down in front of this production, sociably took Strether's arm at the points at which he stopped, surveyed it repeatedly from the right and from the left, inclined a critical head to either quarter, and, while he puffed a still more critical cigarette, animadverted to his companion on this passage and that. Strether sought relief—there were hours when he required it—in repeating himself; it was in truth not to be blinked that Chad had a way. The main question as yet was of what it was a way *to*. It made vulgar questions no more easy; but that was unimportant when all questions save those of his own asking had dropped. That he was free was answer enough, and it was not quite ridiculous that this freedom should itself prove what was difficult to move. His changed state, his lovely home, his beautiful things, his easy talk, his very appetite for Strether, insatiable and, when all was said, flattering—what were such marked matters all but the notes of his freedom? He had the effect of making a present of it, in these handsome forms, to his visitor; which was mainly the reason the visitor was privately, for the time, a little out of countenance. Strether was at this period again and again thrown back on a felt need to remodel somehow his plan. He fairly caught himself shooting rueful glances, shy looks of pursuit, toward the embodied influence, the definite adversary, who had, by a stroke of her own, failed him, and on a fond theory of whose palpable presence he had, under Mrs. Newsome's inspiration, altogether proceeded. He had once or twice, in secret, literally expressed the irritated wish that *she* would come out and find her.

He couldn't quite yet force it upon Woollett that such a career, such a perverted young life, showed after all a certain plausible side, *did* in the case before them flaunt something like an impunity for the social man; but he could at least treat himself to the statement that would prepare him for the sharpest echo. This echo—as distinct, over there, in the dry, thin air, as some shrill "heading" above a column of print—seemed to reach him even as he wrote. "He says there's no woman," he could hear Mrs. Newsome report, in capitals almost of newspaper size, to Mrs. Pocock; and he could focus in Mrs. Pocock the response of the reader of the journal. He could see in the younger lady's face the earnestness of her attention and catch the full scepticism of her but slightly delayed "What is there then?" Just so he could again as little miss the mother's clear decision: "There's plenty of disposition, no doubt, to pretend there isn't." Strether had, after posting his letter, the whole scene out; and it was a scene during which, coming and going, as befell, he kept his eye not least upon the daughter. He had his fine sense of the conviction Mrs. Pocock would take occasion to reaffirm—a conviction bearing, as he had from the first deeply divined it to bear, on Mr. Strether's essential inaptitude. She had looked him in his conscious eye even before he sailed, and that she didn't believe *he* would find the woman had been written in her look. Hadn't she, at the best, but a scant faith in his ability to find women? It wasn't even as if he had found her mother—so much more, to her discrimination, had her mother performed the finding. Her mother had, in a case her private judgment of which remained educative of Mrs. Pocock's critical sense, found the man. The man owed his unchallenged state, in general, to the fact that Mrs. Newsome's discoveries were accepted at Woollett; but he knew in his bones, our friend did, how almost irresistibly Mrs. Pocock would now be moved to show what she thought of his own. Give *her* a free hand, would be the moral, and the woman would soon be found.

His impression of Miss Gostrey after her introduction to Chad was meanwhile the impression of a person almost unnaturally on her guard. He struck himself as at first unable to extract from her what he wished; though indeed *of* what he wished at this special juncture he would doubtless have contrived to make but a crude statement. It sifted and settled nothing to put to her, *tout bête-ment,* as she often said, "Do you like him, eh?"—thanks to his feeling it actually the least of his needs to heap up the evidence in the young man's favor. He repeatedly knocked at her door to let her have it afresh that Chad's case—whatever else of minor interest it might yield—was, first and foremost, a miracle almost monstrous. It was the alteration of the entire man, and was so signal an instance that nothing else, for the intelligent observer, could—*could* it?—signify. "It's a plot," he declared—"there's more in it than meets the eye." He gave the rein to his fancy. "It's a plant!"

His fancy seemed to please her. "Whose then?"

"Well, the party responsible is, I suppose, the fate that waits for one, the dark doom that rides. What I mean is that with such elements one can't count. I've but my poor individual, my modest human, means. It isn't playing the game to turn on the uncanny. All one's energy goes to facing it, to tracking it. One wants, confound it, don't you see?" he confessed with a queer face—"one wants to enjoy anything so rare. Call it then life"—he puzzled it out—"call it poor dear old life simply that springs the surprise. Nothing alters the fact that the surprise is paralyzing, or at any rate engrossing—all, practically, hang it, that one sees, that one *can* see."

Her silences were never dull. "Is that what you've written home?"

He tossed it off. "Oh dear, yes!"

She had another pause while, over her carpets, he had another walk. "If you don't look out you'll have them straight over."

"Oh, but I've said he'll go back."

"And *will* he?" Miss Gostrey asked.

The special tone of it made him, pulling up, look at her long. "What's that but just the question I've spent treasures of patience and ingenuity in giving *you*, by the sight of him—after everything had led up—every facility to answer? What is it but just the thing I came here to-day to get out of you? Will he?"

"No—he won't," she said at last. "He's not free."

The air of it held him. "Then you've all the while known—?"

"I've known nothing but what I've seen; and I wonder," she declared with some impatience, "that you didn't see as much. It was enough to be with him there—"

"In the box? Yes," he rather blankly urged.

"Well—to feel sure."

"Sure of what?"

She got up from her chair, at this, with a nearer approach than she had ever yet shown to dismay at his dimness. She even, fairly pausing for it, spoke with a shade of pity. "Guess!"

It was a shade, fairly, that brought a flush into his face; so that, for a moment, as they stood there, their difference was between them. "You mean that just your hour with him told you so much of his story? Very good; I'm not such a fool, on my side, as that I don't understand you, or as that I didn't in some degree understand *him.* That he has done what he liked most isn't, among any of us, a matter the least in dispute. There's equally little question at this time of day of what it is he does like most. But I'm not talking," he reasonably explained, "of any mere wretch he may still pick up. I'm talking of some person who, in his present situation, may have held her own, may really have counted."

"That's exactly what *I* am!" said Miss Gostrey. But she as quickly made her point. "I thought you thought—or that they think at Woollett—that that's what mere wretches necessarily do. Mere wretches necessarily *don't!*" she declared with spirit. "There must, behind every appearance to the contrary, still be somebody—somebody who's not a mere wretch, since we accept the miracle. What else but such a somebody can such a miracle be?"

He took it in. "Because the fact itself *is* the woman?"

"*A* woman. Some woman or other. It's one of the things that *have* to be."

"But you mean then at least a good one."

"A good woman?" She threw up her arms with a laugh. "I should call her excellent!"

"Then why does he deny her?"

Miss Gostrey thought a moment. "Because she's too good to admit! Don't you see," she went on, "how she accounts for him?"

Strether clearly, more and more, did see; yet it made him also see other things. "But isn't what we want that he shall account for *her?*"

"Well, he does. What you have before you is his way. You must forgive him if it isn't quite outspoken. In Paris such debts are tacit."

Strether could imagine; but still—! "Even when the woman's good?"

Again she laughed out. "Yes, and even when the man is! There's always a caution in such cases," she more seriously explained—"for what it may seem to show. There's nothing that's taken as showing so much here as sudden unnatural goodness."

"Ah then, you're speaking now," Strether said, "of people who are *not* nice."

"I delight," she replied, "in your classifications. But do you want me," she asked, "to give you in the matter, on this ground, the wisest advice I'm capable of? Don't consider her, don't judge her at all in herself. Consider her and judge her only in Chad."

He had the courage at least of his companion's logic. "Because then I shall like her?" He almost looked, with his quick imagination, as if he already did, though seeing at once also the full extent of how little it would suit his book. "But is that what I came out for?"

She had to confess indeed that it wasn't. But there was something else. "Don't make up your mind. There are all sorts of things. You haven't seen him all."

This, on his side, Strether recognized; but his acuteness none the less showed him the danger. "Yes, but if the more I see the better he seems?"

Well, she found something. "That may be—but his disavowal of her isn't, all the same, pure consideration. There's a hitch." She made it out. "It's the effort to sink her."

Strether winced at the image. "To 'sink'—?"

"Well, I mean there's a struggle, and a part of it is just what he hides. Take time—that's the only way not to make some mistake that you'll regret. Then you'll see. He does really want to shake her off."

Our friend had by this time so got into the vision that he almost gasped. "After all she has done for him?"

Miss Gostrey gave him a look which broke the next moment into a wonderful smile. "He's not so good as you think!"

They remained with him, these words, promising him, in their character of warning, considerable help; but the support he tried to draw from them found itself, on each renewal of contact with Chad, defeated by something else. What could it be, this disconcerting force, he asked himself, but the sense, constantly renewed, that Chad *was*—quite, in fact, insisted on being—as good as he thought? It seemed somehow as if he couldn't *but* be as good from the moment he wasn't as bad. There was a succession of days, at all events, when contact with him—and in its immediate effect, as if it could produce no other—elbowed out of Strether's consciousness everything but itself. Little Bilham once more pervaded the scene, but little Bilham became even in a higher degree than he had originally been one of the numerous forms of the inclusive relation; a consequence promoted, to our friend's sense, by two or three incidents with which we have yet to make acquaintance. Waymarsh himself, for the occasion, was drawn into the eddy; it absolutely, though but temporarily, swallowed him down, and there were days when Strether seemed to bump against him as a sinking swimmer might brush a submarine object. The fathomless medium held them—Chad's manner was the fathomless medium; and our friend felt as if they passed each other, in their deep immersion, with the round, impersonal eye of silent fish. It was practically produced between them that Waymarsh was giving him, then, his chance; and the shade of discomfort that Strether drew from the allowance resembled not a little the embarrassment he had known, at school, as a boy, when members of his family had been present at exhibitions. He could perform before strangers, but relatives were fatal, and it was now as if, comparatively, Waymarsh were a relative. He seemed to hear him say " Strike up then!" and to enjoy a foretaste of conscientious domestic criticism. He *had* struck up, so far as he actually could; Chad knew by this time in profusion what he wanted; and what vulgar violence did his fellow-pilgrim expect of him when he had really emptied his mind? It went somehow to and fro that what poor Waymarsh meant was " I told you so—that you'd lose your immortal soul!" but it was also fairly explicit that Strether had his own challenge and that, since they must go to the bottom of things, he wasted no more virtue in watching Chad than Chad wasted in watching him. His dip for duty's sake—where was it worse than Waymarsh's own? For *he* needn't have stopped resisting and refusing, needn't have parleyed, at that rate, with the foe.

The strolls, in Paris, to see something or call somewhere, were, accordingly, inevitable and natural, and the late sessions in the wondrous *troisième,* the lovely home, when men dropped in and the picture composed more suggestively through the haze of tobacco, of music more or less good and of talk more or less polyglot, were on a principle not to be distinguished from that of the mornings and the afternoons. Nothing, Strether had to recognize as he

119

leaned back and smoked, could well less resemble a scene of violence than even the liveliest of these occasions. They were occasions of discussion, none the less, and Strether had never in his life heard so many opinions on so many subjects. There were opinions at Woollett, but only on three or four. The differences were there to match; if they were doubtless deep, though few, they were quiet— they were, as might be said, almost as shy as if people had been ashamed of them. People showed little diffidence about such things, on the other hand, in the Boulevard Malesherbes, and were so far from being ashamed of them—or indeed of anything else— that they often seemed to have invented them to avert those agreements that destroy the taste of talk. No one had ever done that at Woollett, though Strether could remember times when he himself had been tempted to it without quite knowing why. He saw why at present—he had but wanted to promote intercourse.

These, however, were but parenthetic memories; and the turn his affair had, on the whole, taken was positively that, if his nerves were on the stretch, it was because he missed violence. When he asked himself if none would then, in connection with it, ever come at all, he might almost have passed as wondering how to provoke it. It would be too absurd if such a vision as *that* should have to be invoked for relief; it was already marked enough as absurd that he should actually have begun with flutters and dignities on the score of a single accepted meal. What sort of a brute had he expected Chad to be, anyway?—Strether had occasion to make the inquiry, but he was careful to make it in private. He could himself, comparatively recent as it was—it was truly but the fact of a few days since—focus his primal crudity; but he would, on the approach of an observer, as if handling an illicit possession, have slipped the reminiscence out of sight. There were echoes of it still in Mrs. Newsome's letters, and there were moments when these echoes made him exclaim on her want of tact. He blushed of course, at once, still more for the explanation than for the ground of it: it came to him in time to save his manners that she couldn't at the best become tactful as quickly as he. Her tact had to reckon with the Atlantic Ocean, the General Post-Office and the extravagant curve of the globe.

Chad had one day offered tea, in the Boulevard Malesherbes, to a chosen few, a group again including the unobscured Miss Barrace; and Strether had, on coming out, walked away with the acquaintance whom, in his letters to Mrs. Newsome, he always spoke of as the little artist-man. He had had full occasion to mention him as the other party, so oddly, to the only close personal alliance observation had as yet detected in Chad's existence. Little Bilham's way, this afternoon, was not Strether's, but he had none the less kindly come with him, and it was somehow a part of his kindness that, as, awkwardly, it had begun to rain, they suddenly found themselves seated for conversation at a café in which they had taken refuge. He had passed no more crowded hour in Chad's society than the one just ended; he had talked with Miss Barrace, who had reproached him with not having come to see her, and he had above all hit on a happy thought for causing Waymarsh's tension to relax. Something might possibly be done, for the latter, with the idea of his success with that lady, whose quick apprehension of what might amuse her had given Strether a free hand. What had she meant if not to ask whether she couldn't help him with his splendid encumbrance, and mightn't the sacred rage, at any rate, be kept a little in abeyance by thus creating for his comrade's mind, even in a world of irrelevance, the possibility of a relation? What was it but a relation to be regarded as so decorative, and, in especial, on the strength of it, to be whirled away, amid flounces and feathers, in a coupé lined, by what Strether could make out, with dark blue brocade? He himself had never been whirled away—never at least in a coupé and behind a footman; he had driven with Miss Gostrey in cabs, with Mrs. Pocock, a few times, in an open buggy, with Mrs. Newsome in a four-seated cart and, occasionally, in the mountains, on a buckboard; but his friend's actual adventure transcended his personal experience. He now showed his companion soon enough indeed how inadequate, as a general monitor, this last queer quantity could once more feel itself.

"What game, under the sun, is he playing?" He signified the next moment that his allusion was not to the fat gentleman immersed in dominoes on whom his eyes had begun by resting, but to their host of the previous hour, as to whom, there on the velvet bench, with a final collapse of all consistency, he treated himself to the comfort of indiscretion. "Where do you see him come out?"

Little Bilham, in meditation, looked at him with a kindness almost paternal. "Don't you like it over here?"

Strether laughed out—for the tone was indeed droll; he let himself go. "What has that to do with it? The only thing I've any business to like is to feel that I'm moving him. That's why I ask you whether you believe I *am?* Is the creature"—and he did his best to show that he simply wished to ascertain—"honest?"

His companion looked responsible, but looked it through a small dim smile. "What creature do you mean?"

It was on this that they did have, for a little, a mute interchange. "Is it untrue that he's free? How then," Strether asked wondering, "does he arrange his life?"

"Is the creature you mean Chad himself?" little Bilham said.

Strether here, with a rising hope, just thought, "We must take one of them at a time." But his coherence lapsed. "*Is* there some woman? Of whom he's really afraid, of course I mean—or who does with him what she likes."

"It's awfully charming of you," Bilham presently remarked, "not to have asked me that before."

"Oh, I'm not fit for my job!"

The exclamation had escaped our friend, but it made little Bilham more deliberate. "Chad's a rare case!" he luminously observed. "He's awfully changed," he added.

"Then you see it too?"

"The way he has improved? Oh yes—I think every one must see it. But I'm not sure," said little Bilham, "that I didn't like him about as well in his other state."

"Then this *is* really a new state altogether?"

"Well," the young man after a moment returned, "I'm not sure he was really meant by nature to be quite so good. It's like the new edition of an old book that one has been fond of—revised and amended, brought up to date, but not quite the thing that one knew and loved. However that may be, at all events," he pursued, "I don't think, you know, that he's really playing, as you call it, any game. He really wants, I believe, to go back and take up a career. He's capable of one, you know, that will improve and enlarge him still more. He won't then," little Bilham continued to remark, " be my pleasant well-rubbed old-fashioned volume at all. But of course I'm beastly immoral. I'm afraid it would be a funny world altogether—a world with things the way I like them. I ought, I dare say, to go home and go into business myself. Only I'd simply rather die—simply. And I've not the least difficulty in making up my mind not to, and in knowing exactly why, and in defending my ground against all comers. All the same," he wound up, " I assure you I don't say a word against it—for himself, I mean—to Chad. I seem to see it as much the best thing for him. You see he's not happy."

" *Do* I?"—Strether stared. " I've been supposing I see just the opposite—an extraordinary case of the equilibrium arrived at and assured."

" Oh, there's a lot behind it."

" Ah, there you are!" Strether exclaimed. " That's just what I want to get at. You speak of your familiar volume altered out of recognition. Well, who's the editor?"

Little Bilham, for a minute, looked before him in silence. " He ought to get married. *That* would do it. And he wants to."

" Wants to marry her?"

Again, for a moment, Bilham waited, and with his sense that he had information, Strether scarce knew what was coming. " He wants to be free. He isn't used, you see," the young man explained in his lucid way, " to being so good."

Strether hesitated. "Then I may take it from you that he *is* good?"

Bilham had, on his own side, a pause; but there was a quiet ful- ness in the way he made it up. " *Do* take it from me."

" Well then, why isn't he free? He swears to me he is, but mean- while does nothing—except of course that he's so kind to me— to prove it; and couldn't really act much otherwise if he weren't. My question to you just now was exactly on this queer impression of his diplomacy: as if instead of really giving ground his line were to keep me on here and set me a bad example."

As the half-hour meanwhile had ebbed, Strether had paid his score, and the waiter was now in the act of counting out change. Our friend pushed back to him a fraction of it, with which, after an emphatic recognition, the personage in question retreated. " You give too much," little Bilham permitted himself benevolently to observe.

"Oh, I always give too much!" Strether helplessly sighed. "But you don't," he went on as if to get quickly away from the contemplation of that doom, "answer my question. Why isn't he free?"

Little Bilham had got up as if the transaction with the waiter had been a signal, and had already edged out between the table and the divan. The effect of this was that, a minute later, they had quitted the place, the gratified waiter alert again at the open door. Strether had found himself deferring to his companion's abruptness as to a hint that he should be answered as soon as they were more isolated. This happened when, after a few steps in the outer air, they had turned the next corner. There our friend had kept it up. "Why isn't he free if he's good?"

Little Bilham looked him full in the face. "Because it's a virtuous attachment."

This had settled the question so effectually for the time—that is for the next few days—that it had given Strether almost a new lease of life. It must be added, however, that, thanks to his constant habit of shaking the bottle in which life handed him the wine of experience, he presently found the taste of the lees rising, as usual, into his draught. His imagination had in other words already dealt with his young friend's assertion; of which it had made something that sufficiently came out on the very next occasion of his seeing Maria Gostrey. This occasion, moreover, had been determined promptly, by a new circumstance—a circumstance he was the last man to leave her for a day in ignorance of. "When I said to him last night," he immediately began, "that without some definite word from him, now, that will enable me to speak to them over there of our sailing—or at least of mine, giving them some sort of date—my responsibility becomes uncomfortable and my situation awkward; when I said that to him, what do you think was his reply?" And then as, this time, she gave it up: "Why, that he has two particular friends, two ladies, mother and daughter, about to arrive in Paris—coming back from an absence; and that he wants me so furiously to meet them, know them and like them, that I shall oblige him by kindly not bringing our business to a crisis till he has had a chance to see them again himself. Is that," Strether inquired, " the way he's going to try to get off? These are the people," he explained, " that he must have gone down to see before I arrived. They're the best friends he has in the world, and they take more interest than any one else in what concerns him. As I'm his next best, he sees a thousand reasons why we should comfortably meet. He hasn't broached the question sooner because their return was uncertain—seemed, in fact, for the present, impossible. But he more than intimates that—if you can believe it—their desire to make my acquaintance has had to do with their surmounting difficulties."

" They're dying to see you?" Miss Gostrey asked.

" Dying. Of course," said Strether, " they're the virtuous attachment." He had already told her about that—had seen her the day after his talk with little Bilham; and they had then threshed out together the bearing of the revelation. She had helped him to put into it the logic in which little Bilham had left it slightly deficient. Strether had not pressed him as to the object of the preference so unexpectedly described; feeling in the presence of it, with one of his irrepressible scruples, a delicacy from which he had, in the quest of the quite other article, worked himself sufficiently free. He had held off, as on a small principle of pride, from permitting his young friend to mention a name; wishing to make the great point, with this, that Chad's virtuous attachments were none of his business. He had not wanted, from the first, to think too much of his dignity; but that was not a reason for not allowing it any little benefit that might turn up. He had often enough wondered to what degree his interference might pass for interested; so that there was no want of luxury in letting it be seen whenever he could that he didn't interfere. That had of course, at the same time, not deprived him of the further luxury of much private astonishment; which, however, he had reduced to some order before communicating his knowledge. When he had done this, at last, it was with the remark that, surprised as Miss Gostrey might, like himself, at first be, she would probably agree with him on reflection that such an account of the matter did, after all, fit the confirmed appearances. Nothing, certainly, on all the indications, could have been a greater change for him than a virtuous attachment, and since they had been in search of the "word" as the French called it, of that change, little Bilham's announcement—though so long and so oddly delayed—would serve as well as another. She had assured Strether in fact, after a pause, that the more she thought of it the more it did serve; and yet her assurance had not so weighed with him as that, before they parted, he had not ventured to challenge her sincerity. Didn't she believe the attachment *was* virtuous?—he had made sure of her again with the aid of that question. The tidings he brought her on this second occasion were moreover such as would help him to make surer still. She showed at first, none the less, as only amused.

"You say there are two? An attachment to them both then would, I suppose, almost necessarily be innocent."

Our friend took the point, but he had his clue. "Mayn't he be still in the stage of not quite knowing which of them, mother or daughter, he likes best?"

She gave it more thought. "Oh, it must be the daughter—at his age."

"Possibly. Yet what do we know," Strether asked, "about hers? She may be old enough."

"Old enough for what?"

"Why, to marry Chad. That may be, you know, what they want. And if Chad wants it too, and little Bilham wants it, and even *we,* at a pinch, could do with it—that is if she doesn't prevent repatriation—why, it may be plain sailing yet."

It was always the case for him in these counsels that each of his remarks, as it came, seemed to drop into a deeper well. He had at all events to wait a moment to hear the slight splash of this one. "I don't see why if Mr. Newsome wants to marry the young lady, he hasn't already done it, or hasn't been prepared with some statement to you about it. And if he both wants to marry her and is on good terms with them, why isn't he 'free'?"

Strether, responsively, wondered indeed. "Perhaps the girl herself doesn't like him."

"Then why does he speak of them to you as he does?"

Strether's mind echoed the question, but also again met it. "Perhaps it's with the mother that he's on good terms."

"As against the daughter?"

"Well, if she's trying to persuade the daughter to consent to him, what could make him like the mother more? Only," Strether threw out, "why shouldn't the daughter consent to him?"

"Oh," said Miss Gostrey, "mayn't it be that every one else isn't quite so struck with him as you?"

"Doesn't regard him, you mean, as such an 'eligible' young man? *Is* that what I've come to?" he audibly and rather gravely inquired. "However," he went on, "his marriage is what his mother most desires—that is if it will help. And oughtn't *any* marriage to help? They must want him "—he had already worked it out—" to be better off. Almost any girl he may marry will have a direct interest in his taking up his chances. It won't suit *her* at least that he shall miss them."

Miss Gostrey debated. "No—you reason well! But of course, on the other hand, there's always dear old Woollett itself."

"Oh yes," he mused—" there's always dear old Woollett itself."

She waited a moment. "The young lady mayn't find herself able to swallow *that* quantity. She may think it's paying too much; she may weigh one thing against another."

Strether, ever restless in such debates, took a turn about. "It will all depend on who she is. That of course—the proved ability to deal with dear old Woollett; since I'm sure she does deal with it! —is what makes so strongly for Mamie."

"Mamie?"

He stopped short, at her tone, before her; then, though seeing that it represented not vagueness, but a momentary embarrassed fulness, he let his exclamation come. "You surely haven't forgotten about Mamie!"

"No, I haven't forgotten about Mamie," she smiled. "There's no doubt whatever that there's ever so much to be said for her. Mamie's *my* girl!" she roundly declared.

Strether resumed for a minute his walk. "She's really perfectly lovely, you know. Far prettier than any girl I've seen over here yet."

"That's precisely on what I perhaps most build." And she mused a moment in her friend's way. "I should positively like to take her in hand!"

He humored the fancy, though indeed finally to deprecate it.

" Oh, but don't, in your zeal, go over to her! I need you most and can't, you know, be left."

But she kept it up. " I wish they'd send her out to me!"

" If they knew you," he returned, " they would."

" Ah, but don't they?—after all that, as I've understood you, you've told them about me?"

He had paused before her again, but he continued his course. " They *will*—before, as you say, I've done." Then he came out with the point he had wished, after all, most to make. " It seems to give away, now, his game. This is what he has been doing— keeping me along for. He has been waiting for them."

Miss Gostrey drew in her lips. " You see a good deal in it!"

" I doubt if I see as much as you. Do you pretend," he went on, " that you don't see—?"

" Well, what?"—she pressed him as he paused.

" Why, that there must be a lot between them—and that it has been going on from the first, even from before I came."

She took a minute to answer. " Who are they then—if it's so grave?"

" It may not be grave—it may be gay. But at any rate it's marked. Only I don't know," Strether had to confess, " anything about them. Their name, for instance, was a thing that, after little Bilham's information, I found it a kind of refreshment not to feel obliged to follow up."

" Oh," she returned, " if you think you've got off—!"

Her laugh produced in him a momentary gloom. " I don't think I've got off. I only think I'm breathing for about five minutes. I dare say I *shall* have, at the best, still to get on." A look, over it all, passed between them, and the next minute he had come back to good-humor. " I don't, meanwhile, take the smallest interest in their name."

" Nor in their nationality?—American, French, English, Polish?"

" I don't care the least little ' hang,' " he smiled, " for their nationality. It would be nice if they're Polish!" he almost immediately added.

" Very nice indeed." The transition kept up her spirits. " So you see you do care."

He did this contention a modified justice. " I think I should if they *were* Polish. Yes," he thought — "there might be joy in *that*."

"Let us then hope for it." But she came, after this, nearer to the question. "If the girl's of the right age, of course the mother can't be. I mean for the virtuous attachment. If the girl's twenty—and she can't be less—the mother must be at least forty. So it puts the mother out. *She's* too old for him."

Strether, arrested again, considered and demurred. "Do you think so? Do you think any one would be too old for him? *I'm* seventy, and I'm too young. But perhaps the girl," he continued, "*isn't* twenty. Perhaps she's only ten—but such a little dear that Chad finds himself counting her in as an attraction of the acquaintance. Perhaps she's only five. Perhaps the mother's but five-and-twenty—a charming young widow."

Miss Gostrey entertained the suggestion. "She *is* a widow then?"

"I haven't the least idea!" They once more, in spite of this vagueness, exchanged a look—a look that was perhaps the longest yet. It seemed in fact, the next thing, to require to explain itself; which it did as it could. "I only feel what I've told you—that he has some reason."

Miss Gostrey's imagination had taken its own flight. "Perhaps she's *not* a widow."

Strether seemed to accept the possibility with reserve. Still, he accepted it. "Then that's why the attachment—if it's to her—is virtuous."

But she looked as if she scarce followed. "Why is it virtuous if —since she's free—there's nothing to impose on it any condition?"

He laughed at her question. "Oh, I perhaps don't mean as virtuous as *that!* Your idea is that it can be virtuous—in any sense worthy of the name—only if she's *not* free? But what does it become then," he asked, "for *her?*"

"Ah, that's another matter." He said nothing for a moment, and she soon went on. "I dare say you're right, at any rate, about Mr. Newsome's little plan. He *has* been trying you—has been reporting on you to these friends."

Strether, meanwhile, had had time to think more. "Then where's his straightness?"

"Well, as we say, it's struggling up, breaking out, asserting

9   129

itself as it can. We can be on the side, you see, of his straightness. We can help him. But he has made out," said Miss Gostrey. " that you'll do."

" Do for what ?"

" Why, for *them*—for *ces dames*. He has watched you, studied you, liked you—and recognized that *they* must. It's a great compliment to you my dear man; for I'm sure they're particular. You came out for a success. Well," she gayly declared, " you're having it !"

He took it from her with momentary patience, and then turned abruptly away. It was always convenient to him that there were so many fine things in her room to look at. But the examination of two or three of them appeared soon to have determined a speech that had little to do with them. " You don't believe in it !"

" In what ?"

" In the character of the attachment. In its innocence."

But she defended herself. " I don't pretend to know anything about it. Everything's possible. We must see."

" See ?" he echoed with a groan. " Haven't we seen enough ?"

" *I* haven't," she smiled.

" But do you suppose then little Bilham has lied ?"

" You must find out."

It made him almost turn pale. " Find out any *more*?"

He had dropped on a sofa for dismay; but she seemed, as she stood over him, to have the last word. " Wasn't what you came out for to find out *all*?"

PART FIFTH

X

Ì'HE Sunday of the next week was a wonderful day, and Chad
Newsome had let his friend know in advance that he had provided
for it. There had already been a question of his taking him to see
the great Gloriani, who was at home on Sunday afternoons and at
whose house, for the most part, fewer bores were to be met than
elsewhere; but the project, through some accident, had not had instant effect. It had now, however, revived in happier conditions.
Chad had made the point that the celebrated sculptor had a queer
old garden, for which the weather—spring at last frank and fair—
was propitious; and two or three of his other allusions had confirmed for Strether the expectation of something special. He had
by this time, for all introductions and adventures, let himself recklessly go, cherishing the sense that, whatever the young man showed
him, he was showing at least himself. He could have wished, indeed,
so far as this went, that Chad were less of a mere cicerone; for he
was not without the impression—now that the vision of his game,
his plan, his deep diplomacy, did recurrently assert itself—of his
taking refuge from the realities of their intercourse in the offer,
as our friend mentally phrased it, of *panem et circenses*. Our
friend continued to feel rather smothered in flowers, though he
made in his other moments the almost angry inference that this was
only because of his odious ascetic suspicion of any form of beauty.
He periodically assured himself—for his reactions were sharp—
that he should not reach the truth of anything till he had at least
got rid of that.

He had known beforehand that Mme. de Vionnet and her
daughter would probably be on view, an intimation to that effect
having constituted the only reference again made by Chad to his
good friends from the south. The effect of Strether's talk about
them with Miss Gostrey had been quite to consecrate his reluc-

tance to pry; something in the very air of Chad's silence—judged in the light of that talk—offered it to him as a reserve he could markedly match. It shrouded them about with he scarce knew what —a consideration, a distinction; he was in the presence, at any rate—so far as it placed him there—of ladies; and the one thing that was definite for him was that they themselves should be, to the extent of his responsibility, in the presence of a gentleman. Was it because they were very beautiful, very clever, or even very good—was it for one of these reasons that Chad was, so to speak, nursing his effect? Did he wish to spring them, in the Woollett phrase, with a fuller force—to confound his critic, slight though as yet the criticism, with some form of merit exquisitely incalculable? The most he had, at all events, asked of his companion was whether the persons in question were French; and that inquiry had been but a proper comment on the sound of their name. " Yes. That is no!" had been Chad's reply; but he had immediately added that their English was the most charming in the world, so that if Strether were wanting an excuse for not getting on with them he wouldn't in the least find one. Never in fact had Strether—in the mood into which the place had quickly launched him—felt, for himself, less the need of an excuse. Those he might have found would have been, at the worst, all for the others, the people before him, in whose liberty to be as they were he was aware that he positively rejoiced. His fellow-guests were multiplying, and these things, their liberty, their intensity, their variety, their condi- tions at large, were in fusion in the admirable medium of the scene.

The place itself was a great impression—a small pavilion, clear-faced and sequestered, an effect of polished *parquet,* of fine white panel and spare, sallow gilt, of decoration delicate and rare, in the heart of the Faubourg Saint Germain and on the edge of a cluster of gardens attached to old noble houses. Far back from streets and unsuspected by crowds, reached by a long passage and a quiet court, it was as striking to the unprepared mind, he immediately saw, as a treasure dug up; giving him too, more than anything yet, the note of the range of the immeasurable town and sweeping away, as by a last brave brush, his usual landmarks and terms. It was in the garden, a spacious, cherished remnant, out to which a dozen persons had already passed, that Chad's host presently met them; while the tall, bird-haunted trees, all of a twitter with the spring and the weather, and the high party-walls, on the other side of which grave *hôtels* stood off for privacy, spoke of survival, transmission, association, a strong, indifferent, persistent order. The day was so soft that the little party had practically adjourned to the open air, but the open air, in such conditions, was all a chamber of state. Strether had presently the sense of a great convent, a convent of missions, famous for he scarce knew what, a nursery of young priests, of scattered shade, of straight alleys and chapel-bells, that spread its mass in one quarter; he had the sense of names in the air, of ghosts at the windows, of signs and tokens, a whole range of expression, all about him, too thick for prompt discrimination.

This assault of images became for a moment, in the address of the distinguished sculptor, almost formidable: Gloriani showed him, in such perfect confidence, on Chad's introduction of him, a fine, worn handsome face, a face that was like an open letter in a foreign tongue. With his genius in his eyes, his manners on his lips, his long career behind him and his honors and rewards all round, the great artist, in the course of a single sustained look and a few words of delight at receiving him, affected our friend as a dazzling prodigy of type. Strether had seen in museums—in the Luxembourg as well as, more reverently, in other days, in the New York of the billionaires—the work of his hand; knowing too that, after an earlier time in his native Rome, he had migrated, in mid-career, to Paris, where, with a personal lustre almost violent, he shone in a constellation: all of which was more than enough to crown him, for his guest, with the light, with the romance, of glory. Strether, in contact with that element as he had never yet so intimately been, had the consciousness of opening to it, for the happy instant, all the windows of his mind, of letting this rather gray interior drink in, for once, the sun of a clime not marked in his old geography. He was to see again, repeatedly, in remembrance, the medal-like Italian face, in which every line was an artist's own, in which time told only as tone and consecration; and he was to recall in especial, as the penetrating radiance, as the communication of the illustrious spirit itself, the manner in which, while they stood briefly, in welcome and response, face to face, he was held by the sculptor's eyes. He was not soon to forget them, was to think of them, all unconscious, unintending, preoccupied though they were, as the source of the deepest intellectual sounding to which he had ever been exposed. He was in fact quite to cherish his vision of it, to play with it in idle hours; only speaking of it to no one and quite aware he couldn't have spoken without appearing to talk nonsense. Was what it had told him or what it had asked him the greater of the mysteries? Was it the most special flare, unequalled, supreme, of the æsthetic torch, lighting that wondrous world forever, or was it above all the long, straight shaft sunk by a personal acuteness that life had seasoned to steel? Nothing on earth could have been stranger and no one doubtless more surprised than the artist himself, but it was, for all the world, to Strether, in these instants, as if, in respect to his accepted duty, he had positively been on trial. The deep human expertness in Gloriani's charming smile—oh, the terrible life behind it!—was flashed upon him as a test of his stuff.

Chad, meanwhile, after having easily named his companion, had still more easily turned away and was already greeting other persons present. He was as easy, clever Chad, with the great artist as with his obscure compatriot, and as easy with every one else as with either: this fell into its place for Strether and made almost a new light, giving him, as a concatenation, something more he could enjoy. He liked Gloriani, but should never see him again; of that he was sufficiently sure. Chad, accordingly, who was wonderful with both of them, was a kind of link for hopeless fancy, an implication of possibilities—oh, if everything had been different! Strether noted, at all events, that he was thus on terms with illustrious spirits, and also that—yes, distinctly—he had not in the least swaggered about it. Our friend hadn't come there only for this figure of Abel Newsome's son, but it threatened to affect the observant mind as positively central. Gloriani indeed, remembering something and excusing himself, pursued Chad to speak to him, and Strether was left musing on many things. One of them was the question of whether, since he had been tested, he had passed. Did the artist drop him from having made out that he wouldn't do? He really felt, just to-day, that he might do better than usual Hadn't he done well enough, for that matter, in being just so dazzled? and in not having too, as he almost believed, wholly hidden from his host that he knew of the latter's inquiry? Suddenly, across the garden, he saw little Bilham approach, and it was a part of the fit that was on him that, as their eyes met, he guessed also *his* knowledge. If he had said to him on the instant what was uppermost he would have said: "*Have* I passed?—for of course I know one has to pass here." Little Bilham would have reassured him, have told him that he exaggerated, and have adduced happily enough the argument of little Bilham's own very presence; which, in truth, he could see, was as easy a one as Gloriani's own or as Chad's. He himself would perhaps then after a while cease to be frightened, would get the point of view for some of the faces—types tremendously alien, alien to Woollett—that he had already begun to take in. Who were they all, the dispersed groups and couples, the ladies even more unlike those of Woollett than the gentlemen?—this was the inquiry that, when his young friend had greeted him, he did find himself making.

"Oh, they're every one—all sorts and sizes; of course I mean within limits, though limits down perhaps rather more than limits up. There are always artists—he's beautiful, inimitable to the *cher confrère;* and then *gros bonnets* of many kinds—ambassadors, cabinet ministers, bankers, generals; what do I know? even Jews. Above all, always, some awfully nice women—and not too many; sometimes an actress, an artist, a great performer—but only when they're not monsters; and, in particular, the right *femmes du monde.* You can fancy his history on that side—I believe it's fabulous: they *never* give him up. Yet he keeps them down: no one knows how he manages; it's too beautiful and bland. Never too many—and a mighty good thing too; just a perfect choice. But there are not in any way many bores; it has always been so; he has some secret. It's extraordinary. And you don't find it out. He's the same to every one. He doesn't ask questions."

"Ah, doesn't he?" Strether laughed.

Bilham met it with all his candor. "How then should *I* be here?"

"Oh, for what you tell me. You're part of the perfect choice."

Well, the young man took in the scene. "It seems rather good to-day."

Strether followed the direction of his eyes. "Are they all, this time, *femmes du monde?*"

Little Bilham showed his competence. "Pretty well."

This was a category our friend had a feeling for; a light, romantic and mysterious, on the feminine element, in which he enjoyed for a little watching it. "Are there any Poles?"

His companion considered. "I think I make out a Portuguese. But I've seen Turks."

Strether wondered, desiring justice. "They seem, all the women, very harmonious."

"Oh, in closer quarters they come out!" And then, while Strether was aware of fearing closer quarters, though giving himself again to the harmonies, "Well," little Bilham went on, "it *is,* at the worst, rather good, you know. If you like it, you feel it, this way, that shows you're not in the least out. But you always know things," he handsomely added, "immediately."

Strether liked it and felt it only too much; so "I say, don't lay traps for me!" he rather helplessly murmured.

"Well," the young man returned, "he's wonderfully kind to *us.*"

"To us Americans, you mean?"

"Oh no—he doesn't know anything about *that.* That's half the battle here—that you can never hear politics. We don't talk them. I mean to poor young wretches of all sorts. And yet it's always as charming as this; it's as if, by something in the air, our squalor didn't show. It puts us all back—into the last century."

"I'm afraid," Strether said, amused, "that it puts me, rather, forward: oh, ever so far!"

"Into the next? But isn't that only," little Bilham asked, "because you're really of the century before?"

"The century before the last? Thank you!" Strether laughed. "If I ask you about some of the ladies it can't be then that I may hope, as such a specimen of the rococo, to please them."

"On the contrary, they adore—we all adore here—the rococo, and where is there a better setting for it than the whole thing, the pavilion and the garden, together? There are lots of people," little Bilham smiled as he glanced round, "with collections. You'll be secured!"

It made Strether, for a moment, give himself again to contempla tion. There were faces he scarce knew what to make of. Were they charming, or were they only strange? He mightn't talk politics, yet he suspected a Pole or two. The upshot was the question at the back of his head from the moment his friend had joined him. "Have Mme. de Vionnet and her daughter arrived?"

"I haven't seen them yet, but Miss Gostrey has come. She's in the pavilion looking at objects. One can see *she's* a collector," little Bilham added without offence.

"Oh yes, she's a collector, and I knew she was to come. Is Mme. de Vionnet a collector?" Strether went on.

"Rather, I believe; almost celebrated." The young man met, on it, a little, his friend's eyes. "I happen to know—from Chad, whom I saw last night—that they've come back; but only yesterday. He wasn't sure—up to the last. This, accordingly," little Bilham went on, "will be—if they *are* here—their first appearance after their return."

Strether, very quickly, turned these things over. "Chad told you last night? To me he, on our way here, said nothing about it."

"But did you ask him?"

Strether did him the justice. "I dare say not."

"Well," said little Bilham, "you're not a person to whom it's easy to tell things you don't want to know. Though it *is* easy, I admit—it's quite beautiful," he benevolently added, "when you do want to."

Strether looked at him with an indulgence that matched his intelligence. "Is that the deep reasoning on which—about these ladies—you've been yourself so silent?"

Little Bilham considered the depth of his reasoning. "I haven't been silent. I spoke of them to you the other day, the day we sat together after Chad's tea-party."

Strether came round to it. "They then are the virtuous attachment?"

"I can only tell you that it's what they pass for. But isn't that enough? What more than a vain appearance does the wisest of us know? I commend you," the young man declared with a pleasant emphasis, "the vain appearance."

Strether looked more widely round, and what he saw, from face to face, deepened the effect of his young friend's words. "Is it so good?"

"Magnificent."

Strether had a pause. "The husband's dead?"

"Dear no. Alive."

"Oh!" said Strether. After which, as his companion laughed: "How then can it be so good?"

"You'll see for yourself. One does see."

"Chad's in love with the daughter?"

"That's what I mean."

Strether wondered. "Then where's the difficulty?"

"Why, aren't you and I—with our grander, bolder ideas?"

"Oh, mine—!" Strether said rather strangely. But then as if to attenuate: "You mean they won't hear of Woollett?"

Little Bilham smiled. "Isn't that just what you must see about?"

It had brought them, as she caught the last words, into relation with Miss Barrace, whom Strether had already observed—as he had never before seen a lady at a party—moving about alone. Coming within sound of them, she had already spoken, and she took again, through her long-handled glass, all her amused and amusing possession. "How much, poor Mr. Strether, you seem to have to see about! But you can't say," she gayly declared, "that I don't do what I can to help you. Mr. Waymarsh is placed. I've left him in the house with Miss Gostrey."

"The way," little Bilham exclaimed, "Mr. Strether gets the ladies to work for him! He's just preparing to draw in another; to pounce—don't you see him?—on Mme. de Vionnet."

"Mme. de Vionnet? Oh, oh, oh!" Miss Barrace cried in a wonderful crescendo. There was more in it, our friend made out, than met the ear. Was it, after all, a joke that he should be serious about anything? He envied Miss Barrace, at any rate, her power of not being. She seemed, with little cries and protests and quick recognitions, movements like the darts of some fine high-feathered, free-pecking bird, to stand before life as before some full shop-window. You could fairly hear, as she selected and pointed, the tap of her tortoise-shell against the glass. "It's certain that we do need seeing about; only I'm glad it's not I who have to do it.

One does, no doubt, begin that way; then suddenly one finds that one has given it up. It's too much, it's too difficult. You're wonderful, you people," she continued to Strether, "for not feeling those things—by which I mean impossibilities. You never feel them. You face them with a fortitude that makes it a lesson to watch you."

"Ah, but "—little Bilham put it with discouragement—"what do we achieve after all? We see about you and report—when we even go so far as reporting. But nothing's done."

"Oh you, Mr. Bilham," she replied as with an impatient rap on the glass, "you're not worth sixpence! You come over to convert the savages—for I know you verily did, I remember you—and the savages simply convert *you*."

"Not even!" the young man wofully confessed: "they haven't gone through that form. They've simply—the cannibals!—eaten me; converted me if you like, but converted me into food. I'm but the bleached bones of a Christian."

"Well, then, there we are! Only "—and Miss Barrace appealed again to Strether—"don't let it discourage you. You'll break down soon enough, but you'll meanwhile have had your moments. *Il faut en avoir.* I always like to see you while you last. And I'll tell you who *will* last."

"Waymarsh?"—he had already taken her up.

She laughed out as at the alarm of it. "He'll resist even Miss Gostrey: so grand is it not to understand. He's wonderful."

"He is, indeed," Strether conceded. "He wouldn't tell me of this affair—only said he had an engagement; but with such a gloom, you must let me insist, as if it had been an engagement to be hanged. Then, silently and secretly, he turns up here with you. Do you call *that* 'lasting'?"

"Oh, I hope it's lasting!" Miss Barrace said. "But he only, at the best, bears with me. He doesn't understand—not one little scrap. He's delightful. He's wonderful," she repeated.

"Michelangelesque!"—little Bilham completed her meaning. "He *is* a success. Moses, on the ceiling, brought down to the floor; overwhelming, colossal, but somehow portable."

"Certainly, if you mean by portable," she returned, "looking so well in one's carriage. He's too funny beside me in his corner; he looks like somebody, somebody foreign and famous, *en exil;* so that people wonder—it's very amusing—whom I'm taking about. I show him Paris, show him everything, and he never turns a hair. He's like the Indian chief one reads about, who, when he comes up to Washington to see the Great Father, stands wrapped in his blanket and gives no sign. *I* might be the Great Father—from the way he takes everything." She was delighted at this hit of her identity with that personage—it fitted so her character; she declared it was the title she meant henceforth to adopt. "And the way he sits, too, in the corner of my room, only looking at my visitors very hard and as if he wanted to start something! They wonder what he does want to start. But he's wonderful," Miss Barrace once more insisted. "He has never started anything yet."

It presented him none the less, in truth, to her actual friends, who looked at each other in intelligence, with frank amusement on Bilham's part and a shade of sadness on Strether's. Strether's sadness sprang—for the image had its grandeur—from his thinking how little he himself was wrapped in his blanket, how little, in marble halls, all too oblivious of the Great Father, he resembled a really majestic aboriginal. But he had also another reflection. "You've all of you here so much visual sense that you've somehow all 'run' to it. There are moments when it strikes one that you haven't any other."

"Any moral," little Bilham explained, watching serenely, across the garden, the several *femmes du monde.* "But Miss Barrace has a moral distinction," he kindly continued; speaking as if for Strether's benefit not less than for her own.

"*Have* you?" Strether, scarce knowing what he was about, asked of her almost eagerly.

"Oh, not a distinction"—she was mightily amused at his tone —"Mr. Bilham is too good. But I think I may say a sufficiency. Yes, a sufficiency. Have you supposed strange things of me?"—and she fixed him again, through all her tortoise-shell, with the droll interest of it. "You *are* all indeed wonderful. I should awfully disappoint you. I do take my stand on my sufficiency. But I know, I confess," she went on, "strange people. I don't know how it happens; I don't do it on purpose; it seems to be my doom—as if I were, always, one of their habits; it's wonderful! I dare say.

moreover," she pursued with an interested gravity, " that I do, that we all do here, run too much to mere eye. But how can it be helped? We're all looking at each other—and in the light of Paris one sees what things resemble. That's what the light of Paris seems always to show. It's the fault of the light of Paris—dear old light!"

" Dear old Paris!" little Bilham echoed.

" Everything, every one shows," Miss Barrace went on.

'But for what they really are?" Strether asked.

" Oh, I like your Boston ' reallys'! But sometimes—yes."

" Dear old Paris then!" Strether resignedly sighed while, for a moment, they looked at each other. Then he broke out: " Does Mme. de Vionnet do that? I mean really show for what she is?"

Her answer was prompt. " She's charming. She's perfect."

" Then why did you, a minute ago, say ' Oh, oh, oh!' at her name?"

She easily remembered. " Why, just because—! She's wonderful."

" Ah, she too?"—Strether had almost a groan.

But Miss Barrace had meanwhile perceived relief. " Why not put your question straight to the person who can answer it best?"

" No," said little Bilham; " don't put any question; wait, rather—it will be much more fun—to judge for yourself. He has come to take you to her."

On which Strether saw that Chad was again at hand, and he afterwards scarce knew, absurd as it may seem, what had then quickly occurred. The moment concerned him, he felt, more deeply than he could have explained, and he had a subsequent passage of speculation as to whether, on walking off with Chad, he hadn't looked either pale or red. The only thing he was clear about was that, luckily, nothing indiscreet had in fact been said, and that Chad himself was, more than ever, in Miss Barrace's great sense, wonderful. It was one of the connections—though really why it should be, after all, was none so apparent—in which the whole change in him came out as most striking. Strether recalled, as they approached the house, that he had impressed him that first night as knowing how to enter a box. Well, he impressed him scarce less now as knowing how to make a presentation. It did something for Strether's own quality—marked it as estimated; so that our poor friend, conscious and passive, really seemed to feel himself quite handed over and delivered; absolutely, as he would have said, made a present of, given away. As they reached the house a young woman, about to come forth, appeared, unaccompanied, on the steps; at the exchange with whom of a word on Chad's part Strether immediately perceived that, obligingly, kindly, she was there to meet them. Chad had left her in the house, but she had afterwards come half-way and then, the next moment, had joined them in the garden. Her air of youth, for Strether, was at first almost disconcerting, while his second impression was, not less sharply, a degree of relief at there not having just been, with the others, any freedom used about her. It was upon him at a touch that she was no subject for that, and meanwhile, on Chad's introducing him, she had spoken to him, very simply and gently, in an English clearly of the easiest to her, yet unlike any other he had ever heard. It wasn't as if she tried; nothing, he could see after they had been a few minutes together, was as if she tried; but her speech, charming, correct and odd, was like a precaution against her passing for a Pole. There were precautions, he seemed indeed to see, only when there were really dangers.

Later on he was to feel many more of them; but by that time he was to feel other things besides. She was dressed in black, but in black that struck him as light and transparent; she was exceedingly fair, and, though she was as markedly slim, her face had a roundness, with eyes far apart and a little strange. Her smile was natural and dim; her hat not extravagant; he had only perhaps a sense of the clink, beneath her fine black sleeves, of more gold bracelets and bangles than he had ever seen a lady wear. Chad was excellently free and light about their encounter; it was one of the occasions on which Strether most wished he himself might have arrived at such ease and such humor: " Here you are then, face to face at last; you're made for each other—*vous allez voir;* and I bless your union." It was indeed, after he had gone off, as if he had been partly serious too. This latter motion had been determined by an inquiry from him about " Jeanne "; to which her mother had replied that she was probably still in the house with Miss Gostrey, to whom she had lately committed her. " Ah, but you know," the young man had rejoined, " he must see her "; with which, while Strether pricked up his ears, he had started as if to bring her, leaving the other objects of his interest together. Strether wondered to find Miss Gostrey already involved, feeling that he missed a link; but feeling also, with small delay, how much he should like to talk with her of Mme. de Vionnet on this basis of evidence.

The evidence as yet, in truth, was meagre; which, for that matter, was perhaps a little why his expectation had had a drop. There was somehow not a wealth in her; and a wealth was all that, in his simplicity, he had definitely prefigured. Still, it was too much to be sure already that there was but a poverty. They moved away from the house, and, with eyes on a bench at some distance, he proposed that they should sit down. " I've heard a great deal about you," she said as they went; but he had an answer to it that made her stop short. " Well, about *you,* Mme. de Vionnet, I've heard, I'm bound to say, almost nothing "—those struck him as the only words he himself could, with any lucidity, utter; conscious as he was, and as with more reason, of the determination to be, in respect to the rest of his business, perfectly plain and go perfectly straight. It had not at any rate been in the least his idea to spy on Chad's proper freedom. It was possibly, however, at this very instant and under the impression of Mme. de Vionnet's pause, that going straight began to announce itself as a matter for care. She had only, after all, to smile at him ever so gently to make him ask himself if he weren't already going crooked. It might be going crooked to find it of a sudden just only clear that she intended very definitely to be what he would have called nice to him. This was what passed between them while, for another instant, they stood still; he couldn't at least remember afterwards what else it might have been. The thing indeed really unmistakable was that it rolled over him as a wave that he had been, in conditions incalculable and unimaginable, a subject of discussion. He had been on some ground that concerned her, answered for; which gave her an advantage he should never be able to match.

"Hasn't Miss Gostrey," she asked, "said a good word for me?"

What had struck him first was the way he was bracketed with that lady; and he wondered what account Chad would have given of their acquaintance. Something not as yet traceable, at all events, had obviously happened. "I didn't even know of her knowing you."

"Well, now she'll tell you all. I'm so glad you're in relation with her."

This was one of the things—the "all" Miss Gostrey would now tell him—that, with every deference to present preoccupation, was uppermost for Strether after they had taken their seat. One of the others was, at the end of five minutes, that she—oh, incontestably, yes—*differed* less; differed, that is, scarcely at all—well, superficially speaking, from Mrs. Newsome or even from Mrs. Pocock. She was ever so much younger than the one and not so young as the other; but what *was* there in her, if anything, that would have made it impossible he should meet her at Woollett? And wherein was her talk, during their moments on the bench together, not the same as would have been found adequate for a Woollett garden party?—unless perhaps, truly, in not being quite so bright. She observed to him that Mr. Newsome had, to her knowledge, taken extraordinary pleasure in his visit; but there was no good lady at Woollett who wouldn't have been at least up to that. Was there in Chad, by chance, after all, deep down, a principle of aboriginal loyalty that had made him, for sentimental ends, attach himself to elements, happily encountered, that would remind him most of the old air and the old soil? Why, accordingly, be in a flutter— Strether could even put it that way—about this unfamiliar phenomenon of the *femme du monde?* On these terms Mrs. Newsome herself was as much of one. Little Bilham, verily, had testified that they came out, the ladies of the type, in close quarters; but it was just in these quarters—now comparatively close—that he felt Mme. de Vionnet's common humanity. She did come out, and certainly to his relief, but she came out as the usual thing. There might be motives behind, but so could there often be even at Woollett. The only thing was that if she showed him she wished to like him —as the motives behind might conceivably prompt—it would possibly have been more thrilling for him that she should have shown as more vividly alien. Ah, she was neither Turk nor Pole!—which would be indeed flat, once more, for Mrs. Newsome and Mrs. Pocock. A lady and two gentlemen had meanwhile, however, approached their bench, and this accident stayed for the time further developments.

They presently addressed his companion, the brilliant strangers; she rose to speak to them, and Strether noted that the escorted lady, though mature and by no means beautiful, had more of the bold, high look, the range of expensive reference, that he had, as might have been said, made his plans for. Mme. de Vionnet greeted her as "Duchesse" and was greeted in turn, while talk started in French, as "Ma toute-belle"; little facts that had their due, their vivid interest for Strether. Mme. de Vionnet didn't, none the less, introduce him—a note he was conscious of as false to the Woollett scale and the Woollett humanity; though it didn't prevent the Duchess, who struck him as confident and free, very much what he had obscurely supposed duchesses, from looking at him as straight and as hard—for it *was* hard—as if she would have liked, all the same, to know him. "Oh yes, my dear, it's all right, it's *me;* and who are *you,* with your interesting wrinkles and your most effective (is it the handsomest, is it the ugliest?) of noses?"—some such loose handful of bright flowers she seemed, fragrantly enough, to fling at him. Strether almost wondered—at such a pace was he going—if some divination of the influence of either party were what determined Mme. de Vionnet's abstention. One of the gentlemen, in any case, succeeded in placing himself in close relation with our friend's companion; a gentleman rather stout and not very tall, in a hat with a wonderful wide curl to its brim and a frock coat buttoned with an effect of superlative decision. His French had quickly turned to equal English, and it occurred to Strether that he might well be one of the ambassadors. His design was evidently to assert a claim to Mme. de Vionnet's undivided countenance, and he made it good in the course of a minute—led her away with a trick of three words; a trick played with a social art of which Strether, looking after them as the four, whose backs were now all turned, moved off, felt himself no master.

He sank again upon his bench and, while his eyes followed the party, reflected, as he had done before, on Chad's strange communities. He sat there alone for five minutes, with plenty to think of; above all with his sense of having suddenly been dropped by a charming woman overlaid now by other impressions and in fact quite cleared and indifferent. He had not yet had so quiet a surrender; he didn't in the least care if nobody spoke to him more. He might have been, by his attitude, in for something of a march so broad that the want of ceremony with which he had just been used could fall into its place as but a minor incident of the procession. Besides, there would be incidents enough, as he felt when this term of contemplation was closed by the reappearance of little Bilham, who stood before him a moment with a suggestive "Well?" in which he saw himself reflected as disorganized, as possibly floored. He replied with a "Well!" intended to show that he was not floored in the least. No indeed; he gave it out, as the young man sat down beside him, that if, at the worst, he had been overturned at all, he had been overturned into the upper air, the sublimer element with which he had an affinity and in which he might be trusted a while to float. It was not a descent to earth to say, after an instant, in sustained response to the reference: "You're quite sure her husband's living?"

" Oh dear, yes."

" Ah then—!"

" Ah then what?"

Strether had, after all, to think. "Well, I'm sorry for them." But it didn't matter, for the moment, more than that. He assured his young friend he was quite content. They wouldn't stir; were all right as they were. He didn't want to be introduced; had been introduced already about as far as he could go. He had seen moreover an immensity; liked Gloriani, who, as Miss Barrace kept saying, was wonderful; had made out, he was sure, the half-dozen other men who were distinguished, the artists, the critics and, oh, the great dramatist—*him* it was easy to spot; but wanted—no, thanks, really—to talk with none of them; having nothing at all to say and finding it would do beautifully as it was; do beautifully because what it was—well, was just simply too late. And when, after this, little Bilham, submissive and responsive, but with an eye to the consolation nearest, easily threw off some " Better late than never!" all he got in return for it was a sharp " Better early than late!" This note, indeed, the next thing, overflowed, for Strether, into a quiet stream of demonstration that, as soon as he had let himself go, he felt as the real relief. It had consciously gathered to a head, but the reservoir had filled sooner than he knew, and his companion's touch was to make the waters spread. There were some things that had to come in time if they were to come at all. If they didn't come in time they were lost forever. It was the general sense of them that had overwhelmed him with its long, slow rush.

" It's not too late for *you,* on any side, and you don't strike me as in danger of missing the train; besides which people can be in general pretty well trusted, of course—with the clock of their freedom ticking as loud as it seems to do here—to keep an eye on the fleeting hour. All the same, don't forget that you're young— blessedly young; be glad of it, on the contrary, and live up to it. Live all you can; it's a mistake not to. It doesn't so much matter what you do in particular, so long as you have your life. If you haven't had that, what *have* you had? This place and these impressions—mild as you may find them to wind a man up so; all my impressions of Chad and of people I've seen at *his* place—well, have had their abundant message for me, have just dropped *that* into my

149

mind. I see it now. I haven't done so enough before—and now I'm old; too old at any rate for what I see. Oh, I *do* see, at least; and more than you'd believe or I can express. It's too late. And it's as if the train had fairly waited at the station for me without my having had the gumption to know it was there. Now I hear its faint, receding whistle miles and miles down the line. What one loses one loses; make no mistake about that. The affair—I mean the affair of life—couldn't, no doubt, have been different for me; for it's, at the best, a tin mould, either fluted and embossed, with ornamental excrescences, or else smooth and dreadfully plain, into which, a helpless jelly, one's consciousness is poured—so that one 'takes' the form, as the great cook says, and is more or less compactly held by it: one lives, in fine, as one can. Still, one has the illusion of freedom; therefore don't be, like me, without the memory of that illusion. I was either, at the right time, too stupid or too intelligent to have it; I don't quite know which. Of course, at present, I'm a case of reaction against the mistake; and the voice of reaction should, no doubt, always be taken with an allowance. But that doesn't affect the point that the right time is now yours. The right time is *any* time that one is still so lucky as to have. You've plenty; that's the great thing; you're, as I say, damn you, so happily and hatefully young. Don't, at any rate, miss things out of stupidity. Of course I don't take you for a fool, or I shouldn't be addressing you thus awfully. Do what you like so long as you don't make *my* mistake. For it was a mistake. Live!" . . . . Slowly and sociably, with full pauses and straight dashes, Strether had so delivered himself; holding little Bilham, from step to step, deeply and gravely attentive. The end of all was that the young man had turned quite solemn, and that this was a contradiction of the innocent gayety the speaker had wished to promote. He watched for a moment the consequence of his words, and then, laying a hand on his listener's knee and as if to end, properly, with a joke: "And now for the eye I shall keep on you!"

"Oh, but I don't know that I want to be, at your age, too different from you!"

"Ah, prepare, while you're about it," Strether said, "to be more amusing."

Little Bilham continued to think; then at last he had a smile. "Well, you *are* amusing—to *me*."

"*Impayable,* as you say, no doubt. But what am I to myself?" Strether had risen with this, giving his attention now to an encounter that, in the middle of the garden, was in the act of taking place between their host and the lady at whose side Mme. de Vionnet had quitted him. This lady, who appeared within a few minutes to have left her friends, awaited Gloriani's eager approach with words on her lips that Strether couldn't catch, but of which her interesting, witty face seemed to give him the echo. He was sure she was prompt and fine, but also that she had met her match, and he liked—in the light of what he was quite sure was the Duchess's latent insolence—the good-humor with which the great artist asserted equal resources. Were they, this pair, of the " great world "?—and was he himself, for the moment, thus related to them by his observation, *in* it? Then there was something in the great world covertly tigerish, which came to him, across the lawn, in the charming air, as a waft from the jungle. Yet it made him admire most of the two, made him envy, the glossy male tiger, magnificently marked. These absurdities of the stirred sense, fruits of suggestion, ripening on the instant, were all reflected in his next words to little Bilham. " I know—if we talk of that—whom *I* should enjoy being like!"

Little Bilham followed his eyes; but then, as if with a shade of knowing surprise: " Gloriani?"

Our friend had in fact already hesitated, though not on the hint of his companion's doubt, in which there were depths of critical reserve. He had just made out, in the now full picture, something and somebody else; another impression had been superimposed. A young girl in a white dress and a softly plumed white hat had suddenly come into view, and what was next clear was that her course was toward them. What was clearer still was that the handsome young man at her side was Chad Newsome, and what was clearest of all was that she was therefore Mlle. de Vionnet, that she was unmistakably pretty—bright, gentle, shy, happy, wonderful—and that Chad now, with a consummate calculation of effect, was about to present her to his old friend's vision. What was clearest of all indeed was something much more than this, something at the single stroke of which—and wasn't it simply juxtaposition?—all vagueness vanished. It was the click of a spring—he saw the truth. He had by this time also met Chad's look; there was more of it in that; and the truth, accordingly, so far as Bilham's inquiry was concerned, had thrust in the answer. "Oh, Chad!"—it was that rare youth he should have enjoyed being "like." The virtuous attachment would be all there before him; the virtuous attachment would be in the very act of appeal for his blessing; Jeanne de Vionnet, this charming creature, would be—exquisitely, intensely now—the object of it. Chad brought her straight up to him, and Chad was, oh yes, at this moment—for the glory of Woollett or whatever—better still even than Gloriani. He had plucked this blossom; he had kept it, over-night, in water; and at last, as he held it up to wonder, he did enjoy his effect. That was why Strether had felt at first the breath of calculation—and why, moreover, as he now knew, his look at the girl would be, for the young man, a sign of the latter's success. What young man had ever paraded about that way, without a reason, a maiden in her flower? And there was nothing in his reason at present obscure. Her type sufficiently told of it—they wouldn't want her to go to Woollett. Poor Woollett, and what it might miss!—though brave Chad indeed too, and what it might gain! Brave Chad, however, had just excellently spoken. "This is a good little friend of mine who knows all about you and has moreover a message for you. And this, my dear"—he had turned to the child herself—" is the best man in the world, who has it in his power to do a great deal for us and whom I want you to like and revere as nearly as possible as much as I do."

She stood there quite pink, a little frightened, prettier and prettier and not a bit like her mother. There was in this last particular no resemblance but that of youth to youth; and here in fact, suddenly, was Strether's sharpest impression. It went wondering, dazed, embarrassed, back to the woman he had just been talking with; it was a revelation in the light of which he already saw she would become more interesting. So slim and fresh and fair, she had yet put forth this perfection; so that for really believing it of her, for seeing her to any such developed degree as a mother, comparison would be urgent. Well, what was it now but fairly thrust upon him? "Mamma wishes me to tell you before we go," the girl said, "that she hopes very much you'll come to see us very soon. She has something particular to say to you."

"She quite reproaches herself," Chad helpfully explained: "you were interesting her so much when she accidentally suffered you to be interrupted."

"Ah, don't mention it!" Strether murmured, looking kindly from one to the other and wondering at many things.

"And I'm to ask you for myself," Jeanne continued with her hands clasped together as if in some small learnt prayer—"I'm to ask you for myself if you won't positively come."

"Leave it to me, dear—I'll take care of it!" Chad genially declared in answer to this, while Strether himself almost held his breath. What was in the girl was indeed too soft, too unknown for direct dealing; so that one could only gaze at it as at a picture, quite staying one's own hand. But with Chad he was now on ground—Chad he could meet; so pleasant a confidence in that and in everything did the young man freely exhale. There was the whole of a story in his tone to his companion, and he spoke indeed as if already of the family. It made Strether guess the more quickly what it might be about which Mme. de Vionnet was "particular." Having seen him, then, she had found him easy; she wished to have it out with him that some way for the young people must be discovered, some way that would not impose as a condition the transplantation of her daughter. He already saw himself discussing with this lady the attractions of Woollett as a residence for Chad's companion. Was that youth going now to trust her with the affair—so that it would be after all with one of his "lady-friends" that his mother's missionary should be condemned to deal? It was quite as if for an instant the two men looked at each other on this question. But there was no mistaking at last Chad's pride in the display of such a connection. This was what had made him so carry himself while, three minutes before, he was bringing it into view; what had caused his friend, first catching sight of him, to be so struck with his air. It was, in a word, just when he thus finally felt Chad putting things straight off on him that he envied him, as he had mentioned to little Bilham, most. The whole exhibition, however, was but a matter of three or four minutes, and the author of it had soon explained that, as Mme. de

Vionnet was immediately going " on," this could be for Jeanne but a snatch. They would all meet again soon, and Strether was meanwhile to stay and amuse himself—" I'll pick you up again in plenty of time." He took the girl off as he had brought her, and Strether, with the faint, sweet foreignness of her " Au revoir, monsieur!" in his ears as a note almost unprecedented, watched them recede side by side and felt how, once more, her companion's relation to her got an accent from it. They disappeared among the others and apparently into the house; whereupon our friend turned round to give out to little Bilham the conviction of which he was full. But there was no little Bilham any more; little Bilham had, within the few moments, for reasons of his own, proceeded further: a circumstance by which, in its order, Strether was also sensibly affected.

XII

CHAD was not in fact, on this occasion, to keep his promise of coming back; but Miss Gostrey had soon presented herself with an explanation of his failure. There had been reasons, at the last, for his going off with *ces dames;* and he had asked her, with much instance, to come out and take charge of their friend. She did so, Strether felt as she took her place beside him, in a manner that left nothing to desire. He had dropped back on his bench, alone again for a time, and the more conscious, for little Bilham's defection, of his unexpressed thought; in respect to which, however, this next interlocutor was a still more capacious vessel. "It's the child!" he had exclaimed to her almost as soon as she appeared; and though her direct response was for some time delayed he could feel in her meanwhile, the working of this truth. It might have been simply, as she waited, that they were now in presence, altogether, of truth spreading like a flood and not, for the moment, to be offered her in the mere cupful; inasmuch as who should *ces dames* prove to be but persons about whom—once thus face to face with them—she found she might from the first have told him almost everything? This would have freely come had he taken the simple precaution of giving her their name. There could be no better example—and she appeared to note it with high amusement—than the way, making things out already so much for himself, he was at last throwing precautions to the winds. They were neither more nor less, she and the child's mother, than old school-friends—friends who had scarcely met for years, but whom this unlooked-for chance had brought together with a rush. It was a relief, Miss Gostrey hinted, to feel herself no longer groping; she was unaccustomed to grope and, as a general thing, he might well have seen, made straight enough for her clue. With the one she had now picked up in her hands there need be at least no waste of wonder. "She's coming to see me—that's for *you*," Strether's interlocutress continued; "but I don't require it to know where I am."

The waste of wonder might be proscribed; but Strether, characteristically, was even by this time in the immensity of space. "By which you mean that you know where *she* is?"

She just hesitated. "I mean that if she comes to see me I shall—now that I've pulled myself round a bit after the shock—not be at home."

Strether hung poised. "You call it—your recognition—a shock?"

She gave one of her rare flickers of impatience. "It was a surprise, an emotion. Don't be so literal. I wash my hands of her."

Poor Strether's face lengthened. "She's impossible—?"

"She's even more charming than I remembered her."

"Then what's the matter?"

She had to think how to put it. "Well, *I'm* impossible. It's impossible. Everything's impossible."

He looked at her an instant. "I see where you're coming out. Everything's possible." Their eyes had, on it, in fact, an exchange of some duration; after which he pursued: "Isn't it that beautiful child?" Then as she still said nothing: "Why don't you mean to receive her?"

Her answer, in an instant, rang clear. "Because I wish to keep out of the business."

It provoked in him a small wail. "You're going to abandon me *now*?"

"No, I'm only going to abandon her. She'll want me to help her with you. And I won't."

"You'll only help me with her? Well then—!" Most of the persons previously gathered had, in the interest of tea, passed into the house, and they had the gardens mainly to themselves. The shadows were long, the last call of the birds, who had made a home of their own in the noble interspaced quarter, sounded from the high trees in the other gardens as well, those of the old convent and of the old *hôtels;* it was as if our friends had waited for the full charm to come out. Strether's impressions were still present; it was as if something had happened that "nailed" them, made them more intense; but he was to ask himself soon afterwards, that evening, what really *had* happened—conscious as he could remain, after all, that, for a gentleman taken, the first time, into the "great" world, the world of ambassadors and duchesses, the items made a meagre total. It was nothing new to him, however, as we know, that a man might have—at all events such a man as *he* was—an amount of experience out of any proportion to his adventures; so that, though it was doubtless no great adventure to sit on there with Miss Gostrey and hear about Mme. de Vionnet, the hour, the picture, the immediate, the recent, the possible—as well as the communication itself, not a note of which failed to reverberate—only gave the moments more of the taste of history.

It was history, to begin with, that Jeanne's mother had been three-and-twenty years before, at Geneva, schoolmate and good girl-friend to Maria Gostrey, who had moreover enjoyed since then, though interruptedly and above all with a long recent drop, other glimpses of her. Twenty-three years put them both on, no doubt; and Mme. de Vionnet—though she had married straight after school—couldn't be to-day an hour less than thirty-eight. This made her ten years older than Chad—though ten years, also, if Strether liked, older than she looked; the least, at any rate, that a prospective mother-in-law could be expected to do with. She would be of all mothers-in-law the most charming; unless, indeed, through some perversity as yet insupposable, she should utterly belie herself in that relation. There was none, surely, in which, as Maria remembered her, she mustn't be charming; and this, frankly, in spite of the stigma of failure in the tie in which failure always most showed. It was no test there—when indeed *was* it a test there?—for M. de Vionnet had been a brute. She had lived for years apart from him—which was of course always a horrid position; but Miss Gostrey's impression of the matter had been that she could scarce have made a better thing of it had she done it on purpose to show that she was amiable. She was so amiable that nobody had had a word to say; which was, luckily, not the case for her husband. He was so impossible that she had the advantage of all her merits.

It was still history for Strether that the Comte de Vionnet—it being also history that the lady in question was a Countess—should now, under Miss Gostrey's sharp touch, rise before him as a high.

distinguished, polished, impertinent reprobate, the product of a mysterious order; it was history, further, that the charming girl so freely sketched by his companion should have been married, out of hand, by a mother, another figure of striking outline, full of dark personal motive; it was perhaps history most of all that this company was, as a matter of course, governed by such considerations as put divorce out of the question. " *Ces gens-là* don't divorce, you know, any more than they emigrate or abjure—they think it impious and vulgar "; a fact in the light of which they seemed but the more richly special. It was all special; it was all, for Strether's imagination, more or less rich. The girl at the Genevese school, an isolated, interesting, attaching creature, both sensitive, then, and violent, audacious but always forgiven, was the daughter of a French father and an English mother who, early left a widow, had married again—tried afresh with a foreigner; in her career with whom she had apparently given her child no example of comfort. All these people—the people of the English mother's side—had been of condition more or less eminent; yet with oddities and disparities that had often since made Maria, thinking them over, wonder what they really quite rhymed to. It was in any case her belief that the mother, interested and prone to adventure, had been without conscience, had only thought of ridding herself most quickly of a possible, an actual encumbrance. The father, by her impression, a Frenchman with a name one knew, had been a different matter, leaving his child, she clearly recalled, a memory all fondness, as well as an assured little fortune which was unluckily, later on, to make her more or less of a prey. She had been in particular, at school, dazzlingly, though quite booklessly, clever; as polyglot as a little Jewess (which she wasn't, oh no!) and chattering French, English, German, Italian, anything one would, in a way that made a clean sweep, if not of prizes and parchments, at least of every "part," whether memorized or improvised, in the curtained, costumed, school repertory, and, in especial, of all mysteries of race and vagueness of reference, all swagger about "home," among their variegated mates.

It would doubtless be difficult to-day, as between French and English, to name her and place her; she would certainly show, on knowledge, Miss Gostrey felt, as one of those convenient types who didn't keep you explaining—minds with doors as numerous as the many-tongued cluster of confessionals at St. Peter's. You might confess to her with confidence in Roumelian, and even Roumelian sins. Therefore—! But Strether's narrator covered her implication with a laugh; a laugh by which his betrayal of a sense of the lurid in the picture was also perhaps sufficiently protected. He had a moment of wondering, while his friend went on, what sins might be especially Roumelian. She went on, at all events, to the mention of her having met the young thing—again by some Swiss lake —in her first married state, which had appeared for the few intermediate years not at least violently disturbed. She had been lovely at that moment, delightful to *her,* full of responsive emotion, of amused recognitions and amusing reminders; and then, once more, much later, after a long interval, equally but differently charming —touching and rather mystifying for the five minutes of an encounter at a railway station *en province,* during which it had come out that her life was all changed. Miss Gostrey had understood enough to see, essentially, what had happened, and yet had beautifully dreamed that she was herself faultless. There were doubtless depths in her, but she was all right; Strether would see if she wasn't. She was another person, however—that had been promptly marked—from the small child of nature at the Geneva school; a little person quite made over—as foreign women *were,* compared with American—by marriage. Her situation moreover, evidently, had cleared itself up; there would have been—all that was possible—a judicial separation. She had settled in Paris, brought up her daughter, steered her boat. It was no very pleasant boat— especially there—to be in; but Marie de Vionnet would have headed straight. She would have friends, certainly—and very good ones. There she was, at all events—and it was very interesting. Her knowing Mr. Chad didn't in the least prove she hadn't friends; what it proved was what good ones *he* had. "I saw that," said Miss Gostrey, "that night at the Français; it came out for me in three minutes. I saw *her*—or somebody like her. And so," she immediately added, "did you."

"Oh no—not anybody like her!" Strether laughed. "But you mean," he as promptly went on, "that she has had such an influence on him?"

Miss Gostrey was on her feet; it was time for them to go. "She has brought him up for her daughter."

Their eyes, as so often, in candid conference, through their settled glasses, met over it long; after which Strether's again took in the whole place. They were quite alone there now. "Mustn't she rather—in the time then—have rushed it?"

"Ah, she won't of course have lost an hour. But that's just the good mother—the good French one. You must remember that of her—that, as a mother, she's French; and that for them there's a special providence. It precisely, however—that she may not have been able to begin as far back as she would have liked—makes her grateful for aid."

Strether took this in as they slowly moved to the house on their way out. "She counts on me then to put the thing through?"

"Yes—she counts on you. Oh, and first of all of course," Miss Gostrey added, "on her—well, convincing you."

"Ah," her friend returned, "she caught Chad young!"

"Yes, but there are women who are for all your 'times of life.' They're the most wonderful sort."

She had laughed the words out, but they brought her companion, the next thing, to a stand. "Is what you mean that she'll try to make a fool of me?"

"Well, I'm wondering what she *will*—with an opportunity—make."

"What do you call," Strether asked, "an opportunity? My going to see her?"

"Ah, you must go to see her"—Miss Gostrey was a trifle evasive. "You can't do that. You'd have gone to see the other woman. I mean if there had been one—a different sort. It's what you came out for."

It might be; but Strether distinguished. "I didn't come out to see *this* sort."

She had a wonderful look at him now. "Are you disappointed she isn't worse?"

He for a moment entertained the question, then found for it the frankest of answers. "Yes. If she were worse she would be better for our purpose. It would be simpler."

"Perhaps," she admitted. "But won't this be pleasanter?"

160

"Ah, you know," he promptly replied, " I didn't come out—wasn't that just what you originally reproached me with?—for the pleasant."

"Precisely. Therefore I say again what I said at first. You must take things as they come. Besides," Miss Gostrey added, " I'm not afraid for myself."

"For yourself—?"

"Of your seeing her. I trust her. There's nothing she'll say about me. In fact there's nothing she *can*."

Strether wondered—little as he had thought of this. Then he broke out. " Oh, you women!"

There was something in it at which she flushed. " Yes—there we are. We're abysses." At last she smiled. " But I risk her!"

He gave himself a shake. " Well then, so do I!" But he added as they passed into the house that he would see Chad the first thing in the morning.

This was, the next day, the more easily effected that the young man, as it happened, even before he was down, turned up at his hotel. Strether took his coffee, by habit, in the public room; but on his descending for this purpose Chad instantly proposed an adjournment to what he called greater privacy. He had himself, as yet, had nothing—they would sit down somewhere together; and, when, after a few steps and a turn into the boulevard, they had, for their greater privacy, sat down among twenty others, our friend saw in his companion's move a fear of the advent of Waymarsh. It was the first time Chad had, to that extent, given this personage " away "; and Strether found himself wondering of what it was symptomatic. He made out in a moment that the youth was in earnest as he had not yet seen him; which, in its turn, threw a ray perhaps a trifle startling on what they had each, up to that time, been treating as earnestness. It was sufficiently flattering, however, that the real thing—if this *was* at last the real thing—should have been determined, as appeared, precisely by an accretion of Strether's importance. For this was what, quickly enough, it came to—that Chad, rising with the lark, had rushed down to let him know, while his morning consciousness was yet young, that he had made, literally, the afternoon before, a tremendous impression. Mme. de Vionnet wouldn't, couldn't rest till she should have some assurance from him that he *would* consent again to see her. The announcement was made, across their marble-topped table, while the foam of the hot milk was in their cups and its plash still in the air, with the smile of Chad's easiest urbanity; and this expression of his face caused our friend's doubts to gather, on the spot, into a challenge of the lips. " See here "—that was all; he only, for the moment, said again " See here." Chad met it with all his air of straight intelligence, while Strether remembered again that fancy of the first impression of him, the happy young pagan, handsome and hard, but indulgent, whose mysterious measure, under the street-lamp, he had tried mentally to take. The young pagan, while a long look passed between them, sufficiently understood. Strether scarce needed at last to say the rest—" I want to know where I am." But he said it, and he added, before any answer, something more. " Are you engaged to be married—is that your secret?—to the young lady ?"

Chad shook his head with the slow amenity that was one of his ways of conveying that there was time for everything. " I have no secret—though I may have secrets! I haven't at any rate that one. We're not engaged. No."

" Then where's the hitch ?"

" Do you mean why I haven't already started with you ?" Chad, beginning his coffee and buttering his roll, was quite ready to explain. " Nothing would have induced me—nothing will still induce me—not to try to keep you here as long as you can be made to stay. It's too visibly good for you." Strether had himself plenty to say about this, but it was amusing also to measure the march of Chad's tone. He had never been more a man of the world, and it was always, in his company, present to our friend that one was seeing how, in successive connections, a man of the world acquitted himself. Chad kept it up beautifully. " My idea—*voyons!*—is simply that you should let Mme. de Vionnet know you, simply that you should consent to know *her*. I don't in the least mind telling you that, clever and charming as she is, she's ever so much in my confidence. All I ask of you is to let her talk to you. You've asked me about what you call my hitch, and so far as it goes she'll explain it to you. She's herself my hitch, hang it—if you must really have it all out. But in a sense," he hastened in the most wonderful manner to add, "that you'll quite make out for yourself. She's too good a friend, confound her. Too good, I mean, for me to leave without—without—" It was his first hesitation.

"Without what?"

"Well, without my arranging somehow or other the damnable terms of my sacrifice."

"It *will* be a sacrifice then?"

"It will be the greatest loss I ever suffered. I owe her so much."

It was beautiful, the way Chad said these things, and his plea was now confessedly—oh, quite flagrantly and publicly—interesting. The moment really, for Strether, took on an intensity. Chad owed Mme. de Vionnet so much? What *did* that do then but clear up the whole mystery? He was indebted for alterations, and she was thereby in a position to have sent in her bill for expenses incurred in reconstruction. What was this, at bottom, but what had been to be arrived at? Strether sat there arriving at it while he munched toast and stirred his second cup. To do this, with the aid of Chad's pleasant, earnest face, was also to do more besides. No, never before had he been so ready to take him as he was. What was it that had suddenly so cleared up? It was just everybody's character—that is, everybody's but, in a measure, his own. Strether felt *his* character receive, for the instant, a smutch from all the wrong things he had suspected or believed. The person to whom Chad owed it that he could positively turn out such a comfort to other persons—such a person was sufficiently raised above any " breath " by the nature of her work and the young man's steady light. All of which was vivid enough to come and go quickly; though indeed in the midst of it Strether could utter a question. " Have I your word of honor that if I surrender myself to Mme. de Vionnet you'll surrender yourself to *me?*"

Chad laid his hand firmly on his friend's. " My dear man, you have it."

There was finally something in his felicity almost embarrassing and oppressive; Strether had begun to fidget, under it, for the open air and the erect posture. He had signed to the waiter that he wished to pay, and this transaction took some moments, during which he thoroughly felt, while he put down money and pretended

—it was quite hollow—to estimate change, that Chad's higher spirit, his youth, his practice, his paganism, his felicity, his assurance, his impudence, whatever it might be, had consciously scored a success. Well, that was all right, so far as it went; his sense of the thing in question covered our friend for a minute like a veil, through which—as if he had been muffled—he heard his interlocutor ask him if he mightn't take him over about five. "Over" was over the river, and over the river was where Mme. de Vionnet lived, and five was that very afternoon. They got at last out of the place—got out before he answered. He lighted, in the street, a cigarette, which again gave him more time. But it was already sharp for him that there was no use in time. "What does she propose to do to me?" he had presently demanded.

Chad had no delays. "Are you afraid of her?"

"Oh, immensely. Don't you see it?"

"Well," said Chad, "she won't do anything worse to you than make you like her."

"It's just of that I'm afraid."

"Then it's not fair to me."

Strether hesitated. "It's fair to your mother."

"Oh," said Chad, "are you afraid of *her*?"

"Scarcely less. Or perhaps even more. But is this lady against your interests at home?" Strether went on.

"Not directly, no doubt; but she's greatly in favor of them here."

"And what—'here'—does she consider them to be?"

"Well, good relations!"

"With herself?"

"With herself."

"And what is it that makes them so good?"

"What? Well, that's exactly what you'll make out if you'll only go, as I'm supplicating you, to see her."

Strether stared at him with a little of the wanness, no doubt, that the vision of more to "make out" could scarce help producing. I mean *how* good are they?"

"Oh, awfully good."

Again Strether had faltered, but it was brief. It was all very well, but there was nothing now he wouldn't risk. "Excuse me, but I must really—as I began by telling you—know where I am. Is she bad?"

" ' Bad '?"—Chad echoed it, but without a shock. "Is that what's implied—?"

" When relations are good?" Strether felt a little silly, and was even conscious of a foolish laugh, at having it imposed on him to have appeared to speak so. What indeed was he talking about? His stare had relaxed; he looked now all round him. But something in him brought him back, though he still didn't know quite how to turn it. The two or three ways he thought of, and one of them in particular, were, even with scruples dismissed, too ugly. He none the less at last found something. " Is her life without reproach?"

It struck him, directly he had found it, as pompous and priggish; so much so that he was thankful to Chad for taking it only in the right spirit. The young man spoke so immensely to the point that the effect was practically of positive blandness. " Absolutely without reproach. A beautiful life. *Allez donc voir!*" These last words were, in the liberality of their confidence, so imperative that Strether went through no form of assent; but before they separated it had been confirmed that he should be picked up at a quarter to **five.**

PART SIXTH

XIII

It was quite by half-past five—after the two men had been together in Mme. de Vionnet's drawing-room not more than a dozen minutes—that Chad, with a look at his watch and then another at their hostess, said genially, gayly: " I've an engagement, and I know you won't complain if I leave him with you. He'll interest you immensely; and as for her," he declared to Strether, " I assure you, if you're at all nervous, she's perfectly safe."

He had left them to be embarrassed or not by this guarantee, as they could best manage, and embarrassment was a thing that Strether was at first not sure Mme. de Vionnet escaped. He escaped it himself, to his surprise; but he had grown used by this time to thinking of himself as brazen. She occupied, his hostess, in the Rue de Bellechasse, the first floor of an old house to which our visitors had had access from an old clean court. The court was large and open, full of revelations, for our friend, of the habit of privacy, the peace of intervals, the dignity of distances and approaches; the house, to his restless sense, was in the high, homely style of an elder day, and the ancient Paris that he was always looking for — sometimes intensely felt, sometimes more acutely missed—was in the immemorial polish of the wide waxed staircase and in the fine *boiseries,* the medallions, mouldings, mirrors, great clear spaces, of the grayish-white salon into which he had been shown. He seemed to see her, at the outset, in the midst of possessions not vulgarly numerous, but hereditary, cherished, charming. While his eyes, after a little, turned from those of his hostess and Chad freely talked—not in the least about *him,* but about other people, people he didn't know, and quite as if he did know them—he found himself making out, as a background of the occupant, some glory, some prosperity of the first Empire, some Napoleonic glamour, some dim lustre of the great legend; elements clinging still to all the consular chairs and mythological brasses and sphinxes' heads and faded surfaces of satin striped with alternate silk.

The place itself went further back—that he guessed, and how old Paris continued, in a manner, to echo there; but the post-revolutionary period, the world he vaguely thought of as the world of Chateaubriand, of Mme. de Staël, of the young Lamartine, had left its stamp of harps and urns and torches, a stamp impressed on sundry small objects, ornaments and relics. He had never before, to his knowledge, been in the presence of relics, of any special dignity, of a private order—little old miniatures, medallions, pictures, books; books in leather bindings, pinkish and greenish, with gilt garlands on the back, ranged, together with other promiscuous properties, under the glass of brass-mounted cabinets. His attention took them all tenderly into account. They were among the matters that marked Mme. de Vionnet's apartment as something quite different from Miss Gostrey's little museum of bargains and from Chad's lovely home; he recognized it as founded much more on old accumulations that had possibly from time to time shrunken than on any contemporary method of acquisition or form of curiosity. Chad and Miss Gostrey had rummaged and purchased and picked up and exchanged, sifting, selecting, comparing; whereas the mistress of the scene before him, beautifully passive under the spell of transmission—transmission from her father's line, he quite made up his mind—had only received, accepted and been quiet. When she had not been quiet, at least, she had been moved, at the most, to some occult charity for some fallen fortune. There had been objects she or her predecessors might even conceivably, on occasion, needfully have parted with; but Strether couldn't suspect them of having sold old pieces to get " better " ones. They would have felt no difference as to better or worse. He could but imagine their having felt—perhaps in emigration, in proscription, for his sketch was slight and confused—the pressure of want or the obligation of sacrifice.

The pressure of want—whatever might be the case with the other force—was, however, presumably not active now, for the tokens of a chastened ease, after all, still abounded, many marks of a taste whose discriminations might perhaps have been called eccentric. He guessed at intense little preferences and sharp little exclusions, a deep suspicion of the vulgar and a personal view of the right. The general result of this was something for which he had no name, on the spot, quite ready, but something he would have come nearest to naming in speaking of it as the air of supreme respectability, the consciousness, small, still, reserved, but none the less distinct and diffused, of private honor. The air of supreme respectability—that was a strange blank wall for his adventure to have brought him to break his nose against. It had in fact, as he was now aware, filled all the approaches, hovered in the court as he passed, hung on the staircase as he mounted, sounded in the grave rumble of the old bell, as little electric as possible, of which Chad, at the door, had pulled the ancient but neatly-kept tassel; it formed, in short, the clearest medium of its particular kind that he had ever breathed. He would have answered for it at the end of a quarter of an hour that some of the glass cases contained swords and epaulettes of ancient colonels and generals; medals and orders once pinned over hearts that had long since ceased to beat; snuff-boxes bestowed on ministers and envoys; copies of works presented, with inscriptions, by authors now classic. At bottom of it all, for him, was the sense of her rare unlikeness to the women he had known. This sense had grown, since the day before, the more he recalled her, and had been above all singularly fed by his talk with Chad in the morning. Everything, in fine, made her immeasurably new, and nothing so new as the old house and the old objects. There were books, two or three, on a small table near his chair, but they had not the lemon-colored covers with which his eye had begun to dally from the hour of his arrival and to the opportunity of a further acquaintance with which he had, for a fortnight now, altogether succumbed. On another table, across the room, he made out the great *Revue;* but even that familiar face, conspicuous in Mrs. Newsome's parlors, scarce counted here as a modern note. He was sure, on the spot—and he afterwards knew he was right—that this was a touch of Chad's own hand. What would Mrs. Newsome say to the circumstance that Chad's interested " influence " kept her paper-knife in the *Revue?* The interested influence, at any rate, had, as we say, gone straight to the point— had in fact soon left it quite behind.

She was seated, near the fire, on a small stuffed and fringed chair, one of the few modern articles in the room; and she leaned back in it with her hands clasped in her lap and no movement, in all her person, but the fine, prompt play of her deep young face. The fire, under the low white marble, undraped and academic, had burnt down to the silver ashes of light wood; one of the windows, at a distance, stood open to the mildness and stillness, out of which, in the short pauses, came the faint sound, pleasant and homely, almost rustic, of a plash and a clatter of *sabots* from some coach-house on the other side of the court. Mme. de Vionnet, while Strether sat there, was not to shift her posture by an inch. "I don't think you seriously believe in what you're doing," she said; "but all the same, you know, I'm going to treat you quite as if I did."

"By which you mean," Strether directly replied, "quite as if you didn't! I assure you it won't make the least difference with me how you treat me."

"Well," she said, taking that menace bravely and philosophically enough, "the only thing that really matters is that you shall get on with me."

"Ah, but I don't!" he immediately returned.

It gave her another pause; which, however, she happily enough shook off. "Will you consent to go on with me a little—provisionally—as if you did?"

Then it was that he saw how she had, decidedly, come all the way; and there accompanied it an extraordinary sense of her raising from somewhere below him her beautiful suppliant eyes. He might have been perched at his door-step or at his window, and she standing in the road. For a moment he let her stand, and he couldn't, moreover, have spoken. It had been sad, of a sudden, with a sadness that was like a cold breath in his face. "What can I do," he finally asked, "but listen to you as I promised Chadwick?"

"Ah, but what I'm asking you," she quickly said, "is not what Mr. Newsome had in mind." She spoke at present, he saw, as if to take courageously *all* her risk. "This is my own idea and a different thing."

It gave poor Strether, in truth—uneasy as it made him too—something of the thrill of a bold perception justified. "Well," he answered kindly enough, "I was sure a moment since that some idea of your own had come to you."

She seemed still to look up at him, but now more serenely. "I made out you were sure—and that helped it to come. So, you see," she continued, "we do get on."

"Oh, but it appears to me I don't at all meet your request. How can I when I don't understand it?"

"It isn't at all necessary you should understand; it will do quite well enough if you simply remember him. Only feel I trust you—and for nothing so tremendous after all. Just," she said with a wonderful smile, "for common civility."

Strether had a long pause while they sat again face to face, as they had sat, scarce less conscious, before the poor lady had crossed the stream. She was the poor lady for Strether now because, clearly, she had some trouble, and her appeal to him could only mean that her trouble was deep. He couldn't help it; it was not his fault; he had done nothing; but by a turn of the hand she had somehow made their encounter a relation. And the relation profited by a mass of things that were not, strictly, in it or of it; by the very air in which they sat, by the high, cold, delicate room, by the world outside and the little plash in the court, by the first Empire and the relics in the stiff cabinets, by matters as far off as those and by others as near as the unbroken clasp of her hands in her lap and the look her expression had of being most natural when her eyes were most fixed. "You count upon me of course for something really much greater than it sounds."

"Oh, it sounds great enough too!" she laughed at this.

He found himself, in time, on the point of telling her that she was, as Miss Barrace called it, wonderful; but, catching himself up, he said something else instead. "What was it Chad's idea then that you should say to me?"

"Ah, his idea was simply what a man's idea always is—to put every effort off on the woman."

"The 'woman'—?" Strether slowly echoed.

"The woman he likes—and just in proportion as he likes her. In proportion too—for shifting the trouble—as she likes *him*."

Strether followed it; then with an abruptness of his own: "How much do you like Chad?"

"Just as much as *that*—to take all, with you, on myself." But she got, more quickly, away from this. "I've been trembling as if we were to stand or fall by what you may think of me; and I'm even now," she went on wonderfully, "drawing a long breath—and, yes, truly, taking a great courage—from the hope that I don't, in fact, strike you as impossible."

"That's at all events, clearly," he observed after an instant, "the way I don't strike *you*."

"Well," she so far assented, "as you haven't yet said you *won't* have, with me, the little patience I ask for—"

"You draw splendid conclusions? Perfectly. But I don't understand them," Strether pursued. "You seem to me to ask for much more than you need. What, at the worst for you, what at the best for myself, can I, after all, do? I can use no pressure that I haven't used. You come, really, late with your request. I've already done all that, for myself, the case admits of. I've said my say, and here I am."

"Yes, here you are, fortunately!" Mme. de Vionnet laughed. "Mrs. Newsome," she added in another tone, "didn't think you can do so little."

He had an hesitation, but he brought the words out. "Well, she thinks so now."

"Do you mean by that—?" But she also hung fire.

"Do I mean what?"

She still rather faltered. "Pardon me if I touch on it, but if I am saying extraordinary things, why, perhaps, mayn't I? Besides, doesn't it properly concern us to know?"

"To know what?" he insisted, as, after thus beating about the bush, she had again dropped.

She made the effort. "Has she given you up?"

He was amazed afterwards to think how simply and quietly he had met it. "Not yet." It was almost as if he were a trifle disappointed—had expected still more of her freedom. But he went straight on. "Is that what Chad has told you will happen to me?"

She was evidently charmed with the way he took it. "If you mean if we've talked of it—most certainly. And the question is not what has had least to do with my wishing to see you."

"To judge if I'm the sort of man a woman *can*—?"

"Precisely," she exclaimed—"you wonderful gentleman! I do

174

judge—I *have* judged. A woman can't. You're safe—with every right to be. You'd be much happier if you'd only believe it."

Strether was silent a little; then he found himself speaking with a cynicism of confidence of which, even at the moment, the sources were strange to him. "I try to believe it. But it's a marvel," he exclaimed, "how *you* already get at it!"

Oh, she was able to say. "Remember how much I was, through Mr. Newsome—before I saw you—on the way to it. He thinks everything of your strength."

"Well, I can bear almost anything!" our friend briskly interrupted. Deep and beautiful, on this, her smile came back, and with the effect of making him hear what he had said just as she had heard it. He easily enough felt that it gave him away, but what, in truth, had everything done but that? It had been all very well to think at moments that he was holding her nose down and that he had coerced her; what had he, by this time, done but let her see, practically, that he accepted their relation? What was their relation, moreover—though light and brief enough in form as yet—but whatever she might choose to make it? Nothing could prevent her—certainly he couldn't—from making it pleasant. At the back of his head, behind everything, was the sense that she was—there, before him, close to him, in vivid, imperative form—one of the rare women he had so often heard of, read of, thought of, but never met, whose very presence, look, voice, the mere contemporaneous *fact* of whom, from the moment it was at all presented, made a relation of mere recognition. That was not the kind of woman he had ever found Mrs. Newsome, a contemporaneous fact who had been distinctly slow to establish herself; and at present, confronted with Mme. de Vionnet, he felt the simplicity of his original impression of Miss Gostrey. She, certainly, had been a fact of rapid growth; but the world was wide, each day was more and more a new lesson. There were, at any rate, even among the stranger ones, relations and relations. "Of course I suit Chad's grand way," he quickly added. "He hasn't had much difficulty in working me in."

She seemed to deny a little, on the young man's behalf, by the rise of her eyebrows, an intention of any process at all inconsiderate. "You must know how grieved he would be if you were to lose anything. He believes you can keep his mother patient."

Strether wondered, with his eyes on her. "I see. *That's* then what you really want of me. And how am I to do it? Perhaps you'll tell me that."

"Simply tell her the truth."

"And what do you call the truth?"

"Well, *any* truth—about us all—that you see yourself. I leave it to you."

"Thank you very much. I like," Strether laughed with a slight harshness, "the way you leave things!"

But she insisted kindly, gently, as if it wasn't so bad. "Be perfectly honest. Tell her all."

"All?" he oddly echoed.

"Tell her the simple truth," Mme. de Vionnet developed in the same tone.

"But what *is* the simple truth? The simple truth is exactly what I'm trying to discover."

Mme. de Vionnet looked about a while, but presently she came back to him. "Tell her, fully and clearly, about *us*."

Strether meanwhile had been staring. "You and your daughter?"

"Yes—little Jeanne and me. Tell her," she just slightly quavered, "you like us."

"And what good will that do me? Or rather"—he caught himself up—"what good will it do *you*?"

She looked graver. "None, you believe, really?"

Strether hesitated. "She didn't send me out to 'like' you."

"Oh," she charmingly remonstrated, "she sent you out to face the facts."

He admitted after an instant that there was something in that. "But how can I face them till I know what they are? Do you want him," he then braced himself to ask, "to marry your daughter?"

She gave a head-shake as noble as it was prompt. "No—not that."

"And he really doesn't want to himself?"

She repeated the movement, but now with a strange light in her face. "He likes her too much."

Strether wondered. "To be willing to consider, you mean, the question of taking her to America?"

"To be willing to do anything with her but be immensely kind and nice—really tender of her. We watch over her, and you must help us. You must see her again."

Strether felt awkward. "Ah, with pleasure—she's so remarkably attractive."

The mother's eagerness with which Mme. de Vionnet jumped at this was to come back to him later as beautiful in its grace. "The dear thing *did* please you?" Then as he met it with the largest "Oh!" of enthusiasm: "She's perfect. She's my joy."

"Well, I'm sure that—if one were near her and saw more of her—she would be mine."

"Then," said Mme. de Vionnet, "tell Mrs. Newsome that!"

He wondered the more. "What good will that do you?" As she only hesitated, however, he brought out something else. "Is your daughter in love with our friend?"

"Ah," she rather startlingly answered, "I wish you'd find out!"

He showed his surprise. "I? A stranger?"

"Oh, you won't be a stranger—presently. You shall see her quite, I assure you, as if you weren't."

It remained for him, none the less, an extraordinary notion. "It seems to me, surely, that if her mother can't—"

"Ah, little girls and their mothers to-day!" she rather inconsequently broke in. But she checked herself with something that she seemed to give out as, after all, more to the point. "Tell her I've been good for him. Don't you think I have?"

It had its effect on him—more than, at the moment, he quite measured. Yet he was consciously enough touched. "Oh, if it's all *you*—!"

"Well, it may not be 'all,'" she interrupted, "but it's to a great extent. Really and truly," she added in a tone that was to take its place with him among things remembered.

"Then it's very wonderful." He smiled at her from a face that he felt as strained, and her own face for a moment kept him so. At last she also got up. "Well, don't you think that for that—"

"I ought to save you?" So it was that the way to meet her— and the way, as well, in a manner, to get off—came over him. He heard himself use the exorbitant word, the very sound of which helped to determine his flight. "I'll save you if I can."

XIV

In Chad's lovely home, however, one evening ten days later, he felt himself present at the collapse of the question of Jeanne de Vionnet's shy secret. He had been dining there in the company of that young lady and her mother, as well as of other persons, and he had gone into the *petit salon,* at Chad's request, on purpose to talk with her. The young man had put this to him as a favor— " I should like so awfully to know what you think of her. It will really be a chance for you," he had said, " to see the *jeune fille*— I mean the type—as she actually is, and I don't think that, as an observer of manners, it's a thing you ought to miss. It will be an impression that—whatever else you take—you can carry home with you, where you'll find again so much to compare it with."

Strether knew well enough with what Chad wished him to compare it, and though he entirely assented, he had not yet, somehow, been so deeply reminded that he was being, as he constantly though mutely expressed it, used. He was as far as ever from making out exactly to what end; but he was none the less constantly accompanied by a sense of the service he rendered. He conceived, only, that this service was highly agreeable to those who profited by it; and he was indeed still waiting for the moment at which he should catch it in the act of proving disagreeable, proving in some degree intolerable, to himself. He failed quite to see how his situation could clear up at all logically except by some turn of events that would give him the pretext of disgust. He was building from day to day on the possibility of disgust, but each day brought forth meanwhile a new and more engaging bend of the road. That possibility was now ever so much further from sight than on the eve of his arrival, and he perfectly felt that, should it come at all, it would have to be at best inconsequent and violent. He struck himself as a little nearer to it only when he asked himself what service, in such a life of utility, he was, after all, rendering Mrs. Newsome. When he wished to help himself to believe that he was still all right he reflected—and in fact with wonder—on the unimpaired frequency of their correspondence; in relation to which what was, after all, more natural than that it should become more frequent just in proportion as their problem became more com plicated?

Certain it is, at any rate, that he now often brought himself balm by the question, with the rich consciousness of yesterday's letter: "Well, what can I do more than that—what can I do more than tell her everything!" To persuade himself that he did tell her, had told her, everything, he used to try to think of particular things he had not told her. When at rare moments, and in the watches of the night he pounced on one it generally showed itself to be—to a deeper scrutiny—not quite truly of the essence. When anything new struck him as coming up, or anything already noted as reappearing, he always immediately wrote, as if for fear that if he didn't he would miss something; and also that he might be able to say to himself from time to time, " She knows it *now,* even while I worry." It was a great comfort to him, in general, not to have left past things to be dragged to light and explained; not to have to produce at so late a stage anything not produced, or anything even veiled and attenuated, at the moment. She knew it now: that was what he said to himself to-night in relation to the fresh fact of Chad's acquaintance with the two ladies—not to speak of the fresher one of his own. Mrs. Newsome knew, in other words, that very night at Woollett, that he himself knew Mme. de Vionnet, and that he had been, conscientiously, to see her; also that he had found her remarkably attractive and that there would probably be a good deal more to tell. But she further knew—or would know very soon — that, again conscientiously, he had not repeated his visit; and that when Chad had asked him on the Countess's behalf—Strether made her out vividly, with a thought at the back of his head, a Countess—if he wouldn't name a day for dining with her, he had replied lucidly: " Thank you very much—impossible." He had begged the young man would present his excuses, and had trusted him to understand that it couldn't really strike one as quite the straight thing. He had not reported to Mrs. Newsome that he had promised to "save" Mme. de Vionnet; but, so far as he was concerned with that reminiscence, he hadn't, at any rate, promised to haunt her house. What Chad had understood could only, in truth, be inferred from Chad's behavior, which had been in this connection as easy as in every other. He was easy, always, when he understood; he was easier still, if possible, when he didn't; he had replied that he would make it all right; and he had proceeded to do this by substituting the present occasion—as he was ready to substitute others—for any, for every occasion as to which his old friend should have a funny scruple.

"Oh, but I'm not a little foreign girl; I'm just as English as I can be," Jeanne de Vionnet had said to him as soon as, in the *petit salon,* he sank, shyly enough on his own side, into the place near her vacated by Mme. Gloriani at his approach. Mme. Gloriani, who was in black velvet, with white lace and powdered hair, and whose somewhat massive majesty melted, at any contact, into the graciousness of some incomprehensible tongue, moved away to make room for the vague gentleman, after benevolent greetings to him which embodied, as he believed, in baffling accents, some recognition of his face from a couple of Sundays before. Then he had remarked—making the most of the advantage of his years—that it frightened him quite enough to find himself dedicated to the entertainment of a little foreign girl. There were girls he wasn't afraid of—he was quite bold with little Americans. Thus it was that she had defended herself to the end—"Oh, but I'm almost American too. That's what mamma has wanted me to be—I mean *like* that; for she has wanted me to have lots of freedom. She has known such good results from it."

She was fairly beautiful to him—a faint pastel in an oval frame: he thought of her already as of some lurking image in a long gallery, the portrait of a small old-time princess of whom nothing was known but that she had died young. Little Jeanne wasn't, doubtless, to die young, but one couldn't, all the same, bear on her lightly enough. It was bearing hard, it was bearing as *he,* in any case, wouldn't bear, to concern himself, in relation to her, with the question of a young man. Odious, really, the question of a young man; one didn't treat such a person as a maidservant suspected of a "follower." And then young men, young men—well, the thing

180

was their business simply, or was, at all events, hers. She was fluttered, fairly fevered—to the point of a little glitter that came and went in her eyes and a pair of pink spots that stayed in her cheeks—with the great adventure of dining out and with the greater one still, possibly, of finding a gentleman whom she must think of as very, very old, a gentleman with eye-glasses, wrinkles, a long, grizzled mustache. She spoke the prettiest English, our friend thought, that he had ever heard spoken, just as he had believed her a few minutes before to be speaking the prettiest French. He wondered almost wistfully if such a sweep of the lyre didn't react on the spirit itself; and his fancy had, in fact, before he knew it, begun so to stray and embroider that he finally found himself, absent and extravagant, sitting with the child in a friendly silence. Only, by this time, he felt that her flutter had fortunately dropped and that she was more at her ease. She trusted him, liked him, and it was to come back to him afterwards that she had told him things. She had dipped into the waiting medium at last and found neither surge nor chill—nothing but the small splash she could herself make in the pleasant warmth, nothing but the safety of dipping and dipping again. At the end of the ten minutes he was to spend with her his impression—with all it had thrown off and all it had taken in—was complete. She had been free, as she knew freedom, partly to show him that, unlike other little persons she knew, she had imbibed that ideal. She was delightfully quaint about herself, but the vision of what she had imbibed was what most held him. It really consisted, he was soon enough to feel, in just one great little matter, the fact that, whatever her nature, she was thoroughly—he had to cast about for the word, but it came —bred. He couldn't of course, on so short an acquaintance, speak for her nature, but the idea of breeding was what she had meanwhile dropped into his mind. He had never yet known it so sharply presented. Her mother gave it, no doubt; but her mother, to make that less sensible, gave so much else besides, and on neither of the two previous occasions, extraordinary woman, Strether felt, anything like what she was giving to-night. Little Jeanne was a case, an exquisite case of education; whereas the Countess, whom it so amused him to think of by that denomination, was a case, also exquisite, of—well, he didn't know what.

"He has wonderful taste, *notre jeune homme*": this was what Gloriani said to him on turning away from the inspection of a small picture suspended near the door of the room. The high celebrity in question had just come in, apparently in search of Mlle. de Vionnet, but while Strether had got up from beside her their fellow-guest, with his eye sharply caught, had paused for a long look. The thing was a landscape, of no size, but of the French school, as our friend was glad to feel he knew, and also of a quality—which he liked to think he should have also guessed; its frame was large out of proportion to the canvas, and he had never seen a person look at anything, he thought, just as Gloriani, with his nose very near and quick movements of the head from side to side and bottom to top, examined this feature of Chad's collection. The artist used that word the next moment, smiling courteously, wiping his nippers and looking round him further—paying the place, in short, by the very manner of his presence and by something Strether fancied he could make out in this particular glance, such a tribute as, to the latter's sense, settled many things once for all. Strether was conscious at this instant, for that matter, as he had not yet been, of how, round about him, quite without him, they *were* consistently settled. Gloriani's smile, deeply Italian, he considered, and finely inscrutable, had had for him, during dinner, at which they were not neighbors, an indefinite greeting; but the quality in it was gone that had appeared on the other occasion to turn him inside out; it was as if even the momentary link supplied by the doubt between them had snapped. He was conscious now of the final reality, which was that there was not so much a doubt as a difference altogether; all the more that over the difference the famous sculptor seemed to signal almost condolingly, yet oh how vacantly! as across some great flat sheet of water. He threw out the bridge of a charming hollow civility on which Strether wouldn't have trusted his own full weight a moment. That idea, even though but transient and perhaps belated, had performed the office of putting Strether more at his ease, and the blurred picture had already dropped—dropped with the sound of something else said and with his becoming aware, by another quick turn, that Gloriani was now on the sofa talking with Jeanne, while he himself had in his ears again the familiar friendliness and the elusive meaning of the " Oh, oh, oh!" that had made him, a fortnight before, challenge Miss Barrace in vain. She had always the air, this picturesque and original lady, who struck him, so oddly, as both antique and modern—she had always the air of taking up some joke that one had already had out with her. The point itself, no doubt, was what was antique, and the use she made of it what was modern. He felt just now that her good-natured irony did bear on something, and it troubled him a little that she wouldn't be more explicit, only assuring him, with the pleasure of observation so visible in her, that she wouldn't tell him more for the world. He could take refuge but in asking her what she had done with Waymarsh, though it must be added that he felt himself a little on the way to a clue after she had answered that this personage was, in the other room, engaged in conversation with Mme. de Vionnet. He stared a moment at the image of such a conjunction; then, for Miss Barrace's benefit, he wondered. "Is she too then under the charm—?"

"No, not a bit"—Miss Barrace was prompt. "She makes nothing of him; she's bored; she won't help you with him."

"Oh," Strether laughed, "she can't do everything."

"Of course not—wonderful as she is. Besides, he makes nothing of *her*. She won't take him from me—though she wouldn't, no doubt, having other affairs in hand, even if she could. I've never," said Miss Barrace, "seen her fail with any one before. And to-night, when she's so magnificent, it would seem to her strange—if she minded. So, at any rate, I have him all. *Je suis tranquille!*"

Strether understood, so far as that went; but he was feeling for his clue. "She strikes you to-night as particularly magnificent?"

"Surely. Almost as I've never seen her. Doesn't she you? Why, it's *for* you."

He persisted in his candor. "'For' me—?"

"Oh, oh, oh!" cried Miss Barrace, who persisted in the opposite of that quality.

"Well," he acutely admitted, "she *is* different. She's gay."

"She's gay!" Miss Barrace laughed. "And she has beautiful shoulders—though there's nothing different in that."

"No," said Strether, "one was sure of her shoulders. It isn't her shoulders."

His companion, with renewed mirth and the finest sense, between the puffs of her cigarette, of the drollery of things, appeared to find their conversation highly delightful. " Yes, it isn't her shoulders."

" What then is it?" Strether earnestly inquired.

" Why, it's *she*—simply. It's her mood. It's her charm."

" Of course it's her charm, but we're speaking of the difference."

" Well," Miss Barrace explained, " she's just brilliant, as we used to say. That's all. She's various. She's fifty women."

" Ah, but only one "—Strether kept it clear—" at a time."

" Perhaps. But in fifty times—!"

" Oh, we sha'n't come to that," our friend declared; and the next moment he had moved in another direction. " Will you answer me a plain question? Will she ever divorce?"

Miss Barrace looked at him through all her tortoise-shell. " Why should she?"

It was not what he had asked for, he signified; but he met it well enough. " To marry Chad."

" Why should she marry Chad?"

" Because I'm convinced she's very fond of him. She has done wonders for him."

" Well then, how could she do more? Marrying a man, or a woman either," Miss Barrace sagely went on, " is never the wonder, for any Jack and Jill can bring *that* off. The wonder is their doing such things without marrying."

Strether considered a moment this proposition. " You mean it's so beautiful for our friends simply to go on so?"

But whatever he said made her laugh. " Beautiful."

He nevertheless insisted. " And *that* because it's disinterested?"

She was now, however, suddenly tired of the question. " Yes, then—call it that. Besides, she'll never divorce. Don't, moreover," she added, " believe everything you hear about her husband."

" He's not then," Strether asked, " a wretch?"

" Oh yes. But charming."

" Do you know him?"

" I've met him. He's *bien aimable*."

" To every one but his wife?"

" Oh, for all I know, to her too—to any, to every woman. I hope

184

you at any rate," she pursued with a quick change, "appreciate the care I take of Mr. Waymarsh."

"Oh, immensely." But Strether was not yet in line. "At all events," he roundly brought out, "the attachment's an innocent one."

"Mine and his? Ah," she laughed, "don't rob it of *all* romance!"

"I mean our friend's here—to the lady we've been speaking of." That was what he had settled to as an indirect, but none the less closely involved, consequence of his impression of Jeanne. That was where he meant to stay. "It's innocent," he repeated—"I see the whole thing."

Mystified by his abrupt declaration, she had glanced over at Gloriani as at the unnamed subject of his allusion, but the next moment she had understood; though indeed not before Strether had noticed her momentary mistake and wondered what might possibly be behind that too. He already knew that the sculptor admired Mme. de Vionnet; but did this admiration also represent an attachment of which the innocence was discussable? He was moving verily in a strange air and on ground not of the firmest. He looked hard for an instant at Miss Barrace, but she had already gone on. "All right with Mr. Newsome? Why, of course she is!" —and she got gayly back to the question of her own good friend. "I dare say you're surprised that I'm not worn out with all I see— it being so much!—of Sitting Bull. But I'm not, you know—I don't mind him; I bear up, and we get on beautifully. I'm very strange; I'm like that; and often I can't explain. There are people who are supposed interesting or remarkable or whatever, and who bore me to death; and then there are others as to whom nobody can understand what anybody sees in them—in whom I see, in short, all sorts of things." Then after she had smoked a moment, "He's touching, you know," she said.

"'Know'?" Strether echoed—"don't I, indeed? We must move you almost to tears."

"Oh, but I don't mean *you!*" she laughed.

"You ought to then, for the worst sign of all—as I must have it for you—is that you can't help me. That's when a woman pities."

"Ah, but I do help you!" she cheerfully insisted.

Again he looked at her hard, and then, after a pause: "No, you don't!"

Her tortoise-shell, on its long chain, rattled down. "I help you with Sitting Bull. That's a good deal."

"Oh that, yes." But Strether hesitated. "Do you mean he talks of me?"

"So that I have to defend you? No, never."

"I see," Strether mused. "It's too deep."

"That's his only fault," she returned—"that everything, with him, is too deep. He has depths of silence—which he breaks only at the longest intervals by a remark. And when the remark comes it's always something he has seen or felt for himself—never a bit *banal*. *That* would be what one might have feared and what would kill me. But never." She smoked again as she thus, with amused complacency, appreciated her acquisition. "And never about you. We keep clear of you. We're wonderful. But I'll tell you what he does do," she continued: "he tries to make me presents."

"Presents?" poor Strether echoed, conscious with a pang that *he* had not yet tried that in any quarter.

"Why, you see," she explained, "he's as fine as ever in the victoria; so that when I leave him, as I often do almost for hours—he likes it so—at the doors of shops, the sight of him there helps me, when I come out, to know my carriage, from afar, in the rank. But sometimes, for a change, he goes with me into the shops, and then I've all I can do to prevent his buying me things."

"He wants to 'treat' you?" Strether almost gasped at all he himself hadn't thought of. He had a sense of admiration. "Oh, he's much more in the real tradition than I. Yes," he mused; "it's the sacred rage."

"The sacred rage, exactly!"—and Miss Barrace, who had not before heard this term applied, recognized its bearing with a clap of her gemmed hands. "Now I do know why he's not *banal*. But I do prevent him all the same—and if you saw what he sometimes selects—from buying I save him hundreds and hundreds. I only take flowers."

"Flowers?" Strether echoed again with a rueful reflection. How many nosegays had her present interlocutor sent?

"Innocent flowers," she pursued, "as much as he likes. And he sends me splendors; he knows all the best places--he has found them for himself; he's wonderful."

"He hasn't told them to *me*," her friend smiled; "he has a life of his own." But Strether had swung back to the consciousness that, for himself, after all, it never would have done. Waymarsh had not Mrs. Waymarsh in the least to consider, whereas Lambert Strether had constantly, in the inmost honor of his thoughts, to consider Mrs. Newsome. He liked moreover to feel how much his friend was in the real tradition. Yet he had his conclusion. "*What* a rage it is!" He had worked it out. "It's an opposition."

She followed, but at a distance. "That's what I feel. Yet to what?"

"Well, he thinks, you know, that *I've* a life of my own. And I haven't!"

"You haven't?" She showed doubt, and her laugh confirmed it. "Oh, oh, oh!"

"No—not of my own. I seem to have a life only for other people."

"Ah, for them and *with* them! Just now, for instance, with—"

"Well, with whom?" he asked before she had had time to say.

His tone had the effect of making her hesitate and even, as he guessed, speak with a difference. "Say with Miss Gostrey. What do you do for *her?*"

It really made him wonder. "Nothing at all!"

XV

Mme. de Vionnet, having meanwhile come in, was at present close to them, and Miss Barrace hereupon, instead of risking a rejoinder, became again, with a look that measured her from top to toe, all mere long-handled appreciative tortoise-shell. She had struck our friend, from the first of her appearing, as dressed for a great occasion, and she met still more than on either of the others the conception reawakened in him at their garden-party, the idea of the *femme du monde* in her habit as she lived. Her bare shoulders and arms were white and beautiful; the materials of her dress, a mixture, as he supposed, of silk and crape, were of a silvery gray so artfully composed as to give an impression of warm splendor; and round her neck she wore a collar of large old emeralds, the green note of which was more dimly repeated, at other points of her apparel, in embroidery, in enamel, in satin, in substances and textures vaguely rich. Her head, extremely fair and exquisitely festal, was like a happy fancy, a notion of the antique, on an old, precious medal, some silver coin of the Renaissance; while her slim lightness and brightness, her gayety, her expression, her decision, contributed to an effect that might have been felt by a poet as half mythological and half conventional. He could have compared her to a goddess still partly engaged in a morning cloud, or to a sea-nymph waist-high in the summer surge. Above all she suggested to him the reflection that the *femme du monde*—in these finest developments of the type—was, like Cleopatra in the play, indeed various and multifold. She had aspects, characters, days, nights—or had them at least, showed them by a mysterious law of her own, when in addition to everything she happened also to be a woman of genius. She was an obscure person, a muffled person one day; and a showy person, an uncovered person the next. He thought of Mme. de Vionnet to-night as showy and uncovered, though he felt the roughness of the formula, because, by one of the short-cuts of genius, she had taken all his categories by surprise. Twice during dinner he had met Chad's eyes in a longish look; but these communications had in truth only stirred up again old ambiguities —so little was it clear from them whether they were an appeal or an admonition. "You see how I'm fixed" was what they appeared to convey; yet how he was fixed was exactly what Strether didn't see. However, perhaps he should see now.

"Are you capable of the very great kindness of going to relieve Newsome, for a few minutes, of the rather crushing responsibility of Mme. Gloriani, while I say a word, if he'll allow me, to Mr. Strether, of whom I've a question to ask? Our host ought to talk a bit to those other ladies, and I'll come back in a minute to your rescue." She made this proposal to Miss Barrace as if her consciousness of a special duty had just flickered up, but that lady's recognition of Strether's little start at it—as at a betrayal on the speaker's part of a domesticated state—was as mute as his own comment; and after an instant, when their fellow-guest had good-naturedly left them, he had been given something else to think of. "Why has Maria so suddenly gone? Do you know?" That was the question Mme. de Vionnet had brought with her.

"I'm afraid I've no reason to give you but the simple reason I've had from her in a note—the sudden obligation to join, in the south, a sick friend who has got worse."

"Ah then, she has been writing you?"

"Not since she went—I had only a brief explanatory word before she started. I went to see her," Strether explained—"it was the day after I called on you—but she was already on her way, and her concierge told me that in case of my coming I was to be informed she had written to me. I found her note when I got home."

Mme. de Vionnet listened with interest and with her eyes on Strether's face; then her delicately-decorated head had a small melancholy motion. "She didn't write to *me*. I went to see her," she added, "almost immediately after I had seen you, and as I assured her I would do when I met her at Gloriani's. She hadn't then told me she was to be absent, and I felt, at her door, as if I understood. She's absent — with all respect to her sick friend, though I know indeed she has plenty—so that I may not see her.
189

She doesn't want to meet me again. Well," she continued with a beautiful conscious mildness, "I liked and admired her beyond every one in the old time, and she knew it—perhaps that's precisely what has made her go—and I dare say I haven't lost her forever." Strether still said nothing; he had a horror, as he now thought of himself, of being in question between women—was in fact already quite enough on his way to that; and there was moreover, as it came to him, perceptibly, something behind these allusions and professions that, should he take it in, would square but ill with his present resolve to simplify. It was as if, for him, all the same, her softness and sadness were sincere. He felt that not less when she soon went on: "I'm extremely glad of her happiness." But it also left him mute—sharp and fine though the imputation it conveyed. What it conveyed was that *he* was Maria Gostrey's happiness, and for the least little instant he had the impulse to challenge the thought. He could have done so, however, only by saying "What then do you suppose to be between us?" and he was wonderfully glad a moment later not to have spoken. He would rather seem stupid any day than fatuous, and he drew back, as well, with a smothered inward shudder, from the consideration of what women—of highly-developed type in particular—might think of each other. Whatever he had come out for, he had not come to go into that; so that he absolutely took up nothing his interlocutress had now let drop. Yet, though he had kept away from her for days, had laid wholly on herself the burden of their meeting again, she had not a gleam of irritation to show him. "Well, about Jeanne now?" she smiled —it had the gayety with which she had originally come in. He felt it, on the instant, to have been, for her, her real errand. But he had been schooling her, of a truth, to say much in proportion to his little. "*Do* you make out that she has a sentiment? I mean for Mr. Newsome."

Almost resentful, Strether could at last be prompt. "How can I make out such things?"

She remained perfectly good-natured. "Ah, but they're beautiful little things, and you make out—don't pretend!—everything in the world. Haven't you," she asked, "been talking with her?"

"Yes, but not about Chad. At least not much."

"Oh, you don't require 'much'!" she reassuringly declared. But she immediately changed her ground. "I hope you remember your promise of the other day."

"To 'save' you, as you called it?"

"I call it so still. You *will?*" she insisted. "You haven't repented?"

He hesitated. "No—but I've been thinking what I meant."

She wondered. "And not, a little, what *I* did?"

"No—that's not necessary. It will be enough if I know what I meant myself."

"And don't you know," she asked, "by this time?"

Again he had a pause. "I think you ought to leave it to me. But how long," he added, "do you give me?"

"It seems to me much more a question of how long you give *me*. Doesn't our friend here himself, at any rate," she went on, "perpetually make me present to you?"

"Not," Strether replied, "by ever speaking of you to me."

"He never does that?"

"Never."

She considered, and, if the fact was disconcerting to her, effectually concealed it. The next minute indeed she had recovered. "No, he wouldn't. But do you *need* that?"

Her emphasis was wonderful, and though his eyes had been wandering he looked at her longer now. "I see what you mean."

"Of course you see what I mean."

Her triumph was gentle, and she really had tones to make justice weep. "I've before me what he owes you."

"Admit, then, that that's something," she said, yet still with the same discretion in her pride.

He took in this note, but he went straight on. "You've made of him what I see, but what I don't see is how in the world you've done it."

"Ah, that's another question!" she smiled. "The point is of what use is it your declining to know me when to know Mr. Newsome—as you do me the honor to find him—*is* just to know me."

"I see," he mused, still with his eyes on her. "I shouldn't have met you to-night."

She raised and dropped her linked hands. "It doesn't matter. If I trust you, why can't you a little trust me too? And why can't you also," she asked in another tone, "trust yourself?" But she gave him no time to reply. "Oh, I shall be so easy for you! And I'm glad, at any rate, you've seen my child."

"I'm glad too," he said; "but she does you no good."

"No good?"—Mme. de Vionnet had a clear stare. "Why, she's an angel of light."

"That's precisely the reason. Leave her alone. Don't try to find out. I mean," he explained, "about what you spoke to me of—the way she feels."

His companion wondered. "Because one really won't?"

"Well, because I ask you, as a favor to myself, not to. She's the most charming young girl I've ever seen. Therefore don't touch her. Don't know—don't want to know. And moreover—yes—you *won't*."

It was an appeal, of a sudden, and she took it in. "As a favor to you?"

"Well—since you ask me."

"Anything, everything you ask," she smiled. "I sha'n't know then—never. Thank you," she added with peculiar gentleness as she turned away.

The sound of it lingered with him, making him fairly feel as if he had been tripped up and had a fall. In the very act of arranging with her for his independence he had, under pressure from a particular perception, inconsistently, quite stupidly, committed himself, and, with her subtlety sensitive, on the spot, to an advantage, she had driven in, by a single word, a little golden nail, the sharp intention of which he signally felt. He had not detached, he had more closely connected himself, and his eyes, as he considered, with some intensity, this circumstance, met another pair which had just come within their range and which struck him as reflecting his sense of what he had done. He recognized them at the same moment as those of little Bilham, who had apparently drawn near on purpose to speak to him, and little Bilham was not, in the conditions, the person to whom his heart would be most closed. They were seated together, a minute later, at the angle of the room obliquely opposite the corner in which Gloriani was still engaged with Jeanne de Vionnet, to whom, at first, and in silence, their attention had been benevolently given. "I can't see for my life," Strether had then

192

observed, " how a young fellow of any spirit—such a one as you, for instance—can be admitted to the sight of that young lady without being hard hit. Why don't you go in, little Bilham?" He remembered the tone into which he had been betrayed on the garden-bench at the sculptor's reception, and this might make up for that by being much more the right sort of thing to say to a young man worthy of any advice at all. " There *would* be some reason."

" Some reason for what?"

" Why, for hanging on here."

" To offer my hand and fortune to Mlle. de Vionnet?"

" Well," Strether asked, " to what lovelier apparition *could* you offer them? She's the sweetest little thing I've ever seen."

" She's certainly immense. I mean she's the real thing. I believe the pale pink petals are folded up there for some wondrous efflorescence in time; to open, that is, to some great golden sun. *I'm* unfortunately but a small farthing candle. What chance, in such a field, for a poor little artist-man?"

" Oh, you're good enough," Strether threw out.

" Certainly, I'm good enough. We're good enough, I consider, *nous autres,* for anything. But she's *too* good. There's the difference. They wouldn't look at me."

Strether, lounging on his divan and still charmed by the young girl, whose eyes had consciously strayed to him, he fancied, with a vague smile—Strether, enjoying the whole occasion as with dormant pulses at last awake and in spite of new material thrust upon him, thought over his companion's words. " Whom do you mean by ' they '? She and her mother?"

" She and her mother. And she has a father too, who, whatever else he may be, can't, certainly, be indifferent to the possibilities she represents. Besides, there's Chad."

Strether was silent a little. " Ah, but he doesn't care for her—not, I mean, it appears, after all, in the sense I'm speaking of. He's *not* in love with her."

" No—but he's her best friend; after her mother. He's very fond of her. He has his ideas about what can be done for her."

" Well, it's very strange!" Strether presently remarked with a sighing sense of fulness.

"Very strange indeed. That's just the beauty of it. Isn't it very much the kind of beauty you had in mind," little Bilham went on, "when you were so wonderful and so inspiring to me the other day? Didn't you adjure me—in accents I shall never forget —to see, while I've a chance, everything I can?—and *really* to see, for it must have been that only that you meant. Well, you did me no end of good, and I'm doing my best. I *do* make it out as a situation."

"So do I!" Strether went on after a moment. But he had the next minute an inconsequent question. "How comes Chad so mixed up, anyway?"

"Ah, ah, ah!"—and little Bilham fell back on his cushions.

It reminded our friend of Miss Barrace, and he felt again the brush of his sense of moving in a maze of mystic, closed allusions. Yet he kept hold of his thread. "Of course I understand really; only the general transformation makes me occasionally gasp. Chad with such a voice in the settlement of the future of a little countess —no," he declared, "it takes more time! You say, moreover," he resumed, "that we're inevitably, people like you and me, out of the running. The curious fact remains that Chad himself isn't. The situation doesn't make for it, but in a different one he could have her if he would."

"Yes, but that's only because he's rich and because there's a possibility of his being richer. They won't think of anything but a great name or a great fortune."

"Well," said Strether, "*he'll* have no great fortune on these lines. He must stir his stumps."

"Is that," little Bilham inquired, "what you were saying to Mme. de Vionnet?"

"No—I don't say much to her. Of course, however," Strether continued, "he can make sacrifices if he likes."

Little Bilham had a pause. "Oh, he's not keen for sacrifices; or thinks, that is, possibly, that he has made enough."

"Well, it *is* virtuous," his companion observed with some decision.

"That's exactly," the young man dropped after a moment, "what I mean."

It kept Strether himself silent a little. "I've made it out for myself," he then went on; "I've really, within the last half-hour, got hold of it. I understand it, in short, at last; which at first—when you originally spoke to me—I didn't. Nor when Chad originally spoke to me either."

"Oh," said little Bilham, "I don't think that at that time you believed me."

"Yes—I did; and I believe Chad too. It would have been odious and unmannerly—as well as quite perverse—if I hadn't. What interest have you in deceiving me?"

The young man hesitated. "What interest have *I*?"

"Yes. Chad *might* have. But you?"

"Ah, ah, ah!" little Bilham exclaimed.

It might, on repetition, as a mystification, have irritated our friend a little; but he knew, once more, as we have seen, where he was, and his being proof against everything was only another attestation that he meant to stay there. "I couldn't, without my own impression, realize. She's a tremendously clever, brilliant, capable woman, and with an extraordinary charm on top of it all— the charm we surely, all of us this evening, know what to think of. It isn't every clever, brilliant, capable woman that has it. In fact it's rare with any woman. So there you are," Strether proceeded as if not for little Bilham's benefit alone. "I understand what a relation with such a woman—what such a high, fine friendship—may be. It can't be vulgar or coarse, anyway—and that's the point."

"Yes, that's the point," said little Bilham. "It can't be vulgar or coarse. And, bless us and save us, it *isn't!* It's, upon my word, the very finest thing I ever saw in my life, and the most distinguished."

Strether, from beside him, and leaning back with him as he leaned, dropped on him a momentary look which filled a short interval and of which he took no notice. He only gazed before him with intent participation. "Of course what it has done for him," Strether, at all events, presently pursued, "of course what it has done for him—that is as to *how* it has so wonderfully worked— is not a thing I pretend to understand. I've to take it as I find it. There he is."

"There he is!" little Bilham echoed. "And it's really and truly she. I don't understand either, even with my longer and closer opportunity. But I'm like you," he added; "I can admire and rejoice even when I'm a little in the dark. You see I've watched it for some three years, and especially for this last. He wasn't so bad before it as I seem to have made out that you think—"

"Oh, I don't think anything now!" Strether impatiently broke in: "that is but what I *do* think! I mean that, originally, for her to have cared for him—"

"There must have been stuff in him? Oh yes, there was stuff indeed, and much more of it than ever showed, I dare say, at home. Still, you know," the young man in all fairness developed, " there was room for her, and that's where she came in. She saw her chance, and she took it. That's what strikes me as having been so fine. But of course," he wound up, " he liked her first."

"Naturally," said Strether.

"I mean that they first met somehow and somewhere—I believe in some American house—and she, without in the least then intending it, made her impression. Then, with time and opportunity, he made his; and after *that* she was as bad as he."

Strether vaguely took it up. "As ' bad '?"

"She began, that is, to care—to care very much. Alone, and in her horrid position, she found it, when once she had started, an interest. It was, it is, an interest; and it did—it continues to do— a lot for herself as well. So she still cares. She cares in fact," said little Bilham thoughtfully, " more."

Strether's theory that it was none of his business was somehow not damaged by the way he took this. " More, you mean, than he?" On which his companion looked round at him, and now, for an instant, their eyes met. " More than he?" he repeated.

Little Bilham, for as long, hung fire. " Will you never tell any one ?"

Strether thought. " Whom should I tell?"

" Why, I supposed you reported regularly—"

" To people at home?"—Strether took him up. " Well, I won't tell them this."

The young man at last looked away. " Then she does now care more than he."

" Oh!" Strether oddly exclaimed.

But his companion immediately met it. "Haven't you, after all, had your impression of it? That's how you've got hold of him."

"Ah, but I haven't got hold of him!"

"Oh, I say!" But it was all little Bilham said.

"It's at any rate none of my business. I mean," Strether explained, "nothing else than getting hold of him is." It appeared, however, to strike him as his business to add: "The fact remains, nevertheless, that she has saved him."

Little Bilham just waited. "I thought that was what *you* were to do."

But Strether had his answer ready. "I'm speaking—in connection with her—of his manners and morals, his character and life. I'm speaking of him as a person to deal with and talk with and live with—speaking of him as a social animal."

"And isn't it as a social animal that you also want him?"

"Certainly; so that it's as if she had saved him *for* us."

"It strikes you accordingly then," the young man threw out, "as for you all to save *her*?"

"Oh, for us 'all'—!" Strether could but laugh at that. It brought him back, however, to the point he had really wished to make. "They've accepted their situation—hard as it is. They're not free—at least she's not; but they take what's left to them. It's a friendship, of a beautiful sort; and that's what makes them so strong. They're straight, they feel; and they keep each other up. It's doubtless she, however, who, as you yourself have hinted, feels it most."

Little Bilham appeared to wonder what he had hinted. "Feels most that they're straight?"

"Well, feels that *she* is, and the strength that comes from it. She keeps *him* up—she keeps the whole thing up. When people are able to, it's fine. She's wonderful, wonderful, as Miss Barrace says; and he is, in his way, too; however, as a mere man, he may sometimes rebel and not feel that he finds his account in it. She has simply given him an immense moral lift, and what that can explain is prodigious. That's why I speak of it as a situation. It *is* one, if there ever was." And Strether, with his head back and his eyes on the ceiling, seemed to lose himself in the vision of it.

His companion attended deeply. "You state it much better than I could."

"Oh, you see, it doesn't concern you."

Little Bilham considered. "I thought you said just now that it doesn't concern you either."

"Well, it doesn't, a bit, as Mme. de Vionnet's affair. But, as we were, again, saying just now, what did I come out for but to save him?"

"Yes—to remove him."

"To save him *by* removal; to win him over to *himself* thinking it best he shall take up business—thinking he must immediately do, therefore, what is necessary to that end."

"Well," said little Bilham after a moment, "you *have* won him over. He does think it best. He has within a day or two again said to me as much."

"And that," Strether asked, "is why you consider that he cares less than she?"

"Cares less for her than she for him? Yes, that's one of the reasons. But other things too have given me the impression. A man, don't you think?" little Bilham presently pursued, "*can't*, in such conditions, care so much as a woman. It takes different conditions to make him, and then perhaps he cares more. Chad," he wound up, "has his possible future before him."

"Are you speaking of his business-future?"

"No—on the contrary; of the other, the future of what you so justly call their situation. M. de Vionnet may live forever."

"So that they can't marry?"

The young man just hesitated. "Not being able to marry is all they've with any confidence to look forward to. A woman—a particular woman—may stand that strain. But can a man?" he propounded.

Strether's answer was as prompt as if he had already, for himself, worked it out. "Not without a very high ideal of conduct. But that's just what we're attributing to Chad. And how, for that matter," he mused, "does his going to America diminish the particular strain? Wouldn't it seem rather to add to it?"

"Out of sight out of mind!" his companion laughed. Then more bravely: "Wouldn't distance lessen the torment?" But before

Strether could reply, " The thing is, you see, Chad ought to marry!" he exclaimed.

Strether, for a little, appeared to think of it. " If you talk of torments, you don't diminish mine!" he then broke out. The next moment he was on his feet with a question. " He ought to marry whom?"

Little Bilham rose more slowly. " Well, some one he *can*—some thoroughly nice girl."

Strether's eyes, as they stood together, turned again to Jeanne. " Do you mean *her*?"

His friend made a sudden strange face. " After being in love with her mother? No."

" But isn't it exactly your idea that he *isn't* in love with her mother?"

His friend once more had a pause. " Well, he isn't at any rate in love with Jeanne."

" I dare say not."

" How *can* he be with any other woman?"

" Oh, that I admit. But being in love isn't, you know, here " —little Bilham spoke in friendly reminder—" thought necessary, in strictness, for marriage."

" And what torment—to call a torment—can there ever possibly be with a woman like that?" As if from the interest of his own question, Strether had gone on without hearing. " Is it for her to have turned a man out so wonderfully, too, only for somebody else?" He appeared to make a point of this, and little Bilham looked at him now. " When it's for each other that people give things up they don't miss them." Then he threw off as with an extravagance of which he was conscious: " Let them face the future together!"

Little Bilham looked at him indeed. " You mean that, after all, he shouldn't go back?"

" I mean that if he gives her up—!"

" Yes?"

" Well, he ought to be ashamed of himself." But Strether spoke with a sound that might have passed for a laugh.

PART SEVENTH

PART SEVENTH

XVI

It was not the first time Strether had sat alone in the great dim church—still less was it the first of his giving himself up, so far as conditions permitted, to its beneficent action on his nerves. He had been to Notre Dame with Waymarsh, he had been there with Miss Gostrey, he had been there with Chad Newsome, and had found the place, even in company, such a refuge from the obsession of his problem that, with renewed pressure from that source, he had not unnaturally recurred to a remedy that seemed so, for the moment, to meet the case. He was conscious enough that it was only for the moment, but good moments—if he could call them good —still had their value for a man who, by this time, struck himself as living almost disgracefully from hand to mouth. Having so well learnt the way, he had lately made the pilgrimage more than once by himself—had quite stolen off, taking an unnoticed chance and making no point of speaking of the adventure when restored to his friends.

His great friend, for that matter, was still absent, as well as remarkably silent; even at the end of three weeks Miss Gostrey had not come back. She wrote to him from Mentone, admitting that he must judge her grossly inconsequent—perhaps, in fact, for the time, odiously faithless; but asking for patience, for a deferred sentence, throwing herself, in short, on his generosity. For her too, she could assure him, life was complicated—more complicated than he could have guessed; she had moreover made certain of him —certain of not wholly missing him on her return—before her disappearance. If furthermore she didn't burden him with letters it was frankly because of her sense of the other great commerce he had to carry on. He himself, at the end of a fortnight, had written twice, to show how his generosity could be trusted; but he reminded himself in each case of Mrs. Newsome's epistolary manner at the times when Mrs. Newsome kept off delicate ground. He sank his problem, he talked of Waymarsh and Miss Barrace, of little Bilham and the set over the river, with whom he had again had tea, and he was easy, for convenience, about Chad and Mme. de Vionnet and Jeanne. He admitted that he continued to see them, he was, decidedly, so confirmed a haunter of Chad's premises, and that young man's practical intimacy with them was so undeniably great; but he had his reason for not attempting to render for Miss Gostrey's benefit the impression of these last days. That would be to tell her too much about himself—it being at present just from himself that he was trying to escape.

This small struggle sprang not a little, in its way, from the same impulse that had now carried him across to Notre Dame; the impulse to let things be, to give them time to justify themselves or at least to pass. He was aware of having no errand in such a place but the desire not to be, for the hour, in certain other places; a sense of safety, of simplification, which, each time he yielded to it, he amused himself by thinking of as a private concession to cowardice. The great church had no altar for his worship, no direct voice for his soul; but it was none the less soothing even to sanctity; for he could feel while there what he couldn't elsewhere, that he was a plain tired man taking the holiday he had earned. He was tired, but he wasn't plain—that was the pity and the trouble of it; he was able, however, to drop his problem at the door very much as if it had been the copper piece that he deposited, on the threshold, in the receptacle of the inveterate blind beggar. He trod the long, dim nave, sat in the splendid choir, paused before the clustered chapels of the east end, and the mighty monument laid upon him its spell. He might have been a student under the charm of a museum—which was exactly what, in a foreign town, in the afternoon of life, he would have liked to be free to be. This form of sacrifice, at any rate, did, for the occasion, as well as another; it made him quite sufficiently understand how, within the precinct, for the real refugee, the things of the world could fall into abeyance. That was the cowardice, probably—to dodge them, to beg the question, not to deal with it in the hard outer light; but his own oblivions were too brief, too vain, to hurt any one but himself, and he had a vague and fanciful kindness for certain persons whom

he met, figures of mystery and anxiety, and whom, with observation
for his pastime, he ranked as those who were fleeing from justice.
Justice was outside, in the hard light, and injustice too; but one
was as absent as the other from the air of the long aisles and the
brightness of the many altars.

Thus it was, at all events, that, one morning some dozen days
after the dinner in the Boulevard Malesherbes at which Mme. de
Vionnet had been present with her daughter, he was called upon
to play his part in an encounter that deeply stirred his imagination. He had the habit, in these contemplations, of watching a fel-
low-visitant, here and there, from a respectable distance, remarking
some note of behavior, of penitence, of prostration, of the absolved,
relieved state; this was the manner in which his vague tenderness
took its course, the degree of demonstration to which, naturally,
it had to confine itself. It had not indeed so felt its responsibility
as when, on this occasion, he suddenly measured the suggestive
effect of a lady whose supreme stillness, in the shade of one of the
chapels, he had two or three times noticed as he made, and made
once more, his slow circuit. She was not prostrate—not in any
degree bowed, but she was strangely fixed, and her prolonged immobility showed her, while he passed and paused, as wholly given
up to the need, whatever it was, that had brought her there. She
only sat and gazed before her, as he himself often sat; but she had
placed herself, as he never did, within the focus of the shrine, and
she had lost herself, he could easily see, as he would only have liked
to do. She was not a wandering alien, keeping back more than she
gave, but one of the familiar, the intimate, the fortunate, for whom
these dealings had a method and a meaning. She reminded our
friend—since it was the way of nine-tenths of his current impressions to act as recalls of things imagined—of some fine, firm,
concentrated heroine of an old story, something he had heard, read,
something that, had he had a hand for drama, he might himself
have written, renewing her courage, renewing her clearness, in
splendidly-protected meditation. Her back, as she sat, was turned
to him, but his impression absolutely required that she should be
young and interesting, and she carried her head, moreover, even
in the sacred shade, with a discernible faith in herself, a kind of
implied conviction of consistency, security, impunity. But what

had such a woman come for if she hadn't come to pray? Strether's reading of such matters was, it must be owned, confused; but he wondered if her attitude were some congruous fruit of absolution, of "indulgence." He knew but dimly what indulgence, in such a place, might mean; yet he had, as with a soft sweep, a vision of how it might indeed add to the zest of active rites. All this was a good deal to have been denoted by a mere lurking figure who was nothing to him; but, the last thing before leaving the church, he had the surprise of a still deeper quickening.

He had dropped upon a seat half-way down the nave and, again in the museum mood, was trying with head thrown back and eyes aloft, to reconstitute a past, to reduce it in fact to the convenient terms of Victor Hugo, whom, a few days before, giving the rein for once in a way to the joy of life, he had purchased in seventy bound volumes, a miracle of cheapness, parted with, he was assured by the shopman, at the price of the red-and-gold alone. He looked, doubtless, while he played his eternal nippers over Gothic glooms, sufficiently rapt in reverence; but what his thought had finally bumped against was the question of where, among packed accumulations, so multiform a wedge would be able to enter. Were seventy volumes in red-and-gold to be perhaps what he should most substantially have to show at Woollett as the fruit of his mission? It was a possibility that held him a minute—held him till he happened to feel that some one, unnoticed, had approached him and paused. Turning, he saw that a lady stood there as for a greeting, and he sprang up as he next perceived that the lady was Mme. de Vionnet, who appeared to have recognized him as she passed near him on her way to the door. She checked, quickly and gayly, a certain confusion in him, came to meet it, turned it back, by an art of her own; the confusion threatened him as he knew her for the person he had lately been observing. She was the lurking figure of the dim chapel; she had occupied him more than she guessed; but it came to him in time, luckily, that he needn't tell her and that no harm, after all, had been done. She herself, for that matter, straightway showed that she felt their encounter as the happiest of accidents—had for him a "You come here too?" that despoiled surprise of every awkwardness.

"I come often," she said; "I love this place; but I'm terrible.

in general, for churches. The old women who live in them all know me; in fact I'm already myself one of the old women. It's like that, at all events, that I foresee I shall end." Looking about for a chair, so that he instantly pulled one nearer, she sat down with him again to the sound of an " Oh, I like so much your also being fond—!"

He confessed the extent of his feeling, though she left the object vague; and he was struck with the tact, the taste of her vagueness, which simply took for granted in him a sense of beautiful things. He was conscious of how much it was affected, this sense, by something subdued and discreet in the way she had arranged herself for her special object and her morning walk—he believed her to have come on foot; the way her slightly thicker veil was drawn— a mere touch, but everything; the composed gravity of her dress, in which, here and there, a dull wine-color seemed to gleam faintly through black; the charming discretion of her small, compact head; the quiet note, as she sat, of her folded, gray-gloved hands. It was, to Strether's mind, as if she sat on her own ground, the light honors of which, at an open gate, she thus easily did him, while all the vastness and mystery of the property stretched off behind. When people were so completely in possession they could be extraordinarily civil; and our friend indeed, at this hour, had a kind of revelation of her heritage. She was romantic for him far beyond what she could have guessed, and again he found his small comfort in the conviction that, subtle though she was, his impression must remain a secret from her. The thing that, once more, made him uneasy for secrets in general was this particular patience she could have with his own want of color; albeit that, on the other hand, his uneasiness pretty well dropped after he had been for ten minutes as colorless as possible and at the same time as responsive.

The moments had already, for that matter, drawn their deepest tinge from the special interest excited in him by his vision of his companion's identity with the person whose attitude before the glimmering altar had so impressed him. This attitude fitted admirably into the stand he had privately taken about her connection with Chad on the last occasion of his seeing them together. It helped him to stick fast at the point he had then reached; it was there, he had resolved, that he *would* stick, and at no moment since had it seemed as easy to do so. Unassailably innocent was a relation that could make one of the parties to it so carry herself. If it wasn't innocent why did she haunt the churches?—into which, given the woman he could believe he made out, she would never have come to flaunt an insolence of guilt. She haunted them for continued help, for strength, for peace—sublime support which, if one were able to look at it so, she found from day to day. They talked, in low, easy tones and with lifted, lingering looks, about the great monument and its history and its beauty—all of which, Mme. de Vionnet professed, came to her most in the other, the outer view. "We'll presently, after we go," she said, "walk round it again if you like. I'm not in a particular hurry, and it will be pleasant to look at it again with you." He had spoken of the great romancer and the great romance, and of what, to his imagination, they had done for the whole, mentioning to her moreover the exorbitance of his purchase, the seventy blazing volumes that were so out of proportion.

"Out of proportion to what?"

"Well, to any other plunge." Yet he felt even as he spoke how at that instant he was plunging. He had made up his mind and was impatient to get into the air; for his purpose was a purpose to be uttered outside, and he had a fear that it might with delay still slip away from him. She, however, took her time; she drew out their quiet gossip as if she had wished to profit by their meeting, and that, precisely, confirmed an interpretation of her manner, of her mystery. While she rose, as he would have called it, to the question of Victor Hugo, her voice itself, the light, low quaver of her deference to the solemnity about them, seemed to make her words mean something that they didn't mean openly. Help, strength, peace, a sublime support—she had not found so much of these things as that the amount wouldn't be sensibly greater for any scrap his appearance of faith in her might enable her to feel in her hand. Every little, in a long strain, helped, and if he happened to affect her as a firm object she could hold on by, he wouldn't jerk himself out of her reach. People in difficulties held on by what was nearest, and he was perhaps, after all, not further off than sources of comfort more abstract. It was as to this he had made up his mind; he had made it up, that is, to give her a sign. The sign would be that—though it was her own affair—he understood; the sign would be that—though it was her own affair—she was free to clutch. Since she took him for a firm object—much as he might to his own sense appear at times to rock—he would do his best to *be* one.

The end of it was that, half an hour later, they were seated together, for an early luncheon, at a wonderful, a delightful house of entertainment on the left bank—a place of pilgrimage for the knowing, they were both aware, the knowing who came, for its great renown, the homage of restless days, from the other end of the town. Strether had already been there three times—first with Miss Gostrey, then with Chad, then with Chad again and with Waymarsh and little Bilham, all of whom he had himself sagaciously entertained; and his pleasure was deep now on learning that Mme. de Vionnet had not yet been initiated. When he had said, as they strolled round the church, by the river, acting at last on what, within, he had made up his mind to, " Will you, if you have time, come to *déjeuner* with me somewhere? For instance, if you know it, over there on the other side, which is so easy a walk—" and then had named the place; when he had done this she stopped short, as for quick intensity, and yet deep difficulty, of response. She took in the proposal as if it were almost too charming to be true; and there had perhaps never yet been for her companion so unexpected a moment of pride—so fine, so odd a case, at any rate, as his finding himself thus able to offer to a person in such universal possession a new, a rare amusement. She had heard of the happy spot, but she asked him in reply to a further question how in the world he could suppose her to have been there. He supposed himself to have supposed that Chad might have taken her, and she guessed this the next moment, to his no small discomfort.

" Ah, let me explain," she smiled, " that I don't go about with him in public; I never have such chances—not having them otherwise— and it's just the sort of thing that, as a quiet creature living in my hole, I adore." It was more than kind of him to have thought of it—though, frankly, if he asked whether she had time, she hadn't a single minute. That, however, made no difference—she would throw everything over. Every duty, at home, domestic, maternal,

social, awaited her; but it was a case for a high line. Her affairs
would go to smash; but hadn't one a right to one's snatch of scandal
when one was prepared to pay? It was on this pleasant basis of
costly disorder, consequently, that they eventually seated themselves,
on either side of a small table, at a window adjusted to the busy
quay and the shining, barge-burdened Seine; where, for an hour,
in the matter of letting himself go, of diving deep, Strether was to
feel that he had touched bottom. He was to feel many things on
this occasion, and one of the first of them was that he had travelled
far since that evening, in London, before the theatre, when his
dinner with Maria Gostrey, between the pink-shaded candles, had
struck him as requiring so many explanations. He had at that
time gathered them in, the explanations—he had stored them up;
but it was at present as if he had either soared above or sunk below
them—he couldn't tell which; he could somehow think of none
that didn't seem to leave the appearance of collapse and cynicism
easier for him than lucidity. How could he wish it to be lucid for
others, for any one, that he, for the hour, saw reasons enough in
the mere way the bright, clean, ordered water-side life came in at
the open window?—the mere way Mme. de Vionnet, opposite him
over their intensely white table-linen, their *omelette aux tomates,*
their bottle of straw-colored Chablis, thanked him for everything almost with the smile of a child, while her gray eyes moved in and
out of their talk, back to the quarter of the warm spring air, in
which early summer had already begun to throb, and then back
again to his face and their human questions.

Their human questions became many before they had done—
many more, as one after the other came up, than our friend's free
fancy had at all foreseen. The sense he had had before, the sense he
had had repeatedly, the sense that the situation was running away
with him, had never been so sharp as now; and all the more that he
could perfectly put his finger on the moment it had taken the bit
in its teeth. That accident had definitely occurred, the other evening, after Chad's dinner; it had occurred, as he fully knew,
at the moment when he interposed between this lady and her
child, when he suffered himself so to discuss with her a matter
closely concerning them that her own subtlety, with its significant
"Thank you!" instantly sealed the occasion in her favor. Again

he had held off for ten days, but the situation had continued **out of** hand in spite of that; the fact that it was running so fast being indeed just *why* he had held off. What had come over him as he recognized her in the nave of the church was that holding off could be but a losing game from the instant she was worked for not only by her subtlety, but by the hand of fate itself. If all the accidents were to fight on her side—and by the actual showing they loomed large—he could only give himself up. This was what he had done in privately deciding then and there to propose she should breakfast with him. What did the success of his proposal in fact resemble but the smash in which a regular runaway properly ends? The smash was their walk, their déjeûner, their omelette, the Chablis, the place, the view, their present talk and his present pleasure in it —to say nothing, wonder of wonders, of her own. To this tune and nothing less, accordingly, was his surrender made good. It sufficiently lighted up at least the folly of holding off. Ancient proverbs sounded, for his memory, in the tone of their words and the clink of their glasses, in the hum of the town and the plash of the river. It *was* clearly better to suffer as a sheep than as a lamb. One might as well perish by the sword as by famine.

"Maria's still away?"—that was the first thing she had asked him; and when he had found the frankness to be cheerful about it in spite of the meaning he knew her to attach to Miss Gostrey's absence, she had gone on to inquire if he didn't tremendously miss her. There were reasons that made him by no means sure, yet he nevertheless answered "Tremendously"; which she took in as if it were all she had wished to prove. Then, "A man in trouble *must* be possessed, somehow, of a woman," she said; "if she doesn't come in one way she comes in another."

"Why do you call me a man in trouble?"

"Ah, because that's the way you strike me." She spoke ever so gently and as if with all fear of wounding him while she sat partaking of his bounty. "*Aren't* you in trouble?"

He felt himself color at the question, and then he hated that— hated to pass for anything so idiotic as woundable. Woundable by Chad's lady, in respect to whom he had come out with such a fund of indifference—was he already at that point? Perversely, meanwhile, however, his pause gave a strange air of truth to her

211

supposition; and what was he in fact but disconcerted at having struck her just in the way he had most dreamed of not doing? "I'm not in trouble yet," he at last smiled. "I'm not in trouble now."

"Well, I'm always so. But that you sufficiently know." She was a woman who, between courses, could be graceful with her elbows on the table. It was a posture unknown to Mrs. Newsome, but it was easy for a *femme du monde.* "Yes—I am 'now'!"

"There was a question you put to me," he presently returned, "the night of Chad's dinner. I didn't answer it then, and it has been very handsome of you not to have sought an occasion for pressing me about it since."

She was instantly all there. "Of course I know what you allude to. I asked you what you had meant by saying, the day you came to see me, just before you left me, that you would save me. And you then said—at our friend's—that you would have really to wait to see, for yourself, what you did mean."

"Yes, I asked for time," said Strether. "And it sounds now, as you put it, like a very ridiculous speech."

"Oh!" she murmured—she was full of attenuation. But she had another thought. "If it does sound ridiculous, why do you deny that you're in trouble?"

"Ah, if I were," he replied, "it wouldn't be the trouble of fearing ridicule. I don't fear it."

"What then do you?"

"Nothing—now." And he leaned back in his chair.

"I like your 'now'!" she laughed across at him.

"Well, it's precisely that it fully comes to me at present that I've kept you long enough. I know by this time, at any rate, what I meant by my speech; and I really knew it the night of Chad's dinner."

"Then why didn't you tell me?"

"Because it was difficult at the moment. I had already at that moment done something for you, in the sense of what I had said the day I went to see you; but I wasn't then sure of the importance I might represent this as having."

She was all eagerness. "And you're sure now?"

"Yes; I see that, practically, I've done for you—had done for you when you put me your question—all that it's as yet possible to me to do. I feel now," he went on, "that it may go further than I thought. What I did after my visit to you," he explained, "was to write straight off to Mrs. Newsome about you, and I'm at last, from one day to the other, expecting her answer. It's this answer that will represent, as I believe, the consequences."

Patient and beautiful was her interest. "I see—the consequences of your speaking for me." And she waited, as if not to hustle him.

He acknowledged it by immediately going on. "The question, you understand, was *how* I should save you. Well, I'm trying it by thus letting her know that I consider you worth saving."

"I see—I see." Her eagerness broke through. "How can I thank you enough?" He couldn't tell her that, however, and she quickly pursued. "You do really, for yourself, consider it?"

His only answer at first was to help her to the dish that had been freshly put before them. "I've written to her again since then—I've left her in no doubt of what I think. I've told her all about you."

"Thanks—not so much. 'All about' me," she went on—"yes."

"All it seems to me," said Strether, "you've done for him."

"Ah, and you might have added all it seems to *me!*" She laughed again, while she took up her knife and fork, as in the cheer of these assurances. "But you're not sure how she'll take it."

"No, I'll not pretend I'm sure."

"*Voilà.*" And she waited a moment. "I wish you'd tell me about her."

"Oh," said Strether with a slightly strained smile, "all that need concern you about her is that she's really a grand person."

Mme. de Vionnet seemed to demur. "Is that all that need concern me about her?"

But Strether neglected the question. "Hasn't Chad talked to you?"

"Of his mother? Yes, a great deal—immensely. But not from your point of view."

"He can't," our friend returned, "have said any ill of her."

"Not the least bit. He has given me, like you, the assurance that she's really grand. But her being really grand is somehow just

213

what has not seemed to simplify our case. Nothing," she continued, " is further from me than to wish to say a word against her; but of course I feel how little she can like being told of her owing me anything. No woman ever enjoys such an obligation to another woman."

This was a proposition Strether couldn't contradict. "And yet what other way could I have expressed to her what I felt? It's what there was most to say about you."

"Do you mean then that she *will* be good to me?"

"It's what I'm waiting to see. But I've little doubt she would," he added, " if she could comfortably see you."

It seemed to strike her as a happy, a beneficent thought. "Oh then, couldn't that be managed? Wouldn't she come out? Wouldn't she if you so put it to her? *Did* you by any possibility?" she faintly quavered.

"Oh no"—he was prompt. "Not that. It would be, much more, to give an account of you that—since there's no question of *your* paying the visit—I should go home first."

It instantly made her graver. "And are you thinking of that?"

"Oh, all the while, naturally."

"Stay with us—stay with us!" she exclaimed on this. "That's your only way to make sure."

"To make sure of what?"

"Why, that he doesn't break up. You didn't come out to do that to him."

"Doesn't it depend," Strether returned after a moment, "on what you mean by breaking up?"

"Oh, you know well enough what I mean!"

His silence, again, for a little, seemed to denote an understanding. 'You take for granted remarkable things."

"Yes, I do—to the extent that I don't take for granted vulgar ones. You're perfectly capable of seeing that what you came out for was not really at all to do what you would now have to do."

"Ah, it's perfectly simple," Strether good-humoredly pleaded. "I've had but one thing to do—to put our case before him. To put it as it could only be put, here, on the spot—by personal pressure. My dear lady," he lucidly pursued, "my work, you see, is really done, and my reasons for staying on even another day are none of the best. Chad's in possession of our case and professes to do it full justice. What remains is with himself. I've had my rest, my amusement and refreshment; I've had, as we say at Woollett, a lovely time. Nothing in it has been more lovely than this happy meeting with you—in these fantastic conditions to which you've so delightfully consented. I've a sense of success. It's what I wanted. My getting all this good is what Chad has waited for, and I gather that if I'm ready to go he's the same."

She shook her head with a finer, deeper wisdom. "You're not ready. If you're ready why did you write to Mrs. Newsome in the sense you've mentioned to me?"

Strether considered. " I sha'n't go before I hear from her. You're too much afraid of her," he added.

It produced between them a long look from which neither shrank. "I don't think you believe that—believe I've not really reason to fear her."

" She's capable of great generosity," Strether presently declared.

" Well then, let her trust me a little. That's all I ask. Let her recognize, in spite of everything, what I've done."

" Ah, remember," our friend replied, " that she can't effectually recognize it without seeing it for herself. Let Chad go over and show her what you've done, and let him plead with her there for it and, as it were, for *you*."

She measured the depth of this suggestion. " Do you give me your word of honor that if she once has him there she won't do her best to marry him?"

It made her companion, this inquiry, look again awhile out at the view; after which he spoke without sharpness. " When she sees for herself what he is—"

But she had already broken in. " It's when she sees for herself what he is that she'll want to marry him most."

Strether's attitude, that of due deference to what she said, permitted him to attend for a minute to his luncheon. " I doubt if that will come off. It won't be easy to make it."

" It will be easy if he remains there—and he'll remain for the money. The money appears to be, as a probability, so hideously much."

"Well," Strether presently concluded, "nothing *could* really hurt you but his marrying."

She gave a strange light laugh. "Putting aside what may really hurt *him.*"

But her friend looked at her as if he had thought of that too. "The question will come up, of course, of the future that you yourself offer him."

She was leaning back now, but she fully faced him. "Well, let it come up!"

"The point is that it's for Chad to make of it what he can. His being proof against marriage will show what he does make."

"If he *is* proof, yes"—she accepted the proposition. "But for myself," she added, "the question is what *you* make."

"Ah, I make nothing. It's not my affair."

"I beg your pardon. It's just there that, since you've taken it up and are committed to it, it most intensely becomes yours. You're not saving me, I take it, for your interest in myself, but for your interest in our friend. The one, at any rate, is wholly dependent on the other. You can't in honor not see me through," she wound up, "because you can't in honor not see *him.*"

Strange and beautiful to him was her quiet, soft acuteness. The thing that most moved him was really that she was so deeply serious. She had none of the portentous forms of it, but he had never come in contact, it struck him, with a spirit brought to so fine a point. Mrs. Newsome, goodness knew, was serious; but it was nothing to this. He took it all in, he saw it all together. "No," he mused, "I can't in honor not see him."

Her face affected him as with an exquisite light. "You *will* then?"

"I will."

At this she pushed back her chair and was the next moment on her feet. "Thank you!" she said with her hand held out to him across the table and with no less a meaning in the words than her lips had so particularly given them after Chad's dinner. The golden nail she had then driven in pierced a good inch deeper. Yet he reflected that he himself had only meanwhile done what he had made up his mind to on the same occasion. So far as the essence of the matter went he had simply stood fast on the spot on which he had then planted his feet.

XVII

He received three days after this a communication from America, in the form of a scrap of blue paper folded and gummed, not
reaching him through his bankers, but delivered at his hotel by
a small boy in uniform, who, under instructions from the concierge, approached him as he slowly paced the little court. It was
the evening hour, but daylight was long now and Paris more
than ever penetrating. The scent of flowers was in the streets, he
had the whiff of violets perpetually in his nose; and he had attached
himself to sounds and suggestions, vibrations of the air, human and
dramatic, he imagined, as they were not in other places, that came
out for him more and more as the mild afternoons deepened—a
far - off hum, a sharp, near click on the asphalt, a voice calling,
replying, somewhere, and as full of tone as an actor's in a play.
He was to dine at home, as usual, with Waymarsh—they had settled to that for thrift and simplicity; and he now hung about before his friend came down.

He read his telegram in the court, standing still a long time
where he had opened it and giving five minutes, afterwards, to
the renewed study of it. At last, quickly, he crumpled it up as if
to get it out of the way; in spite of which, however, he kept it
there—still kept it when, at the end of another turn, he had
dropped into a chair placed near a small table. Here, with his
scrap of paper compressed in his fist and further concealed by his
folding his arms tight, he sat for some time in thought, gazed before him so straight that Waymarsh appeared and approached him
without catching his eye. The latter, in fact, struck with his appearance, looked at him hard for a single instant and then, as if
determined to that course by some special vividness in it, dropped
back into the *salon de lecture* without addressing him. But the
pilgrim from Milrose permitted himself still to observe the scene

217

from behind the clear glass plate of that retreat. Strether ended, as he sat, by a fresh scrutiny of his compressed missive, which he smoothed out carefully again as he placed it on his table. There it remained for some minutes, until, at last looking up, he saw Waymarsh watching him from within. It was on this that their eyes met—met for a moment during which neither moved. But Strether then got up, folding his telegram more carefully and putting it into his waistcoat pocket.

A few minutes later the friends were seated together at dinner; but Strether had meanwhile said nothing about it, and they eventually parted, after coffee in the court, with nothing said on either side. Our friend had moreover the consciousness that even less than usual was said on this occasion between them, so that it was almost as if each had been waiting for something from the other. Waymarsh had always more or less the air of sitting at the door of his tent, and silence, after so many weeks, had come to play its part in their concert. This note indeed, to Strether's sense, had lately taken a fuller tone, and it was his fancy to-night that they had never quite so drawn it out. Yet it befell, none the less, that he closed the door to confidence when his companion finally asked him if there were anything particular the matter with him. "Nothing," he replied, "more than usual."

On the morrow, at an early hour, however, he found occasion to give an answer more in consonance with the facts. What was the matter had continued to be so all the previous evening, the first hours of which, after dinner, in his room, he had devoted to the copious composition of a letter. He had quitted Waymarsh for this purpose, leaving him to his own resources with less ceremony than their wont, but finally coming down again with his letter unconcluded and going forth into the streets without inquiry for his comrade. He had taken a long, vague walk, and one o'clock had struck before his return and his re-ascent to his room by the aid of the glimmering candle-end left for him on the shelf outside the porter's lodge. He had possessed himself, on closing his door, of the numerous loose sheets of his unfinished composition, and then, without reading them over, had torn them into small pieces. He had thereupon slept—as if it had been in some measure thanks to that sacrifice—the sleep of the just, and had prolonged his rest considerably beyond his custom. Thus it was that when, between nine and ten, the tap of the knob of a walking-stick sounded on his door, he had not yet made himself altogether presentable. Chad Newsome's bright, deep voice, determined quickly enough, none the less, the admission of the visitor. The little blue paper of the evening before, plainly an object the more precious for its escape from premature destruction, now lay on the sill of the open window, smoothed out afresh and kept from blowing away by the superincumbent weight of his watch. Chad, looking about with careless and competent criticism, as he looked wherever he went, immediately espied it and permitted himself to fix it for a moment rather hard. After which he turned his eyes to his host. "It has come then at last?"

Strether paused in the act of pinning his necktie. "Then you know—? You've had one too?"

"No, I've had nothing, and I only know what I see. I see that thing and I guess. Well," he added, "it comes as pat as in a play, for I've precisely turned up this morning—as I would have done yesterday, but it was impossible—to take you."

"To take me?" Strether had turned again to his glass.

"Back, at last, as I promised. I'm ready—I've really been ready this month. I've only been waiting for you—as was perfectly right. But you're better now; you're safe—I see that for myself; you've got all your good. You're looking, this morning, as fit as a flea."

Strether, at his glass, finished dressing; consulting that witness moreover on this last opinion. *Was* he looking preternaturally fit? There was something in it perhaps for Chad's wonderful eye, but he had felt himself, for hours, rather in pieces. Such a judgment, however, was after all but a contribution to his resolve; it testified unwittingly to his wisdom. He was still firmer, apparently—since it shone in him as a light—than he had flattered himself. His firmness indeed was slightly compromised, as he faced about to his friend, by the way this very personage looked—though the case would of course have been worse had not the secret of personal magnificence been at every hour Chad's unfailing possession. There he was in all the pleasant morning freshness of it—strong and sleek and gay, easy and fragrant and fathomless, with happy health in his color, and pleasant silver in his thick young hair, and the right word for everything on the lips that his clear brownness caused to show as red. He had never struck Strether as personally such a success; it was as if now, for his definite surrender, he had gathered himself vividly together. This, sharply and rather strangely, was the form in which he was to be presented to Woollett. Our friend took him in again—he was always taking him in and yet finding that parts of him still remained out; though even thus his image showed through a mist of other things. "I've had a cable," Strether said, "from your mother."

"I dare say, my dear man. I hope she's well."

Strether hesitated. "No—she's not well, I'm sorry to have to tell you."

"Ah," said Chad, "I must have had the instinct of it. All the more reason then that we should start straight off."

Strether had now got together hat, gloves and stick, but Chad had dropped on the sofa as if to show where he wished to make his point. He kept observing his companion's things; he might have been judging how quickly they could be packed. He might even have wished to hint that he would send his own servant to assist. "What do you mean," Strether inquired, "by 'straight off'?"

"Oh, by one of next week's boats. Everything at this season goes out so light that berths will be easy anywhere."

Strether had in his hand his telegram, which he had kept there after attaching his watch, and he now offered it to Chad, who, however, with an odd movement, declined to take it. "Thanks, I had rather not. Your correspondence with mother is your own affair. I'm only *with* you both on it, whatever it is." Strether, at this, while their eyes met, slowly folded the missive and put it in his pocket; after which, before he had spoken again, Chad broke fresh ground. "Has Miss Gostrey come back?"

But when Strether presently spoke, it was not in answer. "It's not, I gather, that your mother is physically ill; her health, on the whole, this spring, seems to have been better than usual. But she's worried, she's anxious; and it appears to have risen within the last few days to a climax. We've tired out, between us, her patience."

"Oh, it isn't *you!*" Chad generously protested.

"I beg your pardon—it *is* me." Strether was mild and melancholy, but firm. He saw it far away and over his companion's head. "It's very particularly me."

"Well, then, all the more reason. *Marchons, marchons!*" said the young man gayly. His host, however, at this, but continued to stand agaze; and he had the next thing repeated his question of a moment before. "Has Miss Gostrey come back?"

"Yes, two days ago."

"Then you've seen her?"

"No—I'm to see her to-day." But Strether wouldn't linger now on Miss Gostrey. "Your mother sends me an ultimatum. If I can't bring you I'm to leave you; I'm to come at any rate myself."

"Ah, but you *can* bring me now," Chad, from his sofa, reassuringly replied.

Strether hesitated. "I don't think I understand you. Why was it that, more than a month ago, you put it to me so urgently to let Mme. de Vionnet speak for you?"

"'Why'?" Chad considered, but he had it at his fingers' ends. "Why but because I knew how well she'd do it? It was the way to keep you quiet and, to that extent, do you good. Besides," he happily and comfortably explained, "I wanted you really to know her and to get the impression of her—and you see the good that *has* done you."

"Well," said Strether, "the way she has spoken for you, all the same—so far as I have given her a chance—has only made me feel how much she wishes to keep you. If you make nothing of that I don't see why you wanted me to listen to her."

"Why, my dear man," Chad exclaimed, "I make everything of it! How can you doubt—?"

"I doubt only because you come to me this morning with your signal to start."

Chad stared, then gave a laugh. "And isn't my signal to start just what you've been waiting for?"

Strether debated; he took another turn. "This last month I've been awaiting, I think, more than anything else, the message I have here."

"You mean you've been afraid of it?"

"Well, I was doing my business in my own way. And I suppose your present announcement," Strether went on, "isn't merely the result of your sense of what I've expected. Otherwise you wouldn't have put me in relation—" But he paused, pulling up.

At this Chad rose. "Ah, *her* wanting me not to go has nothing to do with it! It's only because she's afraid—afraid of the way that, over there, I may get caught. But her fear's groundless."

He had met again his companion's sufficiently searching look. "Are you tired of her?"

Chad gave him in reply to this, with a movement of the head, the strangest slow smile he had ever had from him. "Never."

It had immediately, on Strether's imagination, so deep and soft an effect that our friend could only, for the moment, keep it before him. "Never?"

"Never," Chad obligingly and serenely repeated.

It made his companion take several more steps. "Then *you're* not afraid."

"Afraid to go?"

Strether pulled up again. "Afraid to stay."

The young man looked brightly amazed. "You want me now to 'stay'?"

"If I don't immediately sail, the Pococks will immediately come out. That's what I mean," said Strether, "by your mother's ultimatum."

Chad showed a still livelier, but not an alarmed interest. "She has turned on Sarah and Jim?"

Strether joined him for an instant in the vision. "Oh, and you may be sure, Mamie. *That's* whom she's turning on."

This also Chad saw—he laughed out. "Mamie—to corrupt me?"

"Ah," said Strether, "she's very charming."

"So you've already more than once told me. I should like to see her."

Something happy and easy, something above all unconscious, in the way he said this, brought home again to his companion the facility of his attitude and the enviability of his state. "See her then by all means. And consider too," Strether went on, "that you really give your sister a lift in letting her come to you. You give her a couple of months of Paris, which she hasn't seen, if I'm not mistaken, since just after she was married, and which I'm sure she wants but the pretext to visit."

222

Chad listened, but with all his own knowledge of the world. "She has had it, the pretext, these several years, yet she has never taken it."

"Do you mean *you?*" Strether after an instant inquired.

"Certainly—the lone exile. And whom do you mean?" said Chad.

"Oh, I mean *me.* I'm her pretext. That is—for it comes to the same thing—I'm your mother's."

"Then why," Chad asked, "doesn't mother come herself?"

His friend gave him a long look. "Should you like her to?" And as he for the moment said nothing: "It's perfectly open to you to cable for her."

Chad continued to think. "Will she come if I do?"

"Quite possibly. But try, and you'll see."

"Why don't *you* try?" Chad after a moment asked.

"Because I don't want to."

Chad hesitated. "Don't desire her presence here?"

Strether faced the question, and his answer was the more emphatic. "Don't put it off, my dear boy, on *me!*"

"Well—I see what you mean. I'm sure you'd behave beautifully, but you *don't* want to see her. So I won't play you that trick."

"Ah," Strether declared, "I shouldn't call it a trick. You've a perfect right, and it would be perfectly straight of you." Then he added in a different tone: "You'd have moreover, in the person of Mme. de Vionnet, a very interesting relation prepared for her."

Their eyes, on this proposition, continued to meet, but Chad's, pleasant and bold, never flinched for a moment. He got up at last, and he said something with which Strether was struck. "She wouldn't understand her, but that makes no difference. Mme. de Vionnet would like to see her. She'd like to be charming to her. She believes she could work it."

Strether thought a moment, affected by this, but finally turning away. "She couldn't!"

"You're quite sure?" Chad asked.

"Well, risk it if you like!"

Strether, who uttered this with serenity, had urged a plea for their now getting into the air; but the young man still waited. "Have you sent your answer?"

"No, I've done nothing yet."

"Were you waiting to see me?"

"No, not that."

"Only waiting"—and Chad, with this, had a smile for him—"to see Miss Gostrey?"

"No—not even Miss Gostrey. I wasn't waiting to see any one. I had only waited, till now, to make up my mind—in complete solitude; and, since I of course absolutely owe you the information, was on the point of going out with it quite made up. Have therefore a little more patience with me. Remember," Strether went on, "that that is what, originally, you asked *me* to have. I've had it, you see, and you see what has come of it. Stay on with me."

Chad looked grave. "How much longer?"

"Well, till I make you a sign. I can't myself, you know, at the best, or at the worst, stay forever. Let the Pococks come," Strether repeated.

"Because it gains you time?"

"Yes—it gains me time."

Chad, as if it still puzzled him, waited a minute. "You don't want to get back to mother?"

"Not just yet. I'm not ready."

"You feel," Chad asked in a tone of his own, "the charm of life here?"

"Immensely." Strether faced it. "You've helped me so to feel it that that surely needn't surprise you."

"No, it doesn't surprise me, and I'm delighted. But what, my dear man," Chad went on with conscious queerness, "does it all lead to for you?"

The change of position and of relation, for each, was so oddly betrayed in the question that Chad laughed out as soon as he had uttered it—which made Strether also laugh. "Well, to my having a certitude that has been tested—that has passed through the fire. But, oh," he couldn't help breaking out, "if within my first month here you had been willing to move with me—!"

"Well?" said Chad, while he paused as if for weight of thought.

"Well, we should have been over there by now."

"Ah, but you wouldn't have had your fun!"

"I should have had a month of it; and I'm having now, if you want to know," Strether continued, "enough to last me for the rest of my days."

Chad looked amused and interested, yet still somewhat in the dark; partly perhaps because Strether's estimate of fun had required of him from the first a good deal of elucidation. "It wouldn't do if I left you—?"

"Left me?"—Strether remained blank.

"Only for a month or two—time to go and come. Mme. de Vionnet," Chad smiled, "would look after you in the interval."

"To go back by yourself, I remaining here?" Again, for an instant, their eyes had the question out; after which Strether said: "Grotesque!"

"But I want to see mother," Chad presently returned. "Remember how long it is since I've seen mother."

"Long indeed; and that's exactly why I was originally so keen for moving you. Hadn't you shown us enough how beautifully you could do without it?"

"Oh, but," said Chad wonderfully, "I'm better now."

There was an easy triumph in it that made his friend laugh out again. "Oh, if you were worse, I *should* know what to do with you. In that case, I believe, I'd have you gagged and strapped down, carried on board resisting, kicking. How *much,*" Strether asked, " do you want to see mother?"

"How much?"—Chad seemed to find it, in fact, difficult to say.

"How much."

"Why, as much as you've made me. I'd give anything to see her. And you've left me," Chad went on, "in little enough doubt as to how much *she* wants it."

Strether thought a minute. "Well then, if those things are really your motive, catch the French steamer and sail to-morrow. Of course, when it comes to that, you're absolutely free to do as you choose. From the moment you can't hold yourself, I can only accept your flight."

"I'll fly in a minute then," said Chad, "if you'll stay here."

"I'll stay here till the next steamer—then I'll follow you."

"And do you call that," Chad asked, "accepting my flight?"

"Certainly—it's the only thing to call it. The only way to keep me here, accordingly," Strether explained, "is by staying yourself."

Chad took it in. "All the more that I've really dished you, eh?"

"Dished me?" Strether echoed as inexpressively as possible.

"Why, if she sends out the Pococks it will be that she doesn't trust you; and if she doesn't trust you, that bears upon—well, you know what."

Strether decided after a moment that he did know what, and in consonance with this he spoke. "You see then, all the more, what you owe me."

"Well, if I do see, how can I pay?"

"By not deserting me. By standing by me."

"Oh, I say—!" But Chad, as they went down-stairs, clapped a firm hand, in the manner of a pledge, upon his shoulder. They descended slowly together and had, in the court of the hotel, some further talk, of which the upshot was that they presently separated. Chad Newsome departed, and Strether, left alone, looked about, superficially, for Waymarsh. But Waymarsh had not yet, it appeared, come down, and our friend finally went out without a sight of him.

XVIII

At four o'clock that afternoon he had still not seen him, but he was then, as to make up for this, engaged in talk about him with Miss Gostrey. Strether had kept away from home all day, given himself up to the town and to his thoughts, wandered and mused, been at once restless and absorbed—and all with the present climax of a rich little welcome in the Quartier Marbœuf. "Waymarsh has been, 'unbeknown' to me, I'm convinced"—for Miss Gostrey had inquired—" in communication with Woollett: the consequence of which was, last night, the loudest possible call for me."

"Do you mean a letter to bring you home?"

"No—a cable, which I have at this moment in my pocket: a 'Come back by the first ship.'"

Strether's hostess, it might have been made out, just escaped changing color. Reflection arrived but in time and established a provisional serenity. It was perhaps exactly this that enabled her to say with duplicity: "And you're going—?"

"You almost deserve it when you abandon me so."

She shook her head as if this were not worth taking up. "My absence has helped you—as I've only to look at you to see. It was my calculation, and I'm justified. You're not where you were. And the thing," she smiled, "was for me not to be there either. You can go of yourself."

"Oh, but I feel to-day," he comfortably declared, "that I shall want you yet."

She took him all in again. "Well, I promise you not again to leave you, but it will only be to follow you. You've got your momentum, and you can toddle alone."

He intelligently accepted it. "Yes—I suppose I can toddle. It's the sight of that in fact that has upset Waymarsh. He can bear it—the way I strike him as going—no longer. That's only the climax of his original feeling. He wants me to quit; and he must have written to Woollett that I'm in peril of perdition."

"Ah, good!" she murmured. "But is it only your supposition?"

"I make it out—it explains."

"Then he denies?—or you haven't asked him?"

"I've not had time," Strether said; "I made it out but last night, putting various things together, and I've not been since then face to face with him."

She wondered. "Because you're too disgusted? You can't trust yourself?"

He settled his glasses on his nose. "Do I look in a great rage?"

"You look divine!"

"There's nothing," he went on, "to be angry about. He has done me, on the contrary, a service."

She made it out. "By bringing things to a head?"

"How well you understand!" he almost groaned. "Waymarsh won't in the least, at any rate, when I have it out with him, deny or extenuate. He has acted from the deepest conviction, with the best conscience, and after wakeful nights. He'll recognize that he's fully responsible, and will consider that he has been highly successful; so that any discussion we may have will bring us quite together again—bridge the dark stream that has kept us so thoroughly apart. We shall have at last, in the consequences of his act, something we can definitely talk about."

She was silent a little. "How wonderfully you take it! But you're always wonderful."

He had a pause that matched her own; then he had, with an adequate spirit, a complete admission. "It's quite true. I'm extremely wonderful just now. I dare say in fact I'm quite fantastic, and I shouldn't be at all surprised if I were mad."

"Then tell me!" she earnestly pressed. As he, however, for the time, answered nothing, only returning the look with which she watched him, she presented herself where it was easier to meet her. "What will Mr. Waymarsh exactly have done?"

"Simply have written a letter. One will have been quite enough. He has told them I want looking after."

"And do you?"—she was all interest.

"Immensely. And I shall get it."

" By which you mean you don't budge ?"

" I don't budge."

" You've cabled ?"

" No—I've made Chad do it."

" That you decline to come ?"

" That *he* declines. We had it out this morning, and I brought him round. He had come in, before I was down, to tell me he was ready—ready, I mean, to return. And he went off, after ten minutes with me, to say he wouldn't."

Miss Gostrey followed with intensity. " Then you've *stopped* him ?"

Strether settled himself afresh in his chair. " I've stopped him. That is for the time. That "—he gave it to her more vividly—" is where I am."

" I see, I see. But where is Mr. Newsome ? He was ready," she asked, " to go ?"

" All ready."

" And sincerely—believing *you* would be ?"

" Perfectly, I think; so that he was amazed to find the hand I had laid on him to pull him over suddenly converted into an engine for keeping him still."

It was an account of the matter Miss Gostrey could weigh. " Does he think the conversion sudden ?"

" Well," said Strether, " I'm not altogether sure what he thinks. I'm not sure of anything that concerns him, except that the more I've seen of him the less I've found him what I originally expected. He's obscure, and that's why I'm waiting."

She wondered. " But for what in particular ?"

" For the answer to his cable."

" And what was his cable ?"

" I don't know," Strether replied; " it was to be, when he left me, according to his own taste. I simply said to him: ' I want to stay, and the only way for me to do so is for *you* to.' That I wanted to stay seemed to interest him, and he acted on that."

Miss Gostrey turned it over. " He wants then himself to stay."

" He half wants it. That is he half wants to go. My original appeal has to that extent worked in him. Nevertheless," Strether pursued, " he won't go. Not, at least, so long as I'm here."

"But you can't," his companion suggested, "stay here always. I wish you could."

"By no means. Still, I want to see him a little further. He is not in the least the case I supposed; he's quite another case. And it's as such that he interests me." It was almost as if for his own intelligence that, deliberate and lucid, our friend thus expressed the matter. "I don't want to give him up."

Miss Gostrey but desired to help his lucidity. She had, however, to be light and tactful. "Up, you mean—a—to his mother?"

"Well, I'm not thinking of his mother now. I'm thinking of the plan of which I was the mouthpiece, which, as soon as we met, I put before him as persuasively as I knew how, and which was drawn up, as it were, in complete ignorance of all that, in this last long period, has been happening to him. It took no account whatever of the impressions I was, here on the spot, immediately to begin to receive from him—impressions of which I feel sure I'm far from having had the last."

Miss Gostrey had a smile of the most genial criticism. "So your idea is—more or less—to stay out of curiosity?"

"Call it what you like! I don't care what it's called—"

"So long as you do stay? Certainly not then. I call it, all the same, immense fun," Maria Gostrey declared; "and to see you work it out will be one of the sensations of my life. It *is* clear you can toddle alone!"

He received this tribute without elation. "I sha'n't be alone when the Pococks have come."

Her eyebrows went up. "The Pococks are coming?"

"That, I mean, is what will happen—and happen as quickly as possible—in consequence of Chad's cable. They'll simply embark. Sarah will come to speak for her mother—with an effect different from *my* muddle."

Miss Gostrey more gravely wondered. "*She* then will take him back?"

"Very possibly—and we shall see. She must at any rate have the chance, and she may be trusted to do all she can."

"And do you *want* that?"

"Of course," said Strether, "I want it. I want to play fair."

But she had lost for a moment the thread. "If it devolves on the Pococks, why do you stay?"

"Just to see that I *do* play fair—and a little also, no doubt, that they do." Strether was luminous as he had never been. "I came out to find myself in presence of new facts—facts that have kept striking me as less and less met by our old reasons. The matter's perfectly simple. New reasons — reasons as new as the facts themselves—are wanted; and of this our friends at Woollett—Chad's and mine—were at the earliest moment definitely notified. If any are producible Mrs. Pocock will produce them; she'll bring over the whole collection. They'll be," he added with a pensive smile, "a part of the ' fun ' you speak of."

She was quite in the current now and floating by his side. "It's Mamie—so far as I've had it from you—who'll be their great card." And then, as his contemplative silence was not a denial, she significantly added: "I think I'm sorry for her."

"I think *I* am!"—and Strether sprang up, moving about a little as her eyes followed him. "But it can't be helped."

"You mean her coming out can't be?"

He explained after another turn what he meant. "The only way for her not to come is for me to go home—as I believe that, on the spot, I could prevent it. But the difficulty as to that is that if I do go home—"

"I see, I see "—she had easily understood. "Mr. Newsome will do the same, and that's not "—she laughed out now—" to be thought of."

Strether had no laugh; he had only a quiet, comparatively placid look that might have shown him as proof against ridicule. "Strange, isn't it?"

They had, in the matter that so much interested them, come so far as this without sounding another name—to which, however, their present momentary silence was full of a conscious reference. Strether's question was a sufficient implication of the weight it had gained with him during the absence of his hostess; and just for that reason a single gesture from her could pass for him as a vivid answer. Yet he was answered still better when she said in a moment: "Will Mr. Newsome introduce his sister—?"

"To Mme. de Vionnet?" Strether spoke the name at last. "I shall be greatly surprised if he doesn't."

She seemed to gaze at the possibility. "You mean you've thought of it and you're prepared."

"I've thought of it, and I'm prepared."

It was to her visitor now that she applied her consideration. "Bon! You *are* magnificent!"

"Well," he answered after a pause and a little wearily, but still standing there before her—"well, that's what, just once in all my dull days, I think I shall like to have been!"

Two days later he had news from Chad of a communication from Woollett in response to their determinant telegram, this missive being addressed to Chad himself and announcing the immediate departure for France of Sarah and Jim and Mamie. Strether had meanwhile, on his own side, cabled; he had but delayed that act till after his visit to Miss Gostrey, an interview by which, as so often before, he felt his sense of things cleared up and settled. His message to Mrs. Newsome, in answer to her own, had consisted of the words: "Judge best to take another month, but with full appreciation of all reinforcements." He had added that he was writing, but he was of course always writing; it was a practice that continued, oddly enough, to relieve him, to make him come nearer than anything else to the consciousness of doing something: so that he often wondered if he had not really, under his recent stress, acquired some hollow trick, one of the specious arts of make-believe. Wouldn't the pages he still so freely despatched by the American post have been worthy of a showy journalist, some master of the great new science of beating the sense out of words? Wasn't he writing against time, and mainly to show he was kind?—since it had become quite his habit not to like to read himself over. On those lines he could still be liberal, yet it was at best a sort of whistling in the dark. It was unmistakable, moreover, that the sense of being in the dark now pressed on him more sharply—creating thereby the need for a louder and livelier whistle. He whistled long and hard after sending his message; he whistled again and again in celebration of Chad's news; there was an interval of a fortnight in which this exercise helped him. He had no great notion of what, on the spot, Sarah

Pocock would have to say, though he had indeed confused pre-monitions; but it shouldn't be in her power to say—it shouldn't be in any one's anywhere to say—that he was neglecting her mother. He might have written before more freely, but he had never written more copiously; and he frankly gave for a reason, at Woollett, that he wished to fill the void created there by Sarah's departure.

The increase of his darkness, however, and the quickening, as I have called it, of his tune, resided in the fact that he was hearing almost nothing. He had for some time been aware that he was hearing less than before, but he was now clearly following a process by which Mrs. Newsome's letters could only, logically, stop. He had not had a line for many days, and he needed no proof—though he was, in time, to have plenty—that she wouldn't have put pen to paper after receiving the hint that had determined her tele-gram. She wouldn't write till Sarah should have seen him and reported on him. It was strange, though it might well be less so than his own behavior appeared at Woollett. It was at any rate significant, and what *was* remarkable was the way his friend's nature and manner put on for him, through this very drop of demonstra-tion, a greater intensity. It struck him really that he had never so lived with her as during this period of her silence; the silence was a sacred hush, a finer, clearer medium, in which her idiosyn-crasies showed. He walked about with her, sat with her, drove with her and dined face-to-face with her—a rare treat " in his life," as he could perhaps have scarce escaped phrasing it; and if he had never seen her so soundless, so, on the other hand, he had never felt her so highly, so almost austerely, herself: pure and by the vulgar estimate " cold," but deep, devoted, delicate, sensitive, noble. Her vividness in these respects became for him, in the special conditions, almost an obsession; and though the obsession sharpened his pulses, adding really to the excitement of life, there were hours at which, to be less on the stretch, he directly sought forgetfulness. He knew it for the queerest of adventures—a circumstance that could play such a part only for Lambert Strether—that in Paris itself, of all places, he should find this ghost of the lady of Woollett more im-portunate than any other presence.

When he went back to Maria Gostrey it was for the change to something else. And yet, after all, the change scarcely operated, for he talked to her of Mrs. Newsome in these days as he had never talked before. He had hitherto observed in that particular a discretion and a law; considerations that at present broke down quite as if relations had altered. They hadn't *really* altered, he said to himself, so much as that came to; for if what had occurred was of course that Mrs. Newsome had ceased to trust him, there was nothing on the other hand to prove that he shouldn't win back her confidence. It was quite his present theory that he would leave no stone unturned to do so; and in fact if he now told Maria things about her that he had never told before, this was largely because it kept before him the idea of the honor of such a woman's esteem. His relation with Maria as well was, strangely enough, no longer quite the same; this truth—though not too disconcertingly—had come up between them on the renewal of their meetings. It was all contained in what she had then almost immediately said to him; it was represented by the remark she had needed but ten minutes to make and that he had not been disposed to gainsay. He could toddle alone, and the difference that showed was extraordinary. The turn taken by their talk had promptly confirmed this difference; his larger confidence on the score of Mrs. Newsome did the rest; and the time seemed already far off when he had held out his small thirsty cup to the spout of her pail. Her pail was scarce touched now, and other fountains had flowed for him; she fell into her place as but one of his tributaries; and there was a strange sweetness—a melancholy mildness that touched him—in her acceptance of the altered order.

It marked for himself the flight of time, or at any rate what he was pleased to think of with irony and pity as the rush of experience; it having been but the day before yesterday that he sat at her feet and held on by her garment and was fed by her hand. It was the proportions that were changed, and the proportions were at all times, he philosophized, the very conditions of perception, the terms of thought. It was as if, with her effective little *entresol* and her wide acquaintance, her activities, varieties, promiscuities, the duties and devotions that took up nine-tenths of her time and of which he got, guardedly, but the side-wind—it was as if she had shrunk to a secondary element and had consented to the shrinkage with the perfection of tact. This perfection had never failed her;

it had originally been greater than his prime measure for it; it had kept him quite apart, kept him out of the shop, as she called her huge general acquaintance, made their commerce as quiet, as much a thing of the home alone—the opposite of the shop—as if she had never another customer. She had been wonderful to him at first, with the memory of her little *entresol* the image to which, on most mornings at that time, his eyes directly opened; but now she mainly figured for him as but part of the bristling total—though of course always as a person to whom he should never cease to be indebted. It would never be given to him certainly to inspire a greater kindness. She had decked him out for others, and he saw at this point at least nothing she would ever ask for. She only wondered and questioned and listened, rendering him the homage of a wistful speculation. She expressed it repeatedly; he was already far beyond her, and she must prepare herself to lose him. There was but one little chance for her.

Often as she had said it he met it—for it was a touch he liked—each time the same way. "My coming to grief?"

"Yes—then I might patch you up."

"Oh, for my real smash, if it takes place, there will be no patching."

"But you surely don't mean it will kill you."

"No—worse. It will make me old."

"Ah, nothing can do that! The wonderful and special thing about you is that you *are,* at this time of day, youth." Then she always made, further, one of those remarks that she had completely ceased to adorn with hesitations or apologies, and that had, by the same token, in spite of their extreme straightness, ceased to produce in Strether the least embarrassment. She made him believe them, and they became thereby as impersonal as truth itself. "It's just your particular charm."

His answer too was always the same. "Of course I'm youth—youth for the trip to Europe. I began to be young, or at least to get the benefit of it, the moment I met you at Chester, and that's what has been taking place ever since. I never had the benefit at the proper time—which comes to saying that I never had the thing itself. I'm having the benefit at this moment; I had it the other day when I said to Chad 'Wait'; I shall have it still again when Sarah

Pocock arrives. It's a benefit that would make a poor show for many people; and I don't know who else but you and I, frankly, could begin to see in it what I feel. I don't get drunk; I don't pursue the ladies; I don't spend money; I don't even write sonnets. But nevertheless I'm making up late for what I didn't have early. I cultivate my little benefit in my own little way. It amuses me more than anything that has happened to me in all my life. They may say what they like—it's my surrender, it's my tribute, to youth. One puts that in where one can—it has to come in somewhere, if only out of the lives, the conditions, the feelings of other persons. Chad gives me the sense of it, for all his gray hairs, which merely make it solid in him and safe and serene; and *she* does the same, for all her being older than he, for all her marriageable daughter, her separated husband, her agitated history. Though they're young enough, my pair, I don't say they're, in the freshest way, their *own* absolutely prime adolescence; for that has nothing to do with it. The point is that they're mine. Yes, they're my youth; since somehow, at the right time, nothing else ever was. What I meant just now therefore is that it would all go—go before doing its work —if they were to fail me."

On which, just here, Miss Gostrey inveterately questioned. "What do you, in particular, call its work?"

"Well, to see me through."

"But through what?"—she liked to get it all out of him.

"Why, through this experience." That was all that would come.

It regularly gave her, none the less, the last word. "Don't you remember how, in those first days of our meeting, it was *I* who was to see you through?"

"Remember? Tenderly, deeply"—he always rose to it. "You're just doing your part in letting me maunder to you thus."

"Ah, don't speak as if my part were small; since whatever else fails you—"

"*You* won't, ever, ever, ever?"—he thus took her up. "Oh, I beg your pardon; you necessarily, you inevitably *will*. Your conditions—that's what I mean—won't allow me anything to do for you."

"Let alone—I see what you mean—that I'm drearily, dreadfully old. I *am;* but there's a service—possible for you to render—that I know, all the same, I shall think of."

"And what will it be?"

This, in fine, however, she would never tell him. "You shall hear only if your smash takes place. As that is really out of the question, I won't expose myself"—a point at which, for reasons of his own, Strether ceased to press.

He came round, for publicity—it was the easiest thing—to the idea that his smash *was* out of the question, and that rendered idle the discussion of what might follow it. He attached an added importance, as the days elapsed, to the arrival of the Pococks; he had even a shameful sense of waiting for it insincerely and incorrectly. He accused himself of making believe to his own mind that Sarah's presence, her impression, her judgment would simplify and harmonize; he accused himself of being so afraid of what they *might* do that he sought refuge, to beg the whole question, in a vain fury. He had abundantly seen at home what they were in the habit of doing, and he had not at present the smallest ground. His clearest vision was when he made out that what he most desired was an account more full and free of Mrs. Newsome's state of mind than any he felt he could now expect from herself; that calculation, at least, went hand in hand with the sharp consciousness of wishing to prove to himself that he was not afraid to look his behavior in the face. If he was by an inexorable logic to pay for it he was literally impatient to know the cost, and he held himself ready to pay in instalments. The first instalment would be precisely this entertainment of Sarah; as a consequence of which, moreover, he should know vastly better how he stood.

PART EIGHTH

XIX

STRETHER rambled alone during these few days; the effect of the incident of the previous week having been to simplify in a marked fashion his mixed relations with Waymarsh. Nothing had passed between them in reference to Mrs. Newsome's summons but that our friend had mentioned to his own the departure of the deputation actually at sea—giving him thus an opportunity to confess to the occult intervention he imputed to him. Waymarsh, however, in the event, confessed to nothing; and though this falsified in some degree Strether's forecast, the latter saw in it, amusedly, the same depth of good conscience out of which the dear man's impertinence had originally sprung. He was patient with the dear man now, and delighted to observe that he had unmistakably put on flesh; he felt his own holiday so successfully large and free that he was full of allowances and charities in respect to those cabined and confined: his instinct toward a spirit so strapped down as Waymarsh's was to walk round it on tiptoe for fear of waking it up to a sense of losses by this time irretrievable. It was all very funny, he knew, and but the difference, as he often said to himself, of tweedledum and tweedledee—an emancipation so purely comparative that it was like the advance of the door-mat on the scraper; yet the present crisis was happily to profit by it and the pilgrim from Milrose to know himself more than ever in the right.

Strether felt that when he heard of the approach of the Pococks the impulse of pity quite sprang up in him beside the impulse of triumph. That was exactly why Waymarsh had looked at him with eyes in which the heat of justice was measured and shaded. He had looked very hard, as if affectionately sorry for the friend—the friend of fifty-five—whose frivolity had had thus to be recorded; becoming, however, but obscurely sententious and leaving his companion to formulate a charge. It was in this general attitude that he had of late altogether taken refuge; with the drop of discussion

241

they were solemnly, sadly superficial; Strether recognized in him the mere portentous rumination to which Miss Barrace had so good-humoredly described herself as assigning a corner of her salon. It was quite as if he knew the step he had taken had been divined; and it was also as if he missed the chance to explain the purity of his motive; but this privation of opportunity should be precisely his small penance: it was not amiss for Strether that he should find himself to that degree uneasy. If he had been challenged or accused, rebuked for meddling or otherwise pulled up, he would probably have shown, on his own system, all the height of his consistency, all the depth of his good faith. Explicit resentment of his course would have made him take the floor, and the thump of his fist on the table would have affirmed him as consciously incorruptible. Was what had now really prevailed with Strether been but a dread of that thump—a dread of wincing a little painfully at what it might invidiously demonstrate? However this might be, at any rate, one of the marks of the situation was a visible lapse, in Waymarsh, of expectation. As if to make up to his comrade for the stroke by which he had played providence, he now conspicuously ignored his movements, withdrew himself from the pretension to share them, stiffened up his sensibility to neglect, and, clasping his large empty hands and swinging his large restless foot, clearly looked to another quarter for relief.

This made for independence on Strether's part, and he had in truth at no moment of his stay been so free to go and come. The early summer brushed the picture over and blurred everything but the near; it made a vast, warm, fragrant medium in which the elements floated together on the best of terms, in which rewards were immediate and reckonings postponed. Chad was out of town again, for the first time since his visitor's first view of him; he had explained this necessity—without detail, yet also without embarrassment; the circumstance was one of those which, in the young man's life, testified to the variety of his ties. Strether was not otherwise concerned with it than as to its so testifying—a pleasant multitudinous image in which he took comfort. He took comfort, by the same stroke, in the swing of Chad's pendulum back from that other swing, the sharp jerk towards Woollett, so stayed by his own hand. He had the entertainment of thinking that if he had for that moment stopped the clock, it was to promote, the next minute, this still livelier motion. He himself did what he had not done before; he took two or three times whole days off—irrespective of others, of two or three that he took with Miss Gostrey, two or three that he took with little Bilham: he went to Chartres and cultivated, before the front of the cathedral, a general easy beatitude; he went to Fontainebleau and imagined himself on the way to Italy; he went to Rouen with a little handbag and inordinately spent the night.

One afternoon he did something quite different; finding himself in the neighborhood of a fine old house across the river, he passed under the great arch of its doorway and asked at the porter's lodge for Mme. de Vionnet. He had already hovered more than once about that possibility, been aware of it, in the course of ostensible strolls, as lurking but round the corner. Only it had perversely happened, after his morning at Notre Dame, that his consistency, as he considered and intended it, had come back to him; whereby he had reflected that the encounter in question had been none of his making; clinging again intensely to the strength of his position, which was precisely that there was nothing in it for himself. From the moment he actively pursued the charming associate of his adventure, from that moment his position weakened, for he was then acting in an interested way. It was only within a few days that he had fixed himself a limit: he promised himself his consistency should end with Sarah's arrival. It was arguing correctly to feel the title to a free hand that this event would give him. If he was not to be let alone he should be merely a dupe to act with delicacy. If he was not to be trusted he could at least take his ease. If he was to be placed under control he became free to try what his position *might* agreeably give him. An ideal rigor would perhaps postpone the trial till after the Pococks had shown their spirit; and it was to an ideal rigor that he had quite promised himself to conform.

Suddenly, however, on this particular day, he felt a particular fear under which everything collapsed. He knew abruptly that he was afraid of himself—and yet not in relation to the effect on his sensibilities of another hour of Mme. de Vionnet. What he dreaded was the effect of a single hour of Sarah Pocock, as to whom he was visited, in troubled nights, with fantastic waking dreams. She loomed at him larger than life; she increased in volume as she came; she so met his eyes that, his imagination taking, after the first step, all, and more than all, the strides, he already felt her come down on him, already burned, under her reprobation, with the blush of guilt, already consented, by way of penance, to the instant forfeiture of everything. He saw himself recommitted, under her direction, to Woollett, as juvenile offenders are committed to reformatories. It was not of course that Woollett was really a place of discipline; but he knew in advance that Sarah's salon at the hotel would be. His danger, at any rate, in these moods of alarm, was some concession, on this ground, that would involve a sharp rupture with the actual; therefore if he waited to take leave of it he might wholly miss his chance. It was represented with supreme vividness by Mme. de Vionnet, and that is why, in a word, he waited no longer. He had seen in a flash that he must anticipate Mrs. Pocock. He was accordingly much disappointed on now learning from the portress that the lady of his quest was not in Paris. She had gone for some days to the country. There was nothing in this accident but what was natural; yet it produced for poor Strether a drop of all confidence. It was suddenly as if he should never see her again, and as if moreover he had brought it on himself by not having been quite kind to her.

It was the advantage of his having let his fancy lose itself for a little in the gloom that the prospect, by reaction, began really to brighten from the moment the deputation from Woollett alighted on the platform of the station. They had come straight from Havre, having sailed from New York to that port, and having also, thanks to a happy voyage, made land with a promptitude that left Chad Newsome, who had meant to meet them at the dock, belated. He had received their telegram, with the announcement of their immediate further advance, just as he was taking the train for Havre, so that nothing had remained for him but to await them in Paris. He hastily picked up Strether, at the hotel, for this purpose, and he even, with easy pleasantry, suggested the attendance of Waymarsh as well—Waymarsh, at the moment his cab rattled up, being engaged, under Strether's contemplative range, in a grave perambulation of the familiar court. Waymarsh had learned from his companion, who had already had a note, delivered by hand, from

Chad, that the Pococks were due, and had ambiguously, though, as always, impressively, glowered at him over the circumstance; carrying himself in a manner in which Strether was now expert enough to recognize his uncertainty, in the premises, as to the best tone. The only tone he really liked was a full tone—which was necessarily difficult in the absence of a full knowledge. The Pococks were a quantity as yet unmeasured, and, as he had practically brought them over, so Waymarsh had to that extent exposed himself. He wanted to feel right about it, but he could only, at the best, for the time, feel vague. " I shall look to you, you know, immensely," our friend had said, " to help me with them," and he had been quite conscious of the effect of the remark, and of others of the same sort, on his comrade's sombre sensibility. He had insisted on the fact that he would quite like Mrs. Pocock—one could be certain he would: he would be with her about everything, and she would also be with *him,* and Miss Barrace's nose, in short, would find itself out of joint.

Strether had woven this web of cheerfulness while they waited in the court for Chad; he had sat smoking cigarettes to keep himself quiet, while before him, caged and leonine, his fellow-traveller paced and turned. Chad Newsome was doubtless to be struck, when he arrived, with the sharpness of their opposition at this particular hour; he was to remember, as a part of it, how Waymarsh came with him and with Strether to the street and stood there with a face half wistful and half rueful. They talked of him, the two others, as they drove, and Strether put Chad in possession of much of his own strained sense of things. He had already, a few days before, named to him the wire that he was convinced their friend had pulled—a confidence that had made, on the young man's part, quite hugely for curiosity and diversion. The effect of the matter, moreover, Strether could see, was sharp; he saw, that is, how Chad judged a system of influence in which Waymarsh had served as a determinant—an impression just now quickened again; with the whole bearing of such a fact on the youth's view of his relations. As it came up between them that they might now regard their friend as a feature of the control of these latter now sought to be exerted from Woollett, Strether felt indeed how it would be stamped all over him, half an hour later, for Sarah Pocock's eyes, that he was as much on Chad's "side" as Waymarsh had probably described him. He was letting himself, at present, go; there was no denying it; it might be desperation, it might be confidence; he should offer himself to the arriving travellers bristling with all the lucidity he had cultivated.

He repeated to Chad what he had been saying, in the court, to Waymarsh; how there was no doubt whatever that his sister would find the latter a kindred spirit, no doubt of the alliance, based on an exchange of views, that the pair would successfully strike up. They would become as thick as thieves—which moreover was but a development of what Strether remembered to have said in one of his first discussions with his mate, struck as he had then already been with the elements of affinity between that personage and Mrs. Newsome herself. "I told him, one day, when he had questioned me on your mother, that she was a person who, when he should know her, would rouse in him, I was sure, a special enthusiasm; and that hangs together with the conviction we now feel—this certitude that Mrs. Pocock will take him into her boat. For it's your mother's own boat that she's pulling."

"Ah," said Chad, "mother's worth fifty of Sally!"

"A thousand; but when you presently meet her, all the same, you'll be meeting your mother's representative—just as I shall. I feel like the outgoing ambassador," said Strether, "doing honor to his appointed successor." A moment after speaking as he had just done he felt that he had inadvertently rather cheapened Mrs. Newsome to her son; an impression audibly reflected, as at first seen, in Chad's prompt protest. He had recently rather failed of apprehension of the young man's attitude and temper—remaining principally conscious of how little worry, at the worst, he wasted; and he studied him at this critical hour with renewed interest. Chad had done exactly what he had promised him a fortnight previous—had accepted without another question his plea for delay. He was waiting cheerfully and handsomely, but also inscrutably and with a slight increase perhaps of the hardness originally involved in his acquired high polish. He was neither excited nor depressed; was easy and acute and deliberate—unhurried, unflurried, unworried, only at most a little less amused than usual. Strether felt him more than ever a justification of the extraordinary process of which his own absurd spirit had been the arena; he knew as their cab rolled along, knew as he had not even yet known, that nothing else than what Chad had done and had been would have led to his present showing. They had made him, these things, what he was, and the business had not been easy; it had taken time and trouble, it had cost, above all, a price. The result, at any rate, was now to be offered to Sally; which Strether, so far as that was concerned, was glad to be there to witness. Would she in the least make it out or take it in, the result, or would she in the least care for it if she did? He scratched his chin as he asked himself by what name, when challenged—as he was sure he should be—he could call it for her. Oh, those were determinations she must herself arrive at; since she wanted so much to see, let her see then and welcome. She had come out in the pride of her competence, yet it hummed in Strether's inner sense that she practically wouldn't see.

That this was moreover what Chad shrewdly suspected was clear from a word that next dropped from him. "They're children; they play at life!"—and the exclamation was significant and reassuring. It implied that he hadn't then, for his companion's sensibility, appeared to give Mrs. Newsome away; and it facilitated our friend's presently asking him if it were his idea that Mrs. Pocock and Mme. de Vionnet should become acquainted. Strether was still more sharply struck, hereupon, with Chad's lucidity. "Why, isn't that exactly—to get a sight of the company I keep—what she has come out for?"

"Yes—I'm afraid it is," Strether unguardedly replied.

Chad's quick rejoinder lighted his precipitation. "Why do you say you're afraid?"

"Well, because I feel a certain responsibility. It's my testimony, I imagine, that will have been at the bottom of Mrs. Pocock's curiosity. My letters, as I've supposed you to understand from the beginning, have spoken freely. I've certainly said my little say about Mme. de Vionnet."

All that, for Chad, was beautifully obvious. "Yes, but you've only spoken handsomely."

"Never more handsomely of any woman. But it's just that tone—!"

" That tone," said Chad, " that has fetched her? I dare say; but I've no quarrel with you about it. And no more has Mme. de Vionnet. Don't you know, by this time, how she likes you?"

" Oh!"—and Strether had, with his groan, a real pang of melancholy. " For all I've done for her!"

" Ah, you've done a great deal."

Chad's urbanity fairly shamed him, and he was at this moment absolutely impatient to see the face Sarah Pocock would present to a force as to which, certainly, despite his own admonitions, she would arrive with no adequate forecast. " I've done *this!*"

" Well, this is all right. She likes," Chad comfortably remarked, " to be liked."

It gave his companion a moment's thought. " And she's sure Mrs. Pocock *will*—?"

" No, I say that for *you*. She likes your liking her; it's so much, as it were," Chad laughed, " to the good. However, she doesn't despair of Sarah either, and is prepared, on her own side, to go all lengths."

" In the way of appreciation?"

" Yes, and of everything else. In the way of general amiability, hospitality and welcome. She's under arms," Chad laughed again; " she's prepared."

Strether took it in; then as if an echo of Miss Barrace were in the air: " She's wonderful."

" You don't begin to know *how* wonderful!"

There was a depth in it, to Strether's ear, of confirmed luxury —almost a kind of unconscious insolence of proprietorship; but the effect of the glimpse was not at this moment to foster speculation; there was something so conclusive in so much graceful and generous assurance. It was a fresh evocation, in fact; and the evocation had, before many minutes, another consequence. " Well, I shall see her oftener now. I shall see her as much as I like— by your leave; which is what I hitherto haven't done."

" It has been," said Chad, but without reproach, " only your own fault. I tried to bring you together, and *she*—my dear fellow, I never saw her more charming to any man. But you've got your extraordinary ideas."

" Well, I *did* have," Strether murmured; while he felt both how

they had possessed him and how they had now lost their authority.
He couldn't have traced the sequence to the end, but it was all
because of Mrs. Pocock. Mrs. Pocock might be because of Mrs.
Newsome, but that was still to be proved. What came over him
was the sense of having stupidly failed to profit where profit would
have been precious. It had been open to him to see so much
more of her, and he had but let the good days pass. Fierce in him
almost was the resolve to lose no more of them, and he whimsically reflected while he drew nearer, at Chad's side, to his destina-
tion, that it was Sarah, after all, who would have touched up his
chance. What her visit of inquisition might achieve in other
directions was as yet all obscure; but it was not obscure that it
would do supremely much to bring two earnest persons together.
He had only to listen to Chad at this moment to feel it; for Chad
was in the act of remarking to him that they of course both
counted on him—he himself and the other earnest person—for cheer
and support. It was brave to Strether to hear him talk as if the
line of wisdom they had struck out was to make things ravishing
to the Pococks. No, if Mme. de Vionnet compassed *that,* compassed the ravishment of the Pococks, Mme. de Vionnet would be
prodigious. It would be a beautiful plan if it succeeded, and it all
came to the question of Sarah's being really bribable. The prece-
dent of his own case helped Strether perhaps but little to consider
she might prove so; it being distinct that her character would make,
rather, for every possible difference. This idea of his own briba-
bility set him apart, for himself; with the further mark, in fact,
that his case was absolutely proved. He liked always, where
Lambert Strether was concerned, to know the worst, and what he
now seemed to know was not only that he was bribable, but that
he had been effectually bribed. The only difficulty was that he
couldn't quite have said with what. It was as if he had sold himself, but hadn't somehow got the cash. That, however, was what,
characteristically, *would* happen to him. It would naturally be his
kind of traffic. While he thought of these things, at any rate, he
reminded Chad of the truth they mustn't lose sight of—the truth
that, with all deference to her susceptibility to new interests, Sarah
would have come out with a high, firm, definite purpose. " She
hasn't come out, you know, to be bamboozled. We may all be ravish-

ing—nothing perhaps can be more easy for us; but she hasn't come out to be ravished. She has come out just simply to take you home."

"Oh, well, with *her* I'll go," said Chad, good-humoredly. "I suppose you'll allow *that.*" And then as, for a minute, Strether said nothing: "Or is your idea that when I've seen her I won't want to go?" As this question, however, again left his friend silent he presently went on: "My own idea, at any rate, is that they shall have, while they're here, a good time."

It was at this that Strether spoke. "Ah, there you are! I think if you really wanted to go—!"

"Well?" said Chad to bring it out.

"Well, you wouldn't trouble about our good time. You wouldn't care what sort of a time we have."

Chad could always take, in the easiest way in the world, any ingenious suggestion. "I see. But can I help it? I'm too decent."

"Yes, you're too decent!" Strether heavily sighed. And he felt, for the moment, as if it were the preposterous end of his mission.

It ministered for the time to this temporary effect that Chad made no rejoinder. But he spoke again as they came in sight of the station. "Do you mean to introduce her to Miss Gostrey?"

As to this Strether was ready. "No."

"But haven't you told me they know about her?"

"I think I've told you your mother knows."

"And won't she have told Sally?"

"That's one of the things I want to see."

"And if you find she *has*—?"

"Will I then, you mean, bring them together?"

"Yes," said Chad with his pleasant promptness: "to show her there's nothing in it."

Strether hesitated. "I don't know that I care very much what she may think there's in it."

"Not if it represents what mother thinks?"

"Ah, what *does* your mother think?" There was in this some sound of bewilderment.

But they were just driving up, and help, of a sort, might, after all, well be at hand. "Isn't that, my dear man, what we're both just going to make out?"

XX

STRETHER quitted the station half an hour later in different company. Chad had taken charge, for the journey to the hotel, of Sarah,
Mamie, the maid and the luggage, all spaciously installed and conveyed; and it was only after the four had rolled away that his companion got into a cab with Jim. A strange new feeling had come
over Strether, in consequence of which his spirits had risen; it was
as if what had occurred on the alighting of the travellers had been
something other than his fear, though his fear had yet not been of an
instant scene of violence. His impression had been nothing but
what was inevitable—he said that to himself; yet relief and reassurance had softly dropped upon him. Nothing could be so odd
as to be indebted for these things to the look of faces and the sound
of voices that had been with him to satiety, as he might have said,
for years; but he now knew, all the same, how uneasy he had been;
that was brought home to him by his present sense of a respite. It
had come, moreover, in the flash of an eye; it had come in the smile
with which Sarah, whom, at the window of her compartment, they
had effusively greeted from the platform, rustled down to them a
moment later, fresh and handsome from her cool June progress
through the charming land. It was only a sign, but enough: she
was going to be gracious and unallusive, she was going to play the
larger game—which was still more apparent, after she had emerged
from Chad's arms, in her direct greeting to the valued friend of
her family.

Strether *was* then, as much as ever, the valued friend of her
family; it was something he could at all events go on with; and the
manner of his response to it expressed even for himself how little
he had liked the prospect of ceasing to figure in that character. He
had always seen Sarah gracious—had in fact rarely seen her shy
or dry; her marked, thin-lipped smile, intense without brightness

251

and as prompt to act as the scrape of a safety-match; the protrusion of her rather remarkably long chin, which in her case represented invitation and urbanity, and not, as in most others, pugnacity and defiance; the penetration of her voice to a distance, the general encouragement and approval of her manner, were all elements with which intercourse had made him familiar, but which he noted to-day almost as if she had been a new acquaintance. This first glimpse of her had given a brief but vivid accent to her resemblance to her mother; he could have taken her for Mrs. Newsome while she met his eyes as the train rolled into the station. It was an impression that quickly dropped; Mrs. Newsome was much handsomer, and while Sarah inclined to the massive, her mother had, at an age, still the girdle of a maid; the latter's chin, also, was rather short than long, and her smile, by good fortune, much more, oh ever so much more, mercifully vague. Strether had seen Mrs. Newsome reserved; he had literally heard her silent; though he had never known her disagreeable. It was the case with Mrs. Pocock that he had known *her* disagreeable, even though he had never known her not affable. She had forms of affability that were in a high degree affirmative; nothing, for instance, had ever been more striking than that she was affable to Jim.

What had told, at any rate, at the window of the train, was her high, clear forehead, that forehead which her friends, for some reason, always thought of as a " brow "; the long reach of her eyes— it came out at this juncture in such a manner as to remind him, oddly enough, also of that of Waymarsh's; and the unusual gloss of her dark hair, dressed and hatted after her mother's refined example, with such an avoidance of extremes that it was always spoken of at Woollett as " their own." Though this analogy dropped as soon as she was on the platform, it had lasted long enough to make him feel all the advantage, as it were, of his relief. The woman at home, the woman to whom he was attached, was before him just long enough to give him again the measure of the wretchedness, in fact really of the shame, of their having to recognize the formation, between them, of a " split." He had taken this measure in solitude and meditation; but the catastrophe, as Sarah steamed up, looked, for its few seconds, unprecedentedly dreadful—or proved, more exactly, absolutely unthinkable; so that his finding something free and familiar to respond to brought with it an instant renewal of his loyalty. He had suddenly sounded the whole depth, had gasped at what he might have lost.

Well, he could now, for the quarter of an hour of their detention, hover about the travellers as soothingly as if their direct message to him was that he had lost nothing. He wasn't going to have Sarah write to her mother that night that he was in any way altered or strange. There had been times enough for a month when it had seemed to him that he was strange, that he was altered, in every way; but that was a matter for himself; he knew at least whose business it was *not*; it was not at all events such a circumstance as Sarah's own unaided lights would help her to. Even if she had come out to flash those lights more than yet appeared, she wouldn't make much headway against mere pleasantness. He counted on being able to be merely pleasant to the end; and if only from incapacity, moreover, to formulate anything different. He couldn't even formulate to himself his being changed and queer; it had taken place, the process, somewhere deep down; Maria Gostrey had caught glimpses of it; but how was he to fish it up, even if he desired, for Mrs. Pocock? This was the spirit then in which he hovered, and with the easier throb in it much indebted, moreover, to the impression of high and established adequacy as a pretty girl promptly produced in him by Mamie. He had wondered vaguely—turning over many things in the fidget of his thoughts—if Mamie *were* as pretty as Woollett published her; as to which issue seeing her now again was to be so swept away by Woollett's opinion that this consequence really let loose for the imagination an avalanche of others. There were positively five minutes in which the last word seemed of necessity to abide with a Woollett represented by a Mamie. This was the sort of truth the place itself would feel; it would send her forth in confidence; it would point to her with triumph; it would take its stand on her with assurance; it would be conscious of no requirement she didn't meet, of no question she couldn't answer.

Well, it was right, Strether slipped smoothly enough into the cheerfulness of saying; granted that a community *might* be best represented by a young lady of twenty-two, Mamie perfectly played the part, played it as if she were used to it, and looked and spoke and dressed the character. He wondered if she mightn't, in the high light of Paris, a cool, full studio-light, becoming, yet treacherous, show as too conscious of these matters; but the next moment he felt satisfied that her consciousness was, after all, empty for its size, rather too simple than too mixed, and that the kind way with her would be not to take many things out of it, but to put as many as possible in. She was robust and conveniently tall; just a trifle too bloodlessly fair perhaps, but with a pleasant, public, familiar radiance that affirmed her vitality. She might have been "receiving" for Woollett, wherever she found herself, and there was something in her manner, her tone, her motion, her pretty blue eyes, her pretty, perfect teeth and her very small, too small, nose, that immediately placed her, to the fancy, between the windows of a hot, bright room in which voices were high—up at that end to which people were brought to be "presented." They were there to congratulate, these images, and Strether's renewed vision, on this hint, completed the idea. What Mamie was like was the happy bride, the bride after the church and just before going away. She wasn't the mere maiden—yet on the other hand she was only as much married as *that*. She was in the brilliant, triumphant, festal stage. Well, might it last her long!

Strether rejoiced in these things for Chad, who was all genial attention to the needs of his friends, besides having arranged that his servant should reinforce him; the ladies were certainly pleasant to see, and Mamie would be at any time and anywhere pleasant to exhibit. She would look extraordinarily like his young wife—the wife of a honeymoon, should he go about with her; but that was his own affair—or perhaps it was hers; it was something, at any rate, she couldn't help. Strether remembered how he had seen him come up with Jeanne de Vionnet in Gloriani's garden, and the fancy he had had about that—the fancy obscured now, thickly overlaid with others; the recollection was during these minutes his only note of trouble. He had often, in spite of himself, wondered if Chad were *not*, with Jeanne, the object of a still and shaded flame. It was on the cards that the child *might* be tremulously in love, and this conviction now flickered up not a bit the less for his disliking to think of it, for its being, in a complicated situation, a complication the more, and for something indescribable in Mamie, something, at all events, that his own mind straightway lent her, something that gave her value, gave her intensity and purpose, as the symbol of an opposition. Little Jeanne wasn't really at all in question—how *could* she be?—yet from the moment Miss Pocock had shaken her skirts on the platform, touched up the immense bows of her hat and settled properly over her shoulder the strap of her morocco-and-gilt travelling-satchel, from that moment little Jeanne was opposed.

It was in the cab with Jim that impressions really crowded on Strether, giving him the strangest sense of length of absence from people among whom he had lived for years. Having them thus come out to him was as if he had returned to find them; and the droll promptitude of Jim's mental reaction threw his own initiation far back into the past. Whoever might or mightn't be suited by what was going on among them, Jim, for one, would certainly be: his instant recognition—frank and whimsical—of what the affair was for *him* gave Strether a glow of pleasure. "I say, you know, this is about my shape, and if it hadn't been for *you*—!" so he broke out as the charming streets met his healthy appetite; and he wound up, after an expressive nudge, with a clap of his companion's knee and an "Oh, you, you—you *are* doing it!" that was charged with rich meaning. Strether felt in it the intention of homage, but, with a curiosity otherwise occupied, postponed taking it up. What he was asking himself for the time was how Sarah Pocock, in the opportunity already given her, had judged her brother—from whom he himself, as they finally, at the station, separated for their different conveyances, had had a look into which he could read more than one message. However Sarah was judging her brother, Chad's conclusion about his sister, and about her husband and her husband's sister, was at the least on the way to be sharp. Strether felt the sharpness, and that, as the look between them was an exchange, what he himself gave back was relatively vague. That comparison of notes, however, could wait; everything struck him as depending on the effect produced by Chad. Neither Sarah nor Mamie had in any way, at the station—where they had had, after all, full time— broken out about it; which, to make up for this, was what our friend had expected of Jim as soon as they should find themselves together.

It was queer to him that he had had that noiseless brush with Chad; an ironic intelligence with this youth on the subject of his relatives, an intelligence carried on under their nose and, as might be said, at their expense—such a matter marked again for him strongly the number of stages he had come; albeit that if the number seemed great the time taken for the final one was but the turn of a hand. He had before this had his moments of wondering if he himself were not perhaps changed even as Chad was changed. Only what in Chad was conspicuous improvement—well, he had no name ready for the action, in his own organism, of his own more timid dose. He should have to see first what this action would be. And for his occult passage with the young man, after all, the direct- ness of it had no greater oddity than the fact that the young man's way with the three travellers should have been so happy a mani- festation. Strether liked him for it, on the spot, as he had not yet liked him; it affected him, while it lasted, as he might have been affected by some light, pleasant, perfect work of art: to that degree that he wondered if they were really worthy of it, took it in and did it justice; to that degree that it would have been scarce a miracle if, there in the luggage-room, while they waited for their things, Sarah had pulled his sleeve and drawn him aside. "You're right; we haven't quite known what you mean, mother and I, but now we see. Chad's magnificent; what can one want more? If *this* be the kind of thing—!" On which they might, as it were, have embraced and begun to work together.

Ah, how much, as it was, for all her bridling brightness—which was merely general and noticed nothing—*would* they work to- gether? Strether knew he was unreasonable; he set it down to his being nervous: people couldn't notice everything and speak of everything in a quarter of an hour. Possibly, no doubt, also, he made too much of Chad's display. Yet, none the less, when, at the end of five minutes, in the cab, Jim Pocock had said nothing either —hadn't said, that is, what Strether wanted, though he had said much else—it all suddenly bounced back to their being either stupid or wilful. It was more probably, on the whole, the former; so that that would be the drawback of the bridling brightness. Yes, they would bridle and be bright; they would make the best of what was before them, but their observation would fail; it would be beyond them; they simply wouldn't understand. Of what use would it be then that they had come?—if they weren't to be intelligent up to *that* point: unless indeed he himself were utterly deluded and extravagant? Was he, on this question of Chad's improvement, fantastic and away from the truth? Did he live in a false world, a world that had grown simply to suit him, and was his present slight irritation—in the face, now, of Jim's silence in particular — but the alarm of the vain thing menaced by the touch of the real? Was this contribution of the real possibly the mission of the Pococks?—had they come to make the work of observation, as *he* had practised observation, crack and crumble, and to reduce Chad to the plain terms in which honest minds could deal with him? Had they come in short to be sane where Strether was destined to feel that he himself had only been silly?

He glanced at such a contingency, but it failed to hold him long when once he had reflected that he would have been silly, in this case, with Maria Gostrey and little Bilham, with Mme. de Vionnet and little Jeanne, with Lambert Strether, in fine, and above all with Chad Newsome himself. Wouldn't it be found to have made more for reality to be silly with these persons than sane with Sarah and Jim? Jim, in fact, he presently made up his mind, was individually out of it; Jim didn't care; Jim hadn't come out either for Chad or for him; Jim, in short, left the moral side to Sally, and indeed simply availed himself now, for the sense of recreation, of the fact that he left almost everything to Sally. He was nothing compared to Sally, and not so much by reason of Sally's temper and will as by that of her more developed type and greater acquaintance with the world. He quite frankly and serenely confessed, as he sat there with Strether, that he felt his type hang far in the rear of his wife's, and still further, if possible, in the rear of his sister's. Their types, he well knew, were recognized and acclaimed; whereas the most a leading Woollett business-man could hope to achieve socially, and, for that matter, industrially, was a certain freedom to play into this general glamour.

The impression he made on our friend was another of the things that marked our friend's road. It was a strange impression, especially as so soon produced; Strether had received it, he judged, all in the twenty minutes; it struck him at least as but in a minor degree the work of the long Woollett years. Pocock was normally and consentingly, though not quite wittingly, out of the question. It was despite his being normal; it was despite his being cheerful; it was despite his being a leading Woollett business-man; and the determination of his fate left him thus perfectly usual—as everything else about it was clearly, to his sense, not less so. He seemed to say that there was a whole side of life on which the perfectly usual *was* for leading Woollett business-men to be out of the question. He made no more of it than that, and Strether, so far as Jim was concerned, desired to make no more. Only Strether's imagination, as always, worked, and he asked himself if this side of life were not somehow connected, for those who figured on it, with the fact of marriage. Would *his* relation to it, had he married ten years before, have become now the same as Pocock's? Might it even become the same should he marry in a few months? Should he ever know himself as much out of the question for Mrs. Newsome as Jim knew himself—in a dim way—for Mrs. Jim?

To turn his eyes in that direction was to be, personally, reassured; he was different from Pocock; he had affirmed himself differently; and he was held, after all, in higher esteem. What none the less came home to him, however, at this hour, was that the society, over there, of which Sarah and Mamie—and, in a more eminent way, Mrs. Newsome herself—were specimens, was essentially a society of women, and that poor Jim wasn't in it. He himself, Lambert Strether, *was,* as yet, in some degree—which was an odd situation for a man; but it kept coming back to him in a whimsical way that he should perhaps find his marriage had cost him his place. This occasion indeed, whatever that fancy represented, was not a time of sensible exclusion for Jim, who was in a state of manifest response to the charm of his adventure. Small and fat and constantly facetious, straw-colored and destitute of marks, he would have been practically indistinguishable had not his constant preference for light-gray clothes, for white hats, for very big cigars and very little stories done what it could for his identity. There were signs in him, though none of them plaintive, of always paying for others; and the principal one perhaps was just this failure of type. It was with this that he paid, rather than with fatigue or waste; and also, doubtless, a little, with the effort of humor—never irrelevant to the conditions, to the relations, with which he was acquainted.

He gurgled his joy as they rolled through the happy streets; he declared that his trip was a regular windfall, and that he wasn't there, he was eager to remark, to hang back from anything; he didn't know quite what Sally had come for, but *he* had come for a good time. Strether indulged him even while wondering if what Sally wanted her brother to go back for was to become like her husband. He trusted that a good time was to be, out and out, the programme for all of them; and he assented liberally to Jim's proposal that, disencumbered and irresponsible—his things were in the omnibus with those of the others—they should take a further turn round before going to the hotel. It wasn't for *him* to tackle Chad—it was Sally's job; and as it would be like her, he felt, to open fire on the spot, it wouldn't be amiss of them to hold off and give her time. Strether, on his side, only asked to give her time; so he jogged with his companion along boulevards and avenues, trying to extract from meagre material some forecast of his catastrophe. He was quick enough to see that Jim Pocock declined judgment, had hovered quite round the outer edge of discussion and anxiety, leaving all analysis of their question to the ladies alone and now only feeling his way toward some small, droll cynicism. It broke out afresh, the cynicism—it had already shown a flicker—in a but slightly deferred: "Well, hanged if I would if *I* were he!"

"You mean you wouldn't in Chad's place—?"

"Give up this to go back and boss the advertising!" Poor Jim, with his arms folded and his little legs out in the open fiacre, drank in the sparkling Paris noon and carried his eyes from one side of their vista to the other. "Why, I want to come out here and live myself. And I want to live while I *am* here too. I feel with *you*— oh you've been grand, old man, and I've twigged—that it ain't right to worry Chad. *I* don't mean to persecute him; I couldn't in conscience. It's thanks to you, at any rate, that I'm here; and I'm sure I'm much obliged. You're a lovely pair."

There were things in this speech that Strether, for the time, let pass. "Don't you then think it important the advertising should be thoroughly taken in hand? Chad *will* be, so far as capacity is concerned," he went on, " the man to do it."

" Where did he get his capacity," Jim asked, " over here?"

" He didn't get it over here, and the wonderful thing is that, over here, he hasn't inevitably lost it. He has a natural turn for business, an extraordinary head. He comes by that," Strether explained, " honestly enough. He's in that respect his father's son, and also—for she's wonderful, in her way, too—his mother's. He has other tastes and other tendencies; but Mrs. Newsome and your wife are quite right about his having that. He's very remarkable."

" Well, I guess he is!" Jim Pocock comfortably sighed. " But if you've believed so in his making us hum, why have you so prolonged the discussion? Don't you know we've been quite anxious about you?"

These questions were not informed with earnestness, but Strether saw he must none the less make a choice and take a line. " Because, you see, I've greatly liked it. I've liked my Paris. I dare say I've liked it too much."

" Oh, you old wretch!" Jim gayly exclaimed.

" But nothing is concluded," Strether went on. " The case is more complex than it looks from Woollett."

" Oh well, it looks bad enough from Woollett!" Jim declared.

" Even after all I've written?"

Jim bethought himself. " Isn't it what you've written that has made Mrs. Newsome pack us off? That, at least, and Chad's not turning up?"

Strether made a reflection of his own. " I see. That she should do something was, no doubt, inevitable, and your wife has therefore, of course, come out to act."

" Oh yes," Jim concurred—" to act. But Sally comes out to act, you know," he lucidly added, " every time she leaves the house. She never comes out but she *does* act. She's acting moreover now for her mother, and that fixes the scale." Then he wound up, opening all his senses to it, with a renewed embrace of pleasant Paris. " We haven't, all the same, at Woollett, got anything like this."

Strether continued to consider. " I'm bound to say for you all that you strike me as having arrived in a very mild and reasonable frame of mind. You don't show your claws. I felt just now in Mrs. Pocock no symptom of that. She isn't fierce," he went on. "I'm such a nervous idiot that I thought she might be."

"Oh, don't you know her well enough," Pocock asked, "to have noticed that she never gives herself away, any more than her mother ever does? They ain't fierce, either of 'em; they let you come quite close. They wear their fur the smooth side out—the warm side in. Do you know what they are?" Jim pursued as he looked about him, giving the question, as Strether felt, but half his care— "do you know what they are? They're about as intense as they can live."

"Yes"—and Strether's concurrence had a positive precipitation, "they're about as intense as they can live."

"They don't lash about and shake the cage," said Jim, who seemed pleased with his analogy; "and it's at feeding-time that they're quietest. But they always get there."

"They do indeed—they always get there!" Strether replied with a laugh that justified his confession of nervousness. He disliked to be talking sincerely of Mrs. Newsome with Pocock; he could have talked insincerely. But there was something he wanted to know, a need created in him by her recent intermission, by his having given, from the first, so much, as now more than ever appeared to him, and got so little. It was as if a queer truth in his companion's metaphor had rolled over him with a rush. She *had* been quiet at feeding-time; she had fed, and Sarah had fed with her, out of the big bowl of all his recent free communication, his vividness and pleasantness, his ingenuity and even his eloquence, while the current of her response had steadily run thin. Jim meanwhile, however, it was true, slipped characteristically into shallowness from the moment he ceased to speak out of the experience of a husband.

"But of course Chad has now the advantage of being there before her. If he doesn't work that for all it's worth—!" He sighed with contingent pity at his brother-in-law's possible want of resource. "He has worked it on *you*, pretty well, eh?" and he asked the next moment if there were anything new at the Varieties, which he pronounced in the American manner. They talked about the Varieties—Strether confessing to a knowledge which produced again on Pocock's part a play of innuendo as vague as a nursery-rhyme, yet as aggressive as an elbow in his side; and they finished their drive under the protection of easy themes. Strether waited to the end, but still in vain, for any show that Jim had seen Chad as different; and he could scarce have explained the discouragement he drew from the absence of this testimony. It was what he had taken his own stand on, so far as he had taken a stand; and if they were all only going to see nothing he had only wasted his time. He gave his friend till the very last moment, till they had come into sight of the hotel; and when poor Pocock only continued cheerful and envious and funny he fairly grew to dislike him, to feel him extravagantly common. If they were *all* going to see nothing!—Strether knew, as this came back to him, that he was also letting Pocock represent for him what Mrs. Newsome wouldn't see. He went on disliking, in the light of Jim's commonness, to talk to him about that lady; yet just before the cab pulled up he knew the extent of his desire for the real word from Woollett.

"Has Mrs. Newsome at all given way—?"

"'Given way'?"—Jim echoed it with the practical derision of his sense of a long past.

"Under the strain, I mean, of hope deferred, of disappointment repeated and thereby intensified."

"Oh, is she prostrate, you mean?"—he had his categories in hand. "Why, yes, she's prostrate—just as Sally is. But they're never so lively, you know, as when they're prostrate."

"Ah, Sarah's prostrate?" Strether vaguely murmured.

"It's when they're prostrate that they most sit up."

"And Mrs. Newsome is sitting up?"

"All night, my boy—for *you!*" And Jim fetched him, with a vulgar little guffaw, a thrust that gave relief to the picture. But he had got what he wanted. He felt on the spot that this *was* the real word from Woollett. "So don't you go home!" Jim added while he alighted and while his friend, letting him profusely pay the cabman, sat on in a momentary muse. Strether wondered if that were the real word too.

XXI

As the door of Mrs. Pocock's salon was pushed open for him, the next day, well before noon, he was reached by a voice with a charming sound that made him just falter before crossing the threshold. Mme. de Vionnet was already on the field, and this gave the drama a quicker pace than he felt it as yet—though his suspense had increased—in the power of any act of his own to do. He had spent the previous evening with all his old friends together; yet he would still have described himself as quite in the dark in respect to a forecast of their influence on his situation. It was strange now, none the less, that, in the light of this unexpected note of her presence, he felt Mme. de Vionnet a part of that situation as she had not even yet been. She was alone, he found himself assuming, with Sarah, and there was a bearing in that—somehow beyond his control—on his personal fate. Yet she was only saying something quite independent and charming—the thing she had come, as a good friend of Chad's, on purpose to say. "There isn't anything at all—? I should be so delighted."

It was clear enough, when they were there before him, how she had been received. He saw this, as Sarah got up to greet him, from something fairly hectic in Sarah's face. He saw furthermore that they were not, as had first come to him, alone together; he was at no loss as to the identity of the broad, high back presented to him in the embrasure of the window furthest from the door. Waymarsh, whom he had to-day not yet seen, whom he only knew to have left the hotel before him and who had taken part, the night previous, on Mrs. Pocock's kind invitation, conveyed by Chad, in the entertainment, informal but cordial, promptly offered by that lady— Waymarsh had anticipated him even as Mme. de Vionnet had done, and, with his hands in his pockets and his attitude unaffected by Strether's entrance, was looking out, in marked detachment, at the

Rue de Rivoli. The latter felt it in the air—it was immense how Waymarsh could mark things—that he had remained deeply dissociated from the overture to their hostess that we have recorded on Mme. de Vionnet's side. He had, conspicuously, tact, besides a stiff general view; and this was why he had left Mrs. Pocock to struggle alone. He would outstay the visitor; he would unmistakably wait; to what had he been doomed for months past but waiting? Therefore she was to feel that she had him in reserve. What support she drew from this was still to be seen, for, although Sarah was vividly bright, she had given herself up, for the moment, to an ambiguous flushed formalism. She had had to reckon more quickly than she expected; but it concerned her first of all to signify that she was not to be taken unawares. Strether arrived precisely in time for her showing it. "Oh, you're too good; but I don't think I feel quite helpless. I have my brother—and these American friends. And then, you know, I've been to Paris. I *know* Paris," said Sally Pocock in a tone that breathed a certain chill on Strether's heart.

"Ah, but a woman, in this tiresome place where everything is always changing, a woman of good will," Mme. de Vionnet threw off, "can always help a woman. I'm sure you 'know'—but we know perhaps different things." She too, visibly, wished to make no mistake; but it was a fear of a different order, and she kept it more out of sight. She smiled in welcome at Strether; she greeted him more familiarly than Mrs. Pocock; she put out her hand to him without moving from her place; and it came to him, in the course of a minute, and in the oddest way, that—yes, positively—she was giving him over to ruin. She was all kindness and ease, but she couldn't help so giving him; she was exquisite, and her being just as she was poured, for Sarah, a sudden rush of meaning into his own equivocations. How could she know how she was hurting him? She wanted to show as simple and humble—in the degree compatible with operative charm; but it was just this that seemed to put him on her side. She struck him as dressed, as arranged, as prepared infinitely to conciliate—with the very poetry of good taste in her view of the conditions of her early call. She was ready to advise about dressmakers and shops; she held herself wholly at the disposition of Chad's family. Strether noticed her card on the table—her coronet and her " Comtesse "—and the imagination was sharp in him of certain private adjustments in Sarah's mind. She had never, he was sure, sat with a " Comtesse " before, and such was the specimen of that class he had been keeping to play on her. She had crossed the sea very particularly for a look at her; but he read in Mme. de Vionnet's own eyes that this curiosity had not been so successfully met as that she herself would not now have more than ever need of him. She looked much as she had looked to him that morning at Notre Dame; he noted in fact the suggestive sameness of her discreet and delicate dress. It seemed to speak— perhaps a little prematurely or too finely—of the sense in which she would help Mrs. Pocock with the shops. The way that lady took her in, moreover, added depth to his impression of what Miss Gostrey, by their common wisdom, had escaped. He winced as he saw himself, but for that timely prudence, ushering in Maria as a guide and an example. There was, however, a touch of relief for him in his glimpse, so far as he had got it, of Sarah's line. She " knew Paris." Mme. de Vionnet had, for that matter, lightly taken this up. " Ah, then you've a turn for that, an affinity that belongs to your family. Your brother, though his long experience makes a difference, I admit, has become one of us in a marvellous way." And she appealed to Strether in the manner of a woman who could always glide off with smoothness into another subject. Wasn't *he* struck with the way Mr. Newsome had made the place his own, and hadn't he been in a position to profit by his friend's wondrous expertness?

Strether felt the bravery, at the least, of her presenting herself so promptly to sound that note, and yet asked himself what other note, after all, she *could* strike from the moment she presented herself at all. She could meet Mrs. Pocock only on the ground of the obvious, and what feature of Chad's situation was more eminent than the fact that he had created for himself a new set of circumstances? Unless she hid herself altogether she could show but as one of these, an illustration of his domiciled, and indeed of his confirmed, condition. And the consciousness of all this, in her charming eyes, was so clear and fine that as she thus publicly drew him into her boat she produced in him such a silent agitation as he was not to fail afterwards to denounce as pusillanimous. " Ah, don't be so charming to me!—for it makes us intimate, and, after all, what *is* between us, when I've been so tremendously on my guard and have seen you but half a dozen times?" He recognized once more the perverse law that so inveterately governed his poor personal aspects: it would be exactly *like* the way things always turned out for him that he should affect Mrs. Pocock and Waymarsh as launched in a relation in which he had really never been launched at all. They were at this very moment—they could only be—attributing to him the full license of it, and all by the operation of her own tone with him; whereas his sole license had been to cling, with intensity, to the brink, not to dip so much as a toe into the flood. But the flicker of his fear on this occasion was not, as may be added, to repeat itself; it sprang up, for its moment, only to die down and then go out forever. To meet his fellow-visitor's invocation and, with Sarah's brilliant eyes on him, answer, *was* quite sufficiently to step into her boat. During the rest of the time her visit lasted he felt himself proceed to each of the proper offices, successively, for helping to keep the adventurous skiff afloat. It rocked beneath him, but he settled himself in his place. He took up an oar, and since he was to have the credit of pulling, he pulled.

"That will make it all the pleasanter if it so happens that we *do* meet," Mme. de Vionnet had further observed in reference to Mrs. Pocock's mention of her initiated state; and she had immediately added that, after all, her hostess couldn't be in need with the good offices of Mr. Strether so close at hand. "It's he, I gather, who has learned to know his Paris, and to love it, better than any one ever before in so short a time; so that between him and your brother, when it comes to the point, how can you possibly want for good guidance? The great thing, Mr. Strether will show you," she smiled, "is just to let one's self go."

"Oh, I've not let myself go very far," Strether answered, feeling quite as if he had been called upon to hint to Mrs. Pocock how Parisians could talk. "I'm only afraid of showing I haven't let myself go far enough. I've taken a good deal of time, but I must quite have had the air of not budging from one spot." He looked at Sarah in a manner that he thought she might take as engaging, and he made, under Mme. de Vionnet's protection, as it were, his first personal point. "What has really happened has been that, all the while, I've done what I came out for."

Yet it only, at first, gave Mme. de Vionnet a chance immediately to take him up. " You've renewed acquaintance with your friend— you've learned to know him again." She spoke with such cheerful helpfulness that they might, in a common cause, have been calling together and pledged to mutual aid.

Waymarsh, at this, as if he had been in question, straightway turned from the window. " Oh yes, Countess—he has renewed acquaintance with *me,* and he *has,* I guess, learned something about me, though I don't know how much he has liked it. It's for Strether himself to say whether he has felt it justifies his course."

" Oh, but *you,*" said the Countess gayly, " are not in the least what he came out for—is he really, Strether?—and I hadn't you at all in my mind. I was thinking of Mr. Newsome, of whom we think so much and with whom, precisely, Mrs. Pocock has given herself the opportunity to take up threads. What a pleasure for you both!" Mme. de Vionnet, with her eyes on Sarah, bravely continued.

Mrs. Pocock met her handsomely, but Strether quickly saw she meant to accept no version of her movements or plans from any other lips. She required no patronage and no support, which were but other names for a false position; she would show in her own way what she chose to show, and this she expressed with a dry glitter that recalled to him a fine Woollett winter morning. " I've never wanted for opportunities to see my brother. We've many things to think of at home, and great responsibilities and occupations, and our home is not an impossible place. We've plenty of reasons," Sarah continued a little piercingly, " for everything we do "—and in short she wouldn't give herself the least little scrap away. But she added as one who was always bland and who could afford a concession: " I've come because—well, because we do come."

" Ah, fortunately!"—Mme. de Vionnet breathed it to the air. Five minutes later they were on their feet for her to take leave, standing together in an affability that had succeeded in surviving a further exchange of remarks: only with the rather marked appearance on Waymarsh's part of a tendency to revert, in a ruminating manner, and as with an instinctive or a precautionary lightening of his tread, to an open window and his point of vantage. The glazed and gilded room, all red damask, ormolu, mirrors, clocks, looked south, and the shutters were bowed upon the summer morning; but the Tuileries garden and what was beyond it, over which the whole

267

place hung, were things visible through gaps; so that the far-spreading presence of Paris came up in coolness, dimness and invitation, in the twinkle of gilt-tipped palings, the crunch of gravel, the click of hoofs, the crack of whips, things that suggested some parade of the circus. "I think it probable," said Mrs. Pocock, "that I shall have the opportunity of going to my brother's. I've no doubt it's very pleasant indeed." She spoke as to Strether, but her face was turned, with an intensity of brightness, to Mme. de Vionnet, and there was a moment during which, while she thus fronted her, our friend expected to hear her add: "I'm much obliged to you, I'm sure, for inviting me there." He guessed that, for five seconds, these words were on the point of coming; he heard them as clearly as if they had been spoken; but he presently knew they had just failed—knew it by a glance, quick and fine, from Mme. de Vionnet, which told him that she too had felt them in the air, but that the point had luckily not been made in any manner requiring notice. This left her free to reply only to what had been said.

"That the Boulevard Malesherbes may be common ground for us offers me the best prospect I see for the pleasure of meeting you again."

"Oh, I shall come to see you, since you've been so good:" and Mrs. Pocock looked her interlocutress well in the eyes. The flush in Sarah's cheeks had by this time settled to a small definite crimson spot that was not without its own bravery; she held her head a good deal up, and it came to Strether that of the two, at this moment, she was the one who most carried out the idea of a Countess. He quite took in, however, that she would really return her visitor's civility: she would not report again at Woollett without at least so much producible history as that in her pocket.

"I want extremely to be able to show you my little daughter," Mme. de Vionnet went on; "and I should have brought her with me if I hadn't wished first to ask your leave. I was in hopes I should perhaps find Miss Pocock, of whose being with you I've heard from Mr. Newsome, and whose acquaintance I should so much like my child to make. If I have the pleasure of seeing her, and you do permit it, I shall venture to ask her to be kind to Jeanne. Mr. Strether will tell you "—she beautifully kept it up—" that my poor girl is gentle and good and rather lonely. They've made friends, he

and she, ever so happily, and he doesn't, I believe, think ill of her.
As for Jeanne herself, he has had the same success with her that I
know he has had, here, wherever he has turned." She seemed to ask
him for permission to say these things, or seemed, rather, to take it,
softly and happily, with the ease of intimacy, for granted, and he
had quite the consciousness now that not to meet her at any point
more than half-way would be odiously, basely to abandon her. Yes,
he was *with* her, and, confronted even in this covert, this semi-safe
fashion with those who where not, he felt, strangely and confusedly,
but excitedly, inspiringly, how much and how far. It was as if he
had positively waited in suspense for something from her that would
let him in deeper, so that he might show her how he could take it.
And what did in fact come as she drew out a little her farewell
served sufficiently the purpose. " As his success is a matter that
I'm sure he'll never mention for himself, I feel, you see, the less
scruple; which it's very good of me to say, you know, by the way,"
she added as she addressed herself to him; " considering how little
direct advantage I've gained from your triumphs with *me*. When
does one ever see you? I wait at home and I languish. You'll
have rendered me the service, Mrs. Pocock, at least," she wound
up, " of giving me one of my much-too-rare glimpses of this gentleman."

" I certainly should be sorry to deprive you of anything that seems
so much, as you describe it, your natural due. Mr. Strether and I
are very old friends," Sarah conceded, " but the privilege of his
society is not a thing I shall quarrel about with any one."

" And yet, dear Sarah," he freely broke in, " I feel, when I hear
you say that, that you don't quite do justice to the important truth
of the extent to which—as you're also mine—I'm *your* natural
due. I should like much better," he laughed, " to see you fight
for me."

She met him, Mrs. Pocock, on this, with an arrest of speech—with
a certain breathlessness, as he immediately fancied, on the score
of a freedom for which she was not quite prepared. It had flared
up—for all the harm he had intended by it—because, confoundedly,
he didn't want any more to be afraid about her than he wanted to
be afraid about Mme. de Vionnet. He had never, naturally, called
her anything but Sarah at home, and though he had perhaps never

quite so markedly invoked her as his "dear," that was somehow partly because no occasion had hitherto laid so effective a trap for it. But something admonished him now that it was too late—unless indeed it were possibly too early; and that he at any rate shouldn't have pleased Mrs. Pocock the more by it. "Well, Mr. Strether—!" she murmured with vagueness, yet with sharpness, while her crimson spots burned a trifle brighter and he was aware that this must be for the present the limit of her response. Mme. de Vionnet had already, however, come to his aid, and Waymarsh, as if for further participation, moved again back to them. It was true that the aid rendered by Mme. de Vionnet was questionable; it was a sign that, for all one might confess to with her, and for all she might complain of not enjoying, she could still insidiously show how much of the material of conversation had accumulated between them.

"The real truth is, you know, that you sacrifice one without mercy to dear old Maria. She leaves no room in your life for anybody else. Do you know," she inquired of Mrs. Pocock, "about dear old Maria? The worst is that Miss Gostrey is really a wonderful woman."

"Oh yes indeed," Strether answered for her, "Mrs. Pocock knows about Miss Gostrey. Your mother, Sarah, must have told you about her; your mother knows everything," he sturdily pursued. "And I cordially admit," he added with his conscious gayety of courage, "that she's as wonderful a woman as you like."

"Ah, it isn't *I* who 'like,' dear Mr. Strether, anything to do with the matter!" Sarah Pocock promptly protested; "and I'm by no means sure I have—from my mother or from any one else—a notion of whom you're talking about."

"Well, he won't let you see her, you know," Mme. de Vionnet sympathetically threw in. "He never lets *me*—old friends as we are: I mean as I am with Maria. He reserves her for his best hours; keeps her consummately to himself; only gives us others the crumbs of the feast."

"Well, Countess, *I've* had some of the crumbs," Waymarsh observed with weight and covering her with his large look; which led her to break in before he could go on.

"*Comment donc,* he shares her with *you?*" she exclaimed in droll stupefaction. "Take care you don't have, before you go much further, rather more of all *ces dames* than you may know what to do with!"

But he only continued in his massive way. "I can post you about the lady, Mrs. Pocock, so far as you may care to hear. I've seen her quite a number of times, and I was practically present when they made acquaintance. I've kept my eye on her right along, but I don't know as there's any real harm in her."

"'Harm'?" Mme. de Vionnet quickly echoed. "Why, she's the dearest and cleverest of all the clever and dear."

"Well, you run her pretty close, Countess," Waymarsh returned with spirit; "though there's no doubt she's pretty well up in things. She knows her way round Europe. Above all, there's no doubt she does love Strether."

"Ah, but we all do that—we all love Strether: it isn't a merit!" their fellow-visitor laughed, keeping to her idea with a good conscience at which our friend was aware that he marvelled, though he trusted also for it, as he met her exquisitely expressive eyes, to some later light.

The prime effect of her tone, however—and it was a truth which his own eyes gave back to her in sad, ironic play—could only be to make him feel that, to say such things to a man in public, a woman must practically think of him as ninety years old. He had turned awkwardly, responsibly red, he knew, at her mention of Maria Gostrey; Sarah Pocock's presence—the particular quality of it—had made this inevitable; and then he had grown still redder in proportion as he hated to have shown anything at all. He felt indeed that he was showing much, as, uncomfortably and almost in pain, he offered up his redness to Waymarsh, who, strangely enough, seemed now to be looking at him with a certain explanatory yearning. Something deep—something built on their old, old relation—passed, in this complexity, between them: he got the side-wind of a loyalty that stood behind all actual queer questions. Waymarsh's dry, bare humor—as it gave itself to be taken—gloomed out to justify itself. "Well, if you talk of Miss Barrace I've *my* chance too," it appeared stiffly to nod, and it granted that it was giving him away, but struggled to say that it did so only to save him. The sombre glow stared it at him till it fairly sounded out—" to save you, poor old man, to save you; to save you in spite of yourself." Yet

It was somehow just this communication that showed him to himself as more than ever lost. Still another result of it was to put before him as never yet that between his comrade and the interest represented by Sarah there was already a basis. Beyond all question now, yes: Waymarsh had been in occult relation with Mrs. Newsome—out, out it all came in the very effort of his face. " Yes, you're feeling my hand "—he as good as proclaimed it; " but only because this at least I *shall* have got out of the damned Old World: that I shall have picked up the pieces into which it has caused you to crumble." It was as if, in short, after an instant, Strether had not only had it from him, but had recognized that, so far as this went, the instant had cleared the air. Our friend understood and approved; he had the sense that they wouldn't otherwise speak of it. This would be all, and it would mark in himself a kind of intelligent generosity. It was with grim Sarah then—Sarah grim for all her grace—-that Waymarsh had begun at ten o'clock in the morning to save him. Well—if he *could,* poor dear man, with his big, narrow kindness! The upshot of which crowded perception was that Strether, on his own side, still showed no more than he absolutely had to. He showed the least possible by saying to Mrs. Pocock after an interval much briefer than our glance at the picture as reflected in him: " Oh, it's as true as they please! There's no Miss Gostrey for any one but me—not the least little peep. I keep her to myself."

" Well, it's very good of you to notify me," Sarah replied without looking at him, and thrown for a moment by this discrimination, as the direction of her eyes showed, upon a dimly desperate little community with Mme. de Vionnet. " But I hope I sha'n't miss her too much."

Mme. de Vionnet instantly rallied. " And, you know—though it might occur to one—it isn't in the least that he's ashamed of her. She's really—in a way—extremely good-looking."

" Ah, but extremely!" Strether laughed while he wondered at the odd part he found thus imposed on him.

It continued to be so by every touch from Mme. de Vionnet. " Well, as I say, you know, I wish you would keep *me* a little more to yourself. Couldn't you name some day for me, some hour—and better soon than late? I will be at home whenever it best suits you. There—I can't say fairer.'

Strether thought a moment, while Waymarsh and Mrs. Pocock affected him as standing attentive. " I did lately call on you. Last week—while Chad was out of town."

" Yes—and I was away, as it happened, too. You choose your moments well. But don't wait for my next absence, for I sha'n't make another," Mme. de Vionnet declared, " while Mrs. Pocock is here."

" That vow needn't keep you long, fortunately," Sarah observed with reasserted suavity. " I shall be at present but a short time in Paris. I have my plans for other countries. I meet a number of charming friends "—and her voice seemed to caress that description of these persons.

" Ah then," her visitor cheerfully replied, " all the more reason! To-morrow, for instance, or next day?" she continued to Strether. " Tuesday would do for me beautifully."

" Tuesday then with pleasure."

" And at half-past five?—or at six?"

It was ridiculous, but Mrs. Pocock and Waymarsh struck him as fairly waiting for his answer. It was indeed as if they were arranged, gathered for a performance, the performance of " Europe " by his confederate and himself. Well, the performance could only go on. " Say five forty-five."

" Five forty-five—good." And now at last Mme. de Vionnet must leave them, though it carried, for herself, the performance a little further. " I *did* hope so much also to see Miss Pocock. Mayn't I still?"

Sarah hesitated, but she rose equal. " She will return your visit with me. She's at present out with Mr. Pocock and my brother."

" I see—of course Mr. Newsome has everything to show them. He has told me so much about her. My great desire is to give my daughter the opportunity of making her acquaintance. I'm always on the lookout for such chances for her. If I didn't bring her to-day, it was only to make sure first that you'd let me." After which the charming woman risked a more intense appeal. " It wouldn't suit *you* also to mention some near time, so that we shall be sure not to lose you?" Strether, on his side, waited, for Sarah likewise had, after all, to perform; and it occupied him to have been thus reminded that she had stayed at home—and on her first morning of Paris—while Chad led the others forth. Oh, she was up to her eyes; if she had stayed at home she had stayed by an understanding, arrived at the evening before, that Waymarsh would come and find her alone. This was beginning well—for a first day in Paris; and the thing might be amusing yet. But Mme. de Vionnet's earnestness was meanwhile beautiful. "You may think me indiscreet, but I've *such* a desire my Jeanne shall know an American girl of the really delightful kind. You see I throw myself for it on your charity."

The manner of this speech gave Strether such a sense of depths below it and behind it as he had not yet had—ministered in a way that almost frightened him to his dim divinations of reasons; but if Sarah still, in spite of it, faltered, this was why he had time for a sign of sympathy with her petitioner. "Let me say then, dear lady, to back your plea, that Miss Mamie is of the most delightful kind of all—is charming among the charming."

Even Waymarsh, though with more to produce on the subject, could get into motion in time. "Yes, Countess, the American girl is a thing that your country must at least allow ours the privilege to say we *can* show you. But her full beauty is only for those who know how to make use of her."

"Ah then," smiled Mme. de Vionnet, "that's exactly what I want to do. I'm sure she has much to teach us."

It was wonderful, but what was scarce less so was that Strether found himself, by the quick effect of it, moved another way. "Oh, that may be! But don't speak of your own exquisite daughter, you know, as if she were not pure perfection. Mlle. de Vionnet," he explained, in considerable form, to Mrs. Pocock, "*is* pure perfection. Mlle. de Vionnet *is* exquisite."

It had been perhaps a little portentous, but "Ah?" Sarah simply glittered.

Waymarsh himself, for that matter, apparently recognized, in respect to the facts, the need of a larger justice, and he had with it an inclination to Sarah. "Miss Jane is strikingly handsome—in the regular French style."

It somehow made both Strether and Mme. de Vionnet laugh out, though at the very moment he caught in Sarah's eyes, as glancing at the speaker, a vague but unmistakable "You too?" It made Waymarsh in fact look consciously over her head. Mme. de Vionnet meanwhile, however, made her point in her own way. "I wish indeed I could offer you my poor child as a dazzling attraction: it would make one's position simple enough! She's as good as she can be, but of course she's different, and the question is now—in the light of the way things seem to go—if she isn't after all, *too* different: too different I mean from the splendid type every one is so agreed that your wonderful country produces. On the other hand, of course, Mr. Newsome, who knows it so well, has, as a good friend, dear kind man that he is, done everything he can—to keep us from fatal benightedness—for my small, shy creature. Well," she wound up after Mrs. Pocock had signified, in a murmur still a little stiff, that she would speak to her own young charge on the question— "well, we shall sit, my child and I, and wait and wait and wait for you." But her last fine turn was for Strether. "Do speak of us in such a way—!"

"As that something can't but come of it? Oh, something *shall* come of it! I take a great interest!" he further declared; and in proof of it, the next moment, he had gone with her down to her carriage.

PART NINTH

XXII

"THE difficulty is," Strether said to Mme. de Vionnet a couple of days later, "that I can't surprise them into the smallest sign of his not being the same old Chad they've been for the last three years glowering at across the sea. They simply won't give any, and as a policy, you know—what you call a *parti pris,* a deep game—that's positively remarkable."

It was so remarkable that our friend had pulled up before his hostess with the vision of it; he had risen from his chair at the end of ten minutes and begun, as a help not to worry, to move about before her quite as he moved before Maria. He had kept his appointment with her to the minute and had been intensely impatient, though divided in truth between the sense of having everything to tell her and the sense of having nothing at all. The short interval had, in the face of their complication, multiplied his impressions—it being meanwhile to be noted, moreover, that he already frankly, already almost publicly, viewed the complication as common to them. If Mme. de Vionnet, under Sarah's eyes, had pulled him into her boat, there was by this time no doubt whatever that he had remained in it and that what he had really most been conscious of for many hours together was the movement of the vessel itself. They were in it together this moment as they had not yet been, and he had not at present uttered the least of the words of alarm or remonstrance that had died on his lips at the hotel. He had other things to say to her than that she had put him in a position; so quickly had his position grown to affect him as quite excitingly, altogether richly, inevitable. That the outlook, however—given the standpoint—had not cleared up half so much as he had reckoned was the first warning she had had to receive from him on his arrival. She had replied with indulgence that he was in too great a hurry, and had remarked soothingly that if she knew how to be

279

patient surely *he* might be. He felt her presence, on the spot, he felt her tone and everything about her, as an aid to that effort; and it was perhaps one of the proofs of her success with him that he seemed so much to take his ease while they talked. By the time he had explained to her why his impressions, though multiplied, still baffled him, it was as if he had been familiarly talking for hours. They baffled him because Sarah—well, Sarah was deep; deeper than she had ever yet had a chance to show herself. He didn't say that this was partly the effect of her opening so straight down, as it were, into her mother, that, given Mrs. Newsome's profundity, the shaft thus sunk might well have a reach; but he was not without the resigned apprehension that, at such a rate of confidence, he was likely soon to be moved to show how already, at moments, it had been for him as if he were dealing directly with Mrs. Newsome. Sarah, to a certainty, would have begun herself to feel it in him— and this naturally put it in her power to torment him the more. From the moment she knew he *could* be tormented—!

"But *why* can you be?"—his companion was surprised at his use of the word.

"Because I'm made so—I think of everything."

"Ah, one must never do that," she smiled. "One must think of as few things as possible."

"Then," he answered, "one must pick them out right. But all I mean is—for I express myself with violence—that she's in a position to watch me. There's an element of suspense for me, and she can see me wriggle. But my wriggling doesn't matter," he pursued. "I can bear it. Besides, I shall wriggle out."

The picture, at any rate, stirred in her an appreciation that he felt to be sincere. "I don't see how a man can be kinder to a woman than you are to me."

Well, kind was what he wanted to be; yet, even while her charming eyes rested on him with the truth of this, he none the less had his humor of honesty. "When I say suspense I mean, you know," he laughed, "suspense about my own case too!"

"Oh yes—about your own case too!" It diminished his magnanimity, but she only looked at him the more tenderly.

"Not, however," he went on, "that I want to talk to you about that. It's my own little affair, and I mentioned it simply as part of Mrs. Pocock's advantage." No, no; though there was a queer present temptation in it, and his suspense was so real that to fidget was a relief, he wouldn't talk to her about Mrs. Newsome, wouldn't work off on her the anxiety produced in him by Sarah's calculated omissions of reference. The effect she produced of representing her mother had been produced—and that was just the immense, the un-canny part of it—without her having so much as mentioned that lady. She had brought no message, had alluded to no question, had only answered his inquiries with hopeless, limited propriety. She had invented a way of meeting them—as if he had been a polite, perfunctory poor relation, of distant degree—that made them al-most ridiculous in him. He couldn't moreover, on his own side, ask much without appearing to publish how he had lately lacked news; a circumstance of which it was Sarah's profound policy not to betray a suspicion. These things, all the same, he wouldn't breathe to Mme. de Vionnet—much as they might make him walk up and down. And what he didn't say—as well as what *she* didn't, for she had also her high decencies—didn't diminish the effect of his being there with her at the end of ten minutes more intimately on the basis of saving her than he had yet had occasion to be. It ended in fact by being quite beautiful between them, the number of things they had a manifest consciousness of not saying. He would have liked to turn her, critically, to the subject of Mrs. Pocock, but he so stuck to the line he felt to be the point of honor and of delicacy that he scarce even asked her what her personal impression had been. He knew it, for that matter, without putting her to trouble; that she wondered how, with such elements, Sarah could still have no charm, was one of the principal things she held her tongue about. Strether would have been interested in her estimate of the elements —indubitably there, some of them, and to be appraised according to taste—but he denied himself even the luxury of this diversion. The way Mme. de Vionnet affected him to-day was in itself a kind of demonstration of the happy employment of gifts. How could a woman think Sarah had charm who struck one as having arrived at it herself by such different roads? On the other hand, of course, Sarah wasn't obliged to have it. He felt as if, somehow, Mme. de Vionnet *was*. The great question meanwhile was what Chad thought of his sister; which was naturally ushered in by that of Sarah's apprehension of Chad. *That* they could talk of, and with a freedom purchased by their discretion in other directions. The difficulty, however, was that they were reduced as yet to conjecture. He had given them in the day or two as little of a lead as Sarah, and Mme. de Vionnet mentioned that she had not seen him since his sister's arrival.

" And does that strike you as such an age ?"

She met it in all honesty. " Oh, I won't pretend I don't miss him. Sometimes I see him every day. Our friendship is like that. Make what you will of it !" she whimsically smiled ; a little flicker of the kind, occasional in her, that had more than once moved him to wonder what he might best make of *her*. " But he's perfectly right," she hastened to add, " and I wouldn't have him fail in any way, at present, for the world. I would sooner not see him for three months. I begged him to be beautiful to them, and he fully feels it for himself."

Strether turned away under his quick perception ; she was so odd a mixture of lucidity and mystery. She fell in at moments with the theory about her that he most cherished, and she seemed at others to blow it into air. She spoke now as if her art were all an innocence, and then again as if her innocence were all an art. " Oh, he's giving himself up, and he'll do so to the end. How can he but want, now that it's within reach, his full impression ?—which is much more important, you know, than either yours or mine. But he's just soaking," Strether said as he came back ; " he's going in, conscientiously, for a saturation. I'm bound to say he *is* very good."

" Ah," she quietly replied, " to whom do you say it ?" And then more quietly still : " He's capable of anything."

Strether more than reaffirmed—" Oh, he's excellent. I more and more like," he insisted, " to see him with them ;" though the oddity of this tone between them grew sharper for him even while they spoke. It placed the young man so before them as the result of her interest and the product of her genius, acknowledged so her part in the phenomenon and made the phenomenon so rare, that, more than ever yet, he might have been on the very point of asking her for some more detailed account of the whole business than he had yet received from her. The occasion almost forced upon him some question as to how she had managed and as to the appearance such miracles presented from her own singularly close standpoint. The moment, in fact, however, passed, giving way to more present history, and he continued simply to mark his appreciation of the happy truth. "It's a tremendous comfort to feel how one can trust him." And then again while, for a little, she said nothing—as if, after all, to *her* trust there might be a special limit: "I mean for making a good show to them."

"Yes," she thoughtfully returned—"but if they shut their eyes to it!"

Strether for an instant had his own thought. "Well, perhaps that won't matter!"

"You mean because he probably—do what they will—won't like them?"

"Oh, 'do what they will'—! They won't do much; especially if Sarah hasn't more—well, more than one has yet made out—to give."

Mme. de Vionnet weighed it. "Ah, she has all her grace!" It was a statement over which, for a little, they could look at each other sufficiently straight, and, though it produced no protest from Strether the effect was somehow as if he had treated it as a joke. "She may be persuasive and caressing with him; she may be eloquent beyond words. She may get hold of him," she wound up— "well, as neither you nor I have."

"Yes, she *may*"—and now Strether smiled. "But he has spent all his time, each day, with Jim. He's still showing Jim round."

She visibly wondered. "Then how about Jim?"

Strether took a turn before he answered. "Hasn't he given you Jim? I mean, before this, done him for you?" He was a little at a loss. "Doesn't he tell you things?"

She hesitated. "No"—and their eyes once more gave and took. "Not as you do. You, somehow, make me see them—or at least feel them. And I haven't asked too much," she added; "I've wanted so, of late, not to worry him."

"Ah, for that, so have I," he said with encouraging assent; so that—as if she had answered everything—they were briefly sociable on it. It threw him back on his other thought, with which he took another turn; stopping again, however, presently, with something of a glow. "You see, Jim's really immense. I think it will be Jim who'll do it."

She wondered. " Get hold of him ?"

" No—just the other thing. Counteract Sarah's spell." And he showed now, our friend, how far he had worked it out. " Jim's intensely cynical."

" Oh, dear Jim !" Mme. de Vionnet vaguely smiled.

" Yes, literally—dear Jim ! He's awful. What *he* wants, Heaven forgive him, is to help us."

" You mean "—she was eager—" help *me?*"

" Well, Chad and me in the first place. But he throws you in too, though without, as yet, seeing you much. Only, so far as he does see you—if you don't mind—he sees you as awful."

" ' Awful ' ?"—she wanted it all.

" A regular bad one—though of course of a tremendously superior kind. Dreadful, delightful, irresistible."

" Ah, dear Jim ! I should like to know him. I *must.*"

" Yes, naturally. But will it do ? You may, you know," Strether suggested, " disappoint him."

She was funny and humble about it. " I can but try. But my wickedness then," she went on, " is my recommendation for him ?"

" Your wickedness and the charms with which, in such a degree as yours, he associates it. He understands, you see, that Chad and I have above all wanted to have a good time, and his view is simple and sharp. Nothing will persuade him—in the light, that is, of my behavior—that I really didn't, quite as much as Chad, come over to have one before it was too late. He wouldn't have expected it of me ; but men of my age, at Woollett—and especially the least likely ones—have been noted as liable to strange outbreaks, belated, uncanny clutches at the unusual, the ideal. It's an effect that a lifetime of Woollett has quite been observed as having ; and I thus give it to you, in Jim's view, for what it's worth. Now his wife and his mother-in-law," Strether continued to explain, " have, as in honor bound, no patience with such phenomena, late or early —which puts Jim, as against his relatives, on the other side. Besides," he added, " I don't think he really wants Chad back. If Chad doesn't come—"

" He'll have "—Mme. de Vionnet quite apprehended—" more of the free hand ?"

"Well, Chad's the bigger man."

"So he'll work now, *en dessous,* to keep him quiet?"

"No—he won't 'work' at all, and he won't do anything *en dessous.* He's very decent, and he won't be a traitor in the camp. But he'll be amused with his own little view of our duplicity, he'll sniff up what he supposes to be Paris from morning till night, and he'll be, as to the rest, for Chad—well, just what he is."

She thought it over. "A warning?"

He met it almost with glee. "You *are* as wonderful as everybody says!" And then to explain all he meant: "I drove him about for his first hour, and do you know what—all beautifully unconscious--he most put before me? Why, that something like *that* is at bottom, as an improvement to his present state, as in fact the real redemption of it, what they think it may not be too late to make of our friend." With which, as, taking it in, she seemed, in her recurrent alarm, bravely to gaze at the possibility, he completed his statement. "But it *is* too late. Thanks to you!"

It drew from her again one of her indefinite reflections. "Oh, 'me'—after all!"

He stood before her so exhilarated by his demonstration that he could fairly be jocular. "Everything's comparative. You're better than *that.*"

"You"—she could but answer him—"are better than anything." But she had another thought. "*Will* Mrs. Pocock come to me?"

"Oh yes—she'll do that. As soon, that is, as my friend Waymarsh—*her* friend now—leaves her leisure."

She showed an interest. "Is he so much her friend as that?"

"Why, didn't you see it all at the hotel?"

"Oh "—she was amused—" 'all' is a good deal to say. I don't know—I forget. I lost myself in *her.*"

"You were splendid," Strether returned—"but 'all' isn't a good deal to say: it's only a little. Yet it's charming so far as it goes. She wants a man to herself."

"And hasn't she got *you*?"

"Do you think she looked at me—or even at you—as if she had?" Strether easily dismissed that irony. "Every one, you see, must strike her as having somebody. You've got Chad—and Chad has got you."

"I see"—she made of it what she could. "And you've got Maria."

Well, he on his side accepted that. "I've got Maria. And Maria has got me. So it goes."

"But Mr. Jim—whom has he got?"

"Oh, he has got—or it's as *if* he had—the whole place."

"But for Mr. Waymarsh"—she recalled—"isn't Miss Barrace before any one else?"

He shook his head. "Miss Barrace is a *raffinée*, and her amusement won't lose by Mrs. Pocock. It will gain rather—especially if Sarah triumphs and she comes in for a view of it."

"How well you know us!" Mme. de Vionnet, at this, frankly sighed.

"No—it seems to me it's *we* that I know. I know Sarah—it's perhaps on that ground only that my feet are firm. Waymarsh will take *her* round, while Chad takes Jim—and I shall be, I assure you, delighted for both of them. Sarah will have had what she requires —she will have paid *her* tribute to the ideal; and he will have done about the same. In Paris it's in the air—so what can one do less? If there's a point that, beyond any other, Sarah wants to make, it's that she didn't come out to be narrow. We shall feel at least *that*."

"Oh," she sighed, "the quantity we seem likely to 'feel'! But what becomes, in these conditions, of the girl?"

"Of Mamie—if we're all provided? Ah, for that," said Strether, "you can trust Chad."

"To be, you mean, all right to her?"

"To pay her every attention as soon as he has polished off Jim. He wants what Jim can give him—and what Jim really won't— though he has had it all, and more than all, from me. He wants in short his own personal impression, and he'll get it—strong. But as soon as he has got it Mamie won't suffer."

"Oh, Mamie mustn't *suffer!*" Mme. de Vionnet soothingly emphasized.

But Strether could reassure her. "Don't fear. As soon as he has done with Jim, Jim will fall to me. And then you'll see."

It was as if, in a moment, she saw already; yet she still waited. Then, "Is she really quite charming?" she asked.

He had got up with his last words and gathered in his hat and gloves. "I don't know; I'm watching. I'm studying the case, as it were—and I dare say I shall be able to tell you."

She wondered. "Is it a case?"

"Yes—I think so. At any rate I shall see."

"But haven't you known her before?"

"Yes," he smiled—"but somehow at home she wasn't a case. She has become one since." It was as if he made it out for himself. "She has become one here."

"So very, very soon?"

He hesitated, laughing. "Not sooner than I did."

"And you became one—?"

"Very, very soon. The day I arrived."

Her intelligent eyes showed her thought of it. "Ah, but the day you arrived you met Maria. Whom has Miss Pocock met?"

He paused again, but he brought it out. "Hasn't she met Chad?"

"Certainly—but not for the first time. He's an old friend." At which Strether had a slow, amused, significant headshake that made her go on: "You mean that for *her* at least he's a new person—that she sees him as different?"

"She sees him as different."

"And how does she see him?"

Strether gave it up. "How can one tell how a deep little girl sees a deep young man?"

"Is every one so deep? Is she too?"

"So it strikes me—deeper than I thought. But wait a little, and, between us, we'll make it out. You'll judge, for that matter, for yourself."

Mme. de Vionnet looked for the moment fairly bent on the chance. "Then she *will* come with her?—I mean Mamie with Mrs. Pocock?"

"Certainly. Her curiosity, if nothing else, will in any case work that. But leave it all to Chad."

"Ah," wailed Mme. de Vionnet, turning away a little wearily, "the things I leave to Chad!"

The tone of it made him look at her with a kindness that showed his vision of her suspense. But he fell back on his confidence. "Oh well—trust him. Trust him all the way." He had indeed no sooner so spoken than the queer displacement of his point of view appeared again to come up for him in the very sound, which drew from him a short laugh, immediately checked. He became still more advisory. "When they do come, give them plenty of Miss Jeanne. Let Mamie see her well."

She looked for a moment as if she placed them face to face. "For Mamie to hate her?"

He had another of his corrective headshakes. "Mamie won't. Trust *them*."

She looked at him hard, and then, as if it were what she must always come back to: "It's *you* I trust. But I was sincere," she said, "at the hotel. I did, I do, want my child—"

"Well?"—Strether waited with deference while she appeared to hesitate as to how to put it.

"Well, to do what she can for me."

Strether, for a little, met her eyes on it; after which something that might have been unexpected to her came from him. "Poor little duck!"

Not more expected for himself indeed might well have been her echo of it. "Poor little duck! But she immensely wants, herself," she said, "to see our friend's cousin."

"Is that what she thinks her?"

"It's what we call the young lady."

He thought again; then with a laugh: "Well, your daughter will help you."

And now at last he took leave of her, as he had been intending for five minutes But she went part of the way with him, accompanying him out of the room and into the next and the next. Her noble old apartment offered a succession of three, the first two of which indeed, on entering, smaller than the last, but each with its faded and formal air, enlarged the office of the antechamber and enriched the sense of approach. Strether fancied them, liked them, and, passing through them with her more slowly now, met a sharp renewal of his original impression. He stopped, he looked back; the whole thing made a vista, which he found high, melancholy and sweet—full, once more, of dim historic shades, of the faint far-away cannon-roar of the great Empire. It was doubtless half the projection of his mind, but his mind was a thing that, among old waxed parquets, pale shades of pink and green, pseudo-classic candelabra, he had always needfully to reckon with. They could easily make him irrelevant. The oddity, the originality, the poetry—he didn't know what to call it—of Chad's connection reaffirmed for him its romantic side. " They ought to see this, you know. They *must.*"

" The Pococks?"—she looked about in deprecation; she seemed to see gaps he didn't.

" Mamie and Sarah—Mamie in particular."

" My shabby old place? But *their* things—!"

" Oh, their things! You were talking of what will do something for you—"

" So that it strikes you," she broke in, " that my poor place may? Oh," she ruefully mused, " that *would* be desperate!"

" Do you know what I wish?" he went on. " I wish Mrs. Newsome herself could have a look."

She stared, missing a little his logic. " It would make a difference?"

Her tone was so earnest that, as he continued to look about, he laughed. " It might!"

" But you've told her, you tell me—"

" All about you? Yes, a wonderful story. But there's all the indescribable—what one gets only on the spot."

" Thank you!" she charmingly and sadly smiled.

" It's all about me here," he freely continued. " Mrs. Newsome feels things."

But she seemed doomed, always, to come back to doubt. " No one feels so much as *you*. No—no one."

" So much the worse then for every one. It's very easy."

They were by this time in the antechamber, still alone together, as she had not rung for a servant. The antechamber was high and square, grave and suggestive too, a little cold and slippery even in summer, and with a few old prints that were precious, Strether divined, on the walls. He stood in the middle, slightly lingering, vaguely directing his glasses, while, leaning against the door-post of the room, she gently pressed her cheek to the side of the recess. " *You* would have been a friend."

" I?"—it startled him a little.

"For the reason you say. You're not stupid." And then abrupt‑ly, as if her bringing it out were somehow founded on that fact: "We're marrying Jeanne."

It affected him on the spot as a move in a game, and he was even then not without the sense that that wasn't the way Jeanne should be married. But he quickly showed his interest, though—as quickly afterwards struck him — with an absurd confusion of mind. "'You'? You and—a—not Chad?" Of course it was the child's father who made the 'we'; but to the child's father it would have cost him an effort to allude. Yet didn't it seem the next minute that M. de Vionnet was, after all, not in question?—since she had gone on to say that it was indeed to Chad she referred and that he had been, in the whole matter, kindness itself.

"If I must tell you all, it is he himself who has put us in the way. I mean in the way of an opportunity that, so far as I can yet see, is all I could possibly have dreamed of. For all the trouble M. de Vionnet will ever take!" It was the first time she had spoken to him of her husband, and he couldn't have expressed how much more intimate with her it suddenly made him feel. It wasn't much, in truth—there were other things, in what she was saying, that were far more; but it was as if, while they stood there together so easily in these cold chambers of the past, the single touch had shown the reach of her confidence. "But our friend," she asked, "hasn't then told you?"

"He has told me nothing."

"Well, it has come with rather a rush—all in a very few days; and hasn't moreover yet taken a form that permits an announce‑ment. It's only for you—absolutely you alone—that I speak; I so want you to know." The sense he had so often had, since the first hour of his disembarkment, of being further and further "in," treated him again, at this moment, to another twinge; but in this wonderful way of her putting him in there continued to be some‑thing exquisitely remorseless. "M. de Vionnet will accept what he *must* accept. He has proposed half a dozen things—each one more impossible than the other; and he wouldn't have found this if he lives to a hundred. Chad found it," she continued with her lighted, faintly flushed, her conscious, confidential face, "in the quietest way in the world. Or rather it found *him*—for everything finds

290

him; I mean finds him right. You'll think we do such things strangely—but at my age," she smiled, "one has to accept one's conditions. Our young man's people had seen her; one of his sisters, a charming woman—we know all about them—had observed her somewhere with me. She had spoken to her brother—turned him on; and we were again observed, poor Jeanne and I, without our in the least knowing it. It was at the beginning of the winter; it went on for some time; it outlasted our absence; it began again on our return; and it luckily seems all right. The young man had met Chad, and he got a friend to approach him—as having a decent interest in us. Mr. Newsome looked well before he leaped; he kept beautifully quiet and satisfied himself fully; then only he spoke. It's what has for some time past occupied us. It seems as if it were what would do; really, really all one could wish. There are only two or three points to be settled—they depend on her father. But this time I think we're safe."

Strether, consciously gaping a little, had fairly hung upon her lips. "I hope so with all my heart." And then he permitted himself: "Does nothing depend on *her*?"

"Ah, naturally; everything did. But she's as pleased as Punch. She has been perfectly free; and he—our young friend—is really a combination. I quite adore him."

Strether just made sure. "You mean your future son-in-law?"

"Future if we all bring it off."

"Ah well," said Strether decorously, "I heartily hope you may." There seemed little else for him to say, though her communication had the oddest effect on him. Vaguely and confusedly he was troubled by it; feeling as if he had even himself been concerned in something deep and dim. He had allowed for depths, but these were greater: and it was as if, oppressively—indeed absurdly—he was responsible for what they had now thrown up to the surface. It was—through something ancient and cold in it—what he would have called the real thing. In short his hostess's news, though he couldn't have explained why, was a sensible shock, and his oppression a weight he felt he must, somehow or other, immediately get rid of. There were too many connections missing to make it tolerable he should do anything else. He was prepared to suffer—before his own inner tribunal--for Chad; he was prepared to suffer even for Mme.

de Vionnet. But he wasn't prepared to suffer for the little girl. So now, having said the proper thing, he wanted to get away. She held him an instant, however, with another appeal.

"Do I seem to you very awful?"

"Awful? Why so?" But he called it to himself, even as he spoke, his biggest insincerity yet.

"Our arrangements are so different from yours."

"Mine?" Oh, he could dismiss that too! "I haven't any arrangements."

"Then you must accept mine; all the more that they're excellent. They're founded on a *vieille sagesse*. There will be much more, if all goes well, for you to hear and to know, and everything, believe me, for you to like. Don't be afraid; you'll be satisfied." Thus she could talk to him of what, of her innermost life—for that was what it came to—he must "accept"; thus she could extraordinarily speak as if, in such an affair, his being satisfied had an importance. It was all a wonder, and it made the whole case larger. He had struck himself at the hotel, before Sarah and Waymarsh, as being in her boat; but where on earth was he now? This question was in the air till her own lips quenched it with another. "And do you suppose *he*—who loves her so—would do anything reckless or cruel?"

He wondered what he supposed. "Do you mean your young man—?"

"I mean yours. I mean Mr. Newsome." It flashed for Strether the next moment a finer light, and the light deepened as she went on. "He takes, thank God, the truest, tenderest, interest in her."

It deepened indeed. "Oh, I'm sure of that!"

"You were talking," she said, "about one's trusting him. You see then how I do."

He wanted but a moment—it all came. "I see—I see." He felt he really did see.

"He wouldn't hurt her for the world, nor—assuming she marries at all—risk anything that might make against her happiness. And —willingly, at least—he would never hurt *me*."

Her face, with what he had by this time grasped, told him more than her words; whether something had come into it, or whether he only read clearer, her whole story—what at least he then took for
292

such—reached out to him from it. With the initiative she now attributed to Chad it all made a sense, and this sense—a light, a lead,
was what had abruptly risen before him. He wanted, once more, to
get off with these things; which was at last made easy, a servant
having, for his assistance, on hearing voices in the hall, just come
forward. All that Strether had made out was, while the man opened
the door and impersonally waited, summed up in his last word. "I
don't think, you know, Chad will tell me anything."

"No—perhaps not yet."

"And I won't as yet speak to him."

"Ah, that's as you'll think best. You must judge."

She had finally given him her hand, which he held a moment.
"How *much* I have to judge!"

"Everything," said Mme. de Vionnet: a remark that was indeed—
with the refined, disguised, suppressed passion of her face—what he
most carried away.

XXIII

So far as a direct approach was concerned Sarah had neglected him, for the week now about to end, with a civil consistency of chill that, giving him a higher idea of her social resource, threw him back on the general reflection that a woman could always be amazing. It indeed helped a little to console him that he felt sure she had for the same period also left Chad's curiosity hanging; though, on the other hand, for his personal relief, Chad could at least go through the various motions—and he made them extraordinarily numerous—of seeing she had a good time. There wasn't a motion on which, in her presence, poor Strether could so much as venture, and all he could do when he was out of it was to walk over for a talk with Maria. He walked over of course much less than usual, but he found a special compensation in a certain half-hour during which, toward the close of a crowded, empty, expensive day, his several companions struck him as so disposed of as to give his manners a rest. He had been with them in the morning, and had called on the Pococks again in the afternoon; but their whole group, he then found, had dispersed after a fashion of which it would amuse Miss Gostrey to hear. He was sorry again, gratefully sorry she was so out of it—she who had really put him in; but she had always, fortunately, her appetite for news. The pure flame of the disinterested burned there, in her cave of treasures, like a lamp in a Byzantine vault. It was just now, as happened, that for so fine a sense as hers a near view would have begun to pay. Within three days, precisely, the situation on which he was to report had shown signs of an equilibrium; his look in at the hotel confirmed his judgment of that appearance. If the equilibrium might only prevail! Sarah was out with Waymarsh, Mamie was out with Chad, and Jim was out alone. Later on, indeed, he himself was booked to Jim; was to take him that evening to the Varieties—which Strether was careful to pronounce as Jim pronounced them.

Miss Gostrey drank it in. "What then to-night do the others do?"

"Well, it has been arranged. Waymarsh takes Sarah to dine at Bignon's."

She wondered. "And what do they do after? They can't come straight home."

"No—they can't come straight home—at least Sarah can't. It's their secret, but I think I've guessed it." Then as she waited: "The circus."

It made her stare a moment longer, then laugh almost to extravagance. "There's no one like you!"

"Like *me?*"—he only wanted to understand.

"Like all of you together—like all of *us:* Woollett, Milrose and their products. We're abysmal—but may we never fill up! Mr. Newsome," she continued, "meanwhile takes Miss Pocock—?"

"Precisely—to the Français: to see what *you* took Waymarsh and me to, a family-bill."

"Ah then, may Mr. Chad enjoy it as *I* did!" But she saw so much in things. "Do they spend their evenings, your young people, like that, alone together?"

"Well—they're young people, but they're old friends."

"I see, I see. And do *they* dine—for a difference—at Brébant's?"

"Oh, where they dine is their secret too. But I've my idea that it will be, very quietly, at Chad's own place."

"She'll come to him there alone?"

They looked at each other a moment. "He has known her from a child. Besides," said Strether with emphasis, "Mamie's remarkable. She's splendid."

She hesitated. "Do you mean she expects to bring it off?"

"Getting hold of him? No—I think not."

"She doesn't want him enough?—or doesn't believe in her power?" On which, as he said nothing, she continued: "She finds she doesn't care for him?"

"No—I think she finds she does. But that's what I mean by so describing her. It's *if* she does that she's splendid. But we'll see," he wound up, "where she comes out."

"You seem to show me sufficiently," Miss Gostrey laughed, "where she goes in! But is her childhood's friend," she asked, "permitting himself recklessly to flirt with her?"

"No—not that. Chad's also splendid. They're *all* splendid!" he declared with a sudden strange sound of wistfulness and envy. "They're at least happy."

"Happy?"—it appeared, with their various difficulties, to surprise her.

"Well—I seem to myself, among them, the only one who isn't."

She demurred. "With your constant tribute to the ideal?"

He had a laugh at his tribute to the ideal, but he explained, after a moment, his impression. "I mean they're living. They're rushing about. I've already had *my* rushing. I'm waiting."

"But aren't you," she asked by way of cheer, "waiting with *me?*"

He looked at her in all kindness. "Yes—if it weren't for that!"

"And you help *me* to wait," she said. "However," she went on, ' I've really something for you that will help you to wait and which you shall have in a minute. Only there's something more I want from you first. I revel in Sarah."

"So do I. If it weren't," he again amusedly sighed, "for *that*—!"

"Well, you owe more to women than any man I ever saw. We do seem to keep you going. Yet Sarah, as I see her, must be great."

"She *is*"—Strether fully assented: "great! Whatever happens, she won't, with these unforgettable days, have lived in vain."

Miss Gostrey had a pause. "You mean she has fallen in love?"

"I mean she wonders if she hasn't—and it serves all her purpose."

"It has indeed," Maria laughed, "served women's purposes before!"

"Yes—for giving in. But I doubt if the idea—as an idea—has ever up to now answered so well for holding out. That's *her* tribute to the ideal—we each have our own. It's her romance—and it seems to me better, on the whole, than mine. To have it in Paris too," he explained—" on this classic ground, in this charged, infectious air, with so sudden an intensity: well, it's more than she expected. She has had in short to recognize the breaking out for her of a real affinity—and with everything to enhance the drama."

Miss Gostrey followed. "Jim, for instance?"

"Jim. Jim hugely enhances. Jim was made to enhance. And then Mrs. Waymarsh. It's the crowning touch—it supplies the color. He's positively separated."

"And she herself unfortunately isn't—that supplies the color too." Miss Gostrey was all there. But somehow—! "Is *he* in love?"

Strether looked at her a long time; then looked all about the room; then came a little nearer. "Will you never tell any one in the world as long as you live?"

"Never." It was charming.

"He thinks Sarah really is. But he has no fear," Strether hastened to add.

"Of her being affected by it?"

"Of *his* being. He likes it, but he knows she can hold out. He's helping her, he's floating her over, by kindness."

Maria rather funnily considered it. "Floating her over in champagne? The kindness of dining her, nose to nose, at the hour when all Paris is crowding to profane delights. and in the—well, in the great temple, as one hears of it, of pleasure?"

"That's just *it,* for both of them," Strether insisted—"and all of a supreme innocence. The Parisian place, the feverish hour, the putting before her of a hundred francs' worth of food and drink, which they'll scarcely touch—all that's the dear man's own romance: the expensive kind, expensive in francs and centimes, in which he abounds. And the circus afterwards—which is cheaper, but which he'll find some means of making as dear as possible—that's also *his* tribute to the ideal. It does for him. He'll see her through. They won't talk of anything worse than you and me."

"Well, we're bad enough, perhaps, thank Heaven," she laughed, "to upset them! Mr. Waymarsh, at any rate. is a hideous old coquette." And the next moment she had dropped everything for a different pursuit. "What you don't appear to know is that Jeanne de Vionnet has become engaged. She's to marry—it has been definitely arranged—young M. de Montbron."

He fairly blushed. "Then—if you know it—it's 'out'?"

"Don't I often know things that are *not* out? However," she said, "this will be out to-morrow. But I see I've counted too much on your possible ignorance; you've been before me, and I don't make you jump as I hoped."

He gave a gasp at her insight. "You never fail! I've *had* my jump. I had it when I first heard."

" Then, if you knew, why didn't you tell me as soon as you came in?"

" Because I had it from her as a thing not yet to be spoken of."

Miss Gostrey wondered. " From Mme. de Vionnet herself?"

" As a probability—not quite a certainty: a good cause in which Chad has been working. So I've waited."

" You need wait no longer," she returned. " It reached me yesterday—roundabout and accidental, but by a person who had had it from one of the young man's own people—as a thing quite settled. I was only keeping it for you."

" You thought Chad wouldn't have told me?"

She hesitated. " Well, if he hasn't—"

" He hasn't. And yet the thing appears to have been practically his doing. So there we are."

" There we are!" Maria candidly echoed.

" That's why I jumped. I jumped," he continued to explain, " because it means, this disposition of the daughter, that there's now nothing else: nothing else but him and the mother."

" Still—it simplifies."

" It simplifies "—he fully concurred. " But that's precisely where we are. It marks a stage in his relation. The act is his answer to Mrs. Newsome's demonstration."

" It tells," Maria asked, " the worst?"

" The worst."

" But is the worst what he wants Sarah to know?"

" He doesn't care for Sarah."

At which Miss Gostrey's eyebrows went up. " You mean she has already dished herself?"

Strether took a turn about; he had thought it out again and again before this, to the end; but the vista seemed each time longer. " He wants his good friend to know the best. I mean the measure of his attachment. She asked for a sign, and he thought of that one. There it is."

" A concession to her jealousy?"

Strether pulled up. " Yes—call it that. Make it lurid—for that makes my problem richer."

" Certainly, let us have it lurid—for I quite agree with you that we want none of our problems poor. But let us also have it clear.

Can he, in the midst of such a preoccupation, or on the heels of it, have seriously cared for Jeanne?—cared, I mean, as a young man at liberty would have cared?"

Well, Strether had mastered it. "I think he can have thought it would be charming if he *could* care. It would be nicer."

" Nicer than being tied up to Marie?"

" Yes—than the discomfort of an attachment to a person he can never hope, short of a catastrophe, to marry. And he was quite right," said Strether. " It would certainly have been nicer. Even when a thing's already nice there mostly *is* some other thing that would have been nicer—or as to which we wonder if it wouldn't. But his question was all the same a dream. He *couldn't* care in that way. He *is* tied up to Marie. The relation is too special and has gone too far. It's the very basis, and his recent lively contribution toward establishing Jeanne in life has been his definite and final acknowledgment to Mme. de Vionnet that he has ceased squirming. I doubt meanwhile," he went on, " if Sarah has at all directly attacked him."

His companion brooded. " But won't he wish, for his own satisfaction, to make his ground good to her?"

" No—he'll leave it to me, he'll leave everything to me. I 'sort of ' feel "—he worked it out—" that the whole thing will come upon me. Yes, I shall have every inch and every ounce of it. I shall be *used* for it—!" And Strether lost himself in the prospect. Then he fancifully expressed the issue. " To the last drop of my blood."

Maria, however, roundly protested. " Ah, you'll please keep a drop for *me*. *I* shall have a use for it!"—which she didn't, however, follow up. She had come back, the next moment, to another matter. " Mrs. Pocock, with her brother, is trusting only to her general charm?"

" So it would seem."

" And the charm's not working?"

Well, Strether put it otherwise, " She's sounding the note of home—which is the very best thing she can do."

" The best for Mme. de Vionnet?"

" The best for home itself. The natural one; the right one."

" Right," Maria asked, " when it fails?"

Strether had a pause. "The difficulty is Jim. Jim's the note of home."

She debated. "Ah, not, surely, the note of Mrs. Newsome."

But he had it all. "The note of the home for which Mrs. Newsome wants him—the home of the business. Jim stands, with his little legs apart, at the door of *that* tent; and Jim *is,* frankly speaking, extremely awful."

Maria stared. "And you in, you poor thing, for your evening with him?"

"Oh, he's all right for *me!*" Strether laughed. "Any one's good enough for *me*. But Sarah shouldn't, all the same, have brought him. She doesn't appreciate him."

His friend was amused with this statement of it. "Doesn't know, you mean, how bad he is?"

Strether shook his head with decision. "Not really."

She hesitated. "Then doesn't Mrs. Newsome?"

It made him frankly do the same. "Well, no—since you ask me."

Maria rubbed it in. "Not really either?"

"Not at all. She rates him rather high." With which indeed, immediately, he took himself up. "Well, he *is* good too, in his way. It depends on what you want him for."

Miss Gostrey, however, wouldn't let it depend on anything—wouldn't have it, and wouldn't want him, at any price. "It suits my book," she said, "that he should be impossible; and it suits it still better," she more imaginatively added, "that Mrs. Newsome doesn't know he is."

Strether, in consequence, had to take it from her, but he fell back on something else. "I'll tell you who does really know."

"Mr. Waymarsh? Never!"

"Never indeed. I'm not *always* thinking of Mr. Waymarsh; in fact I find now I never am." Then he mentioned the person as if there were a good deal in it. "Mamie."

"His own sister?" Oddly enough, it but let her down. "What good will that do?"

"None perhaps. But there—as usual—we are!"

XXIV

There they were yet again, accordingly, for two days more; when
Strether, on being, at Mrs. Pocock's hotel, ushered into that lady's
salon, found himself at first assuming a mistake on the part of the
servant who had introduced him and retired. The occupants had
not come in, for the room looked empty as only a room can look in
Paris, of a fine afternoon, when the faint murmur of the huge col-
lective life, carried on out-of-doors, strays among scattered objects
even as a summer air idles in a lonely garden. Our friend looked
about and hesitated; observed, on the evidence of a table charged
with purchases and other matters, that Sarah had become possessed
—by no aid from *him*—of the last number of the salmon-colored
Revue; noted further that Mamie appeared to have received a present of Fromentin's " Maîtres d'Autrefois " from Chad, who had
written her name on the cover; and pulled up at the sight of a heavy
letter addressed in a hand he knew. This letter, forwarded by a
banker and arriving in Mrs. Pocock's absence, had been placed in
evidence, and it drew from the fact of its being unopened a sudden
queer power to intensify the reach of its author. It brought home
to him the scale on which Mrs. Newsome—for she had been copious
indeed this time—was writing to her daughter while she kept *him* in
durance; and it had altogether such an effect upon him as made him
for a few minutes stand still and breathe low. In his own room, at
his own hotel, he had dozens of well-filled envelopes superscribed in
that character; and there was actually something in the renewal of
his interrupted vision of the character that played straight into the
so frequent question of whether he were not already disinherited beyond appeal. It was such an assurance as the sharp downstrokes of
her pen had not yet had occasion to give him; but they somehow, at
the present crisis, hinted at a probable absoluteness in any decree
of the writer. He looked at Sarah's name and address, in short, as

if he had been looking hard into her mother's face, and then turned from it as if the face had declined to relax. But since it was, in a manner, as if Mrs. Newsome were thereby all the more, instead of the less, in the room, and were conscious, sharply and sorely conscious, of himself, so he felt both held and hushed, summoned to stay at least and take his punishment. By staying, accordingly, he took it—creeping softly and vaguely about and waiting for Sarah to come in. She *would* come in if he stayed long enough, and he had now more than ever the sense of her success in leaving him a prey to anxiety. It was not to be denied that she had had a happy instinct, from the point of view of Woollett, in placing him thus at the mercy of her own initiative. It was very well to try to say he didn't care— that she might break ground when she would, might never break it at all if she wouldn't, and that he had no confession whatever to wait upon her with: he breathed from day to day an air that damnably required clearing, and there were moments when he quite ached to precipitate that process. He couldn't doubt that, should she only oblige him by surprising him just as he then was, a clarifying scene of some sort would result from the concussion.

He humbly circulated, in this spirit, till he suddenly had a fresh arrest. Both the windows of the room stood open to the balcony, but it was only now that, in the glass of the leaf of one of them, folded back, he caught a reflection quickly recognized as the color of a lady's dress. Somebody had been then, all the while, on the balcony, and the person, whoever it might be, was so placed, between the windows, as to be hidden from him; while, on the other hand, the many sounds of the street had covered his own entrance and movements. If the person were Sarah he might on the spot therefore be served to his taste. He might lead her, by a move or two, up to the remedy for his vain tension; as to which, should he get nothing else from it, he would at least have the relief of pulling down the roof on their heads. There was fortunately no one at hand to observe—in respect to his valor—that even on this completed reasoning he still hung fire. He had been waiting for Mrs. Pocock and the sound of the oracle; but he had to gird himself afresh— which he did in the embrasure of the window, neither advancing nor retreating—before provoking the revelation. It was apparently for Sarah to come more into view; he was in that case there at her service. She did, however, as meanwhile happened, come more into view; only she came, luckily, at the last minute, as a contradiction of Sarah. The occupant of the balcony was after all quite another person, a person presented, on a second look, by a charming back and a slight shift of her position, as beautiful, brilliant, unconscious Mamie—Mamie alone at home, Mamie passing her time in her own innocent way, Mamie in short rather shabbily used, but Mamie absorbed, interested and interesting. With her arms on the balustrade and her attention dropped to the street, she allowed Strether to watch her, to consider several things, without her turning round.

But the oddity was that when he *had* so watched and considered he simply stepped back into the room without following up his advantage. He revolved there again for several minutes, quite as with something new to think of and as if the bearings of the possibility of Sarah had been superseded. For frankly, yes, it *had* bearings thus to find the girl in solitary possession. There was something in it that touched him to a point not to have been reckoned beforehand, something that softly, but quite pressingly, spoke to him, and that spoke the more each time he paused again at the edge of the balcony and saw her still unaware. Her companions were, plainly, scattered; Sarah would be off somewhere with Waymarsh and Chad off somewhere with Jim. Strether didn't at all mentally impute to Chad that he was with his 'good friend'; he gave him the benefit of supposing him involved in appearances that, had he had to describe them—for instance to Maria—he would have conveniently qualified as more subtle. It came to him indeed the next thing that there was perhaps almost an excess of refinement in having left Mamie, in such weather, up there alone; however she might in fact have extemporized, under the charm of the Rue de Rivoli, a little makeshift Paris of wonder and fancy. Our friend at any rate now recognized—and it was as if, at the recognition, Mrs. Newsome's fixed intensity had suddenly, with a deep, audible gasp, grown thin and vague—that, day after day, he had been conscious, in respect to his young lady, of something odd and ambiguous, but something into which he could at last read a meaning. It had been, at the most, this mystery, an obsession—oh, an obsession agreeable; and it had just now fallen into its place as at the touch of a spring. I+

had represented the possibility between them of some communication baffled by accident and delay—the possibility even of some relation as yet unacknowledged.

There was always their old relation, the fruit of the Woollett years; but that—and it was what was strangest—had nothing whatever in common with what was now in the air. As a child, as a "bud," and then again as a flower of expansion, Mamie had bloomed for him, freely, in the almost incessantly open doorways of home; where he remembered her as first very forward, as then very backward—for he had carried on at one period, in Mrs. Newsome's parlors (oh, Mrs. Newsome's phases, and his own!), a course of English Literature reinforced by exams and teas—and once more, finally, as very much in advance. But he had kept no great sense of points of contact; it not being in the nature of things at Woollett that the freshest of the buds should find herself in the same basket with the most withered of the winter apples. The child had given sharpness, above all, to his sense of the flight of time; it was but the day before yesterday that he had tripped up on her hoop, yet his experience of remarkable women—destined, it would seem, remarkably to grow—felt itself ready, this afternoon, quite braced itself, to include her. She had, in fine, more to say to him than he had ever dreamed the pretty girl of the moment *could* have; and the proof of the circumstance was that, visibly, unmistakably, she had been able to say it to no one else. It was something she could mention neither to her brother, to her sister-in-law, nor to Chad; though he could just imagine that, had she still been at home, she might have brought it out, as a supreme tribute to age, authority and attitude, for Mrs. Newsome. It was moreover something in which they all took an interest; the strength of their interest was in truth just the reason of her prudence. All this then, for five minutes, was vivid to Strether, and it put before him that, poor child, she had now but her prudence to amuse her. That, for a pretty girl in Paris, struck him, with a rush, as a sorry state; so that, under the impression, he went out to her with a step as hypocritically alert, he was well aware, as if he had just come into the room. She turned, with a start, at his voice; preoccupied with him though she might be, she was just a scrap disappointed. "Oh, I thought you were Mr. Bilham!"

The remark had been at first surprising and our friend's private thought, under the influence of it, temporarily blighted; yet we are able to add that he presently recovered his inward tone, and that many a fresh flower of fancy was to bloom in the same air. Little Bilham—since little Bilham was, somewhat incongruously, expected —appeared behindhand; a circumstance by which Strether was to profit. They came back into the room together, after a little, the couple on the balcony, and amid its crimson-and-gold elegance, with the others still absent, Strether passed forty minutes that he appraised even at the time as far, in the whole queer connection, from his idlest. Yes indeed, since he had the other day so agreed with Maria about the inspiration of the lurid, here was something for his problem that surely didn't make it shrink and that was floated in upon him as part of a sudden flood. He was doubtless not to know till afterwards, on turning them over in thought, of how many elements his impression was composed; but he none the less felt, as he sat with the charming girl, the signal growth of a confidence. For she *was* charming, when all was said—and none the less so for the visible habit and practice of freedom and fluency. She was charming, he was aware, in spite of the fact that if he hadn't found her so he would have found her something he should have been in peril of expressing as "funny." Yes, she was funny, wonderful Mamie, and without dreaming it; she was bland, she was bridal—with never, that he could make out as yet, a bridegroom to support it; she was handsome and portly and easy and chatty, soft and sweet and almost disconcertingly reassuring. She was dressed, if we might so far discriminate, less as a young lady than as an old one—had an old one been supposable to Strether as so committed to vanity; the complexities of her hair missed moreover also the looseness of youth; and she had a mature manner of bending a little, as to encourage and reward, while she held neatly together in front of her a pair of strikingly polished hands: the combination of all of which kept up, about her, the glamour of her " receiving," placed her again perpetually between the windows and within sound of the ice-cream plates, suggested the enumeration of all the names, all the Mr. Brookses and Mr. Snookses, gregarious specimens of a single type, she was happy to " meet."

But if all this was where she was funny, and if what was funnier than the rest was the contrast between her beautiful benevolent patronage—such a hint of the polysyllabic as might make her something of a bore toward middle age—and her rather flat little voice, the voice, naturally, unaffectedly yet, of a girl of fifteen; so Strether, none the less, at the end of ten minutes, felt in her a quiet dignity that pulled things bravely together. If quiet dignity, almost more than matronly, with voluminous, too voluminous clothes, was the effect she proposed to produce, that was an ideal one could like in her when once one had got into relation. The great thing now, for her visitor, was that this was exactly what he had done; it made so extraordinary a mixture of the brief and crowded hour. It was the mark of a relation that he had begun so quickly to find himself sure she was, of all people, as might have been said, on the side and of the party of Mrs. Newsome's original ambassador. She was in *his* interest, and not in Sarah's; and some sign of that was precisely what he had been feeling in her, these last days, as imminent. Finally placed, in Paris, in immediate presence of the situation and of the hero of it—by whom Strether was incapable of meaning any one but Chad—she had accomplished, and really in a manner all unexpected to herself, a change of base; deep, still things had come to pass within her, and by the time she had grown sure of them Strether had become aware of the little drama. When she knew where she was, in short, he had made it out; and he made it out at present still better; though with never a direct word passing between them all the while on the subject of his own predicament. There had been at first, as he sat there with her, a moment during which he wondered if she meant to break ground in respect to his prime undertaking. That door stood so strangely ajar that he was half prepared to be conscious, at any juncture, of her having, of any one's having, quite bounced in. But, friendly, familiar, light of touch and happy of tact, she exquisitely stayed out; so that it was, for all the world, as if to show she could deal with him without being reduced to—well, to scarcely anything.

It fully came up for them then by means of their talking of everything *but* Chad, that Mamie, unlike Sarah, unlike Jim, knew perfectly what had become of him. It fully came up that she had taken to the last fraction of an inch the measure of the change in him, and that she wanted Strether to know what a secret she proposed to make of it. They talked most conveniently—as if they had had **no** chance yet—about Woollett; and that had virtually the effect **of** their keeping the secret more close. The hour took on for Strether, little by little, a queer, sad sweetness of savor; he had such a re- vulsion in Mamie's favor and on behalf of her social value as might have come from remorse at some early injustice. She made him, as under the breath of some vague western whiff, homesick and freshly restless; he could really, for the time, have fancied himself stranded with her, on a far shore, during an ominous calm, in a quaint community of shipwreck. Their little interview was like a picnic on a coral strand; they passed each other, with melancholy smiles and looks sufficiently allusive, such cupfuls of water as they had saved. Especially sharp in Strether meanwhile was the con- viction that his companion really knew, as we have hinted, where she had come out. It was at a very particular place—only *that* she would never tell him; it would be above all what he should have to puzzle for himself. This was what he hoped for, because his interest in the girl wouldn't be complete without it. No more would the appreciation to which she was entitled—so assured was he that the more he saw of her process the more he should see of her pride. She saw, herself, everything; but she knew what she didn't want, and that it was that had helped her. What didn't she want?—there was a pleasure lost for her old friend in not yet knowing, as there would doubtless be a thrill in getting a glimpse. Gently and sociably she kept that dark to him, and it was as if she soothed and beguiled him in other ways to make up for it. She came out with her impression of Mme. de Vionnet—of whom she had " heard so much "; she came out with her impression of Jeanne, whom she had been " dying to see ": she brought it out with a blandness by which her auditor was really stirred that she had been with Sarah early that very after- noon, and after dreadful delays caused by all sorts of things, mainly, eternally, by the purchase of clothes—clothes that unfortunately wouldn't be themselves eternal—to call in the Rue de Bellechasse.

At the sound of these names Strether almost blushed to feel that he couldn't have sounded them first—and yet couldn't, either, have justified his squeamishness. Mamie made them easy as he couldn't have begun to do, and yet it could only have cost her more than he should ever have had to spend. It was as friends of Chad's, friends special, distinguished, desirable, enviable, that she spoke of them, and she beautifully carried it off that much as she had heard of them —though she didn't say how or where, which was a touch of her own —she had found them beyond her supposition. She abounded in their praise, and after the manner of Woollett—which made the manner of Woollett a lovable thing again to Strether. He had never so felt the true inwardness of it as when his blooming companion pronounced the elder of the ladies of the Rue de Bellechasse too fascinating for words and declared of the younger that she was perfectly ideal, a real little monster of charm. "Nothing," she said of Jeanne, "ought ever to happen to her—she's so awfully right as she is. Another touch will spoil her—so she oughtn't to *be* touched."

"Ah, but things, here in Paris," Strether observed, "do happen to little girls." And then, for the joke's and the occasion's sake: "Haven't you found that yourself?"

"That things happen—? Oh, I'm not a little girl. I'm a big battered, blowsy one: *I* don't care," Mamie laughed, "*what* happens."

Strether had a pause while he wondered if it mightn't happen that he should give her the pleasure of learning that he found her nicer than he had really dreamed—a pause that ended when he had said to himself that, so far as it at all mattered for her, she had in fact perhaps already made this out. He risked accordingly a different question—though conscious, as soon as he had spoken, that he seemed to place it in relation to her last speech. "But that Mlle. de Vionnet is to be married—I suppose you've heard of *that*."

For all, he then found, he need fear! "Dear, yes; the gentleman was there: M. de Montbron, whom Mme. de Vionnet presented to us."

"And was he nice?"

Mamie bloomed and bridled with her best reception manner. "Any man's nice when he's in love."

It made Strether laugh. "But is M. de Montbron in love—already—with *you*?"

"Oh, that's not necessary—it's so much better he should be so with *her:* which, thank goodness, I lost no time in discovering for myself. He's perfectly gone—and I couldn't have borne it, for her, if he hadn't been. She's just too sweet."

Strether hesitated. "And through being in love too?"

On which, with a smile that struck him as wonderful, Mamie had a wonderful answer. "She doesn't know if she is or not."

It made him again laugh out. "Oh, but *you* do!"

She was willing to take it that way. "Oh yes, I know everything." And as she sat there rubbing her polished hands and making the best of it—only holding her elbows perhaps a little too much out—the momentary effect for Strether was that every one else, in all their affair, seemed stupid.

"Know that poor little Jeanne doesn't know what's the matter with her?"

It was as near as they came to saying that she was probably in love with Chad; but it was quite near enough for what Strether wanted; which was to be confirmed in his certitude that, whether in love or not, she appealed to something large and easy in the girl before him. Mamie would be fat, too fat, at thirty; but she would always be the person who, at the present sharp hour, had been disinterestedly tender. "If I see a little more of her—as I hope I shall—I think she'll like me enough (for she seemed to like me today), to want me to tell her."

"And *shall* you?"

"Perfectly. I shall tell her the matter with her is that she wants only too much to do right. To do right for her, naturally," said Mamie, "is to please."

"Her mother, do you mean?"

"Her mother first."

Strether waited. "And then?"

"Well, 'then'—Mr. Newsome."

There was something really grand for him in the serenity of this reference. "And last only M. de Montbron?"

"Last only"—she good-humoredly kept it up.

Strether considered. "So that every one, after all, then, will be suited?"

She had one of her few hesitations, but it was a question only of a moment; and it was her nearest approach to being explicit with him about what was between them. "I think I can speak for myself. *I* shall be."

It said indeed so much, told such a story of her being ready to help him, so committed to him that truth, in short, for such use as he might make of it toward those ends of his own with which, patiently and trustfully, she had nothing to do—it so fully achieved all this that he appeared to himself simply to meet it in its own spirit by the last frankness of admiration. Admiration was of itself almost accusatory, but nothing less would serve to show her how nearly he understood. He put out his hand for good-bye with a " Splendid, splendid, splendid!" And he left her, with her splendor, still waiting for little Bilham.

PART TENTH

XXV

STRETHER occupied beside little Bilham, three evenings after his interview with Mamie Pocock, the same deep divan they had enjoyed together on the first occasion of our friend's meeting Mme. de Vionnet and her daughter in the apartment of the Boulevard Malesherbes, where his position affirmed itself again as ministering to an easy exchange of impressions. The present evening had a different stamp; if the company was much more numerous, so, inevitably, were the ideas set in motion. It was on the other hand, however, now strongly marked that the talkers moved, in respect to such matters, round an inner, a protected circle. They knew, at any rate, what really concerned them to-night, and Strether had begun by keeping his companion close to it. Only a few of Chad's guests had dined—that is fifteen or twenty, a few compared with the large concourse offered to sight by eleven o'clock; but number and mass, quantity and quality, light, fragrance, sound, the overflow of hospitality meeting the high tide of response, had all, from the first, pressed upon Strether's consciousness, and he felt himself somehow part and parcel of the most festive scene, as the term was, in which he had ever in his life been engaged. He had perhaps seen, on Fourths of July and on dear old domestic Commencements, more people assembled, but he had never seen so many in proportion to the space, or had at all events never known so great a promiscuity to show so markedly as picked. Numerous as was the company, it had still been made so by selection, and what was above all rare for Strether was that, by no fault of his own, he was in the secret of the principle that had worked. He had not inquired, he had averted his head, but Chad had put him a pair of questions that themselves smoothed the ground. He had not answered the questions, he had replied that they were the young man's own affair; and he had then seen perfectly that the latter's direction was already settled.

Chad had applied for counsel only by way of intimating that he knew what to do; and he had clearly never known it better than in now presenting to his sister the whole circle of his society. This was all in the sense and the spirit of the note struck by him on that lady's arrival; he had taken at the station itself a line that led him without a break, and that enabled him to lead the Pococks—though dazed a little, no doubt, breathless, no doubt, and bewildered—to the uttermost end of the passage accepted by them perforce as pleasant. He had made it, for them, violently pleasant and mercilessly full; the upshot of which was, to Strether's vision, that they had come all the way without discovering that it was really no passage at all. It was a brave blind alley, where to pass was impossible, and where, unless they stuck fast, they would have—which was always awkward —publicly to back out. They were touching bottom, assuredly, tonight; the whole scene represented the terminus of the *cul-de-sac*. So could things go when there was a hand to keep them consistent— a hand that pulled the wire with a skill at which the elder man more and more marvelled. The elder man felt responsible, but he also felt successful, for what had taken place was simply the issue of his own contention, six weeks before, that they properly should wait to see what their friends would have really to say. He had determined Chad to wait, he had determined him to see; he was therefore not to quarrel with the time given up to the business. As much as ever, accordingly, now that a fortnight had elapsed, the situation created for Sarah, and against which she had raised no protest, was that of her having accommodated herself to her adventure as to a pleasure-party surrendered perhaps even somewhat in excess to bustle and to "pace." If her brother had been at any point the least bit open to criticism it might have been on the ground of his spicing the draught too highly and pouring the cup too full. Frankly treating the whole occasion of the presence of his relatives as an opportunity for amusement, he left it, no doubt, but scant margin as an opportunity for anything else. He suggested, invented, abounded — yet all the while with the loosest, easiest rein. Strether, during his own weeks, had gained a sense of knowing Paris; but he saw it afresh, and with fresh emotion, in the form of the knowledge offered to his colleague.

A thousand unuttered thoughts hummed for him in the air of

these observations; not the least frequent of which was that Sarah might well, of a truth, not quite know whither she was drifting. She was in no position not to appear to expect that Chad should treat her handsomely; yet she struck our friend as privately stiffening a little each time she missed the chance of marking the great *nuance*. The great *nuance* was, in brief, that of course her brother must treat her handsomely—she should like to see him not; but that treating her handsomely, none the less, wasn't all in all—treating her handsomely buttered no parsnips; and that in fine there were moments when she felt the fixed eyes of their admirable absent mother fairly screw into the flat of her back. Strether, watching, after his habit, and overscoring with thought, positively had moments of his own in which he found himself sorry for her—occasions on which she affected him as a person seated in a runaway vehicle and turning over the question of a possible jump. *Would* she jump, could she, would *that* be a safe place?—this question, at such instants, sat for him in her lapse into pallor, her tight lips, her conscious eyes. It came back to the main point at issue: would she be, after all, to be squared? He believed, on the whole, she would jump; yet his alternations on this subject were the more especial stuff of his suspense. One thing remained well before him—a conviction that was in fact to gain sharpness from the impressions of this evening: that if she *should* gather in her skirts, close her eyes and quit the carriage while in motion, he would promptly enough become aware. She would alight from her headlong course more or less directly upon him; it would be appointed to him, unquestionably, to receive her entire weight. Signs and portents of the experience thus in reserve for him had, as it happened, multiplied even through the dazzle of Chad's party. It was partly under the nervous consciousness of such a prospect that, leaving almost every one in the two other rooms, leaving those of the guests already known to him as well as a mass of brilliant strangers of both sexes and of several varieties of speech, he had desired five quiet minutes with little Bilham, whom he always found soothing and even, a little, inspiring, and to whom he had actually, moreover, something distinct and important to say.

He had felt of old—for it already seemed long ago—rather humiliated at finding that he could learn in talk with a personage so much his junior the lesson of a certain moral ease; but he had now got used to that—whether or no the mixture of the fact with other humiliations had made it indistinct, whether or no directly from little Bilham's example, the example of his being contentedly just the obscure and acute little Bilham he was. It worked so for him, Strether seemed to see; and our friend had, at private hours, a wan smile over the fact that he himself, after so many more years, was still in search of something that would work. However, as we have said, it worked just now for them equally to have found a corner a little apart. What particularly kept it apart was the circumstance that the music in the salon was admirable, with two or three such singers as it was a privilege to hear in private. Their presence gave a distinction to Chad's entertainment, and the interest of calculating their effect on Sarah was actually so sharp as to be almost painful. Unmistakably, in her single person, the motive of the composition and dressed in a splendor of crimson which affected Strether as a fall through a skylight, she would now be in the forefront of the listening circle and committed by it up to her eyes. Those eyes during the wonderful dinner itself he had not once met; having confessedly—perhaps a little pusillanimously—arranged with Chad that he should be on the same side of the table. But there was no use in having arrived now with little Bilham at an unprecedented point of intimacy unless he could pitch everything into the pot. "You who sat where you could see her, what does she make of it all? By which I mean on what terms does she take it?"

"Oh, she takes it, I judge, as proving that the claim of his family is more than ever justified."

"She isn't then pleased with what he has to show?"

"On the contrary; she's pleased with it as with his capacity to do this kind of thing—more than she has been pleased with anything for a long time. But she wants him to show it *there*. He has no right to waste it on the likes of us."

Strether wondered. "She wants him to move the whole thing over?"

"The whole thing—with an important exception. Everything he has 'picked up'—and the way he knows how. She sees no difficulty in that. She'd run the show herself, and she'll make the handsome concession that Woollett would be, on the whole, in some ways the better for it. Not that it wouldn't be also, in some ways, the better for Woollett. The people there are just as good."

"Just as good as you and these others? Ah, that may be. But such an occasion as this, whether or no," Strether said, "isn't the people. It's what has made the people possible."

"Well then," his friend replied, "there you are. I give you my impression for what it's worth. Mrs. Pocock has *seen;* and that's to-night how she sits there. If you were to have a glimpse of her face, you'd understand me. She has made up her mind—to the sound of expensive music."

Strether took it smoothly in. "Ah then, I shall have news of her."

"I don't want to frighten you, but I think that likely. However," little Bilham continued, "if I'm of the least use to you to hold on by—!"

"You're not of the least!"—and Strether laid an appreciative hand on him to say it. "No one's of the least." With which to mark how gayly he could take it, he patted his companion's knee. "I must meet my fate alone, and I *shall*—oh, you'll see! And yet," he pursued the next moment, "you *can* help me too. You once said to me"—he followed this further—"that you held Chad should marry. I didn't see then so well as I know now that you meant he should marry Miss Pocock. Do you still consider that he should? Because if you do"—he kept it up—"I want you immediately to change your mind. You can help me that way."

"Help you by thinking he should *not* marry?"

"Not marry at all events Mamie."

"And who then?"

"Ah," Strether returned, "that I'm not obliged to say. But Mme. de Vionnet—I suggest—when he can."

"Oh!" said little Bilham with some sharpness.

"Oh, precisely! But he needn't marry at all—I'm at any rate not obliged to provide for it. Whereas in your case I rather feel that I *am*."

Little Bilham was amused. "Obliged to provide for my marrying?"

"Yes—after all I've done to you!"

The young man weighed it. "Have you done as much as that?"

"Well," said Strether, thus challenged, "of course I must remember what you've also done to *me*. We may perhaps call it square. But, all the same," he went on, " I wish awfully you'd marry Mamie Pocock yourself."

Little Bilham laughed out. " Why, it was only the other night, in this very place, that you were proposing to me a different union altogether."

" Mlle. de Vionnet?" Well, Strether easily confessed it. " That I admit, was a vain image. *This* is practical politics. I want to do something good for both of you—I wish you each so well; and you can see in a moment the trouble it will save me to polish you off by the same stroke. She likes you, you know. You console her. And she's splendid."

Little Bilham stared as a delicate appetite stares at an overheaped plate. " What do I console her for?"

It just made his friend impatient. " Oh come, you know!"

" And what proves for you that she likes me?"

" Why, the fact that I found her, three days ago, stopping at home alone all the golden afternoon on the mere chance that you would come to her, and hanging over her balcony on that of seeing your cab drive up. I don't know what you want more."

Little Bilham after a moment found it. " Only just to know what proves to you that I like *her*."

" Oh, if what I've just mentioned isn't enough to make you do it, you're a stony-hearted little fiend. Besides "—Strether encouraged his fancy's flight—" you showed your inclination in the way you kept her waiting, kept her on purpose to see if she cared enough for you."

His companion paid his ingenuity the deference of a pause. " I didn't keep her waiting. I came at the hour. I wouldn't have kept her waiting for the world," the young man honorably declared.

" Better still—then there you are!" And Strether, charmed, held him the faster. " Even if you didn't do her justice, moreover," he continued, " I should insist on your immediately coming round to it. I want awfully to have worked it. I want "—and our friend spoke now with a yearning that was really earnest—" at least to have done *that*."

" To have married me off—without a penny?"

" Well, I sha'n't live long; and I give you my word, now and here,

that I'll leave you every penny of my own. I haven't many, un·
fortunately, but you shall have them all. And Miss Pocock, I think,
has a few. I want," Strether went on, " to have been at least to that
extent constructive—even expiatory. I've been sacrificing so to
strange gods that I feel I want to put on record, somehow, my
fidelity—fundamentally unchanged, after all—to our own. I feel as
if my hands were embrued with the blood of monstrous alien altars—
of another faith altogether. There it is—it's done." And then he
further explained. " It took hold of me because the idea of getting
her quite out of the way for Chad helps to clear my ground."

The young man, at this, bounced about, and it brought them face
to face in admitted amusement. " You want me to marry as a
convenience to Chad?"

" No," Strether debated—" he doesn't care whether you marry or
not. It's as a convenience, simply, to my own plan for him."

"'Simply'!"—and little Bilham's concurrence was in itself a
lively comment. " Thank you. But I thought," he continued,
" you had exactly no plan ' for ' him."

" Well then, call it my plan for myself—which may be well, as
you say, to have none. His situation, don't you see? is reduced now
to the bare facts one has to recognize. Mamie doesn't want him,
and he doesn't want Mamie: so much as that these days have made
clear. It's a thread we can wind up and tuck in."

But little Bilham still questioned. " You can—since you seem so
much to want to. But why should I?"

Poor Strether thought it over, but was obliged of course to admit
that his demonstration did superficially fail. " Seriously, there is
no reason. It's my affair—I must do it alone. I've only my fantas·
tic need of making my dose stiff."

Little Bilham wondered. " What do you call your dose?"

" Why, what I have to swallow. I want my conditions unmiti·
gated."

He had spoken in the tone of talk for talk's sake, and yet with an
obscure truth lurking in the loose folds; a circumstance presently
not without its effect on his young friend. Little Bilham's eyes
rested on him a moment with some intensity; then, suddenly, as if
everything had cleared up, he gave a happy laugh. It seemed to say
that if pretending, or even trying, or still even hoping, to be able to

care for Mamie would be of use, he was all there at his service. "I'll do anything in the world for you!"

"Well," Strether smiled, "anything in the world is all I want. I don't know anything that pleased me in her more," he went on, "than the way that, on my finding her up there all alone, coming on her unawares, and feeling greatly for her being so out of it, she knocked down my tall house of cards with her instant and cheerful allusion to the next young man. It was somehow so the note I needed—her staying at home to receive him."

"It was Chad of course," said little Bilham, "who asked the next young man—I like your name for me!—to call."

"So I supposed—all of which, thank God, is in our innocent and natural manners. But do you know," Strether asked, "if Chad knows—?" And then as his interlocutor seemed at a loss: "Why, where she has come out."

Little Bilham, at this, met his face with a conscious look; it was as if, more than anything yet, the allusion had penetrated. "Do you know yourself?"

Strether lightly shook his head. "There I stop. Oh, odd as it may appear to you, there *are* things I don't know. I only got the sense from her of something very sharp, and yet very deep down, that she was keeping all to herself. That is, I had begun with the belief that she *had* kept it to herself; but face to face with her there I soon made out that there was a person with whom she would have shared it. I had thought she possibly might with *me*—but I saw then that I was only half in her confidence. When, turning to me to greet me—for she was on the balcony, and I had come in without her knowing it—she showed me she had been expecting *you* and was proportionately disappointed, I got hold of the tail of my conviction. Half an hour later I was in possession of all the rest of it. You know what has happened." He looked at his young friend hard—then he felt sure. "For all you say, you're up to your eyes. So there you are."

Little Bilham after an instant pulled half round. "I assure you she hasn't told me anything."

"Of course she hasn't. For what do you suggest that I suppose her to take you? But you've been with her every day, you've seen her freely, you've liked her greatly—I stick to that—and you've

320

made your profit of it. You know what she has been through as well as you know that she has dined here to-night—which must have put her, by the way, through a good deal more."

The young man faced this blast; after which he pulled round the rest of the way. "I haven't in the least said she hasn't been nice to me. But she's proud."

"And quite properly. But not too proud for that."

"It's just her pride that has made her. Chad," little Bilham loyally went on, "has really been as kind to her as possible. It's awkward for a man when a girl's in love with him."

"Ah, but she isn't—now."

Little Bilham sat staring before him; then he sprang up as if his friend's penetration, recurrent and insistent, made him really, after all, too nervous. "No—she isn't now. It isn't in the least," he went on, "Chad's fault. He's really all right. I mean he would have been willing. But she came over with ideas. Those she had got at home. They had been her motive and support in joining her brother and his wife. She was to *save* our friend."

"Ah, like me, poor thing?" Strether also got to his feet.

"Exactly—she had a bad moment. It was very soon distinct to her, to pull her up, to let her down, that, alas, he was, he *is*, saved. There's nothing left for her to do."

"Not even to love him?"

"She would have loved him better as she originally believed him."

Strether wondered. "Of course one asks one's self what notion a little girl forms, where a young man's in question, of such a history and such a state."

"Well, this little girl saw them, no doubt, as obscure, but she saw them, practically, as wrong. The wrong, for her, *was* the obscure. Chad turns out, at any rate, right and good and disconcerting, while what she was all prepared for, primed and girded and wound up for, was to deal with him as the general opposite."

"Yet wasn't her whole point"—Strether weighed it—"that he was to be, that he *could* be, made better, redeemed?"

Little Bilham fixed it all a moment, and then with a small head-shake that diffused a tenderness: "She's too late. Too late for the miracle."

"**Yes**"—his companion saw enough. "Still, if the worst fault of his condition is that it may be all there for her to profit by—?"

"Oh, she doesn't want to 'profit,' in that flat way. She doesn't want to profit by another woman's work—she wants the miracle to have been her own miracle. *That's* what she's too late for."

Strether quite felt how it all fitted; yet there seemed one loose piece. "I'm bound to say, you know, that she strikes one, on these lines, as fastidious—what you call here *difficile*."

Little Bilham tossed up his chin. "Of course she's *difficile*—on any lines! What else in the world *are* our Mamies—the real, the right, ones?"

"I see, I see," our friend repeated, charmed by the responsive wisdom he had ended by so richly extracting. "Mamie is one of the real and the right."

"The very thing itself."

"And what it comes to then," Strether went on, "is that poor awful Chad is simply too good for her."

"Ah, too good was what he was after all to be; but it was she herself, and she herself only, who was to have made him so."

It hung beautifully together, but with still a loose end. "Wouldn't he do for her even if he should, after all, break—"

"With his actual influence?" Oh, little Bilham had for this inquiry the sharpest of all his controls. "How can he 'do'—on any terms whatever—when he's flagrantly spoiled?"

Strether could only meet the question with his passive, his receptive pleasure. "Well, thank goodness, *you're* not! *You* remain for her to save, and I come back, on so beautiful and full a demonstration, to my contention of just now—that of your showing distinct signs of her having already begun."

The most he could further say to himself—as his young friend turned away—was that the charge encountered for the moment no renewed denial. Little Bilham, taking his course back to the music, only shook his good-natured ears an instant, in the manner of a terrier who has got wet; while Strether relapsed into the sense —which had for him in these days most of comfort—that he was free to believe in anything that, from hour to hour, kept him going. He had positively motions and flutters of this conscious hour-to-hour kind, temporary surrenders to irony, to fancy, frequent instinctive snatches at the growing rose of observation, constantly stronger for him, as he felt, in scent and color, and in which he could bury his nose even to wantonness. This last resource was offered him, for that matter, in the very form of his next clear perception—the vision of a prompt meeting, in the doorway of the room, between little Bilham and brilliant Miss Barrace, who was entering as Bilham withdrew. She had apparently put him a question, to which he had replied by turning to indicate his late interlocutor; toward whom, after an interrogation further aided by a resort to that optical machinery that seemed, like her other ornaments, curious and archaic, the genial lady, suggesting more than ever, for her fellow-guest, the old French print, the historic portrait, directed herself with an intention that Strether instantly met. He knew in advance the first note she would sound, and took in, as she approached, all her need of sounding it. Nothing yet had been so " wonderful " between them as the present occasion; and it was her special sense of this quality in occasions that she was there, as she was in most places, to feed. That sense had already been so well fed by the situation about them that she had quitted the other room, forsaken the music, dropped out of the play, abandoned, in a word, the stage itself, that she might stand a minute behind the scenes with Strether and so perhaps figure as one of the famous augurs replying, behind the oracle, to the wink of the other. Seated near him presently where little Bilham had sat, she replied in truth to many things; beginning as soon as he had said to her—what he hoped he said without fatuity—" All you ladies are extraordinarily kind to me."

She played her long handle, which shifted her observation; she saw in an instant all the absences that left them free. " How can we be anything else? But isn't that exactly your plight? ' We ladies '—oh, we're nice, and you must be having enough of us! As one of us, you know, I don't know that I'm crazy about us. But Miss Gostrey, at least, to-night, has left you alone, hasn't she?" With which she again looked about as if Maria might still lurk.

" Oh yes," said Strether; " she's only sitting up for me at home." And then as this elicited from his companion her gay " Oh, oh, oh!" he explained that he meant sitting up in suspense and prayer. " We thought it on the whole better she shouldn't be present; and either way, of course, it's a terrible worry for her." He abounded in the sense of his appeal to the ladies, and they might take their choice of his doing so from humility or from pride. "Yet she inclines to believe I shall come out."

"Oh, I incline to believe too you'll come out!"—Miss Barrace, with her laugh, was not to be behind. "Only the question's about *where,* isn't it? However," she happily continued, "if it's anywhere at all it must be very far on, mustn't it? To do us justice, I think, you know," she laughed, "we do, among us all, want you rather far on. Yes, yes," she repeated in her quick, droll way; "we want you very, *very* far on!" After which she wished to know why he had thought it better Maria shouldn't be present.

"Oh," he replied, "it was really her own idea. I should have wished it. But she dreads responsibility."

"And isn't that a new thing for her?"

"To dread it? No doubt—no doubt. But her nerve has given way."

Miss Barrace looked at him a moment. "She has too much at stake." Then less gravely: "Mine, luckily for me, holds out."

"Luckily for me too"—Strether came back to that. "My own isn't so firm, *my* appetite for responsibility isn't so sharp, as that I haven't felt the very principle of this occasion to be 'the more the merrier.' If we *are* so merry, it's because Chad has understood so well."

"He has understood amazingly," said Miss Barrace.

"It's wonderful!"—Strether anticipated for her.

"It's wonderful!" she, to meet it, intensified; so that, face to face over it, they simply and recklessly laughed. But she presently added: "Oh, I see the principle. If one didn't, one would be lost. But when once one has got hold of it—"

"It's as simple as twice two! From the moment he had to do something—"

"A crowd"—she took him straight up—"was the only thing? Rather, rather: a rumpus of sound," she laughed, "or nothing. Mrs. Pocock's built in, or built out—whichever you call it; she's packed so tight she can't move. She's in splendid isolation"—Miss Barrace embroidered the theme.

Strether followed, but scrupulous of justice. "Yet with every one in the place successively introduced to her."

"Wonderfully—but just so that it does build her out. She's bricked up, she's buried alive!"

Strether seemed for a moment to look at it; but it brought him to a sigh. "Oh, but she's not dead! It will take more than this to kill her."

His companion had a pause that might have been for pity. "No, I can't pretend I think she's finished—or that it's for more than tonight." She remained pensive as if with the same compunction. "It's only up to her chin." Then again for the fun of it: "She can breathe."

"She can breathe!"—he echoed it in the same spirit. "And do you know," he went on, "what's really, all this time, happening to me?—through the beauty of music, the gayety of voices, the uproar, in short, of our revel and the felicity of your wit? The sound of Mrs. Pocock's respiration drowns for me, I assure you, every other. It's literally all I hear."

She focussed him with her clink of chains. "Well—!" she breathed ever so kindly.

"Well, what?"

"She is free from her chin up," she mused; "and that will be enough for her."

"It will be enough for me!" Strether ruefully laughed. "Waymarsh has really," he then asked, "brought her to see you?"

"Yes—but that's the worst of it. I could do you no good. And yet I tried hard."

Strether wondered. "And how did you try?"

"Why, I didn't speak of you."

"I see. That was better."

"Then what would have been worse? For speaking or silent," she lightly wailed, "I somehow 'compromise.' And it has never been any one but you."

"That shows"—he was magnanimous—"that it's something not in you, but in one's self. It's my fault."

She was silent a little. "No, it's Mr. Waymarsh's. It's the fault of his having brought her."

"Ah then," said Strether good-naturedly, "why did he bring her?"

"He couldn't afford not to."

325

"Oh, you were a trophy—one of the spoils of conquest? But why, in that case, since you do 'compromise'—"

"Don't I compromise *him* as well? I do compromise him as well," Miss Barrace smiled. "I compromise him as hard as I can. But for Mr. Waymarsh it isn't fatal. It's—so far as his wonderful relation with Mrs. Pocock is concerned—favorable." And then, as he still seemed slightly at sea: "The man who had succeeded with *me,* don't you see? For her to get him from me was such an added incentive."

Strether saw, but as if his path was still strewn with surprises. "It's 'from' you then that she has got him?"

She was amused at his momentary muddle. "You can fancy my fight! She believes in her triumph. I think it has been part of her joy."

"Oh, her joy!" Strether sceptically murmured.

"Well, she thinks she has had her own way. And what is to-night, for her, but a kind of apotheosis? Her frock's really good."

"Good enough to go to heaven in? For after a real apotheosis," Strether went on, "there's nothing *but* heaven. For Sarah there's only to-morrow."

"And you mean that she won't find to-morrow heavenly?"

"Well, I mean that I somehow feel to-night—on her behalf—too good to be true. She has had her cake; that is she's in the act now of having it, of swallowing the largest and sweetest piece. There won't be another left for her. Certainly *I* haven't one. It can only, at the best, be Chad." He continued to make it out as for their common entertainment. "He may have one, as it were, up his sleeve; yet it's borne in upon me that if he had—"

"He wouldn't"—she quite understood—"have taken all *this* trouble? I dare say not, and, if I may be quite free and dreadful, I very much hope he won't take any more. Of course I won't pretend now," she added, "not to know what it's a question of."

"Oh, every one knows, I think, now," poor Strether thoughtfully admitted; "and it's strange enough and funny enough that one should feel everybody here at this very moment as knowing and watching and waiting."

"Yes—isn't it indeed funny?" Miss Barrace quite rose to it. "That's the way we *are* in Paris." She was always pleased with a new contribution to that queerness. "It's wonderful! But, you know," she declared, "it all depends on you. I don't want to turn the knife in your vitals, but that's naturally what you just now meant by our all being on top of you. We know you as the hero of the drama and we're gathered to see what you'll do."

Strether looked at her a moment with a light perhaps slightly obscured. "I think that must be why the hero has taken refuge in this corner. He's scared at his heroism—he shrinks from his part."

"Ah, but we nevertheless believe that he'll play it. That's why," Miss Barrace kindly went on, "we take such an interest in you. We feel that you'll come up to the scratch." And then as he seemed perhaps not quite to take fire: "Don't let him do it."

"Don't let Chad go?"

"Yes, keep hold of him. With all this"—and she indicated the general tribute—"he has done enough. We love him here—he's charming."

"It's beautiful," said Strether, "the way you all can simplify when you will."

But she gave it to him back. "It's nothing to the way *you* will when you must."

He winced at it as at the very voice of prophecy, and it kept him a moment quiet. He detained her, however, on her appearing about to leave him alone in the rather cold clearance their talk had made. "There positively isn't a sign of a hero to-night; the hero's dodging and shirking, the hero's ashamed. Therefore, you know, I think, what you must all *really* be occupied with is the heroine."

Miss Barrace took a minute. "The heroine?"

"The heroine. I've treated her," said Strether, "not a bit like a hero. Oh," he sighed, "I don't do it well!"

She eased him off. "You do it as you can." And then after another hesitation: "I think she's satisfied."

But he remained compunctious. "I haven't been near her. I haven't looked at her."

"Ah then, you've lost a good deal!"

He showed that he knew it. "She's more wonderful than ever?"

"Than ever. With Mr. Pocock."

Strether wondered. "Mme. de Vionnet—with Jim?"

"Mme. de Vionnet—with 'Jim.'" Miss Barrace was historic.

"And what is she doing with him?"

"Ah, you must ask *him!*"

Strether's face lighted again at the prospect. "It *will* be amusing to do so." Yet he continued to wonder. "But she must have some idea."

"Of course she has—she has twenty ideas. She has in the first place," said Miss Barrace, swinging a little her tortoise-shell, "that of doing her part. Her part is to help *you.*"

It came out as nothing had come yet; links were missing and connections unnamed, but it was suddenly as if they were at the heart of their subject. "Yes; how much more she does it," Strether gravely reflected, "than I help *her!*" It all came over him as with the near presence of the beauty, the grace, the intense, dissimulated spirit with which he had, as he said, been putting off contact. "*She* has courage."

"Ah, she has courage!" Miss Barrace quite agreed; and it was as if, for a moment, they saw the quantity in each other's face.

But indeed the whole thing was present. "How much she must care!"

"Ah, there it is. She does care. But it isn't, is it," Miss Barrace considerately added, "as if you had ever had any doubt of that?"

Strether seemed suddenly to like to feel that he really never had. "Why, of course it's the whole point."

"*Voilà!*" Miss Barrace smiled.

"It's why one came out," Strether went on. "And it's why one has stayed so long. And it's also"—he abounded—"why one's going home. It's why, it's why—"

"It's why everything!" she concurred. "It's why she might be to-night—for all she looks and shows, and for all your friend 'Jim' does—about twenty years old. That's another of her ideas; to be, for him, and to be quite easily and charmingly, as young as a little girl."

Strether assisted at his distance. "'For him'? For Chad—?"

"For Chad, in a manner, naturally always. But in particular, to-night, for Mr. Pocock." And then as her friend still stared: "Yes, it *is* of a bravery! But that's what she has: her high sense of duty."

It was more than sufficiently before them. "When Mr. Newsome has his hands so embarrassed with his sister—"

"It's quite the least"—Strether filled it out—"that she should take his sister's husband? Certainly—quite the least. So she has taken him."

"She has taken him." It was all Miss Barrace had meant.

Still, it remained enough. "It must be funny."

"Oh, it *is* funny." That of course essentially went with it.

But it brought them back. "How indeed then she must care!" In answer to which Strether's interlocutress dropped a comprehensive "Ah!" which perhaps expressed a slight impatience at the time he took to get used to it. She herself had got used to it long before.

XXVI

When, one morning, within the week, he perceived the whole thing to be really at last upon him, Strether's immediate feeling was all relief. He had known this morning that something was about to happen—known it, in a moment, by Waymarsh's manner when Waymarsh appeared before him during his brief consumption of coffee and a roll in the small, slippery *salle à manger* so associated with rich rumination. Strether had taken there of late various lonely and absent-minded meals; he communed there, even at the end of June, with a suspected chill, the air of old shivers mixed with old savors, the air in which so many of his impressions had perversely matured; the place meanwhile renewing its message to him by the very circumstance of his single state. He now sat there, for the most part, to sigh softly, while he vaguely tilted his *carafe,* over the vision of how much better Waymarsh was occupied. That was really his success, by the common measure—to have led this companion so on and on. He remembered how, at first, there had been scarce a squatting-place he could beguile him into passing; the actual sequel to which, at last, was that there was scarce one that could arrest him in his rush. His rush—as Strether vividly and amusedly figured it—continued to be all with Sarah, and contained perhaps, moreover, the word of the whole enigma, whipped up in its fine, full-flavored froth the very principle, for good or for ill, of his own, of Strether's, outlook. It might, after all, to the end, only be that they had united to save him, and indeed, so far as Waymarsh was concerned, that *had* to be the spring of action. Strether was glad, at all events, in connection with the case, that the saving he required was not more scant; so defined a luxury was it, in certain lights, just to lurk there out of the full glare. He had moments of quite seriously wondering whether Waymarsh wouldn't, in fact, thanks to old friendship and a conceivable indulgence, make about as good terms for him as he might make for himself. They wouldn't be the same terms, of course; but they might have the advantage that he himself probably should be able to make none at all.

He was never, in the morning, very late, but Waymarsh had already been out, and, after a peep into the dim refectory, he presented himself with much less than usual of his large looseness. He had made sure, through the expanse of glass exposed to the court, that they would be alone; and there was now in fact that about him that pretty well took up the room. He was dressed in the garments of summer; and save that his white waistcoat was redundant and bulging, these things favored, they determined, his expression. He wore a straw hat such as his friend had not yet seen in Paris, and he showed a buttonhole freshly adorned with a magnificent rose. Strether read, on the instant, his story—how, astir for the previous hour, the sprinkled newness of the day, so pleasant, at that season, in Paris, he was fairly panting with the pulse of adventure and had been with Mrs. Pocock, unmistakably, to the Marché aux Fleurs. Strether really knew in this vision of him a joy that was akin to envy; so reversed, as he stood there, did their old positions seem; so comparatively doleful now showed, by the sharp turn of the wheel, the posture of the pilgrim from Woollett. He wondered, this pilgrim, if he had originally looked to Waymarsh so brave and well, so remarkably launched, as it was at present the latter's privilege to appear. He recalled that his friend had remarked to him even at Chester that his aspect belied his plea of prostration; but there certainly could not have been, for an issue, an aspect less concerned than Waymarsh's with the menace of decay. Strether had at any rate never resembled a southern planter of the great days—which was the image picturesquely suggested by the happy relation between the fuliginous face and the wide panama of his visitor. This type, it further amused him to guess, had been, on Waymarsh's part, the object of Sarah's care; he was convinced that her taste had not been a stranger to the conception and purchase of the hat, any more than her fine fingers had been guiltless of the bestowal of the rose. It came to him in the current of thought, as things so oddly did come, that *he* had never risen with the lark to attend a brilliant woman to the Marché aux Fleurs; that could be fastened on him in connection neither with Miss Gostrey nor with Mme. de Vionnet;

the practice of getting up early for adventures could indeed in no manner be fastened on him. It came to him in fact that just here was his usual case: he was forever missing things through his general genius for missing them, while others were forever picking them up through a contrary bent. And it was others who looked abstemious and he who looked greedy; it was he, somehow, who finally paid, and it was others who mainly partook. Yes, he should go to the scaffold yet for he wouldn't know quite whom. He almost, for that matter, felt on the scaffold now, and really quite enjoying it. It worked out as *because* he was anxious there—it worked out as for this reason that Waymarsh was so blooming. It was *his* trip for health, for a change, that proved the success—which was just what Strether, planning and exerting himself, had desired it should be. That truth already sat full-blown on his companion's lips; benevolence breathed from them as with the warmth of active exercise, and also, a little, as with the bustle of haste.

" Mrs. Pocock, whom I left a quarter of an hour ago at her hotel, has asked me to mention to you that she would like to find you at home here in about another hour. She wants to see you; she has something to say—or considers, I believe, that you may have: so that I asked her myself why she shouldn't come right round. She hasn't *been* round yet—to see our place; and I took upon myself to say that I was sure you'd be glad to have her. The thing's therefore, you see, to keep right here till she comes."

The announcement was sociably, even though, after Waymarsh's wont, somewhat solemnly made; but Strether quickly felt other things in it than these light features. It was the first approach to a meaning; it quickened his pulse; it simply meant at last that he should have but himself to thank if he didn't know where he was. He had finished his breakfast; he pushed it away and was on his feet. There were plenty of elements of surprise, but only one of doubt. " The thing's for *you* to keep here too?" Waymarsh had been slightly ambiguous.

He wasn't ambiguous, however, after this inquiry; and Strether's understanding had probably never before opened so wide and effective a mouth as it was to open during the next five minutes. It was no part of his friend's wish, as appeared, to help to receive Mrs. Pocock; he quite understood the spirit in which she was to present

herself, but his connection with her visit was limited to his having—
well, as he might say—perhaps a little promoted it. He had thought,
and had let her know it, that Strether possibly would think she
might have been round before. At any rate, as turned out, she had
been wanting herself, quite a while, to come. "I told her," said
Waymarsh, "that it would have been a bright idea if she had only
carried it out before."

Strether pronounced it so bright as to be almost dazzling.
"But why *hasn't* she carried it out before? She has seen me every
day—she had only to name her hour. I've been waiting and waiting."

"Well, I told her you had. And she has been waiting too." It
was, in the oddest way in the world, on the showing of this
tone, a genial, new, pressing, coaxing Waymarsh; a Waymarsh
conscious with a different consciousness from any he had yet betrayed, and actually rendered by it almost insinuating. He lacked
only time for full persuasion, and Strether was to see in a moment
why. Meantime, however, our friend perceived, he was announcing
a step of some magnanimity on Mrs. Pocock's part, so that he could
deprecate a sharp question. It was his own high purpose in fact to
have smoothed sharp questions to rest. He looked his old comrade
very straight in the eyes, and he had never conveyed to him in so
mute a manner so much kind confidence and so much good advice.
Everything that was between them was again in his face, but matured and shelved and finally disposed of. "At any rate," he added,
"she's coming now."

Considering how many pieces had to fit themselves, it all fell, in
Strether's brain, into a close, rapid order. He saw on the spot what
had happened, and what probably would yet; and it was all funny
enough. It was perhaps just this freedom of appreciation that
wound him up to his flare of high spirits. "What is she coming
for?—to kill me?"

"She's coming to be very, *very* kind to you, and you must let me
say that I greatly hope you'll not be less so to herself."

This was spoken by Waymarsh with much gravity of admonition,
and as Strether stood there he knew he had but to make a movement to take the attitude of a man gracefully receiving a present.
The present was that of the opportunity dear old Waymarsh had

flattered himself he had divined in him the slight soreness of not having yet thoroughly enjoyed; so he had brought it to him thus, as on a little silver breakfast-tray, familiarly though delicately— without oppressive pomp; and he was to bend and smile and acknowledge, was to take and use and be grateful. He was not—that was the beauty of it—to be asked to deflect too much from his dignity. No wonder the old boy bloomed in this bland air of his own distillation. Strether felt for a moment as if Sarah were actually walking up and down outside. Wasn't she hanging about the porte-cochère while her friend thus summarily opened a way? Strether would meet her but to take it, and everything would be for the best in the best of possible worlds. He had never so much known what any one meant as, in the light of this demonstration, he knew what Mrs. Newsome did. It had reached Waymarsh from Sarah, but it had reached Sarah from her mother, and there was no break in the chain by which it reached *him*. "Has anything particular happened," he asked after a minute—" so suddenly to determine her? Has she heard anything unexpected from home?"

Waymarsh, on this, it seemed to him, looked at him harder than ever. "'Unexpected'?" He had a brief hesitation; then, however, he was firm. "We're leaving Paris."

"Leaving? That *is* sudden."

Waymarsh showed a different opinion. "Less so than it may seem. The purpose of Mrs. Pocock's visit is to explain to you in fact that it's *not*."

Strether didn't at all know if he had really an advantage—anything that would practically count as one; but he enjoyed for the moment—as for the first time in his life—the sense of so carrying it off. He wondered—it was amusing—if he felt as the impudent feel. "I shall take great pleasure, I assure you, in any explanation. I shall be delighted to receive Sarah."

The sombre glow just darkened in his comrade's eyes; but he was struck with the way it died out again. It was too mixed with another consciousness—it was too smothered, as might be said, in flowers. He really, for the time, regretted it—poor dear old sombre glow! Something straight and simple, something heavy and empty, had been eclipsed in its company; something by which he had best known his friend. Waymarsh wouldn't *be* his friend, somehow, without the occasional ornament of the sacred rage, and the right to the sacred rage—inestimably precious for Strether's charity—he also seemed in a manner, and at Mrs. Pocock's elbow, to have forfeited. Strether remembered the occasion, early in their stay, when, on that very spot, he had come out with his earnest, his ominous "Quit it!"—and, so remembering, felt it hang by a hair that he didn't himself now utter the same note. Waymarsh was having a good time—that was the truth that was embarrassing for him, and he was having it then and there, he was having it in Europe, he was having it under the very protection of circumstances of which he didn't in the least approve; all of which placed him in a false position, with no issue possible—none, at least, by the grand manner. It was practically in the manner of any one—it was all but in poor Strether's own—that, instead of taking anything up, he merely made the most of having to be himself explanatory. "I'm not leaving for the United States direct. Mr. and Mrs. Pocock and Miss Mamie are thinking of a little trip before their own return, and we've been talking for some days past of our joining forces. We've settled it that we do join and that we sail together the end of next month. But we start to-morrow for Switzerland. Mrs. Pocock wants some scenery. She hasn't had much yet."

He was brave in his way too, keeping nothing back, confessing to all there was, and only leaving Strether to make certain connections. "Is what Mrs. Newsome has cabled her daughter an injunction to break off short?"

The grand manner indeed, at this, just raised its head a little. "I know nothing about Mrs. Newsome's cables."

Their eyes met on it with some intensity—during the few seconds of which something happened quite out of proportion to the time. It happened that Strether, looking thus at his friend, didn't take his answer for truth—and that something more again occurred in consequence of *that*. Yes—Waymarsh just *did* know about Mrs. Newsome's cables: to what other end than that had they dined together at Bignon's? Strether almost felt, for the instant, that it was to Mrs. Newsome herself the dinner had been given; and, for that matter, quite felt how she must have known about it and, as he might think, protected and consecrated it. He had a quick, blurred view of daily cables, questions, answers, signals: clear enough was his vision of the expense that, when so exalted, the lady at home was prepared to incur. Vivid not less was his memory of what, during his long observation of her, some of her exaltations had cost her. Distinctly, she was exalted now, and Waymarsh, who imagined himself standing there on his own feet, was truly but suspended in an air of her making. The whole reference of his errand seemed to mark her for Strether as by this time consentingly familiar to him, and nothing yet had so despoiled her of a special shade of consideration. "You don't know," he asked, "whether Sarah has been directed from home to try me on the matter of my also going to Switzerland?"

"I know," said Waymarsh as manfully as possible, "nothing whatever about her private affairs; though I believe her to be acting in conformity with things that have my highest respect." It was as manful as possible, but it was still the small manner—as it had to be to convey so sorry a statement. He knew everything, Strether more and more felt, that he thus disclaimed, and his little punishment was just in this doom to a second fib. What falser position—given the man—could the most vindictive mind impose? He ended by squeezing through a passage in which, three months before, he would certainly have stuck fast. "Mrs. Pocock will probably be ready herself to answer any inquiry you may put to her. But," he continued, " *but—!*" He faltered on it.

"But what? Don't put her too many?"

Waymarsh looked large, but the harm was done; he couldn't, do what he would, help looking rosy. "Don't do anything you'll be sorry for."

It was an attenuation, Strether guessed, of something else that had been on his lips; it was a sudden drop to directness, and was thereby the voice of sincerity. He had fallen to the supplicating note, and that immediately, for our friend, made a difference and reinstated him. They were in communication as they had been, that first morning, in Sarah's salon and in her presence and Mme. de Vionnet's; and the same recognition of a great good-will was again, after all, possible. Only the amount of response Waymarsh had then taken for granted was doubled, decupled now. This came out when he presently said: "Of course I needn't assure you *I* hope you'll come with us." Then it was that his implications and expectations loomed up for Strether as almost pathetically gross.

The latter patted his shoulder while he thanked him, giving the go-by to the question of joining the Pococks; he expressed the joy he felt at seeing him go forth again so brave and free, and he in fact almost took leave of him on the spot. "I shall see you again of course before you go; but I'm meanwhile much obliged to you for arranging so conveniently for what you've told me. I shall walk up and down in the court there—dear little old court which we've each bepaced so, this last couple of months, to the tune of our flights and our drops, our hesitations and our plunges: I shall hang about there, all impatience and excitement, please let Sarah know, till she graciously presents herself. Leave me with her without fear," he laughed; "I assure you I sha'n't hurt her. I don't think, either, that she'll hurt *me:* I'm in a situation in which damage was some time ago discounted. Besides, *that* isn't what worries you—but don't, don't explain! We're all right as we are: which was the degree of success our adventure was pledged to for each of us. We weren't, it seemed, all right as we were before; and we've got over the ground, all things considered, quickly. I hope you'll have a lovely time in the Alps."

Waymarsh fairly looked up at him as from the foot of them. "I don't know as I *ought* really to go."

It was the conscience of Milrose in the very voice of Milrose, but, oh, it was feeble and flat! Strether suddenly felt quite ashamed for him; he breathed a greater boldness. "*Let* yourself, on the contrary, go—in all agreeable directions. These are precious hours—at our age they mayn't recur. Don't have it to say to yourself at Milrose, next winter, that you hadn't courage for them." And then as his comrade queerly stared: "Live up to Mrs. Pocock."

"Live up to her?"

"You're a great help to her."

Waymarsh looked at it as at one of the uncomfortable things that were certainly true and that it was yet ironical to say. "It's more then than you are."

"That's exactly your own chance and advantage. Besides," said Strether, "I do in my way contribute. I know what I'm about."

Waymarsh had kept on his great panama, and, as he now stood

nearer the door, his last look, beneath the shade of it, had turned again to darkness and warning. "So do I! See here, Strether."

"I know what you're going to say. 'Quit this'?"

"Quit this!" But it lacked its old intensity; nothing of it remained; it went out of the room with him.

XXVII

Almost the first thing, strangely enough, that, about an hour later, Strether found himself doing in Sarah's presence was to remark articulately on this failure, in their friend, of what had been superficially his great distinction. It was as if—he alluded of course to the grand manner—the dear man had sacrificed it to some other advantage; which would be of course only for himself to measure. It might be simply that he was physically so much more sound than on his first coming out; this was all prosaic, comparatively cheerful and vulgar. And fortunately, if one came to that, his improvement in health was really itself grander than any manner it could be conceived as having cost him. " You yourself alone, dear Sarah " —Strether took the plunge—" have done him, it strikes me, in these three weeks, as much good as all the rest of his time together."

It was a plunge because somehow the range of reference was, in the conditions, " funny," and made funnier still by Sarah's attitude, by the turn the occasion had, with her appearance, so sensibly taken. Her appearance was really indeed funnier than anything else—the spirit in which he felt her to be there as soon as she *was* there, the shade of obscurity that cleared up for him as soon as he was seated with her in the small *salon de lecture* that had, for the most part, in all the weeks, witnessed the wane of his early vivacity of discussion with Waymarsh. It was an immense thing, quite a tremendous thing, for her to have come: this truth opened out to him in spite of his having already arrived for himself at a fairly vivid view of it. He had done exactly what he had given Waymarsh his word for—had walked and re-walked the court while he awaited her advent; acquiring in this exercise an amount of light that affected him at the time as flooding the scene. She had decided upon the step in order to give him the benefit of a doubt, in order to be able to say to her mother that she had, even to abjectness, smoothed the way for him. The doubt had been as to whether he mightn't take her as not having smoothed it—and the admonition had possibly come from Waymarsh's more detached spirit. Waymarsh had at any rate, certainly, thrown his weight into the scale— he had pointed to the importance of depriving their friend of a grievance. She had done justice to the plea, and it was to set herself right with a high ideal that she actually sat there in her state. Her calculation was sharp in the immobility with which she held her tall parasol-stick upright and at arm's length, quite as if she had struck the place to plant her flag; in the separate precautions she took not to show as nervous; in the aggressive repose in which she did quite nothing but wait for him. Doubt ceased to be possible from the moment he had taken in that she had arrived with no proposal whatever; that her concern was simply to show what she had come to receive. She had come to receive his submission, and Waymarsh was to have made it plain to him that she would expect nothing less. He saw fifty things, her host, at this convenient stage; but one of those he most saw was that their anxious friend had not quite had the hand required of him. Waymarsh *had,* however, uttered the request that she might find him mild, and while hanging about the court before her arrival he had turned over with zeal the different ways in which he could be so. The difficulty was that if he was mild he wasn't, for her purpose, conscious. If she wished him conscious —as everything about her cried aloud that she did—she must accordingly be at costs to make him so. Conscious he *was,* for himself— but only of too many things; so she must choose the one she required.

Practically, however, it at last got itself named, and when once that had happened they were quite at the centre of their situation. One thing had really done as well as another; when Strether had spoken of Waymarsh's leaving him, and that had necessarily brought on a reference to Mrs. Pocock's similar intention, the jump was but short to supreme lucidity. Light became indeed after that so intense that Strether would doubtless have but half made out, in the prodigious glare, by which of the two the issue had been in fact precipitated. It was, in their contracted quarters, as much there between them as if it had been something suddenly spilled, with a crash and a splash, on the floor. The form of his submission was to be an engagement to acquit himself within the twenty-four hours. "He'll go in a moment if you give him the word—he assures me on his honor he'll do that:" this came in its order, out of its order, in respect to Chad, after the crash had occurred. It came repeatedly during the time taken by Strether to feel that he was even more fixed in his rigor than he had supposed—the time he was not above adding to a little by telling her that such a way of putting it on her brother's part left him sufficiently surprised. She wasn't at all funny at last—she was really fine; and he felt easily where she was strong—strong for herself. It had not yet so come home to him that she was nobly and appointedly officious. She was acting in interests grander and clearer than that of her poor little personal, poor little Parisian equilibrium, and all his consciousness of her mother's moral pressure profited by this proof of its sustaining force. She would be held up; she would be strengthened; he needn't in the least be anxious for her. What would, once more, have been distinct to him had he tried to make it so, was that, as Mrs. Newsome was essentially all moral pressure, the presence of this element was almost identical with her own presence. It wasn't perhaps that he felt he was dealing with her straight, but it was certainly as if she had been dealing straight with *him*. She was reaching him, somehow, by the lengthened arm of the spirit, and he was having to that extent to take her into account; but he was not reaching her in turn, not making her take *him;* he was only reaching Sarah, who appeared to take so little of him. "Something has clearly passed between you and Chad," he presently said, "that I think I ought to know something more about. Does he put it all," he smiled, "on me?"

"Did you come out," she asked, "to put it all on *him?*"

But he replied to this no further than, after an instant, by saying: "Oh, it's all right. Chad, I mean, is all right in having said to you—well anything he may have said. I'll *take* it all—what he does put on me. Only I must see him before I see you again."

She hesitated, but she brought it out. "Is it absolutely necessary you should see me again?"

"Certainly, if I'm to give you any definite word about anything."

"Is it your idea then," she returned, "that I shall keep on meeting you only to be exposed to fresh humiliation?"

341

He fixed her a longer time. "Are your instructions from Mrs. Newsome that you shall, even at the worst, absolutely and irretrievably break with me?"

"My instructions from Mrs. Newsome are, if you please, my affair. You know perfectly what your own were, and you can judge for yourself of what it can do for you to have made what you have of them. You can perfectly see, at any rate, I'll go so far as to say, that if I wish not to expose myself, I must wish still less to expose *her*." She had already said more than she had quite expected; but, though she had also pulled up, the color in her face showed him he should, from one moment to the other, have it all. He now indeed felt the high importance of his having it. "What is your conduct," she broke out as if to explain—"what is your conduct but an outrage to women like *us*? I mean your acting as if there can be a doubt—as between us and such another—of his duty?"

He thought a moment. It was rather much to deal with at once; not only the question itself, but the sore abysses it revealed. "Of course they're totally different kinds of duty."

"And do you pretend that he has any at all—to such another?"

"Do you mean to Mme. de Vionnet?" He uttered the name not to affront her, but yet again to gain time—time that he needed for taking in something still other and larger than her demand of a moment before. It was not at once that he could see all that was in her actual challenge; but when he did he found himself just checking a low, vague sound, a sound which was perhaps the nearest approach his vocal chords had ever known to a growl. Everything Mrs. Pocock had failed to give a sign of recognizing in Chad as a particular part of a transformation—everything that had lent intention to this particular failure—affected him as gathered into a large, loose bundle and thrown, in her words, into his face. The missile made him to that extent catch his breath; which, however, he presently recovered. "Why, when a woman is at once so charming and so beneficent—"

"You can sacrifice mothers and sisters to her without a blush, and can make them cross the ocean on purpose to feel the more, and take from you the straighter, *how* you do it?"

Yes, she had taken him up as short and as sharply as that; but he tried not to flounder in her grasp. "I don't think there's anything

I've done in any such calculated way as you describe. Everything has come as a sort of indistinguishable part of everything else. Your coming out belonged closely to my having come before you, and my having come was a result of our general state of mind. Our general state of mind had proceeded, on its side, from our queer ignorance, our queer misconceptions and confusions—from which, since then, an inexorable tide of light seems to have floated us into our perhaps still queerer knowledge. Don't you *like* your brother as he is," he went on, "and haven't you given your mother an intelligible account of all that that comes to ?"

It put to her also, doubtless, his own tone, too many things; this at least would have been the case had not his final challenge directly helped her. Everything, at the stage they had reached, directly helped her, because everything betrayed in him such a basis of intention. He saw—the odd way things came out!—that he would have been held less monstrous had he only been a little wilder. What exposed him was just his poor old trick of quiet inwardness, what exposed him was his *thinking* such offence. He had not in the least, however, the desire to irritate that Sarah imputed to him, and he could only at last temporize, for the moment, with her indignant view. She was altogether more inflamed than he had expected, and he would probably understand this better when he should learn what had occurred for her with Chad. Till then her view of his particular blackness, her clear surprise at his not clutching the pole she held out, must pass as extravagant. "I leave you to flatter yourself," she returned, "that what you speak of is what *you've* beautifully done. When a thing has been already described in such a lovely way—!" But she caught herself up, and her comment on his description rang out sufficiently loud. "Do you consider her even an apology for a decent woman ?"

Ah, there it was at last! She put the matter more crudely than, for his own mixed purposes, he had yet had to do; but, essentially, it was all one matter. It was so much—so much; and she treated it, poor lady, as so little. He grew conscious, as he was now apt to do, of a strange smile, and the next moment he found himself talking like Miss Barrace. "She has struck me from the first as wonderful. I've been thinking too, moreover, that, after all, she would probably have represented even for yourself something rather new and rather good."

He was to have given Mrs. Pocock with this, however, but her best opportunity for a sound of derision. "Rather new? I hope so with all my heart!"

"I mean," he explained, "that she might have affected you by her exquisite amiability—a real revelation, it has seemed to myself; her high rarity, her distinction of every sort."

He had been, with these words, consciously a little "precious"; but he had had to be—he couldn't give her the truth of the case without them; and it seemed to him, moreover, now, that he didn't care. He had at all events not served his cause, for she sprang at its exposed side. "A 'revelation'—to *me:* I've to come to such a woman for a revelation? You talk to me about 'distinction'—*you*, you who've had your privilege?—when the most distinguished woman we shall either of us have seen in this world sits there insulted, in her loneliness, by your incredible comparison!"

Strether forbore, with an effort, from straying; but he looked all about him. "Does your mother herself make the point that she sits insulted?"

Sarah's answer came so straight, so "pat," as might have been said, that he felt on the instant its origin. "She has confided to my judgment and my tenderness the expression of her personal sense of everything, and the assertion of her personal dignity."

They were the very words of the lady of Woollett—he would have known them in a thousand; her parting charge to her child. Mrs. Pocock, accordingly, spoke to this extent by book, and the fact immensely moved him. "If she does really feel as you say, it's of course very, very dreadful. I've given sufficient proof, one would have thought," he added, "of my deep admiration for Mrs. Newsome."

"And pray what proof would one have thought you'd *call* sufficient? That of thinking this person here so far superior to her?"

He wondered again; he waited. "Ah, dear Sarah, you must *leave* me this person here!"

In his desire to avoid all vulgar retorts, to show how, even perversely, he clung to his rag of reason, he had softly almost wailed this plea. Yet he knew it to be perhaps the most positive declaration he had ever made in his life, and his visitor's reception of it virtually gave it that importance. "That's exactly what I'm delighted to do. God knows *we* don't want her! You take good care not to meet," she observed in a still higher key, "my question about their life. If you do consider it a thing one can even *speak* of, I congratulate you on your taste!"

The life she alluded to was of course Chad's and Mme. de Vionnet's, which she thus bracketed together in a way that made him wince a little; there being nothing for him but to take home her full intention. It was none the less his inconsequence that while he had himself been enjoying for weeks the view of the brilliant woman's specific action, he just suffered from any characterization of it by other lips. "I think tremendously well of her, at the same time that I seem to feel her 'life' to be really none of my business. It's my business, that is, only so far as Chad's own life is affected by it; and what has happened, don't you see? is that Chad's has been affected so beautifully. The proof of the pudding's in the eating"—he tried, with no great success, to help it out with a touch of pleasantry, while she let him go on as if to sink and sink. He went on, however, well enough, as well as he could do without fresh counsel; he indeed shouldn't stand quite firm, he felt, till he should have re-established his communications with Chad. Still, he could always speak for the woman he had so definitely promised to "save." This wasn't quite, for her, the air of salvation; but as that chill fairly deepened what did it become but a reminder that one might, at the worst, perish *with* her? And it was simple enough—it was rudimentary: not, not to give her away. "I find in her more merits than you would probably have patience with my counting over. And do you know," he inquired, "the effect you produce on me by alluding to her in such terms? It's as if you had some motive in not recognizing all she has done for your brother, and so shut your eyes to each side of the matter, in order, whichever side comes up, to get rid of the other. I don't, you must allow me to say, see how you can with any pretence to candor get rid of the side nearest you."

"Near me—*that* sort of thing?" And Sarah gave a jerk back of her head that well might have nullified any active proximity.

It kept her friend himself at his distance, and he respected for a moment the interval. Then, with a last persuasive effort, he bridged it. "You don't, on your honor, appreciate Chad's fortunate development?"

"Fortunate?" she echoed again. And indeed she was prepared. "I call it hideous."

Her departure had been for some minutes marked as imminent, and she was already at the door that stood open to the court, from the threshold of which she delivered herself of this judgment. It rang out so loud as to produce for the time the hush of everything else. Strether quite, as an effect of it, breathed less bravely; he could acknowledge it, but simply enough. "Oh, if you think *that—!*"

"Then all's at an end? So much the better. I do think that!" She passed out as she spoke and took her way straight across the court, beyond which, separated from them by the deep arch of the porte-cochère, the low victoria that had conveyed her from her own hotel was drawn up. She made for it with decision, and the manner of her break, the sharp shaft of her rejoinder, had an intensity by which Strether was at first kept in arrest. She had let fly at him as from a stretched cord, and it took him a minute to recover from the sense of being pierced. It was not the penetration of surprise; it was that, much more, of certainty; his case being put for him as he had as yet only put it to himself. She was away, at any rate; she had distanced him—with rather a grand spring, an effect of pride and ease, after all; she had got into her carriage before he could overtake her, and the vehicle was already in motion. He stopped half-way; he stood there in the court only seeing her go and noting that she gave him no other look. The way he had put it to himself was that all quite *might* be at an end. Each of her movements, in this resolute rupture, reaffirmed, reinforced that idea. Sarah passed out of sight in the sunny street, while, planted there in the centre of the comparatively gray court, he continued merely to look before him. It probably *was* all at an end.

PART ELEVENTH

XXVIII

He went late that evening to the Boulevard Maleshcrbes, having
his impression that it would be vain to go early, and having also,
more than once in the course of the day, made inquiries of the
concierge. Chad had not come in and had left no intimation; he had
affairs, apparently, at this juncture—as it occurred to Strether he so
well might have—that kept him long abroad. Our friend asked once
for him at the hotel in the Rue de Rivoli, but the only contribution
offered there was the fact that every one was out. It was with the idea
that he would have to come home to sleep that Strether went up
to his rooms, from which, however, he was still absent, though, from
the balcony, a few moments later, his visitor heard eleven o'clock
strike. Chad's servant had by this time answered for his reappearance; he *had,* the visitor learned, come quickly in to dress
for dinner and vanish again. Strether spent an hour in waiting
for him—an hour full of strange suggestions, persuasions, recognitions; one of those that he was to recall, at the end of his adventure, as the particular handful that most had counted. The mel-
lowest lamplight and the easier chair had been placed at his disposal by Baptiste, subtlest of servants; the novel half uncut, the
novel lemon-colored and tender, with the ivory knife athwart it
like the dagger in a contadina's hair, had been pushed within the
soft circle—a circle which, for some reason, affected Strether as
softer still after the same Baptiste had remarked that, in the absence of a further need of anything by Monsieur, he would betake
himself to bed. The night was hot and heavy and the single lamp
sufficient; the great flare of the lighted city, rising high, spending
itself afar, played up from the Boulevard and, through the vague
vista of the successive rooms, brought objects into view and added
to their dignity. Strether found himself in possession as he never
yet had been; he had been there alone, had turned over books

and prints, had invoked, in Chad's absence, the spirit of the place, but never at the witching hour and never with a relish quite so like a pang.

He spent a long time on the balcony; he hung over it as he had seen little Bilham hang the day of his first approach, as he had seen Mamie hang over her own the day little Bilham himself might have seen her from below; he passed back into the rooms, the three that occupied the front and that communicated by wide doors; and, while he circulated and rested, tried to recover the impression that they had made on him three months before, to catch again the voice in which they had seemed then to speak to him. That voice, he had to note, failed audibly to sound; which he took as the proof of all the change in himself. He had heard, of old, only what he *could* then hear; what he could do now was to think of three months ago as a point in the far past. All voices had grown thicker and meant more things; they crowded on him as he moved about—it was the way they sounded together that wouldn't let him be still. He felt, strangely, as sad as if he had come for some wrong, and yet as excited as if he had come for some freedom. But the freedom was what was most in the place and the hour; it was the freedom that most brought him round again to the youth of his own that he had long ago missed. He could have explained little enough to-day either why he had missed it or why, after years and years, he should care that he had; the main truth of the actual appeal of everything was none the less that everything represented the substance of his loss, put it within reach, within touch, made it, to a degree it had never been, an affair of the senses. That was what it became for him at this singular time, the youth he had long ago missed—a queer concrete presence, full of mystery, yet full of reality, which he could handle, taste, smell, the deep breathing of which he could positively hear. It was in the outside air as well as within; it was in the long watch, from the balcony, in the summer night, of the wide late life of Paris, the unceasing soft, quick rumble, below, of the little lighted carriages that, in the press, always suggested the gamblers he had seen of old at Monte-Carlo pushing up to the tables. This image was before him when he at last became aware that Chad was behind.

"She tells me you put it all on *me*"—he had arrived, after this,

promptly enough at that information; which expressed the matter
however, quite as the young man appeared willing for the moment
to leave it. Other things, with this advantage of their virtually
having the night before them, came up for them, and had, as
well, the odd effect of making the occasion, instead of hurried and
feverish, one of the largest, loosest and easiest to which Strether's
whole adventure was to have treated him. He had been pursuing
Chad from an early hour and had overtaken him only now; but
now the delay was repaired by their being so exceptionally confronted. They had foregathered enough, of course, in all the various times; they had again and again, since that first night at
the theatre, been face to face over their question; but they had
never been so alone together as they were actually alone—their
talk had not yet been so supremely for themselves. And if many
things, moreover, passed before them, none passed more distinctly
for Strether than that striking truth about Chad of which he had
been so often moved to take note: the truth that everything came
happily back with him to his knowing how to live. It had been
seated in his pleased smile—a smile that pleased exactly in the right
degree—as his visitor turned round, on the balcony, to greet his
advent; his visitor in fact felt on the spot that there was nothing
their meeting would so much do as bear witness to that facility. He
surrendered himself, accordingly, to so approved a gift; for what
was the meaning of the facility but that others *did* surrender themselves? He didn't want, luckily, to prevent Chad from living; but
he was quite aware that even if he had he would himself have
thoroughly gone to pieces. It was in truth essentially by bringing
down his personal life to a function all subsidiary to the young
man's own that he held together. And the great point, above all,
the sign of how completely Chad possessed the knowledge in question, was that one thus became, not only with a proper cheerfulness, but with wild native impulses, the feeder of his stream.
Their talk had, accordingly, not lasted three minutes without
Strether's feeling basis enough for the excitement in which he had
waited. This overflow fairly deepened, wastefully abounded, as
he observed the smallness of anything corresponding to it on the
part of his friend. That was exactly this friend's happy case; he
" put out " his excitement, or whatever other emotion the matter

involved, as he put out his washing; than which no arrangement could make more for domestic order. It was quite for Strether himself, in short, to feel a personal analogy with the laundress bringing home the triumphs of the mangle.

When he had reported on Sarah's visit, which he did very fully, Chad answered his question with perfect candor. " I positively referred her to you—told her she must absolutely see you. This was last night, and it all took place in ten minutes. It was our first free talk—really the first time she had tackled me. She knew I also knew what her line had been with yourself; knew moreover how little you had been doing to make anything difficult for her. So I spoke for you frankly—assured her you were all at her service. I assured her I was too," the young man continued; " and I pointed out how she could perfectly, at any time, have got at me. Her difficulty has been simply her not finding the moment she fancied."

" Her difficulty," Strether returned, " has been simply that she finds she's afraid of you. She's not afraid of me, Sarah, one little scrap; and it was just because she has seen how I can fidget when I give my mind to it, that she has felt her best chance, rightly enough, to be in making me as uneasy as possible. I think she's at bottom as pleased to have you put it on me as you yourself can possibly be to put it."

" But what in the world, my dear man," Chad inquired in objection to this luminosity, " have I done to make Sally afraid?"

" You've been ' wonderful, wonderful,' as we say—we poor people who watch the play from the pit; and that's what has, admirably, made her. Made her all the more effectually that she could see you didn't set about it on purpose—I mean set about affecting her as with fear."

Chad cast a pleasant backward glance over his possibilities of motive. " I've only wanted to be kind and friendly, to be decent and attentive—and I still only want to be."

Strether smiled at his comfortable clearness. " Well, there can certainly be no way for it better than by my taking the onus. It reduces your personal friction and your personal offence to almost nothing."

Ah, but Chad, with his completer conception of the friendly, wouldn't quite have this! They had remained on the balcony, where, after their day of great and premature heat, the midnight air was delicious; and they leaned back, in turn, against the balustrade, all in harmony with the chairs and the flower-pots, the cigarettes and the starlight. "The onus isn't *really* yours—after our agreeing so to wait together and judge together. That was all my answer to Sally," Chad pursued—"that we have been, that we are, just judging together."

"I'm not afraid of the burden," Strether explained; "I haven't come in the least that you should take it off me. I've come very much, it seems to me, to double up my forelegs in the manner of the camel when he gets down on his knees to make his back convenient. But I've supposed you, all this while, to have been doing a lot of special and private judging—about which I haven't troubled you; and I've only wished to have your conclusion first from you. I don't ask more than that; I'm quite ready to take it as it has come."

Chad turned up his face to the sky with a slow puff of his smoke. "Well, I've seen."

Strether waited a little. "I've left you wholly alone; haven't, I think I may say, since the first hour or two—when I merely preached patience—so much as breathed on you."

"Oh, you've been awfully good!"

"We've both been good then—we've played the game. We've given them the most liberal conditions."

"Ah," said Chad, "splendid conditions! It was open to them, open to them"—he seemed to make it out, as he smoked, with his eyes still on the stars. He might, in quiet sport, have been reading their horoscope. Strether wondered meanwhile what had been open to them, and he finally let him have it. "It was open to them simply to let me alone; to have made up their minds, on really seeing me for themselves, that I could go on well enough as I was."

Strether assented to this proposition with full lucidity, his companion's plural pronoun, which stood all for Mrs. Newsome and her daughter, having no ambiguity for him. There was nothing, apparently, to stand for Mamie and Jim: and this added to our friend's sense of Chad's knowing what he thought. "But they've made up their minds to the opposite—that you *can't* go on as you are."

"No," Chad continued in the same way; "they won't have it for a minute."

Strether on his side also reflectively smoked. It was as if their high place really represented some moral elevation from which they could look down on their recent past. "There never was the smallest chance, do you know, that they *would* have it for a moment."

"Of course not—no real chance. But if they were willing to think that there was—!"

"They weren't willing." Strether had worked it all out. "It wasn't for you they came out, but for me. It wasn't to see for themselves what you're doing, but what *I'm* doing. The first branch of their curiosity was inevitably destined, under my culpable delay, to give way to the second; and it's on the second that, if I may use the expression and you don't mind my marking the invidious fact, they've been of late exclusively perched. When Sarah sailed it was me, in other words, they were after."

Chad took it in both with intelligence and with indulgence. "It *is* rather a business then—what I've let you in for!"

Strether had again a brief pause; which ended in a reply that seemed to dispose once for all of this element of compunction. Chad was to treat it, at any rate, so far as they were again together, as having done so. "I was 'in' when you found me."

"Ah, but it was you," the young man laughed, "who found *me*."

"I only found you out. It was you who found me in. It was all in the day's work for them, at all events, that they should come. And they've greatly enjoyed it," Strether declared.

"Well, I've tried to make them," said Chad.

His companion did himself presently the same justice. "So have I. I tried even this very morning—while Mrs. Pocock was with me. She enjoys for instance, almost as much as anything else, not being, as I've said, afraid of me; and I think I gave her help in that."

Chad took a deeper interest. "Was she very, very nasty?"

Strether debated. "Well, she was the most important thing—she was definite. She was—at last—crystalline. And I felt no remorse. I saw that they *must* have come."

"Oh, I wanted to see them for myself; so that if it were only for *that*—!" Chad's own remorse was as small.

This appeared almost all Strether wanted. "Isn't your having seen them for yourself then *the* thing, beyond all others, that has come of their visit?"

Chad looked as if he thought it nice of his old friend to put it so. "Don't you count it as anything that you're dished—if you *are* dished? *Are* you, my dear man, dished?"

It sounded as if he were asking if he had caught cold or hurt his foot, and Strether, for a minute, but smoked and smoked. "I want to see her again. I must see her."

"Of course you must." Then Chad hesitated. "Do you mean—a—mother herself?"

"Oh, your mother—that will depend."

It was as if Mrs. Newsome had somehow been placed by the words very far off. Chad, however, endeavored in spite of this to reach the place. "What do you mean it will depend on?"

Strether, for all answer, gave him a longish look. "I was speaking of Sarah. I must positively—though she quite cast me off—see *her* again. I can't part with her that way."

"Then she *was* awfully unpleasant?"

Again Strether exhaled. "She was what she had to be. I mean that from the moment they're not delighted they can only be—well what I admit she was. We gave them," he went on, "their chance to be delighted, and they've walked up to it. and looked all round it, and not taken it."

"You can bring a horse to water—!" Chad suggested.

"Precisely. And the tune to which, this morning, Sarah wasn't delighted—the tune to which, to adopt your metaphor, she refused to drink—leaves us on that side nothing more to hope."

Chad had a pause; and then as if consolingly: "It was never of course really the least on the cards that they *would* be 'delighted.'"

"Well, I don't know, after all," Strether mused. "I've had to come as far round. However"—he shook it off—"it's doubtless *my* performance that's absurd."

"There are certainly moments," said Chad, "when you seem to me too good to be true. Yet if you *are* true," he added, "that seems to be all that need concern me."

"I'm true, but I'm incredible. I'm fantastic and ridiculous—I don't explain myself even *to* myself. How can *they* then," Strether asked, " understand me? So I don't quarrel with them."

"I see. They quarrel," said Chad rather comfortably, " with *us*." Strether noted once more the comfort, but his young friend had already gone on. " I should feel greatly ashamed, all the same, if I didn't put it before you again that you ought to think, after all, tremendously well. I mean before giving up beyond recall—" With which insistence, as from a certain delicacy, dropped.

Ah, but Strether wanted it. " Say it all, say it all."

" Well, at your age, and with what—when all's said and done— mother might do for you and be for you."

Chad had said it all, from his natural scruple, only to that extent; so that Strether, after an instant, himself took a hand. " My absence of an assured future. The little I have to show toward the power to take care of myself. The way, the wonderful way, she would certainly take care of me. Her fortune, her kindness, and the constant miracle of her having been disposed to go even so far. Of course, of course "—he summed it up. " There are those sharp facts."

Chad had meanwhile thought of another still. " And don't you really care— ?"

His friend slowly turned round to him. " Will you go?"

" I'll go if you'll say you now consider I should. You know," he went on, " I was ready six weeks ago."

" Ah," said Strether, " that was when *you* didn't know *I* wasn't! You're ready at present because you do know it."

" That may be," Chad returned; " but, all the same, I'm sincere. You talk about taking the whole thing on your shoulders, but in what light do you regard me that you think me capable of letting you pay?" Strether patted his arm, as they stood together against the parapet, reassuringly—seeming to wish to contend that he *had* the wherewithal; but it was again round this question of purchase and price that the young man's sense of fairness continued to hover. " What it literally comes to for you, if you'll pardon my putting it so, is that you give up money. Possibly a good deal of money."

" Oh," Strether laughed, " if it were only just enough you'd still be justified in putting it so! But I've on my side to remind you

too that *you* give up money; and more than 'possibly'—quite cer·
tainly, as I should suppose—a good deal."

"True enough; but I've got a certain quantity," Chad returned
after a moment. "Whereas you, my dear man, you—"

"I can't be at all said"—Strether took him up—"to have a
'quantity' certain or uncertain? Very true. Still, I sha'n't
starve."

"Oh, you mustn't *starve!*" Chad pacifically emphasized; and so,
in the pleasant conditions, they continued to talk; though there
was, for that matter, a pause in which the younger companion
might have been taken as weighing again the delicacy of his then
and there promising the elder some provision against the possibility
just mentioned. This, however, he presumably thought best not
to do, for at the end of another minute they had moved in quite a
different direction. Strether had broken in by returning to the
subject of Chad's passage with Sarah and inquiring if they had
arrived, in the event, at anything in the nature of a "scene." To
this Chad replied that they had, on the contrary, kept tremendously
polite; adding, moreover, that Sally was after all not the woman
to have made the mistake of not being. "Her hands are a good
deal tied, you see. I got so, from the first," he sagaciously observed, "the start of her."

"You mean she has taken so much from you?"

"Well, I couldn't of course, in common decency, give less: only
she hadn't expected, I think, that I would give her nearly so much.
And she began to take it before she knew it."

"And she began to like it," said Strether, "as soon as she began
to take it!"

"Yes, she has liked it—also more than she expected." After
which Chad observed: "But she doesn't like *me*. In fact she hates
me."

Strether's interest grew. "Then why does she want you at
home?"

"Because when you hate, you want to triumph; and if she should
get me neatly stuck there she *would* triumph."

Strether followed afresh, but looking as he went. "Certainly—in
a manner. But it would scarce be a triumph worth having if,
once entangled, feeling her dislike, and possibly conscious in time

of a certain quantity of your own, you should, on the spot, make yourself unpleasant to her."

"Ah," said Chad, "she can bear *me*—could bear me at least at home. It's my being there that would be her triumph. She hates me in Paris."

"She hates in other words—"

"Yes, *that's* it!"—Chad had quickly understood this understanding; which formed, on the part of each, as near an approach as they had yet made to naming Mme. de Vionnet. The limitations of their distinctness didn't, however, prevent its fairly lingering in the air that it was this lady Mrs. Pocock hated. It added one more touch, moreover, to their established recognition of the rare intimacy of Chad's association with her. He had himself never yet so twitched away the last light veil from this phenomenon as in presenting himself as confounded and submerged in the sentiment she had engendered at Woollett. "And I'll tell you who hates me too," he immediately went on.

Strether knew as immediately whom he meant; but with as prompt a protest. "Ah, no! Mamie doesn't hate—well," he caught himself in time—"anybody at all. Mamie's beautiful."

Chad shook his head. "That's just why I mind it. She certainly doesn't like me."

"How much do you mind it? What would you do for her?"

"Well, I'd like her if she'd like me. Really, really," Chad declared.

It gave his companion a moment's pause. "You asked me just now if I don't, as you said, 'care' about a certain person. You rather tempt me therefore to put the question in my turn. Don't *you* care about a certain other person?"

Chad looked at him hard in the lamplight of the window. "The difference is that *I* don't want to."

Strether wondered. "'Don't want' to?"

"I try not to—that is I *have* tried. I've done my best. You can't be surprised," the young man easily went on, "when you yourself set me on it. I was indeed," he added, "already on it a little; but you set me harder. It was six weeks ago that I thought I had come out."

Strether took it well in. "But you haven't come out!"

"I don't know—it's what I *want* to know," said Chad. "And **if** I could have sufficiently wanted—by myself—to go back, I think **I** might have found out."

"Possibly"—Strether considered. "But all you were able to achieve was to want to want to! And even then," he pursued, "only till our friends there came. Do you want to want to still?" As with a sound half dolorous, half droll and all vague and equivocal, Chad buried his face for a little in his hands, rubbing it in a whimsical way that amounted to an evasion, he brought it out more sharply. "*Do* you?"

Chad kept for a time his attitude, but at last he looked up, and then, abruptly, "Jim *is* a damned dose!" he declared.

"Oh, I don't ask you to abuse or describe or in any way pronounce upon your relatives; I simply put it to you once more whether you're *now* ready. You say you've 'seen.' Is what you've seen that you can't resist?"

Chad gave him a strange smile—the nearest approach he had ever shown to a troubled one. "Can't you *make* me not resist?"

"What it comes to," Strether went on very gravely now and as if he had not heard him, "what it comes to is that more has been done for you, I think, than I've ever seen done—attempted perhaps, but never so successfully done—by one human being for another."

"Oh, an immense deal certainly"—Chad did it full justice. "And you yourself are adding to it."

It was without heeding this either that his friend continued. "And our friends there won't have it."

"No, they simply won't."

"They demand you on the basis, as it were, of repudiation and ingratitude; and what has been the matter with me," Strether went on, "is that I haven't seen my way to working with you for repudiation."

Chad appreciated this. "Then as you haven't seen yours, you naturally haven't seen mine. There it is." After which he proceeded, with a certain abruptness, to a sharp interrogation. "*Now* do you say she doesn't hate me?"

Strether hesitated. "'She'—?"

"Yes—mother. We called it Sarah, but it comes to the same thing."

"Ah," Strether objected, "not to the same thing as her hating *you.*"

On which—though as if. for an instant, it had hung fire—Chad remarkably replied: "Well, if they hate my good friend, *that* comes to the same thing." It had a note of inevitable truth that made Strether take it as enough, feel he wanted nothing more. The young man spoke in it for his "good friend" more than he had ever yet directly spoken, confessed to such deep identities between them as he might play with the idea of working free from, but which at a given moment, could still draw him down like a whirlpool. And meanwhile he had gone on. "Their hating you too, moreover—that also comes to a good deal."

"Ah," said Strether, "your mother doesn't."

Chad, however, loyally stuck to it—loyally, that is, to Strether. "She *will* if you don't look out."

"Well, I do look out. I *am,* after all, looking out. That's just why," our friend explained, "I want to see her again."

It drew from Chad again the same question. "To see mother?"

"To see—for the present—Sarah."

"Ah then, there you are! And what I don't for the life of me make out," Chad pursued with resigned perplexity, "is what you *gain* by it."

Oh, it would have taken his companion too long to say! "That's because you have, I verily believe, no imagination. You've other qualities. But no imagination, don't you see? at all."

"I dare say. I do see." It was an idea in which Chad showed interest. "But haven't you yourself rather too much?"

"Oh, *rather—!*" So that, after an instant, under this reproach and as if it were at last a fact really to escape from, Strether made his move for departure.

ONE of the features of the restless afternoon passed by him after Mrs. Pocock's visit was an hour spent, shortly before dinner, with Maria Gostrey, whom, of late, in spite of so sustained a call on his attention from other quarters, he had by no means neglected. And that he was still not neglecting her will appear from the fact that he was with her again at the same hour on the very morrow—with no less fine a consciousness, moreover, of being able to hold her ear. It continued inveterately to occur, for that matter, that whenever he had taken one of his greater turns he came back to where she so faithfully awaited him. None of these excursions had, on the whole, been livelier than the pair of incidents—the fruit of the short interval since his previous visit—on which he had now to report to her. He had seen Chad Newsome late the night before, and he had had that morning, as a sequel to this conversation, a second interview with Sarah. "But they're all off," he said, "at last."

It puzzled her a moment. "All?—Mr. Newsome with them?"

"Ah, not yet! Sarah and Jim and Mamie. But Waymarsh with them—for Sarah. It's too beautiful," Strether continued; "I find I don't get over that—it's always a fresh joy. But it's a fresh joy too," he added, "that—well, what do you think? Little Bilham also goes. But he of course goes for Mamie."

Miss Gostrey wondered. "'For' her? Do you mean they're already engaged?"

"Well," said Strether, "say then for *me*. He'll do anything for me; just as I will, for that matter—anything I can—for him. Or for Mamie either. *She'll* do anything for me."

Miss Gostrey gave a substantial sigh. "The way you reduce people to subjection!"

"It's certainly, on one side, wonderful. But it's quite equalled, on another, by the way I don't. I haven't reduced Sarah, since yes terday; though I've succeeded in seeing her again, as I'll presently tell you. The others, however, *are* all right. Mamie, by that blessed law of ours, *must* have a young man."

"But what must poor Mr. Bilham have? Do you mean they'll *marry* for you?"

"I mean that, by the same blessed law, it won't matter a grain if they don't—I sha'n't have in the least to worry."

She saw, as usual, what he meant. "And Mr. Jim?—who goes for *him?*"

"Oh," Strether had to admit, "I couldn't manage *that*. He's thrown, as usual, on the world; the world which, after all, by his account—for he has prodigious adventures—seems very good to him. He fortunately—'over here,' as he says—finds the world everywhere; and his *most* prodigious adventure," he went on, "has been of course of the last few days."

Miss Gostrey, already knowing, instantly made the connection. "He has seen Marie de Vionnet again?"

"He went, all by himself, the day after Chad's party—didn't I tell you?—to tea with her. By her invitation—all alone."

"Quite like *you!*" Maria smiled.

"Oh, but he's more wonderful about her than I am!" And then as his friend showed how she could believe it, filling it out, fitting it on to old memories of the wonderful woman: "What I should have liked to manage would have been *her* going."

"To Switzerland with the party?"

"For Jim—and for symmetry. If it had been workable, moreover, for a fortnight, she'd have gone. She's ready"—he followed up his renewed vision of her—"for anything."

Miss Gostrey went with him a minute. "She's too perfect!"

"She *will*, I think," he pursued, "go to-night to the station."

"To see him off?"

"With Chad—marvellously—as part of their general attention. And she does it"—it kept before him—"with a light, light grace, a free, free gayety, that may well softly bewilder Mr. Pocock."

It kept her so before him that his companion had after an instant a friendly comment. "As, in short, it has softly bewildered *you*. Are you really in love with her?" Maria threw off.

"It's of no importance I should know," he replied. "It matters so little—has nothing to do, practically, with either of us."

"All the same"—Maria continued to smile—"they go, the five, as I understand you, and you and Mme. de Vionnet stay."

"Oh, and Chad." To which Strether added: "And you."

"Ah, 'me'!"—she gave a small impatient wail again, in which something of the unreconciled seemed suddenly to break out. "I don't stay, it somehow seems to me, much to my advantage. In the presence of all you cause to pass before me I've a tremendous sense of privation."

Strether hesitated. "But your privation, your keeping out of everything, has been—hasn't it?—by your own choice."

"Oh yes; it has been necessary—that is, it has been better for you. What I mean is only that I seem to have ceased to serve you."

"How can you tell that?" he asked. "You don't know how you serve me. When you cease—"

"Well?" she said as he dropped.

"Well, I'll *let* you know. You can be quiet till then."

She thought a moment. "Then you positively like me to stay?"

"Don't I treat you as if I did?"

"You're certainly very kind to me. But that," said Maria, "is for myself. It's getting late, as you see, and Paris turning rather hot and dusty. People are scattering, and some of them, in other places, want me. But if you want me here—!"

She had spoken as resigned to his word, but he had of a sudden a still sharper sense than he would have expected of desiring not to lose her. "I want you here."

She took it as if the words were all she had wished; as if they brought her, gave her something that was the compensation of her case. "Thank you," she simply answered. And then as he looked at her a little harder, "Thank you very much," she repeated.

It had broken as with a slight arrest into the current of their talk, and it held him a moment longer. "Why, two months, or whatever the time was, ago, did you so suddenly dash off? The reason you afterwards gave me for having kept away three weeks was not the real one."

She recalled. "I never supposed you believed it was. Yet," she continued, "if you didn't guess it, that was just what helped you."

He looked away from her on this; he indulged, so far as space permitted, in one of his slow absences. "I've often thought of it, but never to feel that I could guess it. And you see the consideration with which I've treated you in never asking till now."

"Now then—why *do* you ask?"

"To show you how I miss you when you're not here, and what it does for me."

"It doesn't seem to have done," she laughed, "all it might! However," she added, "if you've really never guessed the truth, I'll tell it you."

"I've never guessed it," Strether declared.

"Never?"

"Never."

"Well then, I dashed off, as you say, so as not to have the confusion of being there if Marie de Vionnet should tell you anything to my detriment."

He looked, however, as if he still doubted. "You even then would have had to face it on your return."

"Oh, if I had found reason to believe it something very bad, I would have left you altogether."

"So then," he continued, "it was only on guessing she had been on the whole merciful that you ventured back?"

Maria kept it together. "I owe her thanks. Whatever her temptation, she didn't separate us. That's one of my reasons," she went on, "for admiring her so."

"Let it pass then," said Strether, "for one of mine as well. But what would have been her temptation?"

"What are ever the temptations of women?"

He thought—but hadn't, naturally, to think too long. "Men?"

"She would have had you, with it, more for herself. But she saw she could have you without it."

"Oh, 'have' me!" Strether a trifle ambiguously sighed. "*You*," he handsomely declared, "would have had me at any rate *with* it."

"Oh, 'have' you!"—she echoed it as he had done. "I do have you, however," she less ironically said, "from the moment you express a wish."

He stopped before her, full of the disposition. "I'll express fifty."

364

Which indeed begot in her, with a certain inconsequence, a return of her small wail. " Ah, there you are!"

There, if it were so, he continued for the rest of the time to be, and it was as if to show her how she could still serve him that, coming back to the departure of the Pococks, he gave her the view, vivid with a hundred more touches than we can reproduce, of what had happened for him that morning. He had had ten minutes with Sarah at her hotel, ten minutes reconquered, by irresistible pressure, from the time over which he had already described her to Miss Gostrey as having, at the end of their interview at his own establishment, passed the great sponge of the future. He had caught her by not announcing himself, had found her in her sitting-room with a dressmaker and a *lingère,* whose accounts she appeared to have been more or less ingenuously settling, and who soon withdrew. Then he had explained to her how he had succeeded, late the night before, in keeping his promise of seeing Chad. " I told her I'd take it all."

" You'd ' take ' it ?"

" Why, if he doesn't go."

Maria waited. " And who takes it if he does ?" she inquired with a certain grimness of gayety.

" Well," said Strether, " I think I take, in any event, everything."

" By which I suppose you mean," his companion brought out after a moment, " that you definitely understand you now lose everything."

He stood before her again. " It does come perhaps to the same thing. But Chad, now that he has seen, doesn't really want it."

She could believe that, but she made, as always, for clearness. " Still, what, after all, *has* he seen ?"

" What they want of him. And it's enough."

" It contrasts so unfavorably with what Mme. de Vionnet wants ?"

" It contrasts—just so ; all round, and tremendously."

" Therefore, perhaps, most of all with what *you* want ?"

" Oh," said Strether, " what I want is a thing I've ceased to measure or even to understand."

But his friend none the less went on. " Do you want Mrs. Newsome—after such a way of treating you ?"

It was a straighter way of dealing with this lady than they had as yet—such was their high form—permitted themselves; but it seemed not wholly for this that he delayed a moment. "I dare say it has been, after all, the only way she could have imagined."

"And does that make you want her any more?"

"I've tremendously disappointed her," Strether thought it worth while to mention.

"Of course you have. That's rudimentary; that was plain to us long ago. But isn't it almost as plain," Maria went on, "that you've even yet your straight remedy? Really drag him away, as I believe you still can, and you'd cease to have to count with her disappointment."

"Ah then," he laughed, "I should have to count with yours!"

But this barely struck her now. "What, in that case, should you call counting? You haven't come out where you are, I think, to please *me*."

"Oh," he insisted, "that too, you know, has been part of it. I can't separate—it's all one; and that's perhaps why, as I say, I don't understand." But he was ready to declare again that this didn't in the least matter; all the more that, as he affirmed, he *hadn't* really as yet "come out." "She gives me after all, on its coming to the pinch, a last mercy, another chance. They don't sail, you see, for five or six weeks more, and they haven't—she admits that—expected Chad would take part in their tour. It's still open to him to join them, at the last, at Liverpool."

Miss Gostrey considered. "How in the world is it 'open' unless you open it? How can he join them at Liverpool if he but sinks deeper into his situation here?"

"He has given her—as I explained to you that she let me know yesterday—his word of honor to do as I say."

Maria stared. "But if you say nothing!"

Well, he, as usual, walked about on it. "I did say something this morning. I gave her my answer—the word I had promised her after hearing from himself what *he* had promised. What she demanded of me yesterday, you'll remember, was the engagement then and there to make him take up this vow."

"Well then," Miss Gostrey inquired, "was the purpose of your visit to her only to decline?"

"No; it was to ask, odd as that may seem to you, for another delay."

"Ah, that's weak!"

"Precisely!" She had spoken with impatience, but, so far as that at least, he knew where he was. "If I *am* weak I want to find it out. If I don't find it out I shall have the comfort, the little glory, of thinking I'm strong."

"It's all the comfort, I judge," she returned, "that you *will* have!"

"At any rate," he said, "it will have been a month more. Paris may grow, from day to day, hot and dusty, as you say; but there are other things that are hotter and dustier. I'm not afraid to stay on; the summer here must be amusing in a wild—if it isn't a tame—way of its own: the place at no time more picturesque. I think I shall like it. And then," he benevolently smiled for her, "there will be always you."

"Oh," she objected, "it won't be as a part of the picturesqueness that I shall stay, for I shall be the plainest thing about you. You may, you see, at any rate," she pursued, "have nobody else. Mme. de Vionnet may very well be going off, mayn't she?—and Mr. Newsome by the same stroke: unless, indeed, you've had an assurance from them to the contrary. So that if your idea's to stay for them "—it was her duty to suggest it—" you may be left in the lurch. Of course if they do stay "—she kept it up—" they would be part of the picturesqueness. Or else indeed you might join them somewhere."

Strether seemed to face it as if it were a happy thought; but the next moment he spoke more critically. "Do you mean that they'll probably go off together?"

She just considered. "I think it will be treating you quite without ceremony if they do; though, after all," she added, "it would be difficult to see, now, quite what degree of ceremony properly meets your case."

"Of course," Strether conceded, "my attitude toward them is extraordinary."

"Just so; so that it will be hard to see what style of proceeding on their own part can altogether match it. The attitude of their own that won't pale in its light they've doubtless still to work out. The really handsome thing, perhaps," she presently threw off, " *would* be for them to withdraw into more secluded conditions, offering at the same time to share them with you." He looked at her, on this, as if some generous irritation—all on his behalf—had suddenly again flickered in her; and what she next said, indeed, half explained it. "Don't really be afraid to tell me if what now holds you *is* the pleasant prospect of the empty town, with plenty of seats in the shade, cool drinks, deserted museums, drives to the Bois in the evening, and our wonderful woman all to yourself." And she kept it up still more. "The handsomest thing of *all*, when one makes it out, would, I dare say, be that Mr. Chad should for a while go off by himself. It's a pity, from that point of view," she wound up, "that he does *not* pay his mother a visit. It would at least occupy your interval." The thought in fact held her a moment. "*Why* doesn't he pay his mother a visit? Even a week, at this good moment, would do."

"My dear lady," Strether replied—and he had it even to himself surprisingly ready—"my dear lady, his mother has paid *him* a visit. Mrs. Newsome has been with him, this month, with an intensity that I'm sure he has thoroughly felt; he has lavishly entertained her, and she has let him have her thanks. Do you suggest he shall go back for more of them?"

Well, she succeeded after a little in shaking it off. "I see. It's what you don't suggest—what you haven't suggested. And you know."

"So would you, my dear," he kindly said, "if you had so much as seen her."

"As seen Mrs. Newsome?"

"No, Sarah—which, both for Chad and for myself, has served all the purpose."

"And served it in a manner," she responsively mused, "so extraordinary!"

"Well, you see," he partly explained, "what it comes to is that she's all cold thought; so that Sarah could serve it to us cold without its really losing anything. So it is that we know what she thinks of us."

Maria had followed, but she had an arrest. "What I've never made out, if you come to that, is what you think—I mean you personally—of *her*. Don't you so much, when all's said, as care a little?"

"That," he answered with no loss of promptness, "is what even Chad himself asked me last night. He asked me if I don't mind the loss—well, the loss of an opulent future. Which, moreover," he hastened to add, "was a perfectly natural question."

"I call your attention, all the same," said Miss Gostrey, "to the fact that I don't ask it. What I venture to ask is whether it's to Mrs. Newsome herself that you're indifferent."

"I haven't been so"—he spoke with all assurance. "I've been the very opposite. I've been, from the first moment, preoccupied with the impression everything might be making on her—quite oppressed, haunted, tormented by it. I've been interested *only* in her seeing what I've seen. And I've been as disappointed in her refusal to see it as she has been in what has appeared to her the perversity of my insistence."

"Do you mean that she has shocked you as you've shocked her?"

Strether hesitated. "I'm doubtless not so shockable. But, on the other hand, I've gone much further to meet her. She, on her side, hasn't budged an inch."

"So that you're now at last"—Maria pointed the moral—"in the sad stage of recriminations."

"No—it's only to you I speak. I've been like a lamb to Sarah. I've only put my back to the wall. It's to *that* one naturally staggers when one has been violently pushed there."

She watched him a moment. "Thrown over?"

"Well, I feel so that I've landed somewhere, that I think I must have been thrown."

She turned it over, but as hoping to clarify much rather than to harmonize. "The thing is that I suppose you've been disappointing—"

"Quite from the very first of my arrival? I dare say. I admit I was surprising even to myself."

"And then, of course," Maria went on, "I had much to do with it."

"With my being surprising—?"

"That will do," she laughed, "if you're too delicate to call it *my* being! Naturally," she added, "you came over more or less for surprises."

"Naturally!"—he valued the reminder.

"But they were to have been all for you"—she continued to piece it out—"and none of them for *her*."

Once more he stopped before her as if she had touched the point. "That's just her difficulty—that she doesn't admit surprises. It's a fact that, I think, describes and represents her; and it falls in with what I tell you—that she's all, as I've called it, fine cold thought. She had, to her own mind, worked the whole thing out in advance, and worked it out for me as well as for herself. Whenever she has done that, you see, there's no room left; no margin, as it were, for any alteration. She's filled as full, packed as tight, as she'll hold, and if you wish to get anything more or different either out or in—"

"You've got to make over, altogether, the woman herself?"

"What it comes to," said Strether, "is that you've got morally and intellectually to get rid of her."

"Which would appear," Maria returned, "to be practically what you've done."

But her friend threw back his head. "I haven't touched her. She won't *be* touched. I see it now as I've never done; and she hangs together with a perfection of her own," he went on, "that does suggest a kind of wrong in *any* change in her composition. It was at any rate," he wound up, "the woman herself, as you call her, the whole moral and intellectual being or block, that Sarah brought me over to take or to leave."

It turned Miss Gostrey to deeper thought. "Fancy having to take at the point of the bayonet a whole moral and intellectual being or block!"

"It was in fact," said Strether, "what, at home, I *had* done. But somehow, over there, I didn't quite know it."

"One never does, I suppose," Miss Gostrey concurred, "realize in advance, in such a case, the size, as you may say, of the block. Little by little it looms up. It has been looming for you more and more, till at last you see it all."

"I see it all," he absently echoed, while his eyes might have been fixing some particularly large iceberg in a cool blue northern sea. "It's magnificent!" he then rather oddly exclaimed.

But his friend, who was used to this kind of inconsequence in

him, kept the thread. " There's nothing so magnificent—for making others feel you—as to have no imagination."

It brought him straight round. " Ah, there you are! It's what
I said last night to Chad. That he himself, I mean, has none."

" Then it would appear," Maria suggested, " that he has, after
all, something in common with his mother."

" He has in common that he makes one, as you say, ' feel ' him.
And yet," he added, as if the question were interesting, " one feels
others too, even when they have plenty."

Miss Gostrey continued suggestive. " Mme. de Vionnet?"

" *She* has plenty."

" Certainly—she had quantities of old. But there are different
ways of making one's self felt."

" Yes, it comes, no doubt, to that. You now—"

He was benevolently going on, but she wouldn't have it. " Oh,
I *don't* make myself felt; so my quantity needn't be settled. Yours,
you know," she went on, " is monstrous. No one has ever had so
much."

It struck him for a moment. " That's what Chad also said."

" There *you* are then—though it isn't for him to complain of
it!"

" Oh, he doesn't complain of it," said Strether.

" That's all that would be wanting! But à propos of what," Maria
went on, " did the question come up?"

" Well, of his asking me what it is I gain."

She had a pause. " Then, as I've asked you too, it settles *my* case.
Oh, you *have,*" she repeated, " treasures of imagination."

But he had been for an instant thinking away from this, and he
came up in another place. " And yet Mrs. Newsome—it's a thing
to remember—*has* imagined, did, that is, imagine, and apparently
still does, horrors about what I should have found. I was booked, by
her vision—extraordinarily intense, after all—to find them; and
that I didn't, that I couldn't, that, as she evidently felt, I wouldn't
—this evidently didn't at all, as they say, ' suit ' her book. It was
more than she could bear. That was her disappointment."

" You mean you were to have found Chad himself horrible?"

" I was to have found the woman."

" Horrible?"

"Found her as she imagined her." And Strether paused as if for his own expression of it he could add no touch to that picture.

His companion had meanwhile thought. "She imagined stupidly —so it comes to the same thing."

"Stupidly? Oh!" said Strether.

But she insisted. "She imagined meanly."

He had it, however, better. "It couldn't but be ignorantly."

"Well, intensity with ignorance—what do you want worse?"

This question might have held him, but he let it pass. "Sarah isn't ignorant—now; she keeps up the theory of the horrible."

"Ah, but she's intense—and that by itself will do sometimes as well. If it doesn't do, in this case, at any rate, to deny that Marie's charming, it will do at least to deny that she's good."

"What I claim is that she's good for Chad."

"You *don't* claim"—she seemed to like it clear—"that she's good for *you*."

But he continued without heeding. "That's what I wanted them to come out for—to see for themselves if she's bad for him."

"And now that they've done so, they won't admit that she's good even for anything?"

"They do think," Strether presently admitted, "that she's on the whole about as bad for me. But they're consistent, of course, inasmuch as they've their clear view of what's good for both of us."

"For you, to begin with"—Maria, all responsive, confined the question for the moment—"to eliminate from your existence and if possible even from your memory, the dreadful creature that *I* must gruesomely shadow forth for them, even more than to eliminate the distincter evil—thereby a little less portentous—of the person whose confederate you've suffered yourself to become. However, that's comparatively simple. You can easily, at the worst, after all, give me up."

"I can easily at the worst, after all, give you up." The irony was so obvious that it needed no care. "I can easily at the worst, after all, even forget you."

"Call that then workable. But Mr. Newsome has much more to forget. How can *he* do it?"

"Ah, there again we are! That's just what I was to have made him do; just where I was to have worked with him and helped."

372

She took it in silence and without attenuation—as if perhaps from very familiarity with the facts; and her thought made a connection without showing the links. "Do you remember how we used to talk at Chester and in London about my seeing you through?" She spoke as of far-off things and as if they had spent weeks at the places she named.

"It's just what you *are* doing."

"Ah, but the worst—since you've left such a margin—may be still to come. You may yet break down."

"Yes, I may yet break down. But will you take me—?"

He had hesitated, and she waited. "Take you—?"

"For as long as I can bear it."

She also debated. "Mr. Newsome and Mme. de Vionnet may, as we were saying, leave town. How long do you think you can bear it without them?"

Strether's reply to this was at first another question. "Do you mean in order to get away from me?"

Her answer had an abruptness. "Don't find me rude if I say I should think they'd want to!"

He looked at her hard again—seemed even for an instant to have an intensity of thought under which his color changed. But he smiled. "You mean after what they've done to me?"

"After what *she* has."

At this, however, with a laugh, he was all right again. "Ah but she hasn't done it yet!"

XXX

HE had taken the train, a few days after this, from a station—as well as *to* a station—selected almost at random; such days, whatever should happen, were numbered, and he had gone forth under the impulse—artless enough, no doubt—to give the whole of one of them to that French ruralism, with its cool special green, into which he had hitherto looked only through the little oblong window of the picture-frame. It had been as yet, for the most part, but a land of fancy for him—the background of fiction, the medium of art, the nursery of letters; practically as distant as Greece, but practically, also, almost as consecrated. Romance could weave itself, for Strether's sense, out of elements mild enough; and even after what he had, as he felt, lately " been through," he could thrill a little at the chance of seeing something somewhere that would remind him of a certain small Lambinet that had charmed him, long years before, at a Boston dealer's, and that he had, quite absurdly, never forgotten. It had been offered, he remembered, at a price he had been instructed to believe the lowest ever named for a Lambinet, a price he had never felt so poor as on having to recognize, all the same, as possibilities for an hour; it had been the only adventure of his life in connection with the purchase of a work of art. The adventure, it will be perceived, was modest; but the memory, beyond all reason and by some accident of association, was sweet. The little Lambinet abode with him as the picture he *would* have bought—the particular production that had made him for the moment overstep the modesty of nature. He was quite aware that if he were to see it again he should perhaps have a drop or a shock, and he never found himself beyond any dream of his. He *had* dreamed—had turned and twisted wishing that the wheel of time would turn it up again, just as he had seen it in the maroon-colored, sky-lighted inner shrine of Tremont Street. It would be a different thing, however, to see the remembered mixture resolved back into its elements—to assist at the restoration to nature of the whole far-away hour: the dusty day in Boston, the background of the Fitchburg Depot, of the maroon-colored sanctum, the special-green vision, the ridiculous price, the poplars, the willows, the rushes, the river, the sunny, silvery sky, the shady, woody horizon.

He observed in respect to his train almost no condition save that it should stop a few times after getting out of the *banlieue;* he threw himself on the general amiability of the day for the hint of where to alight. His theory of his excursion was that he could alight anywhere—not nearer Paris than an hour's run—on catching a suggestion of the particular note required. It made its sign, the suggestion—weather, air, light, color and his mood all favoring—at the end of some eighty minutes; the train pulled up just at the right spot, and he found himself getting out as securely as if to keep an appointment. It will be felt of him that he could amuse himself, at his age, with very small things if it be again noted that his appointment was only with a superseded Boston fashion. He had not gone far without the quick confidence that it would be quite sufficiently kept. The oblong gilt frame disposed its enclosing lines; the poplars and willows, the reeds and river—a river of which he didn't know, and didn't want to know, the name—fell into a composition, full of felicity, within them; the sky was silver and turquoise and varnish; the village on the left was white and the church on the right was gray; it was all there, in short—it was what he wanted: it was Tremont Street, it was France, it was Lambinet. Moreover he was freely walking about in it. He did this last, for an hour, to his heart's content, making for the shady, woody horizon and boring so deep into his impression and his idleness that he might fairly have got through them again and reached the maroon-colored wall. It was a wonder, no doubt, that the taste of idleness, for him, should not need more time to sweeten; but it had in fact taken the few previous days; it had been sweetening, in truth, ever since the retreat of the Pococks. He walked and walked as if to show himself how little he had now to do; he had nothing to do but turn off to some hillside where he might stretch himself and hear the poplars rustle, and whence—in the course of an afternoon so spent, an afternoon richly suffused, too, with the sense of a book in his pocket—he should sufficiently command the scene to be able to pick out just the right little rustic inn for an experiment in respect to dinner. There was a train back to Paris at 9.20, and he saw himself partaking, at the close of the day, with the enhancements of a coarse white cloth and a sanded floor, of something fried and felicitous, washed down with authentic wine; after which he might, as he liked, either stroll back to his station in the gloaming or propose for the local *carriole* and converse with his driver, a driver who naturally wouldn't fail of a stiff clean blouse, of a knitted nightcap and of the genius of response—who, in fine, would sit on the shafts, tell him what the French people were thinking, and remind him, as indeed the whole episode would incidentally do, of Maupassant. Strether heard his lips, for the first time in French air, as this vision assumed consistency, emit sounds of expressive intention without fear of his company. He had been afraid of Chad and of Maria and of Mme. de Vionnet; he had been most of all afraid of Waymarsh, in whose presence, so far as they had mixed together in the light of the town, he had never without somehow paying for it aired either his vocabulary or his accent. He usually paid for it by meeting immediately afterwards Waymarsh's eye.

Such were the liberties with which his fancy played after he had turned off to the hillside that did really and truly, as well as most amiably, await him beneath the poplars, the hillside that made him feel, for a murmurous couple of hours, how happy had been his thought. He had the sense of success, of a finer harmony in things; nothing but what had turned out, as yet, according to his plan. It most of all came home to him, as he lay on his back on the grass, that Sarah had really gone, that his tension was really relaxed; the peace diffused in these ideas might be delusive, but it hung about him, none the less, for the time. It fairly, for half an hour, sent him to sleep; he pulled his straw hat over his eyes—he had bought it the day before with a reminiscence of Waymarsh's—and lost himself anew in Lambinet. It was as if he had found out he was tired—tired not from his walk, but from that inward exercise which had known, on the whole, for three months, so little intermission. That was it—when once they were off he had dropped; this, moreover, was what he had dropped to, and now he was touching bottom. He was kept luxuriously quiet, soothed and amused, by the consciousness of what he had found at the end of his descent. It was very much what he had told Maria Gostrey he should like to stay on for, the hugely distributed Paris of summer, alternately dazzling and dusky, with a weight lifted for him off its columns and cornices, and with shade and air in the flutter of awnings as wide as avenues. It was present to him without attenuation that, reaching out, the day after making the remark, for some proof of his freedom, he had gone that very afternoon to see Mme. de Vionnet. He had gone again the next day but one, and the effect of the two visits, the after-sense of the couple of hours spent with her, was almost that of fulness and frequency. The brave intention of frequency, so great with him from the moment of his finding himself unjustly suspected at Woollett, had remained rather theoretic, and one of the things he could muse about under his poplars was the source of the special shyness that had still made him careful. He had surely got rid of it now, this special shyness; what had become of it if it had not, precisely, within the week, rubbed off?

It struck him now in fact as sufficiently plain that if he had still been careful he had been so for a reason. He had really feared, in his behavior, a lapse from good faith; if there was a danger of one's liking such a woman too much, one's best safety was in waiting at least till one had the right to do so. In the light of the last few days the danger was fairly vivid; so that it was proportionately fortunate that the right was likewise established. It seemed to our friend that he had on each occasion profited to the utmost by the latter: how could he have done so more, he at all events asked himself, than in having immediately let her know that, if it was all the same to her, he preferred not to talk about anything tiresome? He had never in his life so sacrificed an armful of high interests as in that remark; he had never so prepared the way for the comparatively frivolous as in addressing it to Mme. de Vionnet's intelligence. It had not been till later that he quite recalled how in conjuring away everything but the pleasant he had conjured away almost all they had hitherto talked about; it was not till later, even, that he remembered how, with their new tone, they had not so much as mentioned the name of Chad himself. One of the things that most lingered with him on his hillside was this delightful facility, with such a woman, of arriving at a new tone; he thought, as he lay on his back, of all the tones she might make possible if one were to try her, and at any rate of the probability that one could trust her to fit them to occasions. He had wanted her to feel that, as he was disinterested now, so she herself should be, and she had showed she felt it, and he had showed he was grateful, and it had been, for all the world, as if he were calling for the first time. They had had other, but irrelevant, meetings; it was quite as if, had they sooner known how much they *really* had in common, there were quantities of comparatively dull matters they might have skipped. Well, they were skipping them now, even to graceful gratitude, even to handsome "Don't mention it!"—and it was amazing what could still come up without reference to what had been going on between them. It might have been, on analysis, nothing more than Shakespeare and the musical glasses; but it had served all the purpose of his appearing to have said to her: "Don't like me, if it's a question of liking me, for anything obvious and clumsy that I've, as they call it, 'done' for you: like me—well, like me, hang it, for anything else you choose. So, by the same propriety, don't be for me simply the person I've come to know through my awkward connection with Chad—was ever anything, by the way, *more* awkward? Be for me, please, with all your admirable tact and trust, just whatever I may show you it's a present pleasure to me to think you." It had been a large indication to meet; but if she hadn't met it what *had* she done, and how had their time together slipped along so smoothly, mild but not slow, and melting, liquefying, into his happy illusion of idleness? He could recognize on the other hand that he had probably not been without reason, in his prior, his restricted state, for keeping an eye on his liability to lapse from good faith.

He really continued in the picture—that being for himself his situation—all the rest of this rambling day; so that the charm was still, was indeed more than ever, upon him when, towards six o'clock, he found himself amicably engaged with a stout, white-capped, deepvoiced woman at the door of the *auberge* of the biggest village, a village that affected him as a thing of whiteness, blueness and crookedness, set in coppery green, and that had the river flowing behind or before it—one couldn't say which; at the bottom, in particular, of the inn-garden. He had had other adventures before this; had kept along the height, after shaking off slumber; had admired, had almost coveted, another small old church, all steep roof and dim slate-color without and all whitewash and paper flowers within; had lost his way and had found it again; had conversed with rustics who struck him perhaps a little more as men of the world than he had expected; had acquired at a bound a fearless facility in French; had had, as the afternoon waned, a watery *bock,* all pale and Parisian, in the café of the furthest village, which was not the biggest; and had all the while not once overstepped the oblong gilt frame. The frame had drawn itself out for him, as much as you please; but that was just his luck. He had finally come down again to the valley, to keep within touch of stations and trains, turning his face to the quarter from which he had started; and thus it was that he had at last pulled up before the hostess of the Cheval Blanc, who met him, with a rough readiness that was like the clatter of sabots over stones, on their common ground of a *côtelette de veau à l'oseille* and a subsequent lift. He had walked many miles and knew not that he was tired; but he still knew that he was amused, and even that, though he had been alone all day, he had never yet so struck himself as engaged with others and in midstream of his drama. It might have passed for finished, his drama, with its catastrophe all but reached: it had, however, none the less been vivid again for him as he thus gave it its fuller chance. He had only had to be at last well out of it to feel it, oddly enough, still going on.

For this had been all day, at bottom, the spell of the picture—that it was essentially, more than anything else, a scene and a stage, that the very air of the play was in the rustle of the willows and the tone of the sky. The play and the characters had, without his knowing it till now, peopled all his space for him, and it seemed somehow quite happy that they should offer themselves, in the conditions so supplied, with a kind of inevitability. It was as if the conditions made them not only inevitable, but so much more nearly natural and right as that they were at least easier, pleasanter, to put up with. The conditions had nowhere so asserted their difference from those of Woollett as they appeared to him to assert it in the little court of the Cheval Blanc while he arranged with his hostess for a comfortable climax. They were few and simple, scant and humble, but they were *the thing,* as he would have called it, even to a

greater degree than Mme. de Vionnet's old, high salon, where the
ghost of the Empire walked. "The" thing was the thing that implied the greatest number of other things of the sort he had had to
tackle; and it was queer, of course, but so it was—the implication
here was complete. Not a single one of his observations but somehow fell into a place in it; not a breath of the cooler evening that
wasn't somehow a syllable of the text. The text was simply, when
condensed, that in *these* places such things were, and that if it was
in them one elected to move about one had to make one's account
with what one lighted on. Meanwhile, at all events, it was enough
that they did affect one—so far as the village aspect was concerned
—as whiteness, crookedness and blueness set in coppery green; there
being positively, for that matter, an outer wall of the White Horse
that was painted the most improbable shade. That was part of the
amusement—as if to show that the fun was harmless; just as it was
enough, further, that the picture and the play seemed supremely
to melt together in the good woman's broad sketch of what she could
do for her visitor's appetite. He felt, in short, a confidence, and it
was general, and it was all he wanted to feel. It suffered no shock
even on her mentioning that she had in fact just laid the cloth for
two persons who, unlike Monsieur, had arrived by the river—in a
boat of their own; who had asked her, half an hour before, what
she could do for them, and had then paddled away to look at something a little further up—from which promenade they would presently return. Monsieur might meanwhile, if he liked, pass into the
garden, such as it was, where she would serve him, should he wish
it—for there were tables and benches in plenty—a "bitter" before
his repast. Here she would also report to him on the possibility of
a conveyance to his station, and here, at any rate, he would have the
agrément of the river.

It may be mentioned without delay that Monsieur had the *agrément* of everything, and in particular, for the next twenty minutes,
of a small and primitive pavilion that, at the garden's edge, almost
overhung the water, testifying, in its somewhat battered state, to
much fond frequentation. It consisted of little more than a platform, slightly raised, with a couple of benches and a table, a protecting rail and a projecting roof; but it raked the full gray-blue
stream, which, taking a turn a short distance above, passed out of

sight to reappear much higher up; and it was clearly in esteemed requisition for Sundays and other feasts. Strether sat there and, though hungry, felt at peace; the confidence that had so gathered for him deepened with the lap of the water, the ripple of the surface, the rustle of the reeds on the opposite bank, the faint diffused coolness and the slight rock of a couple of small boats attached to a rough landing-place hard by. The valley on the further side was all copper-green level and glazed pearly sky, a sky hatched across with screens of trimmed trees, which looked flat, like *espaliers;* and, though the rest of the village straggled away in the near quarter, the view had an emptiness that made one of the boats suggestive. Such a river set one afloat almost before one could take up the oars —the idie play of which would be moreover the aid to the full impression. This perception went so far as to bring him to his feet; but that movement, in turn, made him feel afresh that he was tired, and while he leaned against a post and continued to look out he saw something that gave him a sharper arrest.

XXXI

What he saw was exactly the right thing — a boat advancing round the bend and containing a man who held the paddles and a lady, at the stern, with a pink parasol. It was suddenly as if these figures, or something like them, had been wanted in the picture, had been wanted, more or less, all day, and had now drifted into sight, with the slow current, on purpose to fill up the measure. They came slowly, floating down, evidently making for the landing-place near their spectator and presenting themselves to him not less clearly as the two persons for whom his hostess was already preparing a meal. For two very happy persons he found himself straightway taking them—a young man in shirt-sleeves, a young woman easy and fair, who had pulled pleasantly up from some other place and, being acquainted with the neighborhood, had known what this particular retreat could offer them. The air quite thickened, at their approach, with further intimations; the intimation that they were expert, familiar, frequent—that this wouldn't, at all events, be the first time. They knew how to do it, he vaguely felt— and it made them but the more idyllic; though at the very moment of the impression, as happened, their boat seemed to have begun to drift wide, the oarsman letting it go. It had by this time, none the less, come much nearer—near enough for Strether to fancy the lady in the stern had, for some reason, taken account of his being there to watch them. She had remarked on it sharply, yet her companion had not turned round; it was in fact almost as if our friend had felt her bid him keep still. She had taken in something as a result of which their course had wavered, and it continued to waver while they just stood off. This little effect was sudden and rapid, so rapid that Strether's sense of it was separate only for an instant from a sharp start of his own. He too had, within the minute, taken in something, taken in that he knew the lady whose parasol,

382

shifting as if to hide her face, made so fine a pink point in the shining scene. It was too prodigious, a chance in a million; but, if he knew the lady, the gentleman, who still presented his back and kept off, the gentleman, the coatless hero of the idyl, who had responded to her start, was, to match the marvel, none other than Chad.

Chad and Mme. de Vionnet were, then, like himself, taking a day in the country—though it was as queer as fiction, as farce, that their country could happen to be exactly *his;* and she had been the first at recognition, the first to feel, across the water, the shock—for it appeared to come to that—of their wonderful accident. Strether became aware, with this, of what was taking place—that her recognition had been even stranger for the pair in the boat, that her immediate impulse had been to control it, and that she was quickly and intensely debating with Chad the risk of betrayal. He saw they would show nothing if they could feel sure he hadn't made them out; so that he had before him for a few seconds his own hesitation. It was a sharp, fantastic crisis that had popped up as if in a dream, and it had had only to last the few seconds to make him feel it as quite horrible. They were thus, on either side, *trying* the other side, and all for some reason that broke the stillness like some unprovoked harsh note. It seemed to him again, within the limit, that he had but one thing to do—to settle their common question by some sign of surprise and joy. He hereupon gave large play to these things, agitating his hat and his stick and loudly calling out—a demonstration that brought him relief as soon as he had seen it answered. The boat, in mid-stream, still went a little wild—which seemed natural, however, while Chad turned round, half springing up; and his good friend, after blankness and wonder, began gayly to wave her parasol. Chad dropped afresh to his paddles and the boat headed round, amazement and pleasantry filling the air meanwhile, and relief, as Strether continued to fancy, superseding mere violence. Our friend went down to the water under this odd impression as of violence averted—the violence of their having "cut" him, out there in the eye of nature, on the assumption that he wouldn't know it. He awaited them with a face from which he was conscious of not being able quite to banish this idea that they would have gone on, not seeing and not knowing, missing their dinner and disappointing their hostess, had he himself taken a line to match. That, at least, was what darkened his vision for the moment. Afterwards, after they had bumped at the landing-place and he had assisted their getting ashore, everything found itself sponged over by the mere miracle of the encounter.

They could so much better, at last, on either side, treat it as a wild fable than as anything else, that the situation was made elastic by the amount of explanation called into play. Why indeed —apart from oddity—the situation should have been really stiff, was a question naturally not practical at the moment, and in fact, so far as we are concerned, a question tackled, later on and in private, only by Strether himself. He was to reflect later on and in private that it was mainly *he* who had explained—as he had had moreover comparatively little difficulty in doing. He was to have, at all events, meanwhile, the worrying thought of their perhaps secretly suspecting him of having plotted this coincidence, taking such pains as might be to give it the semblance of an accident. That possibility—as their imputation—didn't of course bear looking into for an instant; yet the whole incident was so manifestly, arrange it as they would, an awkward one, that he could scarce keep disclaimers in respect to his own presence from rising to his lips. Disclaimers of intention would have been as tactless as his presence was, practically, gross; and the narrowest escape they either of them had was his lucky escape, in the event, from making any. Nothing of the sort, so far as surface and sound were involved, was even in question; surface and sound all made for their common ridiculous good fortune, for the general *invraisemblance* of the occasion, for the charming chance that they had, the others, in passing, ordered some food to be ready, the charming chance that he had himself not eaten, the charming chance, even more, that their little plans, their hours, their train, in short, from *là-bas,* would all match for their return together to Paris. The chance that was most charming of all, the chance that drew from Mme. de Vionnet her clearest, gayest *" Comme cela se trouve!"* was the announcement made to Strether after they were seated at table, the word given him by their hostess in respect to his carriage for the station, on which he might now count. It settled the matter for his friends as well; the conveyance—it *was* all too lucky!—would serve for them; and nothing was more delightful than his being in a position to make the train so definite. It might have been, for themselves—to hear Mme. de Vionnet—almost unnaturally vague, a detail left to be fixed; though Strether indeed was afterwards to remember that Chad had promptly enough intervened to forestall this appearance, laughing at his companion's flightiness and making the point that he had, after all, in spite of the bedazzlement of a day out with her, known what he was about.

Strether was to remember afterwards, further, that this had had for him the effect of forming Chad's almost sole intervention; and indeed he was to remember further still, in subsequent meditation, many things that, as it were, fitted together. Another of them was, for instance, that the wonderful woman's overflow of surprise and amusement was wholly into French, which she struck him as speaking with an unprecedented command of idiomatic turns, but in which she got, as he might have said, somewhat away from him, taking all at once little brilliant jumps that he could but lamely match. The question of his own French had never come up for them; it was the one thing she wouldn't have permitted—it belonged, for a person who had been through much, to mere boredom; but the present result was odd, fairly veiling her identity, shifting her back into a mere voluble class or race to the intense audibility of which he was by this time inured. When she spoke the charming slightly strange English he best knew her by, he seemed to feel her as a creature, among all the millions, with a language quite to herself, the real monopoly of a special shade of speech, beautifully easy for her, yet of a color and a cadence that were both inimitable and matters of accident. She came back to these things after they had shaken down in the inn-parlor and knew, as it were, what was to become of them; it was inevitable that loud ejaculation over the prodigy of their convergence should at last wear itself out. Then it was that his impression took fuller form—the impression, destined only to deepen, to complete itself, that they had something to put a face upon, to carry off and make the best of, and that it was she who, admirably on the whole, was doing this. It was familiar to him of course that they had something to put a face upon; their friendship, their connection, took any amount of explaining—that would have been made familiar by his twenty minutes with Mrs.

Pocock if it hadn't already been so. Only, his theory, as we know, had bountifully been that the facts were, specifically, none of his business, and were, over and above, so far as one had to do with them, intrinsically beautiful; and this might have prepared him for anything, as well as rendered him proof against mystification. When he reached home that night, however, he knew he had been, at bottom, neither prepared nor proof; and since we have spoken of what he was, after his return, to recall and interpret, it may as well immediately be said that his real experience of these few hours put on, in that belated vision—for he scarce went to bed till morning—the aspect that is most to our purpose.

He then knew more or less how he had been affected—he but half knew at the time. There had been plenty to affect him even after, as has been said, they had shaken down; for his consciousness, though muffled, had its sharpest moments during this passage, a marked drop into innocent, friendly Bohemia. They then had put their elbows on the table, deploring the premature end of their two or three dishes; which they had tried to make up with another bottle while Chad joked a little spasmodically, perhaps even a little irrelevantly, with the hostess. What it all came to had been that fiction and fable *were,* inevitably, in the air, and not as a simple term of comparison, but as a result of things said; also that they were blinking it, all round, and that they yet needn't, so much as that, have blinked it—though indeed if they hadn't Strether didn't quite see what else they could have done. Strether didn't quite see *that* even at an hour or two past midnight, even when he had, at his hotel, for a long time, without a light and without undressing, sat back on his bedroom sofa and stared straight before him. He was, at that point of vantage, in full possession, to make of it all what he could. He kept making of it that there had been simply a *lie* in the charming affair—a lie on which one could now, detached and deliberate, perfectly put one's finger. It was with the lie that they had eaten and drunk and talked and laughed, that they had waited for their *carriole* rather impatiently, and had then got into the vehicle and, sensibly subsiding, driven their three or four miles through the darkening summer night. The eating and drinking, which had been a resource, had had the effect of having served its turn; the talk and laughter had done as much; and it was during their somewhat tedious progress to the station, during the waits there, the further delays, their submission to fatigue, their silences in the dim compartment of the much-stopping train, that he pre-pared himself for reflections to come. It had been a performance, Mme. de Vionnet's manner, and though it had to that degree falter-ed toward the end, as through her ceasing to believe in it, as if she had asked herself, or Chad had found a moment surreptitiously to ask her, what, after all, was the use, a performance it had none the less quite handsomely remained, with the final fact about it that it was, on the whole, easier to keep up than to abandon.

From the point of view of presence of mind it had been very wonderful indeed, wonderful for readiness, for beautiful assurance, for the way her decision was taken on the spot, without time to confer with Chad, without time for anything. Their only confer-ence could have been the brief instants in the boat before they con-fessed to recognizing the spectator on the bank, for they had not been alone together a moment since and must have communicated all in silence. It was a part of the deep impression for Strether, and not the least of the deep interest, that they *could* so communi-cate—that Chad, in particular, could let her know he left it to her. He habitually left things to others, as Strether was so well aware, and it in fact came over our friend in these meditations that there had been as yet no such vivid illustration of his famous knowing how to live. It was as if he had humored her to the extent of let-ting her lie without correction—almost as if, really, he would be coming round in the morning to set the matter, as between Strether and himself, right. Of course he couldn't quite come; it was a case in which a man was obliged to accept the woman's version, even when fantastic; if she had, with more flurry than she cared to show, elected, as the phrase was, to represent that they had left Paris that morning, and with no design but of getting back within the day— if she had so sized-up, in the Woollett phrase, their necessity, she knew best her own measure. There were things, all the same, it was impossible to blink and which made this measure an odd one— the too evident fact, for instance, that she had not started out for the day dressed and hatted and shod, and even, for that matter, pink parasol'd, as she had been in the boat. From what did the drop in her assurance proceed as the tension increased—from what

did this slightly baffled ingenuity spring but from her consciousnes·
of not presenting, as night closed in, with not so much as a shaw·
to wrap her round, an appearance that matched her story? She
admitted that she was cold, but only to blame her imprudence,
which Chad suffered her to give such account of as she might. Her
shawl and Chad's overcoat, and her other garments, and his, those
they had each worn the day before, were at the place, best known to
themselves—a quiet retreat enough, no doubt—at which they had
been spending the twenty-four hours, to which they had fully
meant to return that evening, from which they had so remarkably
swum into Strether's ken, and the tacit repudiation of which had
been thus the essence of her comedy. Strether saw how she had
perceived in a flash that they couldn't quite look to going back there
under his nose; though, honestly, as he gouged deeper into the matter, he was somewhat surprised, as Chad likewise had perhaps been,
at the uprising of this scruple. He seemed even to divine that she
had entertained it rather for Chad than for herself, and that, as the
young man had lacked the chance to enlighten her, she had had to
go on with it, he meanwhile mistaking her motive.

He was rather glad, none the less, that they had in point of fact
not parted at the Cheval Blanc, that he had not been reduced to
giving them his blessing for an idyllic retreat down the river. He
had had in the actual case to make believe more than he liked, but
this was nothing, it struck him, to what the other event would have
required. Could he, literally, quite have faced the other event?
Would he have been capable of making the best of it with them?
This was what he was trying to do now; but with the advantage of
his being able to give more time to it a good deal counteracted by
his sense of what, over and above the central fact itself, he had to
swallow. It was the quantity of make-believe involved, and so
vividly exemplified, that most disagreed with his spiritual stomach.
He moved, however, from the consideration of that quantity—to
say nothing of the consciousness of that organ—back to the other
feature of the show, the deep, deep truth of the intimacy revealed.
That was what, in his vain vigil, he oftenest reverted to: intimacy,
at such a point, was *like* that—and what in the world else would
one have wished it to be like? It was all very well for him to feel
the pity of its being so much like lying; he almost blushed, in the

dark, for the way he had dressed the possibility in vagueness, as a little girl might have dressed her doll. He had made them—and by no fault of their own—momentarily pull it for him, the possibility, out of this vagueness; and must he not therefore take it now as they had had simply, with whatever thin attenuations, to give it to him? The very question, it may be added, made him feel lonely and cold. There was the element of the awkward all round, but Chad and Mme. de Vionnet had at least the comfort that they could talk it over together. With whom could *he* talk of such things?—unless indeed always, at almost any stage, with Maria? He foresaw that Miss Gostrey would come again into requisition on the morrow: though it was not to be denied that he was already a little afraid of her "What on earth—that's what I want to know now—had you then supposed?" He recognized at last that he had really been trying, all along, to suppose nothing. Verily, verily, his labor had been lost. He found himself supposing everything.

PART TWELFTH

STRETHER couldn't have said he had during the previous hours definitely expected it; yet when, later on, that morning—though no later indeed than for his coming forth at ten o'clock—he saw the concierge produce, on his approach, a *petit bleu* delivered since his letters had been sent up, he recognized the appearance as the first symptom of a sequel. He then knew he had been thinking of some early sign from Chad as more likely, after all. than not; and this would be, precisely, the early sign. He took it so for granted that he opened the *petit bleu* just where he had stopped, in the pleasant cool draught of the *porte-cochère*—only curious to see where the young man would, at such a juncture, break out. His curiosity, however, was more than gratified; the small missive, whose gummed edge he had detached without attention to the address, not being from the young man at all, but from the person whom the case gave him, on the spot, as still more worth while. Worth while or not, he went round to the nearest telegraph-office, the big one on the Boulevard, with a directness that almost confessed to a fear of the danger of delay. He might have been thinking that if he didn't go before he *could* think, he wouldn't perhaps go at all. He at any rate kept, in the lower side-pocket of his morning coat, a very deliberate hand on his blue missive, crumpling it up rather tenderly than harshly. He wrote a reply, on the Boulevard, also in the form of a *petit bleu* —which was quickly done, under pressure of the place, inasmuch as, like Mme. de Vionnet's own communication, it consisted of the fewest words. She had asked him if he could do her the very great kindness of coming to see her that evening at half-past nine, and he answered, as if nothing were easier, that he would present himself at the hour she named. She had added a line of postscript, to the effect that she would come to him elsewhere and at his own hour if he preferred; but he took no notice of this, feeling that if he saw her at all half the value of it would be in seeing her where he had already seen her best. He mightn't see her at all; that was one of the reflections he made after writing and before he dropped his closed card into the box; he mightn't see any one at all any more at all; he might make an end as well now as ever, leaving things as they were, since he was doubtless not to leave them better, and taking his way home so far as should appear that a home remained to him. This alternative was for a few minutes so sharp that if he at last did deposit his missive it was perhaps because the pressure of the place had an effect.

There was none other, however, than the common and constant pressure, familiar to our friend under the rubric of *Postes et Télégraphes*—the something in the air of these establishments; the vibration of the vast, strange life of the town, the influence of the types, the performers concocting their messages; the little prompt Paris women, arranging, pretexting goodness knew what, driving the dreadful needle-pointed public pen at the dreadful sand-strewn public table: implements that symbolized for Strether's too interpretative innocence something more acute in manners, more sinister in morals, more fierce in the national life. After he had put in his paper, he had ranged himself, he was really amused to think, on the side of the fierce, the sinister, the acute. He was carrying on a correspondence, across the great city, quite in the key of the *Postes et Télégraphes* in general; and it was fairly as if the acceptance of that fact had come from something in his state that sorted with the occupation of his neighbors. He was mixed up with the typical tale of Paris, and so were they, poor things—how could they all together help being? They were no worse than he, in short, and he no worse than they—if, queerly enough, no better; and at all events he had settled his hash, so that he went out to begin, from that moment, his day of waiting. The great settlement was, as he felt, in his preference for seeing his correspondent in her own best conditions. *That* was part of the typical tale, the part most significant in respect to himself. He liked the place she lived in, the picture that, each time, squared itself, large and high and clear, around her: every occasion of seeing it was a pleasure of a different shade. Yet what, precisely, was he doing with shades of pleasure now, and why hadn't he, properly and logically, compelled her to commit herself to whatever of disadvantage and penalty the situation might throw up? He might have proposed, as for Sarah Pocock, the cold hospitality of his own *salon de lecture,* in which the chill of Sarah's visit seemed still to abide and shades of pleasure were dim; he might have suggested a stone bench in the dusty Tuileries or a penny chair at the back part of the Champs Élysées. These things would have been a trifle stern, and sternness alone now wouldn't be sinister. An instinct in him cast about for some form of discipline in which they might meet—some awkwardness they would suffer from, some danger, or at least some grave inconvenience, they would incur. This would give a sense—which the spirit required, rather ached and sighed in the absence of—that somebody was paying something somewhere and somehow, that they were at least not all floating together on the silver stream of impunity. Just, instead of that, to go and see her late in the evening, as if, for all the world—well, as if he were as much in the swim as anybody else: this had as little as possible in common with the disciplinary form.

Even when he had felt that objection melt away, however, the practical difference was small; the long stretch of his interval took the color it would, and if he lived on thus with the sinister from hour to hour it proved an easier thing than one might have supposed in advance. He reverted in thought to his old tradition, the one he had been brought up on and which even so many years of life had but little worn away; the notion that the state of the wrongdoer, or at least this person's happiness, presented some special difficulty. What struck him now, rather, was the ease of it—for nothing, in truth, appeared easier. It was an ease he himself fairly tasted of for the rest of the day; giving himself quite up; not so much as trying to dress it out, in any particular whatever, as a difficulty; not, after all, going to see Maria—which would have been, in a manner, a result of such dressing; only idling, lounging, smoking, sitting in the shade, drinking lemonade and consuming ices. The day had turned to heat and eventual thunder, and he now and again went back to his hotel to find that Chad had not been there. He had not yet struck himself, since leaving Woollett, so much as a loafer, though there had been times when he believed himself touching bottom. This was a deeper depth than any, and with no foresight, scarcely with a care, as to what he should bring up. He almost wondered if he didn't *look* demoralized and disreputable; he had the fanciful vision, as he sat and smoked, of some accidental, some motived, return of the Pococks, who would be passing along the Boulevard and would catch this view of him. They would have distinctly, on his appearance, every ground for scandal. But fate failed to administer even *that* sternness; the Pococks never passed and Chad made no sign. Strether meanwhile continued to hold off from Miss Gostrey, keeping her till to-morrow; so that by evening his irresponsibility, his impunity, his luxury, had become—there was no other word for them—immense.

Between nine and ten, at last, in the high, clear picture—he was moving in these days, as in a gallery, from clever canvas to clever canvas—he drew a long breath: it was so presented to him from the first that the spell of his luxury wouldn't be broken. He wouldn't have, that is, to become responsible—this was, admirably, in the air: she had sent for him, precisely, to let him feel it, so that he might go on with the comfort—comfort already established, hadn't it been?—of regarding his ordeal, the ordeal of the weeks of Sarah's stay and of their climax, as safely traversed and left behind him. Didn't she just wish to assure him that *she* now took it all and so kept it; that he was absolutely not to worry any more, was only to rest on his laurels and continue generously to help her? The light in her beautiful, formal room was dim, though it would do, as everything would always do; the hot night had kept out lamps, but there was a pair of clusters of candles that glimmered over the chimney-piece like the tall tapers of an altar. The windows were all open, their redundant hangings swaying a little, and he heard once more, from the empty court, the small plash of the fountain. From beyond this, and as from a great distance—beyond the court, beyond the *corps de logis* forming the front—came, as if excited and exciting, the vague voice of Paris. Strether had all along been subject to sudden gusts of fancy in connection with such matters as these—odd starts of the historic sense, suppositions and divinations with no warrant but their intensity. Thus and so, on the eve of the great recorded dates, the days and nights of revolution, the sounds had come in, the omens, the beginnings broken out. They were the smell of revolution, the smell of the public temper—or perhaps simply the smell of blood.

It was at present queer beyond words, "subtle," he would have risked saying, that such suggestions should keep crossing the scene; but it was doubtless the effect of the thunder in the air, which had hung about all day without release. His hostess was dressed as for thunderous times, and it fell in with the kind of imagination **we** have just attributed to him that she should be in simplest, coolest white, of a character so old-fashioned, if he were not mistaken, that Madame Roland, on the scaffold, must have worn something like it. This effect was enhanced by a small black fichu, or scarf, of crape or gauze, disposed quaintly round her bosom and now completing, **as** by a mystic touch, the pathetic, the noble analogy. Poor Strether in fact scarce knew what analogy was evoked for him as the charming woman, receiving him and making him, as she could do such things, at once familiarly and gravely welcome, moved over her great room with her image almost repeated in its polished floor, which had been fully bared for summer. The associations of the place, all felt again; the gleam here and there, in the subdued light, of glass and gilt and parquet, with the quietness of her own note as the centre—these things were at first as delicate as if they had been ghostly, and he was sure in a moment that, whatever he should find he had come for, it wouldn't be for an impression that had previously failed him. That conviction came to him at the outset, and, seeming singularly to simplify, certified to him that the objects about would help him, would really help them both. No, he might never see them again—this was only too probably the last time; and he should certainly see nothing in the least degree like them. He should soon be going to where such things were not, and it would be a small mercy for memory, for fancy, to have, in that stress, a loaf on the shelf. He knew in advance he should look back on the perception actually sharpest with him as on the view of something old, old, old, the oldest thing he had ever personally touched; and he also knew, even while he took his companion in as the feature among features, that memory and fancy couldn't help being enlisted for her. She might intend what she would, but this was beyond anything she could intend, with things from far back—tyrannies of history, facts of type, values, as the painters said, of expression—all working for her and giving her the supreme chance, **the** chance of the happy, the really luxurious few, the chance, on **a** great occasion, to be natural and simple. She had never, with him, been more so; or if it was the perfection of art it would never—and that came to the same thing—be proved against her.

What was truly wonderful was her way of differing so from time to time without detriment to her simplicity. Caprices, he was sure she felt, were before anything else bad manners, and that judgment in her was by itself a thing making more for safety of intercourse than anything that, in his various own past intercourses, he had had to reckon on. If therefore her presence was now quite other than the one she had shown him the night before, there was nothing of violence in the change—it was all harmony and reason. It gave him a mild, deep person, whereas he had had, on the occasion to which their interview was a direct reference, a person committed to movement and surface and abounding in them; but she was, in either character, more remarkable for nothing than for her bridging of intervals, and this now fell in with what he understood he was to leave to her. The only thing was that, if he was to leave it *all* to her, why, exactly, had she sent for him? He had had, vaguely, in advance, his explanation, his view of the probability of her wishing to set something right, to deal in some way with the fraud so lately practised on his presumed credulity. Would she attempt to carry it further, or would she blot it out? Would she throw over it some more or less happy color, or would she do nothing about it at all? He perceived soon enough at least that, however reasonable she might be, she was not vulgarly confused, and it herewith pressed upon him that their eminent "lie," Chad's and hers, was simply, after all, such an inevitable tribute to good taste as he couldn't have wished them not to render. Away from them, during his vigil, he had seemed to wince at the amount of comedy involved; whereas in his present posture he could only ask himself how he should enjoy any attempt from her to take the comedy back. He shouldn't enjoy it at all; but, once more and yet once more, he could trust her. That is he could trust her to make deception right. As she presented things the ugliness—goodness knew why—went out of them; none the less too that she could present them, with an art of her own, by not so much as touching them. She let the matter, at all events, lie where it was—where the previous twenty-four hours had placed it; appearing merely to circle about it respectfully, tenderly, almost piously, while she took up another question.

She knew she hadn't really thrown dust in his eyes; this, the previous night, before they separated, had practically passed between them; and, as she had sent for him to see what the difference thus made for him might amount to, so he was conscious at the end of five minutes that he had been tried and tested. She had settled with Chad after he left them that she would, for her satisfaction, assure herself of this quantity, and Chad had, as usual, let her have her way. Chad was always letting people have their way when he felt that it would somehow turn his wheel for him; it somehow always did turn his wheel. Strether felt, oddly enough, before these facts, freshly and consentingly passive; they again so rubbed it into him that the couple thus fixing his attention were intimate, that his intervention had absolutely aided and intensified their intimacy, and that, in fine, he must accept the consequence of that. He had absolutely become, himself, with his perceptions and his mistakes, his concessions and his reserves, the funny mixture, as it must seem to them, of his braveries and his fears, the general spectacle of his art and his innocence, almost an added link and certainly a common, priceless ground for them to meet upon. It was as if he had been hearing their very tone when she brought out a reference that was comparatively straight. " The last twice that you've been here, you know, I never asked you," she said with an abrupt transition—they had been pretending, before this, to talk simply of the charm of the day before and of the interest of the country they had seen. The effort was confessedly vain; not for such talk had she invited him; and her impatient reminder was of their having done for it all the needful on his coming to her after Sarah's flight. What she hadn't asked him then was to state to her where and how he stood for her; she had been resting on Chad's report of their midnight hour together in the Boulevard Malesherbes. The thing, therefore, she at present desired was ushered in by this recall of the two occasions on which, disinterested and merciful, she had not worried him. To-night, truly, she *would* worry him, and this was her appeal to him to let her risk it. He was not to mind if she bored him a little: she had behaved, after all—hadn't she?—so awfully, awfully well.

XXXIII

" Oh, you're all right, you're all right," he almost impatiently declared; his impatience being moreover not for her pressure, but for
her scruple. More and more distinct to him was the tune to which
she would have had the matter out with Chad; more and more vivid
for him the idea that she had been nervous as to what he might be
able to " stand." Yes, it had been a question if he had " stood"
what the scene on the river had given him, and, though the young
man had doubtless opined in favor of his recuperation, her own last
word must have been that she should feel easier in seeing for herself. That was it, unmistakably; she *was* seeing for herself. What
he could stand was thus, in these moments, in the balance for
Strether, who reflected, as he became fully aware of it, that he must
properly brace himself. He wanted fully to appear to stand all he
might; and there was a certain command of the situation for him
in this very wish not to look too much at sea. She was ready with
everything, but so, sufficiently, was he; that is he was at one point
the more prepared of the two, inasmuch as, for all her cleverness, she
couldn't produce on the spot—and it was surprising—an account of
the motive of her note. He had the advantage that his pronouncing
her " all right " gave him for an inquiry. " May I ask, delighted as
I've been to come, if you've wished to say something special?" He
spoke as if she might have seen he had been waiting for it—not indeed with discomfort, but with natural interest. Then he saw that
she was a little taken aback, was even surprised herself at the detail
she had neglected—the only one ever yet; having somehow assumed
he would know, would recognize, would leave some things not to be
said. She looked at him, however, an instant as if to convey that if
he wanted them *all*—!

" Selfish and vulgar—that's what I must seem to you. You've
done everything for me, and here I am as if I were asking for more.

But it isn't," she went on, "because I'm afraid—though I *am* of course afraid, as a woman in my position always is. I mean it isn't because one lives in terror—it isn't because of *that* one is selfish, for I'm ready to give you my word to-night that I don't care; don't care what still may happen and what I may lose. I don't ask you to raise your little finger for me again, nor do I wish so much as to mention to you what we've talked of before, either my danger or my safety, or his mother, or his sister, or the girl he may marry, or the fortune he may make, or miss, or the right or the wrong, of any kind, he may do. If after the help one has had from you one can't either take care of one's self or simply hold one's tongue, one must renounce all claim to be an object of interest. It's in the name of what I *do* care about that I've tried still to keep hold of you. How can I be indifferent," she asked, " to how I appear to you?" And as he found himself unable immediately to say: " Why, if you're going, *need* you, after all? Is it impossible you should stay on—so that one mayn't lose you?"

" Impossible I should live with you here instead of going home?"

" Not 'with' us, if you object to that, but near enough to us, somewhere, for us to see you—well," she beautifully brought out, " when we feel we *must.* How shall we not sometimes feel it? I've wanted to see you often when I couldn't," she pursued, " all these last weeks. How sha'n't I then miss you now, with the sense of your being gone forever?" Then as if the straightness of this appeal, taking him unprepared, had visibly left him wondering: "Where *is* your 'home'; moreover, now—what has become of it? I've made a change in your life, I know I have; I've upset everything in your mind as well; in your sense of—what shall I call it?— all the decencies and possibilities. It gives me a kind of detestation—" She pulled up short.

Oh, but he wanted to hear. " Detestation of what?"

" Of everything—of life."

" Ah, that's too much," he laughed—" or too little!"

" Too little, precisely "—she was eager. " What I hate is myself —when I think that one has to take so much, to be happy, out of the lives of others, and that one isn't happy even then. One does it to cheat one's self and to stop one's mouth—but that is only, at the best, for a little. The wretched self is always there, always making one somehow a fresh anxiety. What it comes to is that it's not, that it's never, a happiness, any happiness at all, to *take*. The only safe thing is to give. It's what plays you least false." Interesting, touching, strikingly sincere as she let these things come from her, she yet puzzled and troubled him—so fine was the quaver of her quietness. He felt what he had felt before with her, that there was always more behind what she showed, and more and more again behind that. "You know so, at least," she added, "where you are!"

"*You* ought to know it indeed then; for isn't what you've been giving exactly what has brought us together this way? You've been making, as I've so fully let you know I've felt," Strether said, "the most precious present I've ever seen made, and if you can't sit down peacefully on that performance, you *are,* no doubt, born to torment yourself. But you ought," he wound up, "to be easy."

"And not trouble you any more, no doubt—not thrust on you even the wonder and the beauty of what I've done; only let you regard our business as over, and well over, and see you depart in a peace that matches my own! No doubt, no doubt, no doubt," she nervously repeated—"all the more that I don't really pretend I believe you couldn't, for yourself, *not* have done what you have. I don't pretend you feel yourself victimized, for this evidently is the way you live, and it's what—we're agreed—is the best way. Yes, as you say," she continued after a moment, "I ought to be easy and rest on my work. Well then, here I am, doing so. I *am* easy. You will have it for your last impression. When is it you say you go?" she asked with a quick change.

He took some time to reply—his last impression was, more and more, so mixed a one. It produced in him a vague disappointment, a drop that was deeper even than the fall of his elation the previous night. The good of what he had done, if he had done so much, wasn't there to enliven him quite to the point that would have been ideal for a grand gay finale. Women were thus endlessly absorbent, and to deal with them was to walk on water. What was at bottom the matter with her, embroider as she might and disclaim as she might—what was at bottom the matter with her was simply Chad himself. It was of Chad she was, after all, renewedly afraid; the strange strength of her passion was the very strength of her fear;

she clung to *him,* Lambert Strether, as to a source of safety she had tested, and, generous, graceful, truthful as she might try to be, exquisite as she was, she dreaded the term of his being within reach. With this sharpest perception yet, it was like a chill in the air to him, it was almost appalling, that a creature so fine could be, by mysterious forces, a creature so exploited. For, at the end of all things, they *were* mysterious: she had but made Chad what he was— so why could she think she had made him infinite? She had made him better, she had made him best, she had made him anything one would; but it came to our friend with supreme queerness that he was none the less only Chad. Strether had the sense that *he,* a little, had made him too; his high appreciation had, as it were, consecrated her work. The work, however admirable, was nevertheless of the strict human order, and in short it was marvellous that the companion of mere earthly joys, of comforts, aberrations—however one classed them—within the common experience, should be so transcendently prized. It might have made Strether hot or shy, as such secrets of others, brought home, sometimes do make us; but he was held there by something so hard that it was fairly grim. This was not the discomposure of last night; that had quite passed— such discomposures were a detail; the real coercion was to see a man ineffably adored. There it was again—it took women, it took women; if to deal with them was to walk on water, what wonder that the water rose? And it had never, surely, risen higher than round this woman. He presently found himself taking a long look from her, and the next thing he knew he had uttered all his thought. "You're afraid for your life!"

It drew out her long look, and he soon enough saw why. A spasm came into her face, the tears she had already been unable to hide overflowed at first in silence, and then, as the sound suddenly comes from a child, quickened to gasps, to sobs. She sat and covered her face with her hands, giving up all attempt at a manner. "It's how you see me, it's how you see me"—she caught her breath with it— "and it's as I *am,* and as I must take myself, and of course it's no matter." Her emotion was at first so incoherent that he could only stand there at a loss, stand with his sense of having upset her, though of having done it by the truth. He had to listen to her in a silence that he made no immediate effort to attenuate, feeling her doubly woful amid all her dim, diffused elegance; consenting to it as he had consented to the rest, and even conscious of some vague inward irony in the presence of such a fine, free range of bliss and bale. He couldn't say it was *not* no matter; for he was serving her to the end, he now knew, anyway—quite as if what he thought of her had nothing to do with it. It was actually moreover as if he didn't think of her at all, as if he could think of nothing but the passion, mature, abysmal, pitiful, she represented, and the possibilities she betrayed. She was older for him to-night, visibly less exempt from the touch of time; but she was as much as ever the finest and subtlest creature, the happiest apparition, it had been given him, in all his years, to meet; and yet he could see her there as vulgarly troubled, in very truth, as a maidservant crying for her young man. The only thing was that she judged herself as the maidservant wouldn't; the weakness of which wisdom too, the dishonor of which judgment, seemed but to sink her lower. Her collapse, however, no doubt, was briefer and she had in a manner recovered herself before he intervened. "Of course, I'm afraid for my life. But that's nothing. It isn't that."

He was silent a little longer, as if thinking what it might be. "There's something I have in mind that I can still do."

But she threw off at last, with a sharp, sad headshake, drying her eyes, what he could still do. "I don't care for that. Of course, as I've said, you're acting, in your wonderful way, for yourself; and what's for yourself is no more my business—though I may reach out unholy hands so clumsily to touch it—than if it were something in Timbuctoo. It's only that you don't snub me, as you've had fifty chances to do—it's only your beautiful patience that makes one forget one's manners. In spite of your patience, all the same," she went on, "you'd do anything rather than be with us here, even if that were possible. You'd do everything for us but be mixed up with us—which is a statement you can easily answer to the advantage of your own manners. You can say 'What's the use of talking of things that at the best are impossible?' What *is*, of course, the use? It's only my little madness. You'd talk if you were tormented. And I don't mean now about *him*. Oh, for him—!" Positively, strangely, bitterly, as it seemed to Strether, she gave "him," for the moment, away. "You don't care what I think of you; but I happen to care what you think of me. And what you *might*," she added. " What you perhaps even did."

He gained time. " What I did—?"

" Did think before. Before this. *Didn't* you think—?"

But he had already stopped her. " I didn't think anything. I never think a step further than I'm obliged to."

" That's perfectly false, I believe," she returned—" except that you may, no doubt, often pull up when things become *too* ugly; or even, I'll say, to save you a protest, too beautiful. At any rate, even so far as it's true, we've thrust on you appearances that you've had to see and that have therefore made your obligation. Ugly or beautiful—it doesn't matter what we call them—you were getting on without them, and that's where we're detestable. We bore you— that's where we are. And we may well—for what we've cost you. All you can do *now* is not to think at all. And I who should have liked to seem to you—well, sublime!"

He could only, after a moment, re-echo Miss Barrace. " You're wonderful!"

" I'm old and abject and hideous "—she went on as without hearing him. " Abject above all. Or old above all. It's when one's old that it's worst. I don't care what becomes of it—let what *will;* there it is. It's a doom—I know it; you can't see it more than I do myself. Things have to happen as they will." With which she came back again to what, face to face with him, had so quite broken down. " Of course you wouldn't, even if possible, and no matter what may happen to you, be near us. But think of me, think of me—!" She exhaled it into air.

He took refuge in repeating something he had already said and that she had made nothing of. " There's something I believe I can still do. And he put out his hand for good-by.

She again made nothing of it; she went on with her insistence. " That won't help you. There's nothing to help you."

" Well, it may help *you*," he said.

She shook her head. " There's not a grain of certainty in my future; for the only certainty is that I shall be the loser in the end."

She hadn't taken his hand, but she moved with him to the door " That's cheerful." he laughed, " for your benefactor!"

"What's cheerful for *me*," she replied, "is that we might, you and I, have been friends. That's it—that's it. You see how, as I say, I want everything. I've wanted you too."

"Ah, but you've *had* me!" he declared, at the door, with an emphasis that made an end.

XXXIV

His purpose had been to see Chad the next day, and he had prefigured seeing him by an early call; having, in general, never stood
on ceremony in respect to visits in the Boulevard Malesherbes. It
had been more often natural for him to go there than for Chad to
come to the small hotel, the attractions of which were scant; yet it
nevertheless, at present, at the eleventh hour, did suggest itself to
Strether to begin by giving the young man a chance. It struck him
that, in the inevitable course, Chad would be " round," as Waymarsh used to say—Waymarsh who already, somehow, seemed long
ago. He hadn't come the day before, because it had been arranged
between them that Mme. de Vionnet should see their friend first;
but now that this passage had taken place he would present himself, and their friend wouldn't have long to wait. Strether assumed, he became aware, on this reasoning, that the interesting
parties to the arrangement would have met betimes, and that the
more interesting of the two—as she was after all—would have communicated to the other the issue of her appeal. Chad would know
without delay that his mother's messenger had been with her, and,
though it was perhaps not quite easy to see how she could qualify
what had occurred, he would at least have been sufficiently advised
to feel he could go on. The day, however, brought, early or late,
no word from him, and Strether felt, as a result of this, that a
change had practically come over their intercourse. It was perhaps
a premature judgment; or it only meant perhaps—how could he
tell?—that the wonderful pair he protected had taken up again together the excursion he had accidentally checked. They might have
gone back to the country, and gone back but with a long breath
drawn; that indeed would best mark Chad's sense that reprobation
had not rewarded Mme. de Vionnet's request for an interview. At
the end of the twenty-four hours, at the end of the forty-eight, there

was still no overture; so that Strether filled up the time, as he had so often filled it before, by going to see Miss Gostrey.

He proposed amusements to her; he felt expert now in proposing amusements; and he had thus, for several days, an odd sense of leading her about Paris, of driving her in the Bois, of showing her the penny steamboats—those from which the breeze of the Seine was to be best enjoyed—that might have belonged to a kindly uncle doing the honors of the capital to an intelligent niece from the country. He found means even to take her to shops she didn't know, or that she pretended she didn't; while she, on her side, was, like the country maiden, all passive, modest and grateful—going in fact so far as to emulate rusticity in occasional fatigues and bewilderments. Strether described these vague proceedings to himself, described them even to her, as a happy interlude; the sign of which was that the companions said for the time no further word about the matter they had talked of to satiety. He proclaimed satiety at the outset, and she quickly took the hint, as docile both in this and in everything else as the intelligent, obedient niece. He told her as yet nothing of his late adventure—for as an adventure it now ranked with him; he pushed the whole business temporarily aside and found his interest in the fact of her beautiful assent. She left questions unasked—she who for so long had been all questions; she gave herself up to him with an understanding of which mere mute gentleness might have seemed the sufficient expression. She knew his sense of his situation had taken still another step—of that he was quite aware; but she conveyed that, whatever had thus happened for him, it was thrown into the shade by what was happening for herself. This—though it mightn't to a detached spirit have seemed much— was the major interest, and she met it with a new directness of response, measuring it from hour to hour with her grave hush of acceptance. Touched as he had so often been by her before, he was, for his part too, touched afresh; all the more that, though he could be duly aware of the principle of his own mood, he couldn't be equally so of the principle of hers. He knew, that is, in a manner— knew roughly and resignedly—what he himself was hatching; whereas he had to take the chance of what he called to himself Maria's calculations. It was all he needed that she liked him enough for what they were doing, and even should they do a good deal more would still like him enough for that; the essential freshness of a relation so simple was a cool bath to the soreness produced by other relations. These others appeared to him now horribly complex; they bristled with fine points, points all unimaginable beforehand, points that pricked and drew blood; a fact that gave to an hour with his present friend on a *bateau-mouche,* or in the afternoon shade of the Champs Elysées, something of the innocent pleasure of handling rounded ivory. His relation with Chad personally—from the moment he had got his point of view—had been of the simplest; yet this also struck him as bristling after a third and a fourth blank day had passed. It was as if, at last, however, his care for such indications had dropped; there came a fifth blank day, and he ceased to inquire or to heed.

They now took on to his fancy, Miss Gostrey and he, the image of the Babes in the Wood; they could trust the merciful elements to let them continue at peace. He had been great already, as he knew, at postponements; but he had only to get afresh into the rhythm of one to feel its fine attraction. It amused him to say to himself that he might, for all the world, have been going to die—die resignedly; the scene was filled for him with so deep a death-bed hush, so melancholy a charm. That meant the postponement of everything else—which made so for the quiet lapse of life; and the postponement in especial of the reckoning to come—unless indeed the reckoning to come were to be one and the same thing with extinction. It faced him, the reckoning, over the shoulder of much interposing experience—which also faced him; and one would float to it, doubtless, duly, through these caverns of Kublai Khan. It was really behind everything; it hadn't merged in what he had done; his final appreciation of what he had done—his appreciation on the spot—would provide it with its main sharpness. The spot, so focussed, was of course Woollett, and he was to see, at the best, what Woollett would be with everything there changed for him. Wouldn't *that* revelation practically amount to the wind-up of his career? Well, the summer's end would show; his suspense had meanwhile exactly the sweetness of vain delay; and he had with it, we should mention, other pastimes than Maria's company—plenty of separate musings in which his luxury failed him but at one point. He was well in port, the outer sea behind him, and it was only a matter of getting ashore. There was a question that came and went for him, however, as he rested against the side of his ship, and it was a little to get rid of the obsession that he prolonged his hours with Miss Gostrey. It was a question about himself, but it could only be settled by seeing Chad again; it was indeed his principal reason for wanting to see Chad. After that it wouldn't signify—it was a ghost that certain words would easily lay to rest. Only the young man must be there to take the words. Once they were taken he wouldn't have a question left; none, that is, in connection with this particular affair. It wouldn't then matter even to himself that he might now have been guilty of speaking *because* of what he had forfeited. That was the refinement of his supreme scruple—he wished so to leave what he had forfeited out of account. He wished not to do anything because he had missed something else, because he was sore or sorry or impoverished, because he was maltreated or desperate; he wished to do everything because he was lucid and quiet, just the same for himself on all essential points as he had ever been. Thus it was that, while he virtually hung about for Chad, he kept mutely putting it, "You've been chucked, old boy; but what has that to do with it?" It would have sickened him to feel vindictive.

These tints of feeling indeed were doubtless but the iridescence of his idleness, and they were presently lost in a new light from Maria. She had a fresh fact for him before the week was out, and she practically met him with it on his appearing one night. He had not on this day seen her, but had planned presenting himself in due course to ask her to dine with him somewhere out of doors, on one of the terraces, in one of the gardens, in which the Paris of summer abounded. It had then come on to rain, so that, disconcerted, he changed his mind; dining alone at home, a little stuffily and stupidly, and waiting on her afterwards to make up his loss. He was sure within a minute that something had happened; it was so in the air of the rich little room that he had scarcely to name his thought. Softly lighted, the whole color of the place, with its vague values, was in cool fusion—an effect that made the visitor stand for a little agaze. It was as if in doing so now he had felt a recent presence—his recognition of the passage of which his hostess in turn divined. She had scarcely to say it—"Yes, she has been

410

here, and this time I received her." It was not till a minute later that she added: "There being, as I understand you, no reason *now—!*"

"None for your refusing?"

"No—if you've done what you've had to do."

"I've certainly so far done it," Strether said, "as that you needn't fear the effect, or the appearance, of coming between us. There's nothing between us now but what we ourselves have put there, and not an inch of room for anything else whatever. Therefore you're only beautifully *with* us as always—though doubtless now, if she has talked to you, rather more with us than less. Of course if she came," he added, "it was to talk to you."

"It was to talk to me," Maria returned; on which he was further sure that she was practically in possession of what he himself had not yet told her. He was even sure she was in possession of things he himself couldn't have told; for the consciousness of them was now all in her face and accompanied there with a shade of sadness that marked in her the close of all uncertainties. It came out for him more than ever yet that she had had from the first a knowledge she believed him not to have had, a knowledge the sharp acquisition of which might be destined to make a difference for him. The difference for him might not inconceivably be an arrest of his independence and a change in his attitude—in other words, a revulsion in favor of the principles of Woollett. She had really prefigured the possibility of a shock that would send him swinging back to Mrs. Newsome. He had not, it was true, week after week, shown signs of receiving it, but the possibility had been none the less in the air. What Maria, accordingly, had had now to take in was that the shock had descended, and that he hadn't, all the same, swung back. He had grown clear, in a flash, on a point long since settled for herself; but no reapproximation to Mrs. Newsome had occurred in consequence. Mme. de Vionnet had by her visit held up the torch to these truths, and what now lingered in poor Maria's face was the somewhat smoky light of the scene between them. If the light, however, was not, as we have hinted, the glow of joy, the reasons for this also were perhaps discernible to Strether even through the blur cast over them by his natural modesty. She had held herself for months with a firm hand; she had not interfered on any chance

—and chances were specious enough—that she might interfere to her profit. She had turned her back on the dream that Mrs. Newsome's rupture, their friend's forfeiture—the engagement, the relation itself, broken beyond all mending—might furnish forth her advantage; and, to stay her hand from promoting these things, she had, on private, difficult, but rigid, lines, played strictly fair. She couldn't therefore but feel that, though, as the end of all, the facts in question had been stoutly confirmed, her ground for personal, for what might have been called interested, elation remained rather vague. Strether might easily have made out that she had been asking herself, in the hours she had just sat through, if there were still for her, or were only not, a fair shade of uncertainty. Let us hasten to add, however, that what he at first made out on this occasion he also at first kept to himself. He only asked what in particular Mme. de Vionnet had come for; and as to this his companion was ready.

" She wants tidings of Mr. Newsome, whom she appears not to have seen for some days."

" Then she has not been away with him again?"

" She seemed to think," Maria answered, " that he might have gone away with *you*."

" And did you tell her I know nothing of him?"

She had her indulgent headshake. " I've known nothing of what you know. I could only tell her I would ask you."

" Then I've not seen him for a week—and of course I've wondered." His wonderment showed at this moment as sharper, but he presently went on. " Still, I dare say I can put my hand on him. Did she strike you," he asked, " as anxious?"

" She's always anxious."

" After all I've done for her?" And he had one of the last flickers of his occasional mild mirth. " To think that that was just what I came out to prevent!"

She took it up but to reply. " You don't regard him then as safe?"

" I was just going to ask you how, in that respect, you regard Mme. de Vionnet."

She looked at him a little. " What woman was *ever* safe? She told me," she added—and it was as if at the touch of the connec-

412

tion—" of your extraordinary meeting in the country. After that *à quoi se fier?*"

" It was, as an accident, in all the possible or impossible chapter," Strether conceded, " amazing enough. But still, but still—"

" But still she didn't mind?"

" She doesn't mind anything."

" Well then, as you don't either, we may all sink to rest!"

He appeared to agree with her, but he had his reservation. " I do mind Chad's disappearance."

" Oh, you'll get him back. But now you know," she said, " why I went to Mentone." He had sufficiently let her see that he had by this time gathered things together, but there was nature in her wish to make them clearer still. " I didn't want you to put it to me."

" To put it to you— ?"

" The question of what you were at last—a week ago—to see for yourself. I didn't want to have to lie for her. I felt that to be too much for me. A man of course is always expected to do it—to do it, I mean, for a woman; but not a woman for another woman; unless perhaps on the tit-for-tat principle, as an indirect way of protecting herself. I don't need protection, so that I was free to 'funk' you— simply to dodge your test. The responsibility was too much for me. I gained time, and when I came back the need of a test had blown over."

Strether serenely recovered it. " Yes; when you came back little Bilham had shown me what's expected of a gentleman. Little Bilham had lied like one."

" And like what had you believed him?"

" Well," said Strether, " it was but a technical lie—he classed the attachment as virtuous. That was a view for which there was much to be said—and the virtue came out for me hugely. There was of course a great deal of it. I got it full in the face, and I haven't, you see, done with it yet."

" What I see, what I saw," Maria returned, " is that you dressed up even the virtue. You were wonderful—you were beautiful, as I've had the honor of telling you before; but, if you wish really to know," she sadly confessed, " I never quite knew *where* you were. There were moments," she explained, " when you struck me as grandly cynical; there were others when you struck me as grandly vague."

Her friend considered. "I had phases. I had flights."

"Yes, but things must have a basis."

"A basis seemed to me just what her beauty supplied."

"Her beauty of person?"

"Well, her beauty of everything. The impression she makes. She has such variety, and yet such harmony."

She considered him with one of her deep returns of indulgence—returns out of all proportion to the irritations they flooded over. "You're complete."

"You're always too personal," he good-humoredly said; "but that's precisely how I wondered and wandered."

"If you mean," she went on, "that she was, from the first, for you, the most charming woman in the world, nothing is more simple. Only that was an odd foundation."

"For what I reared on it?"

"For what you didn't!"

"Well, it was all not a fixed quantity. And it had for me—it has still—such elements of strangeness. Her greater age than his, her different world, traditions, associations; her other opportunities, liabilities, standards."

His friend listened with respect to his enumeration of these disparities; then she disposed of them at a stroke. "Those things are nothing when a woman is hit. It's very awful. She was hit."

Strether, on his side, did justice to that plea. "Oh, of course I saw she was hit. That she was hit was what we were busy with; that she was hit was our great affair. But somehow I couldn't think of her as down in the dust. And as put there by *our* little Chad!"

"Yet wasn't 'your' little Chad just your miracle?"

Strether admitted it. "Of course I moved among miracles. It was all phantasmagoric. But the great fact was that so much of it was none of my business—as I saw my business. It isn't even now."

His companion turned away on this, and it might well have been yet again with the sharpness of a fear of how little his philosophy could bring her personally. "I wish *she* could hear you!"

"Mrs. Newsome?"

" No—not Mrs. Newsome; since I understand you that it doesn't matter now what Mrs. Newsome hears. Hasn't she heard everything?"

" Practically—yes." He had thought a moment, but he went on. " You wish Mme. de Vionnet could hear me?"

" Mme. de Vionnet." She had come back to him. " She thinks just the contrary of what you say. That you distinctly judge her."

He turned over the scene as the two women thus placed together for him seemed to give it. " She might have known—!"

" Might have known you don't?" Miss Gostrey asked as he let it drop. " She was sure of it at first," she pursued as he said nothing; " she took it for granted, at least, as any woman in her position would. But after that she changed her mind; she believed you believed—"

" Well?"—he was curious.

" Why, in her sublimity. And that belief had remained with her, I make out, till the accident of the other day opened your eyes. For that it did," said Maria, " open them—"

" She can't help "—he had taken it up—" being aware? No," he mused; " I suppose she thinks of that even yet."

" Then they were closed? There you are! However, if you still see her as the most charming woman in the world, it comes to the same thing. And if you'd like me to tell her that you do still so see her—!" Miss Gostrey, in short, offered herself for service to the end.

It was an offer he could temporarily entertain; but he decided. " She knows perfectly how I see her."

" Not favorably enough, she mentioned to me, to wish ever to see her again. She told me you had taken a final leave of her. She says you've done with her."

" So I have."

Maria had a pause; then she spoke as if for conscience. " She wouldn't have done with you. She feels she has lost you—yet that she might have been better for you."

" Oh, she has been quite good enough!" Strether laughed.

" She thinks you and she might at any rate have been friends."

" We might certainly. That's just "—he continued to laugh— " why I'm going."

It was as if Maria could feel with this then, at last, that she had done her best for each. But she had still an idea. "Shall I tell her that?"

"No. Tell her nothing."

"Very well, then." To which, in the next breath, Miss Gostrey added: "Poor dear thing!"

Her friend wondered; then with raised eyebrows: "Me?"

"Oh, no. Marie de Vionnet."

He accepted the correction, but he wondered still. "Are you so sorry for her as that?"

It made her think a moment—made her even speak with a smile. But she didn't really retract. "I'm sorry for us all!"

XXXV

He was to delay no longer to re-establish communication with Chad, and we have just seen that he had spoken to Miss Gostrey of this intention on hearing from her of the young man's absence. It was not moreover only the assurance so given that prompted him; it was the need of causing his conduct to square with another profession still—the motive he had described to her as his sharpest for now getting away. If he was to get away because of some of the relations involved in staying, the cold attitude toward them might look pedantic in the light of lingering on. He must do both things; he must see Chad, but he must go. The more he thought of the former of these duties the more he felt himself make a subject of insistence of the latter. They were alike intensely present to him as he sat in front of a quiet little café into which he had dropped on quitting Maria's entresol. The rain that had spoiled his evening with her was over; for it was still to him as if his evening *had* been spoiled—though it mightn't have been wholly the rain. It was late when he left the café, yet not too late; he couldn't in any case go straight to bed, and he would walk round by the Boulevard Malesherbes—rather far round—on his way home. Present enough always was the small circumstance that had originally pressed for him the spring of so big a difference—the accident of little Bilham's appearance on the balcony of the mystic troisième at the moment of his first visit, and the effect of it on his sense of what was then before him. He recalled his watch, his wait, and the recognition that had proceeded from the young stranger, that had played frankly into the air and had presently brought him up— things smoothing the way for his first straight step. He had since had occasion, a few times, to pass the house without going in; but he had never passed it without again feeling how it had then spoken to him. He stopped short to-night, on coming to sight of it: it

was as if his last day were oddly copying his first. The windows
of Chad's apartment were open to the balcony—a pair of them
lighted; and a figure that had come out and taken up little Bilham's attitude, a figure whose cigarette-spark he could see, leaned
on the rail and looked down at him. It denoted, however, no reappearance of his younger friend; it quickly defined itself in the
tempered darkness as Chad's more solid shape; so that Chad's was
the attention that, after he had stepped forward into the street and
signalled, he easily engaged; Chad's was the voice that, sounding
into the night with promptness and seemingly with joy, greeted
him and called him up.

That the young man had been visible there in just this position
expressed somehow for Strether that, as Maria Gostrey had reported, he had been absent and silent; and our friend drew breath
on each landing—the lift, at that hour, having ceased to work—
before the implications of the fact. He had been, for a week, intensely away, away to a distance and alone; but he was more back
than ever, and the attitude in which Strether had surprised him
was something more than a return—it was clearly a conscious surrender. He had arrived but an hour before, from London, from
Lucerne, from Homburg, from no matter where—though the visitor's fancy, on the staircase, liked to fill it out; and after a bath,
a talk with Baptiste and a supper of light cold clever French things,
which one could see the remains of there in the circle of the
lamp, pretty and ultra-Parisian, he had come into the air again for
a smoke, was occupied at the moment of Strether's approach in
what might have been called taking up his life afresh. His life,
his life!—Strether paused anew, on the last flight, at this final
rather breathless sense of what Chad's life was doing with Chad's
mother's emissary. It was dragging him, at strange hours, up the
staircases of the rich; it was keeping him out of bed at the end
of long, hot days; it was transforming beyond recognition the simple, subtle, conveniently uniform thing that had anciently passed
with him for a life of his own. Why should it concern him that
Chad was to be fortified in the pleasant practice of smoking on
balconies, of supping on salads, of feeling his special conditions
agreeably reaffirm themselves, of finding reassurance in compari-
sons and contrasts? There was no answer to such a question but

that he was still practically committed—he had perhaps never yet so much known it. It made him feel old, and he would buy his railway-ticket—feeling, no doubt, older—the next day; but he had meanwhile come up four flights, counting the entresol, at midnight and without a lift, for Chad's life. The young man, hearing him by this time, and with Baptiste sent to rest, was already at the door; so that Strether had before him, in full visibility, the cause in which he was laboring and even, with the troisième fairly gained, panting a little.

Chad offered him, as always, a welcome in which the cordial and the formal—so far as the formal was the respectful—handsomely met; and after he had expressed a hope that he would let him put him up for the night Strether was in full possession of the key, as it might have been called, to what had lately happened. If he had just thought of himself as old, Chad was, at sight of him, thinking of him as older: he wanted to put him up for the night just because he was ancient and weary. It could never be said the tenant of these quarters wasn't nice to him; a tenant who, if he might indeed now keep him, was probably prepared to work it all still more thoroughly. Our friend had in fact the impression that, with the minimum of encouragement, Chad would propose to keep him indefinitely; an impression in the lap of which one of his own possibilities seemed to sit. Mme. de Vionnet had wished him to stay—so why didn't that happily fit? He could enshrine himself for the rest of his days in his young host's *chambre d'ami* and draw out these days at his young host's expense: there could scarce be greater logical expression of the countenance he had been moved to give. There was literally a minute—it was strange enough—during which he grasped the idea that as he *was* acting, as he could only act, he was inconsistent. The sign that the inward forces he had obeyed really hung together would be that—in default, always, of another career—he should promote the good cause by mounting guard on it. These things, during his first minutes, came and went; but they were, after all, practically disposed of as soon as he had mentioned his errand. He had come to say good-bye—yet that was only a part; so that from the moment Chad accepted his farewell the question of a more ideal affirmation gave way to something else. He proceeded with the rest of his business.

"You'll be a brute, you know—you'll be guilty of the last infamy—if you ever forsake her."

That, uttered there at the solemn hour, uttered in the place that was full of her influence, was the rest of his business; and when once he had heard himself say it he felt that his message had never before been spoken. It placed his present call immediately on solid ground, and the effect of it was to enable him quite to play with what we have called the key. Chad showed no shade of embarrassment, but had none the less been troubled for him after their meeting in the country; had had fears and doubts on the subject of his comfort. He was disturbed, as it were, only *for* him, and had positively gone away to ease him off, to let him down—if it wasn't indeed, more precisely, to screw him up—the more gently. Seeing him now fairly jaded, he had come, with characteristic good-humor, all the way to meet him, and what Strether thereupon supremely made out was that he would abound for him, to the end, in conscientious assurances. This was what was between them while the visitor remained; so far from having to go over old ground, he found his entertainer keen to agree to everything. It couldn't be put too strongly for him that he would be a brute. "Oh, rather!—if I should do anything of *that* sort. I hope you believe I really feel it."

"I want it," said Strether, "to be my last word of all to you. I can't say more, you know; and I don't see how I can do more, in every way, than I've done."

Chad took this, almost artlessly, as a direct allusion. "You've seen her?"

"Oh yes—to say good-bye. And if I had doubted the truth of what I tell you—"

"She'd have cleared up your doubt?" Chad understood—"rather"—again! It even kept him briefly silent. But he made that up. "She must have been wonderful."

"She *was*." Strether candidly admitted—all of which practically told as a reference to the conditions created by the accident of the previous week.

They appeared for a little to be looking back at it; and that came out still more in what Chad next said. "I don't know what you've really thought, all along; I never did know—for anything,

with you, seemed to be possible. But of course—of course—"
Without confusion, with nothing but indulgence, he broke down,
he pulled up. "After all, you understand. I spoke to you, originally, only as I *had* to speak. There's only one way—isn't there?—
about such things. However," he smiled with a final philosophy.
"I see it's all right."

Strether met his eyes with a sense of multiplying thoughts.
What was it that made him at present, late at night and after
journeys, so renewedly, so substantially young? Strether saw in
a moment what it was—it was that he was younger again than
Mme. de Vionnet. He himself said immediately none of the
things that he was thinking; he said something quite different.
"You *have* really been to a distance?"

"I've been to England." Chad spoke cheerfully and promptly,
but gave no further account of it than to say: "One must sometimes get off."

Strether wanted no more facts—he only wanted to justify, as
it were, his question. "Of course you do as you're free to do.
But I hope, this time, that you didn't go for *me*."

"For very shame at bothering you really too much? My dear
man," Chad laughed, "what *wouldn't* I do for you?"

Strether's easy answer for this was that it was a disposition he
had precisely come to profit by. "Even at the risk of being in
your way I've waited on, you know, for a definite reason."

Chad took it in. "Oh yes—for us to make, if possible, a still
better impression." And he stood there happily exhaling his full
general consciousness. "I'm delighted to gather that you feel
we've made it."

There was a pleasant irony in the words, which his guest, preoccupied and keeping to the point, didn't take up. "If I had my
sense of wanting the rest of the time—the time of their being
still on this side," he continued to explain—"I know now why I
wanted it."

He was as grave, as distinct, as a demonstrator before a blackboard, and Chad continued to face him like an intelligent pupil.
"You wanted to have been put through the whole thing."

Strether again, for a moment, said nothing; he turned his eyes
away, and they lost themselves, through the open window, in the

dusky outer air. "I shall learn from the Bank here where they're now having their letters, and my last word, which I shall write in the morning and which they're expecting as my ultimatum, will so immediately reach them." The light of his plural pronoun was sufficiently reflected in his companion's face as he again met it; and he completed his demonstration. He pursued indeed as if for himself. "Of course I've first to justify what I shall do."

"You're justifying it beautifully!" Chad declared.

"It's not a question of advising you not to go," Strether said, "but of absolutely preventing you, if possible, from so much as thinking of it. Let me accordingly appeal to you by all you hold sacred."

Chad showed a surprise. "What makes you think me capable—?"

"You'd not only be, as I say, a brute; you'd be," his companion went on in the same way, "a criminal of the deepest dye."

Chad gave a sharper look, as if to gauge a possible suspicion. "I don't know what should make you think I'm tired of her."

Strether didn't quite know either, and such impressions, for the imaginative mind, were always too fine, too floating, to produce on the spot their warrant. There was none the less for him, in the very manner of his host's allusion to satiety as a thinkable motive, a slight breath of the ominous. "I feel how much more she can do for you. She hasn't done it all yet. Stay with her at least till she has."

"And leave her *then*?"

Chad had kept smiling, but its effect in Strether was a shade of dryness. "Don't leave her *before*. When you've got all that can be got—I don't say," he added a trifle grimly. "That will be the proper time. But as, for you, from such a woman, there will always be something to be got, my remark's not a wrong to her." Chad let him go on, showing every decent deference, showing perhaps also a candid curiosity for this sharper accent. "I remember you, you know, as you were."

"An awful ass, wasn't I?"

The response was as prompt as if he had pressed a spring; it had a ready abundance at which he even winced; so that he took a moment to meet it. "You certainly then wouldn't have seemed worth all you've let me in for. You've defined yourself better. Your value has quintupled."

" Well then, wouldn't that be enough— ?"

Chad had risked it jocosely, but Strether remained blank.
" Enough ?"

" If one *should* wish to live on one's accumulations ?" After
which, however, as his friend appeared cold to the joke, the young
man as easily dropped it. " Of course I really never forget, night
or day, what I owe her. I owe her everything. I give you my word
of honor," he frankly rang out, " that I'm not a bit tired of her."
Strether, at this, only gave him a stare: the way youth could express itself was again and again a wonder. He meant no harm,
though he might after all be capable of much; yet he spoke of
being " tired " of her almost as he might have spoken of being
tired of roast mutton for dinner. " She has never, for a moment
yet, bored me—never been wanting, as the cleverest women sometimes are, in tact. She has never talked about her tact—as even
they too sometimes talk; but she has always had it. She has never
had it more "—he handsomely made the point—" than just lately."
And he scrupulously went further. " She has never been anything
I could call a burden."

Strether, for a moment, said nothing; then he spoke gravely,
with his shade of dryness deepened. " Oh, if you didn't do her
justice—!"

" I *should* be a beast, eh ?"

Strether devoted no time to saying what he would be; *that,*
visibly, would take them far. If there was nothing for it but to
repeat, however, repetition was no mistake. " You owe her everything—very much more than she can ever owe you. You've in other
words duties to her, of the most positive sort; and I don't see what
other duties—as the others are presented to you—can be held to
go before them."

Chad looked at him with a smile. " And you know of course
about the others, eh ?—since it's you yourself who have done the
presenting."

" Much of it,—yes—and to the best of my ability. But not all
—from the moment your sister took my place."

" She didn't," Chad returned. " Sally took a place, certainly; but
it was never, I saw from the first moment, to be yours. No one
—with us—will ever take yours. It wouldn't be possible."

"Ah, of course," sighed Strether, "I knew it. I believe you're right. No one in the world, I imagine, was ever so portentously solemn. There I am," he added with another sigh, as if weary enough, on occasion, of this truth. "I was made so."

Chad appeared, for a little, to consider the way he was made; he might, for this purpose, have measured him up and down. His conclusion favored the fact. "*You* have never needed any one to make you better. There has never been any one good enough. They *couldn't*," the young man declared.

His friend hesitated. "I beg your pardon. They *have*."

Chad showed, not without amusement, his doubt. "Who then?"

Strether—though a little dimly—smiled at him. "Women—too."

"'Two'?"—Chad stared and laughed. "Oh, I don't believe, for such work, in any more than one! So you're proving too much. And what *is* beastly, at all events," he added, "is losing you."

Strether had set himself in motion for departure, but at this he paused. "Are you afraid?"

"Afraid—?"

"Of doing wrong. I mean away from my eye." Before Chad could speak, however, he had taken himself up. "I *am*, certainly," he laughed, "prodigious."

"Yes, you spoil us for all the stupid—!" This might have been, on Chad's part, in its extreme emphasis, almost too freely extravagant; but it was full, plainly enough, of the intention of comfort. it carried with it a protest against doubt and a promise, positively, of performance. Picking up a hat in the vestibule he came out with his friend, came down-stairs, took his arm, affectionately, as to help and guide him, treating him if not exactly as aged and infirm, yet as a noble eccentric who appealed to tenderness, and keeping on with him, while they walked, to the next corner and the next. "You needn't tell me, you needn't tell me!"—this again as they proceeded, he wished to make Strether feel. What he needn't tell him was now at last, in the geniality of separation, anything at all it concerned him to know. He knew, up to the hilt—that really came over Chad; he understood, felt, recorded his vow; and they lingered on it as they had lingered in their walk to Strether's hotel the night of their first meeting. The latter took, at this hour, all he could get; he had given all he had had to give; he was as depleted as if he had spent his last sou. But there was just one thing for which, before they broke off, Chad seemed disposed slightly to bargain. His companion needn't, as he said, tell him, but he might himself mention that he had been getting some news of the art of advertisement. He came out quite suddenly with this announcement, while Strether wondered if his revived interest were what had taken him, with strange inconsequence, over to London. He appeared at all events to have been looking into the question and had encountered a revelation. Advertising scientifically worked presented itself thus as the great new force. "It really does the thing, you know."

They were face to face under the street-lamp as they had been the first night, and Strether, no doubt, looked blank. "Affects, you mean, the sale of the object advertised?"

"Yes—but affects it extraordinarily; really beyond what one had supposed. I mean of course when it's done as one makes out that, in our roaring age, it *can* be done. I've been finding out a little; though it doubtless doesn't amount to much more than what you originally, so awfully vividly—and all, very nearly, that first night —put before me. It's an art like another, and infinite like all the arts." He went on as if for the joke of it—almost as if his friend's face amused him. "In the hands, naturally, of a master. The right man must take hold. With the right man to work it *c'est un monde.*"

Strether had watched him quite as if, there on the pavement, without a pretext, he had begun to dance a fancy step. "Is what you're thinking of that you yourself, in the case you have in mind, would be the right man?"

Chad had thrown back his light coat and thrust each of his thumbs into an armhole of his waistcoat; in which position his fingers played up and down. "Why, what is he but what you yourself, as I say, took me for when you first came out?"

Strether felt a little faint, but he coerced his attention. "Oh yes, and there's no doubt that, with your natural parts, you'd have much in common with him. Advertising is clearly, at this time of day, the secret of trade. It's quite possible it will be open to you —giving the whole of your mind to it—to make the whole place

425

num with you. Your mother's appeal is to the whole of your mind, and that's exactly the strength of her case."

Chad's fingers continued to twiddle, but he had something of a drop. "Ah, we've been through my mother's case!"

"So I thought. Why then do you speak of the matter?"

"Only because it was part of our original discussion. To wind up where we began. My interest's purely platonic. There, at any rate, the fact is—the fact of the possible. I mean the money in it."

"Oh, damn the money in it!" said Strether. And then as the young man's fixed smile seemed to shine out more strange: "Shall you give your friend up for the money in it?"

Chad preserved his handsome grimace as well as the rest of his attitude. "You're not altogether—in your so great 'solemnity'— kind. Haven't I been drinking you in—showing you all I feel you're worth to me? What have I done, what am I doing, but cleave to her to the death? The only thing is," he good-humoredly explained, "that one can't but have it before one, in the cleaving— the point where the death comes in. Don't be afraid for *that*. It's pleasant to a fellow's feelings," he developed, "to 'size-up' the bribe he applies his foot to."

"Oh then, if all you want's a kickable surface, the bribe's enormous."

"Good. Then there it goes! Chad administered his kick with fantastic force and sent an imaginary object flying. It was accordingly as if they were once more rid of the question and could come back to what really concerned him. "Of course I shall see you to-morrow."

But Strether scarce heeded the plan proposed for this; he had still the impression—not the slighter for the simulated kick—of an irrelevant hornpipe or jig. "You're restless."

"Ah," returned Chad as they parted, "you're exciting."

XXXVI

He had, however, within two days, another separation to face. He had sent Maria Gostrey a word early, by hand, to ask if he might come to breakfast; in consequence of which, at noon, she awaited him in the cool shade of her little Dutch-looking dining-room. This retreat was at the back of the house, with a view of a scrap of old garden that had been saved from modern ravage; and, though he had on more than one other occasion had his legs under its small and peculiarly polished table of hospitality, the place had never before struck him as so sacred to pleasant knowledge, to intimate charm, to antique order, to a neatness that was almost august. To sit there was, as he had told his hostess before, to see life reflected for the time in ideally kept pewter; which was somehow becoming, improving to life, so that one's eyes were held and comforted. Strether's were comforted, at all events, now—and the more that it was the last time—with the charming effect, on the board bare of a cloth and proud of its perfect surface, of the small old crockery and old silver, matched by the more substantial pieces happily disposed about the room. The specimens of vivid Delf, in particular, had the dignity of family portraits; and it was in the midst of them that our friend resignedly expressed himself. He spoke even with a certain philosophic humor. "There's nothing more to wait for; I seem to have done a good day's work. I've let them have it all round. I've seen Chad, who has been to London and come back. He tells me I'm 'exciting,' and I seem indeed pretty well to have upset every one. I've at any rate excited *him*. He's distinctly restless."

"You've excited *me*," Miss Gostrey smiled. "*I'm* distinctly restless."

"Oh, you were that when I found you. It seems to me I've rather got you out of it. What's this," he asked as he looked about him, "but a haunt of ancient peace?"

427

"I wish with all my heart," she presently replied, "I could make you treat it as a haven of rest." On which they fronted each other, across the table, as if things unuttered were in the air.

Strether seemed, in his way, when he next spoke, to take some of them up. "It wouldn't give me—that would be the trouble—what it will, no doubt, still give you. I'm not," he explained, leaning back in his chair, but with his eyes on a small ripe round melon—"in real harmony with what surrounds me. You *are*. I take it too hard. You *don't*. It makes—that's what it comes to in the end—a fool of me." Then at a tangent, "What has he been doing in London?" he demanded.

"Ah, one may go to London," Maria laughed. "You know *I* did."

Yes—he took the reminder. "And you brought *me* back." He brooded there opposite to her, but without gloom. "Whom has Chad brought? He's full of ideas. And I wrote to Sarah," he added, "the first thing this morning. So I'm square. I'm ready for them."

She neglected certain parts of this speech in the interest of others. "Marie said to me the other day that she felt him to have the makings of an immense man of business."

"There it is. He's the son of his father!"

"But *such* a father!"

"Ah, just the right one, from that point of view! But it isn't his father in him," Strether added, "that troubles me."

"What is it then?" He came back to his breakfast; he partook presently of the charming melon, which she liberally cut for him; and it was only after this that he met her question. Then, moreover, it was but to remark that he would answer her presently. She waited, she watched, she served him and amused him, and it was perhaps with this last idea that she soon reminded him of his having never even yet named to her the article produced at Woollett. "Do you remember our talking of it in London—that night at the play?" Before he could say yes, however, she had put it to him for other matters. Did he remember, did he remember—this and that of their first days? He remembered everything, bringing up with humor even things of which she professed no recollection, things she vehemently denied; and falling back above all on the great interest of their early time, the curiosity felt by both of them as to where he would "come out." They had so assumed it was to be in some wonderful place—they had thought of it as so very *much* out. Well, that was doubtless what it had been—since he had come out just there. He was out, in truth, as far as it was possible to be, and must now rather bethink himself of getting in again. He found on the spot the image of his recent history; he was like one of the figures of the old clock at Berne. *They* came out, on one side, at their hour, jigged along their little course in the public eye, and went in on the other side. He too had jigged his little course—him too a modest retreat awaited. He offered now, should she really like to know, to name the great product of Woollett. It would be a great commentary on everything. At this she stopped him off; she not only had no wish to know, but she wouldn't know for the world. She had done with the products of Woollett—for all the good she had got from them. She desired no further news of them, and she mentioned that Mme. de Vionnet herself had, to her knowledge, lived exempt from the information he was ready to supply. She had never consented to receive it, though she would have taken it, under stress, from Mrs. Pocock. But it was a matter about which Mrs. Pocock appeared to have had little to say—never sounding the word—and it didn't signify now. There was nothing, clearly, for Maria Gostrey that signified now—save one sharp point, that is, to which she came in time. "I don't know whether it's before you as a possibility that, left to himself, Mr. Chad may, after all, go back. I judge that it *is* more or less so before you, from what you just now said of him."

Her guest had his eyes on her, kindly but attentively, as if foreseeing what was to follow this. "I don't think it will be for the money." And then as she seemed uncertain: "I mean that he'll give her up."

"Then he *will* give her up?"

Strether waited a moment, rather slow and deliberate now, drawing out a little this last soft stage, pleading with her in various suggestive and unspoken ways for patience and understanding. "What were you just about to ask me?"

"Is there anything he can do that would make you patch it up?"

"With Mrs. Newsome?"

Her assent, as if she had had a delicacy about sounding the name, was only in her face; but she added with it: "Or is there anything he can do that would make *her* try it?"

"To patch it up with me?" His answer came at last in a conclusive headshake. "There's nothing any one can do. It's over. Over for both of us."

Maria wondered, seemed a little to doubt. "Are you so sure for her?"

"Oh yes—sure now. Too much has happened. I'm different for her."

She took it in then, drawing a deeper breath. "I see. So that as she's different for *you*—"

"Ah, but," he interrupted, "she's not." And as Miss Gostrey wondered again: "She's the same. She's more than ever the same. But I do what I didn't before—I *see* her."

He spoke gravely and as if responsibly—since he had to pronounce; and the effect of it was slightly solemn, so that she simply exclaimed "Oh!" Satisfied and grateful, however, she showed in her own next words an acceptance of his statement. "What then do you go home to?"

He had pushed his plate a little away, occupied with another side of the matter; taking refuge, in fact, in that side and feeling so moved that he soon found himself on his feet. He was affected in advance by what he believed might come from her, and he would have liked to forestall it and deal with it tenderly; yet in the presence of it he wished still more to be—though as smoothly as possible—deterrent and conclusive. He put her question by for the moment; he told her more about Chad. "It would have been impossible to meet me more than he did last night on the question of the infamy of not sticking to her."

"Is that what you called it for him—'infamy'?"

"Oh, rather! I described to him in detail the base creature he'd be, and he quite agrees with me about it."

"So that it's really as if you had nailed him?"

"Quite really as if—! I told him I should curse him."

"Oh," she smiled, "you *have* done it." And then having thought again: "You *can't* after that propose—!" Yet she scanned his face.

"Propose again to Mrs. Newsome?"

She hesitated afresh, but she brought it out. "I've never believed, you know, that you did propose. I always believed it was really she—and, so far as that goes, I can understand it. What I mean is," she explained, "that with such a spirit—the spirit of curses!—your breach is past mending. She has only to know what you've done to him never again to raise a finger."

"I've done," said Strether, "what I could—one can't do more. He protests his devotion and his horror. But I'm not sure I've saved him. He protests too much. He asks how one can dream of his being tired. But he has all life before him."

Maria saw what he meant. "He's formed to please."

"And it's our friend who has formed him." Strether felt in it the strange irony.

"So it's scarcely his fault!"

"It's at any rate his danger. I mean," said Strether, "it's hers. But she knows it."

"Yes, she knows it. And is your idea," Miss Gostrey asked, "that there was some other woman in London?"

"Yes. No. That is I *have* no ideas. I'm afraid of them. I've done with them." And he put out his hand to her. "Good-bye."

It brought her back to her unanswered question. "To what do you go home?"

"I don't know. There will always be something."

"To a great difference," she said as she kept his hand.

"A great difference—no doubt. Yet I shall see what I can make of it."

"Shall you make anything so good—?" But, as if remembering what Mrs. Newsome had done, it was as far as she went.

He had sufficiently understood. "So good as this place at this moment? So good as what *you* make of everything you touch?" He took a minute to say, for, really and truly, what stood about him there in her offer—which was as the offer of exquisite service, of lightened care, for the rest of his days—might well have tempted. It built him softly round, it roofed him warmly over, it rested, all so firm, on selection. And what ruled selection was beauty and knowledge. It was awkward, it was almost stupid, not to seem to prize such things; yet, none the less, so far as they made his opportunity, they made it only for a moment. She would moreover under-stand—she always understood.

That indeed might be, but meanwhile she was going on. "There's nothing, you know, I wouldn't do for you."

"Oh yes—I know."

"There's nothing," she repeated, "in all the world."

"I know. I know. But all the same I must go." He had got it at last. "To be right."

"To be right?"

She had echoed it in vague deprecation, but he felt it already clear for her. "That, you see, is my only logic. Not, out of the whole affair, to have got anything for myself."

She thought. "But, with your wonderful impressions, you'll have got a great deal."

"A great deal"—he agreed. "But nothing like *you*. It's you who would make me wrong!"

Honest and fine, she couldn't pretend she didn't see it. Still, she could pretend a little. "But why should you be so dreadfully right?"

"That's the way that—if I must go—you yourself would be the first to want me. And I can't do anything else."

So then she had to take it, though still with her defeated protest. "It isn't so much your *being* 'right'—it's your horrible sharp eye for what makes you so."

"Oh, but you're just as bad yourself. You can't resist me when I point that out."

She sighed it at last all comically, all tragically, away. "I can't indeed resist you."

"Then, there we are!" said Strether.

THE END